MR. GRIER AND THE GOVERNESS

THE BRAZEN BEAUTIES

SOPHIE BARNES

MR. GRIER AND THE GOVERNESS

The Brazen Beauties

Copyright © 2022 by Sophie Barnes

Cover Design by The Killion Group, Inc.

ALSO BY SOPHIE BARNES

Novels

Brazen Beauties
Mr. Grier and the Governess
Mr. Dale and The Divorcée

Diamonds in the Rough
The Dishonored Viscount
Her Scottish Scoundrel
The Formidable Earl
The Forgotten Duke
The Infamous Duchess
The Illegitimate Duke
The Duke of Her Desire
A Most Unlikely Duke

The Crawfords
Her Seafaring Scoundrel
More Than a Rogue
No Ordinary Duke

Secrets at Thorncliff Manor

Christmas at Thorncliff Manor

His Scandalous Kiss

The Earl's Complete Surrender

Lady Sarah's Sinful Desires

At The Kingsborough Ball

The Danger in Tempting an Earl

The Scandal in Kissing an Heir

The Trouble with Being a Duke

The Summersbys

The Secret Life of Lady Lucinda

There's Something About Lady Mary

Lady Alexandra's Excellent Adventure

Standalone Titles

The Girl Who Stepped Into The Past

How Miss Rutherford Got Her Groove Back

Novellas

Diamonds in the Rough

The Roguish Baron

The Enterprising Scoundrels

Mr. Donahue's Total Surrender

The Townsbridges

An Unexpected Temptation

A Duke for Miss Townsbridge

Falling for Mr. Townsbridge

Lady Abigail's Perfect Match

When Love Leads To Scandal

Once Upon a Townsbridge Story

The Honorable Scoundrels

The Duke Who Came To Town

The Earl Who Loved Her

The Governess Who Captured His Heart

Standalone Titles

Sealed with a Yuletide Kiss

The Secrets of Colchester Hall

Mistletoe Magic

Miss Compton's Christmas Romance

CHAPTER ONE

Somerset, 1820

Numbed by the cold, by the final loss that now gave her freedom, and the guilt this awareness stirred in her breast, Olivia Poole stared at the headstone before her. A frosty March drizzle dampened her black cloak. The smell of wet leaves and dirt teased her nose. Extending one hand, she traced the names adorning the uneven granite, the last one freshly carved.

Jonathan Mathis Poole.

A tear or two would be expected – a welcome relief even – but she had no more to shed. She'd spilled them all when death had reached out for her beloved sister, Agnes, thirteen years earlier. Her mother had died two years later, and now Olivia stood in the churchyard again, bidding her final farewell to her father, the vicar. Most men rushed to marry off their daughters to reduce the financial burden on the rest of the family. But Papa had been different. Instead of considering daughters a disadvantage, he'd used them to plan for the future. A vicar was after all installed for life. Retirement wasn't an option unless he had the means to hire a curate who could assist him with his duties. And since Papa's parish was poor and his salary meager, he'd worried about the cost, which would be paid out of his own pocket.

Hands balled at her sides, Olivia swallowed that thought and stared at the ground. Flowers, already drooping, adorned the newly dug grave. Did she miss him? No. A twinge of renewed guilt pierced her heart as she read his name. Distant, devout, and unforgiving, Jonathan Poole had been a hard man to love. But there was one thing for which Olivia would always thank him, and that was his insistence that she receive a broad education.

As much as she'd loathed the strictness with which each lesson had been delivered, she was grateful now for the knowledge he had imparted to her. His reason for teaching her Latin, German, and French, for ensuring she was mathematically skilled, no longer mattered. For although she was now five and thirty, unmarried and without prospects, he had, in his effort to save the cost of hiring a curate, given her the tools with which to make something of herself.

Intent on making the fresh start she not only needed but knew she deserved, Olivia picked up her travelling bag and turned away from the past. With steady footfalls she followed the wet gravel path out onto the street. It was time for her to live, not only for her own sake, but for Agnes's too.

She gripped her bag as she approached the inn, hastening her steps when she spotted the coach. Water dripped from the brim of her bonnet, and in her hurry she stepped into a puddle. The icy water seeped inside one of her half–boots and soaked her wool stocking.

"Drat."

Setting her jaw she ignored the discomfort. Just a few more strides and she'd reach the coach. Her hand dove into her pocket, retrieving the ticket she'd purchased the previous day.

"Will you be passing through Varney?" she asked a man who was in the process of loading bags. She wanted to verify that she had the right coach. Having never left Treadmire before and with only a few funds at her disposal, she'd no desire to end up in the wrong part of the country.

He shoved a trunk into the boot, then peered at her from beneath the wide brim of his hat while raindrops slid over his shoulders, glossing the capes on his greatcoat. "Aye."

"And you're one of the coachmen?" Just to be sure she'd approached the right person.

"That I am."

Olivia took a step forward and held out her ticket,

the paper sagging between her wet fingers. "Will you be able to drop me off at Sutton Hall?"

He nodded and glanced at her bag. "I can pack that in with the rest if ye like. Or ye can keep it in yer lap."

Olivia paused to consider. Her stomach twisted at the idea of letting her only belongings out of her sight. "I'll keep it in my lap."

"Suit yerself." The man pulled the brim of his hat a bit lower and strode to the front of the coach where he placed one foot on the step. "Ye'd best get in if ye want to come with us."

Propelled by a mixture of dread and excitement, Olivia pulled the door open. Four passengers, crammed inside the confined space, greeted her with varying degrees of curiosity. Recognizing the Brennants and Mr. Marsh, all parishioners, Olivia offered a smile in the hope they'd be willing to make some room.

"You can squeeze in next to me," Mrs. Brennant offered after a moment. She was a robust woman, roughly twenty years Olivia's senior. Her husband, a broad-shouldered fellow, flattened his mouth but said nothing. Olivia was grateful, for although Mr. Marsh and the younger man who occupied the bench across from the Brennants were slimmer, Olivia would much prefer sitting next to another woman.

"Thank you." Olivia climbed inside, squeezed herself into the tiny slot of a space she'd been allocated, bag in lap, and barely managed to shut the door before the conveyance rocked into motion.

"Where are you off to, Miss Poole?" Mrs. Brennant

inquired while Olivia clasped her chilled hands to her mouth, attempting to breathe warm air onto them.

"To Varney," Olivia told her.

"Varney?" Mr. Marsh frowned. "What's in Varney?"

"Opportunity," Olivia said, realizing belatedly that she'd rather not share her dire circumstances with the Treadmire townsfolk. She sighed in response to the unspoken expectation that she elaborate further. "I plan to seek a position advertised in the paper."

"But..." Mrs. Brennant's voice faltered. She shifted her shoulder, pressing Olivia into the side of the coach as it rounded a corner and picked up speed.

Water droplets on the glass hampered Olivia's vision when she glanced toward the river where she and Agnes had learned to swim. Her heart gave a squeeze as the coach clattered across the bridge.

"Your father was a vicar," Mrs. Brennant added. "A gentleman, by all accounts."

Torn away from the view at those words, Olivia clutched her bag more fiercely. These people, save the stranger of course, had been at the service. They'd offered their condolences and had welcomed Papa's replacement who'd arrived last week. But even though the Pooles had been a part of Treadmire for well over thirty years, they'd mostly kept to themselves. Neither the Brennants nor Mr. Marsh could know what life had been like behind the vicarage doors.

Olivia swallowed. "Social rank doesn't always constitute wealth, Mrs. Brennant."

"No, I don't suppose it does."

Thankfully, nothing more was said on the matter. Olivia returned her attention to the dismal view of naked trees and barren fields in the hope of avoiding more uncomfortable questions. Much to her relief, the Brennants seemed to accept her disinclination to chat and chose to engage Mr. Mathis instead.

The carriage bounced along the country road, taking Olivia farther away from the only place she'd ever known. Her eyes slid shut as exhaustion took over. There had been so much to do since Papa's death she'd not had time to rest until now. Not when she'd had a funeral to organize and a future to worry about. The incumbent, a curate from a neighboring parish who'd already been appointed when her father's health worsened, had given her one week to vacate the premises. With no relations left, she'd had no choice but to make her own way in the world.

So she'd set her mind to finding a position. Given her education, she'd hoped to become a teacher or governess, but such required references and acquiring that would take time. Right now, her most pressing concern was gaining an income. Once this was done, she could take her time looking for better employment. So she was prepared to accept a lower position, and since the only options advertised in the local paper had been for charwoman, laundress, and housemaid, it hadn't been hard to decide which to aim for.

A hand gripped her arm, gently shaking, and Olivia's eyes flew open.

"Miss Poole?" Mrs. Brennant's voice called her to attention.

Olivia blinked. Mr. Brennant was sitting opposite now where the stranger had been before. The young man had probably alighted while she'd been sleeping. She straightened as she realized the carriage was no longer moving. "Yes?"

"This must be your stop," Mrs. Brennant informed her. "The rest of us are continuing onward."

Olivia leaned forward and peered through the rain–streaked window. A large building, wedged between the sky and the ground, sat in the distance with sprawling expanses of nothingness stretching to either side. She opened the door and called to the coachmen. "Is this Sutton Hall?"

"It is. Time to get off or ye'll have to find yer own way back from the village."

She scrambled forward, bag in hand, and clambered from the coach, out into the dismal weather. The muddied road was slick, forcing her to brace herself against the carriage door before she lost her footing.

"Go on," yelled one of the coachmen. "Ye've kept us from our schedule long enough."

Olivia bid a hasty farewell to the Brennants and Mr. Mathis, then shut the door and stepped away from the coach. The snap of a whip preceded the rattle of carriage wheels as the horses were forced into motion.

Clutching her bag with frigid fingers, Olivia turned toward the imposing edifice looming at the end of a long, tree–lined driveway. Built from grey stone, it appeared to be three stories tall, large enough to encompass all of Treadmire.

She sucked in a breath. "Good lord."

Sutton Hall surpassed Olivia's wildest expectations. It also reawakened the nervous flutter she'd felt in her stomach that morning when she'd climbed into the coach. But a thrill of excitement also assailed her as she began walking, eager to get out of the rain.

The words her sister had spoken when she knew her end was near reminded Olivia of her purpose.

"Promise me, Livy. You must live the life I shall be denied."

"It will not come to that," she had insisted. Olivia's throat tightened with the memory. The sun had warmed the air that day, offering Agnes a pleasant reprieve from her constant struggle to breathe. So they'd taken a blanket outside for a picnic beneath the old cherry tree in the garden.

"You have the list," Agnes had said, her head in Olivia's lap. "Promise me you will find the means to escape this place, so you can have all of these great experiences."

"I have a better plan," Olivia said, brushing stray locks from her sister's cheek, "and that is for you to have them yourself."

A smile had pulled at Agnes's lips – so vibrant it embedded itself into Olivia's memory forever. "On days like today I feel as though such a thing might be possible, but if it isn't and I must go, then it will be up to you."

Unwilling to disappoint her sister, Olivia had sworn to do as she asked. One month later, shaking with sorrow, she'd dressed Agnes for burial. That day, so achingly beautiful despite its bleakness, had marked her mother's denial of God while prompting her father to cling more firmly to his faith. For Olivia's part, she no longer knew what she believed, except that life was unfair.

A wind swept over her shoulders and Olivia quickened her pace. The rain had turned to sleet and it blew in her face, the icy chill seeping into her bones as she pressed onward. Frozen fingers curled around the handle of her traveling bag while one soaked foot slid back and forth inside her boot with every step she took.

Determined, Olivia plodded through the worsening weather until she reached the end of the driveway. Pausing briefly to catch her breath, she swiped the rain from her eyes and stared at her destination. A pair of square columns guarded the massive front door while an endless number of windows, each at least as tall as she, left her dazed. The tax on those alone was inconceivable.

A spark of hope ignited within her and she forgot her discomfort for a moment. This was what she needed – the means by which to earn her way and get one step closer to keeping her promise to Agnes.

Intent on getting out of the rain and on with her new life, Olivia tightened her grip on her bag and recommenced walking. The front entrance wasn't for her. She needed to find the one meant for servants.

With heavy feet scraping the gravel, she staggered toward the side of the building and rounded a corner. There it was, not too far – a stairwell leading down toward the basement entrance. Relief poured through her, her goal just a few more paces away. And then she was finally descending the stairs to an area where a pump stood with several buckets stacked nearby. A wide window offered a glimpse of Sutton Hall's kitchen, a space that looked to be ten times larger than the kitchen at the vicarage.

Olivia sucked in a breath and approached a green door. Hesitant, yet eager to get indoors, she raised her hand and knocked.

A young man with a white footman's wig perched on his head answered her call. He wore a stunning black jacket adorned with gold braiding, breeches to match, and a very costly looking brocade waistcoat. His eyes widened and his lips parted, and then he promptly stepped to one side and ushered her in with such speed Olivia nearly stumbled right into his arms.

The door swung shut behind her. "I..."

He didn't wait for her to say anything more before he grabbed her by the arm and pulled her inside. The door closed and before she could utter another word, she was being steered into the kitchen and over to the heavenly warmth from a wide iron range where a plump woman was in the process of pouring something into a pot.

The woman's eyes widened the moment she spotted Olivia. "Who's your new friend, Roger?"

"I've no idea, Mrs. Bradley," said the footman, "but she can certainly do with some drying off."

"No doubt about that." Mrs. Bradley eyed the puddle beginning to form at Olivia's feet and clucked her tongue. "Poor thing. You look as though you were dragged from the river. Do you have a name, dear?"

"O...Olivia Poole."

"I don't suppose you're willing to tell us what's brought you all the way here on a day like today?"

"A..." Goodness, she could not keep her teeth from chattering. "An...ad...advertisement."

"Well, I'd advise you to have a seat over there by the fire." Mrs. Bradley gestured toward a chair. "Warm yourself and...would you like a hot cup of tea?"

Olivia almost fell to her knees in gratitude. She nodded. "Pl...please."

"Nancy," Mrs. Bradley instructed, "bring me a brick for the oven, would you?"

A young girl with frizzy blonde hair leapt into action. Mrs. Bradley spun away and began bustling about while Roger guided Olivia to a chair. Tremors swept through her body as she set her bag on the floor. With trembling fingers she struggled to undo the soggy bow tied beneath her chin and finally managed to remove her bonnet, which she set aside on the corner of a nearby work table. She took off her cloak next and hung it across another chair's back so it could dry.

After taking her seat, she stuck out her hands and breathed a sigh of relief as the warmth from the fire soothed away the chill in her fingers.

"I hope you do…don't mind," Olivia said, indicating her discarded garments.

"Of course not," said Roger

Mrs. Bradley handed Olivia a steaming cup of tea. "We're just glad you found your way here before you caught your death out there in that dreadful weather."

Moved by the woman's geniality, Olivia had to gulp down a breath to stop tears from welling. Unaccustomed as she was to words of kindness and with bone-weary tiredness wearing her down, Mrs. Bradley's words threatened to break her for the first time in over a decade.

"Tha…thank you."

"You're most welcome." Mrs. Bradley shifted her gaze to Roger. "We probably ought to inform Mrs. Hodgins of Miss Poole's arrival and of the state she's in."

"I'll see to it right away."

Roger strode off just as Nancy arrived with the brick. "Let's get those wet boots off then."

Olivia gaped at her. "I can't possibly."

"You can and you must," Mrs. Bradley's voice was firm. "The stockings too, I'll wager."

"But—"

"Don't risk your health just because you're too shy to show us your toes. Besides, taking ill will only give us more work." Mrs. Bradley smiled and glanced toward Olivia's bag. "I trust you've some dry clothes in there."

Olivia nodded and took a hasty sip of her tea. Truth

be told, the idea of drying her feet and getting them warm was much too tempting for her to offer much resistance. She set her cup aside and searched her bag for a fresh pair of stockings. As soon as she found them, she removed her boots, her wet stockings too. She quickly put on the dry ones and then the brick was pushed under her feet.

Ahh. Heaven.

Her relief, however, was short lived, evaporating as soon as Roger returned with a mild–faced woman who wasted no time introducing herself as Mrs. Hodgins, the housekeeper.

Oh dear.

Trailing water through the kitchen and keeping the servants from their work while they tended to her was not the sort of first impression Olivia had wanted to make on the woman in charge of hiring her. "I apologize for the inconvenience I've caused."

"Can you walk?" Mrs. Hodgins asked.

Could she walk? Olivia blinked. Did she truly look so wretched?

"Yes."

Mrs. Hodgins glanced at Olivia's feet, then at the sopping wet stockings she'd hung to dry on a chair. Her eyebrows rose and Olivia slumped, certain her chance of employment had been extinguished.

But to her dismay, Mrs. Hodgins quietly asked. "Do you have a dry pair of shoes?"

Olivia swallowed. "I've a pair of slippers."

"Put them on and come with me." She waited while

Olivia readied herself, then guided her out of the kitchen, along a hallway, and into a small room containing a desk and two chairs. "Please have a seat and tell me why you've come."

Olivia stared at her. "To seek the position you advertised in the paper. The opening was for a house-maid and... Please tell me it's still available and I haven't come here for nothing?"

Sympathy stole into Mrs. Hodgins's eyes, causing Olivia's spirit to plummet. "I'm sorry, Miss Poole. That advertisement was posted more than a week ago."

Olivia drew a ragged breath, the tears she'd managed to keep at bay until now finally spilling onto her cheeks. She'd come all this way, had spent a whole ten shillings on the coach fare, and could think of nowhere else to go. The helplessness she experienced as this awareness sank in was absolutely terrifying.

Hands clutched together, she held herself upright by sheer force of will as she asked the only question pressing upon her mind at the moment. "What on earth am I to do now?"

CHAPTER TWO

Mary Hodgins considered the unhappy woman who sat before her. Her black clothing indicated she might be in mourning, possibly over a husband, given her age. Desperation showed in her twisted expression, in the tears sliding over her cheeks. Judging from the dark splotches under her eyes, she hadn't slept well in weeks.

Sympathizing, Mary took a second to ponder her options. As housekeeper she had some authority, and she dearly wanted to help Miss Poole whose hope of employment had just been shattered.

First things first...

"You shall have a hot bath and a change of clothes," Mary said.

Miss Poole wiped at her eyes. A small shake of her head conveyed her confusion. "But if I'm not to be hired then..."

"We can discuss your situation tomorrow." One thing was certain – Mary wouldn't send anyone outside in this weather. "For now we'll make sure the clothes you're presently wearing are laundered, and you eat a proper meal before getting tucked into bed."

"I..." Fresh tears appeared. It was enough to make Mary's eyes sting as well. "Thank you, Mrs. Hodgins. I can't begin to tell you how grateful I am."

"Think nothing of it." Mary pressed her lips together, willing her own emotions into submission before she stood. "Now, let's gather your things and inform the maids so they can get you settled."

Mary left Miss Poole in Betsy's and Fiona's care a few minutes later and went in search of Mr. Dover, the butler. Her heels clicked against the stone floor as she walked to his pantry, the large bunch of keys hanging from her waist jingling as she went.

Not finding him there, she checked the time and decided to head upstairs since he was likely ensuring all was as it should be before Miss Edwards came down to supper. She arrived in the dining room and found Mr. Dover at the far end of the dining table, inspecting not one but two place settings. Roger watched, patiently waiting for his verdict. White coffered ceilings, a large gilt mirror hanging opposite three tall windows, and gleaming candelabras holding dozens of costly wax candles provided the room with the perfect balance between good taste and opulence. It was one of Mary's favorite rooms in the house.

Her pulse leapt a little when Mr. Dover raised his

kindly gaze to meet hers. Foolishness. At almost sixty years of age, she was much too old to be swept off her feet. They both were.

"I gather Miss Chadwick is joining Miss Edwards this evening?" Try as she might, Mary failed to keep her dislike of the governess from her voice. In her opinion, the woman was too haughty by half and treated Mr. Grier's sixteen–year–old ward too sternly.

"Indeed." He straightened to better face her. A flicker of warmth in his eyes and the hint of a smile made her feel slightly giddy.

She firmed her expression, just to be sure she gave nothing away, and glanced at Roger before returning her full attention to Mr. Dover. "There has been a development. Do you have time to talk before supper is served?"

Mr. Dover held her gaze briefly, gave his pocket watch a quick check, and turned to Roger. "Return to the kitchen and make sure the soup is ready to be served in eight minutes." He waited for the door to close before addressing her. "It's not like you to chase me down like this, though I can't say I mind."

Mary started. Was Mr. Dover flirting with her?

Surely not. And yet, they had gotten closer in recent years. After their former master's death, they'd assisted each other in helping his son run the household with as little fuss as possible.

Nonsense. They were just united in a common cause, that was all, and he was merely being friendly. "A woman has arrived."

"Yes. Roger mentioned as much. Said she looked like a soggy dishrag."

Mary winced on Miss Poole's behalf, though she couldn't deny the apt description. "She was hoping to obtain the housemaid position, but since it's already been filled by Fiona, I'm not sure how to help her."

"As you want to do, I'm sure."

This was said kindly, without reproach. Mary produced a weak smile. "Turning her out would be wrong, especially in this weather. If something bad were to happen to her, I'd never forgive myself. So I've asked Betsy and Fiona to make sure she gets a bath and a bed for the night. I hope you won't object."

"How can I do so without appearing the villain?" Mr. Dover took a deep breath and expelled it. "Mr. Grier left the two of us in charge during his absence. As long as we're in agreement we may do as we wish, although we're not in a position to create additional jobs, which still presents a problem with regard to this woman. What's her name?"

"Olivia Poole."

"And what do we know about her?"

Mary reflected on her brief conversation and what she'd observed. "Rather than wait for the weather to clear, she thwarted it in the hope of gaining employment, which means she must be low on funds. Her attire was black, including her bonnet, which would suggest a state of mourning. That's really all I can say. I didn't get around to her references. I thought it best to make sure she could stay the night first."

"Hmm." He gave her a critical look. "We'll need to be extra careful about securing the silver. What's your plan?"

"To inquire about potential positions at Oldbridge House in the morning. If that fails, I'll try to find something for her in Varney proper."

"Very good. Now if you'll—"

A loud series of clipped remarks spoken in French cut him off. Mary bristled, immediately recognizing Miss Chadwick's voice. It came from the drawing room on the opposite side of the dining room door. Additional words followed and although Mary failed to understand what was being said – or practically shouted – she recognized a harsh reprimand when she heard it.

She raised her chin and glanced at Mr. Dover, whose posture had stiffened. A frown of disapproval knit his brow as he glared at the door. "If I didn't know any better, I'd think one of Bonaparte's generals was barking orders in there. We ought to sack her."

"I'm not sure we can."

"Mr. Grier was very clear," Mary reminded him. "If you and I are in agreement, we are permitted to step in and—"

Another terse remark from the drawing room had Mary clenching her teeth in anger.

"Miss Chadwick's father is a renowned barrister," Mr. Dover muttered. "So while she may be beneath Mr. Grier and Miss Edwards in station, she's above the rest of the servants, including us. We cannot dismiss her so easily. Certainly not without Miss Edwards's support, and even then we would need a compelling reason."

Their conversation was interrupted by Roger's return. He paused in the doorway. "Forgive me. You did say eight minutes."

"Quite right." Mr. Dover gestured for Roger to set his tray on the sideboard. "If you will excuse me, Mrs. Hodgins, I've duties to attend to."

Mary nodded, left the dining room, and was heading toward the kitchen when Betsy crossed the hallway with what appeared to be a bundle of Miss Poole's discarded clothes.

"Miss Poole's having her bath," Betsy said. "Fiona is making up the spare bed in Louise's room."

Mary thanked her. Like most of Sutton Hall's staff, save Miss Chadwick, Miss Edwards's personal maid was a good natured woman so it was unlikely she'd mind.

Happy knowing she'd done her part to help a person in need, Mary continued to the kitchen in order to speak with Tabby, the assistant cook. "We'll need an additional serving tonight for our guest. Can you manage?"

Tabby produced a broad smile. "I'm not about to let anyone starve."

"Of course not." Mary glanced around. "Let me know if I'm able to offer an extra pair of hands."

Mrs. Bradley whirled toward her, a horrified look in her eyes. "Don't you worry yourself, Mrs. Hodgins. I'll help Tabby if need be."

"Are you certain?"

"Yes." Glancing sideways, Mrs. Bradley drew Mary's attention to Betsy, who'd arrived with Miss Poole. "Lord knows you've enough to attend to."

Unable to argue, Mary thanked Mrs. Bradley and Tabby for their assistance and showed Miss Poole to the servant's hall where they found Louise mending a frill on a gown. Mary introduced Miss Poole to everyone and showed her where to sit. She wore a slate grey gown to replace the black one, and the added color in her cheeks made her look healthier now than when she'd arrived.

"We'll have a proper meal in a couple of hours," Mary informed her, "and then you can get some rest."

"Is there anything I can do to help?"

Considering how exhausted Miss Poole looked, Mary's immediate instinct was to tell her she needn't worry, but the earnestness with which she'd asked gave Mary pause. "You may assist Betsy in setting the table."

It was Mary's intention to speak with the woman after supper in an attempt to learn more about her. Any information she provided would help Mary and Mr. Dover find work for her elsewhere. But when Miss Poole dozed off at the table, Mary decided the conversation would have to wait until the next day. And since dealing with a leak in the storeroom ceiling kept her busy the following morning, she didn't have time for Miss Poole until well after ten.

"Do you have any references?" Mr. Dover asked once the three of them finally managed to gather in

Mary's sitting room. An extra chair had been brought in so he could sit as well.

Miss Poole shook her head. "I'm afraid not."

Mr. Dover raised an eyebrow. "That pretty much rules out Oldbridge House,"

"I don't follow," Miss Poole said, eyeing them each in turn.

"We were trying to think of a way in which to help you. As there are no vacancies here, we thought of asking at nearby houses. Oldbridge House came to mind but Lady Oldbridge won't take you on unless you have a letter of character."

Miss Poole stared at Mary, then at Mr. Dover. "Your kindness is quite overwhelming."

"We know what it's like to fall on hard times." Mary recalled her own stroke of bad luck several decades ago and the chance Mr. Grier's mother had given her then. "We also know what it means to be given a helping hand."

"Do you have some experience to compensate for your lack of references?" Mr. Dover asked.

Miss Pooled nodded. "I kept the Treadmire vicarage in order for over two decades – cooking, cleaning, and laundering, until my father's recent death. I'm accustomed to hard work."

"I have not heard of Treadmire," Mr. Dover remarked after he and Mary had offered condolences.

"It's a small parish roughly four hours south of here by coach."

"Your father," Mary commented. "Was he the vicar?"

"Yes."

"And yet..." Mary chose to leave the rest of her thought unspoken. Miss Poole had clearly fallen on hard times if she was being forced into service. No sense in pointing that out. She cleared her throat. "Perhaps we can—"

Someone knocked on the door. A series of angry shouts followed. What on earth? The knocking continued with greater insistence.

Mr. Dover stood, his brow knit with displeasure. Mary didn't blame him. Such a disturbance was most unusual and lacked the decorum they expected from the rest of the servants. He pulled the door open. "What in blazes do you..."

No other words were spoken as he stepped aside, admitting Miss Edwards, who looked as though she was ready to march into hell and murder the devil. Considering how agreeable she normally was, something awful must have happened to make her lose her temper.

Mary rose to her feet, as did Miss Poole. And then Miss Chadwick arrived.

Of course.

"I want her gone," Miss Edwards fumed, each word a blade slicing the air.

"That isn't up to you." Miss Chadwick's haughty voice grated on Mary's nerves.

"She locked me in the dining room." Miss Edwards's voice shook with anger. "I'd still be there if Roger hadn't heard me shouting for help."

Taken aback by this revelation, Mary turned to Miss Chadwick. "What would possess you to do such a thing?"

Miss Chadwick arched her brows and stared down her nose at Mary. "I would suggest you ask Miss Edwards."

Annoyed with the woman, Mary forced herself to calmly inquire, "What happened, Miss Edwards?"

Rather than give a response, Miss Edwards glared at her. A triumphant smirk curled Miss Chadwick's lips. Her next remark, directed at Miss Edwards, was spoken in French. Mary recognized the sound of the language, even though she understood none of the words.

Miss Edwards spun to face her, and an angry series of equally incomprehensible words filled the air.

Miss Chadwick's expression hardened.

"English, if you please," Mr. Dover insisted.

Ignoring him completely, the governess narrowed her gaze on Miss Edwards and said something neither Mary nor Mr. Dover had any hope of understanding.

Miss Poole on the other hand gasped. And then, before Mary could work out what was happening, the mouseish woman pulled Miss Edwards behind her. It was like watching a helpless kitten turn into a tiger.

Her spine straightened, her chin rose, and then she spoke in an unyielding voice that brooked no nonsense. "You will do no such thing."

Silence followed for a good three seconds before Miss Chadwick responded. "How dare you interfere?"

"How dare you threaten to strike your charge?" Miss Poole countered.

Mary shared a disbelieving look with Mr. Dover, whose expression had turned thunderous.

"She insulted me," said Miss Chadwick.

"For good reason, I'm sure," Miss Poole snapped.

"Mr. Grier will not approve when he learns what—"

"If he is worth his salt," Miss Poole gritted, "he won't approve of his ward being terrorized by any of his servants."

The scathing remarks that flowed from Miss Chadwick's lips in response to this were hard to follow. To Mary's surprise, it didn't shock her as much as it probably should have. Not when she'd always suspected Miss Chadwick of being a vile person at heart. It confounded her to think Mr. Grier had hired her and could only surmise he'd not been aware of her true character when he'd done so.

"I think we've heard enough," Mr. Dover said, his voice more forceful than before. He glanced at Miss Edwards. "Is it true? Has Miss Chadwick tried to intimidate you?"

"I was tasked with preparing her for her debut," Miss Chadwick interrupted. "When she misbehaves as she has just done there must be—"

"Do shut up," Mr. Dover ordered, prompting Mary to press her lips together to keep from smiling. It was a serious situation after all, but seeing the dear man lose control was quite a novelty.

"She had a frog in her room," Miss Chadwick

shouted, jabbing a finger in Miss Edwards's direction. "Mice too."

"Which you fed to a cat," Miss Edwards snapped. "While they were alive!"

"Good lord," Mary muttered. She stared at Miss Edwards, horrified at the sight of a tear trickling down her cheek. She cleared her throat, and managed to speak in a calm voice. "Miss Chadwick was right to reprimand you for bringing such creatures into the house. However, I cannot support the manner in which she handled the situation. So, if you wish for her to leave Sutton Hall, I shall support the decision."

"As will I," said Mr. Dover.

"Mr. Grier will hear of this," Miss Chadwick seethed.

"He most certainly shall," Mary assured her without so much as batting an eyelid.

"Please pack your things," Miss Edwards told Miss Chadwick.

Miss Chadwick sent them all a scathing look before quitting their presence, slamming the door behind her as she departed. Mary expelled a deep breath while Mr. Dover closed his eyes as if in relief. Miss Poole remained tense, as though she feared her interference might affect Mary's and Mr. Dover's offer to help her.

If anything, it gave Mary an idea.

She met Mr. Dover's gaze briefly before addressing Miss Poole. "Perhaps it would be prudent of you to reveal the extent of your education before we proceed any further."

Miss Poole blinked. "I...um... I was taught by my father."

"And?" Mr. Dover prompted when Miss Poole said nothing more.

Miss Poole gave them a tentative look, then cleared her throat and said, "As I've mentioned, he was a vicar. But his parish was poor, so he feared he'd lack the funds required to hire a cleric. My sister and I were therefore trained to perform such duties."

"Then you must be well versed in Latin," Mary remarked.

Miss Poole nodded.

"What about mathematics, history, and geography?" Mr. Dover asked.

Miss Poole bit her lip and fidgeted with her fingers. She hesitated briefly before admitting, "I have an acceptable amount of knowledge in all three subjects." Swallowing, she quietly added, "I also speak German."

"Well, I'll be," Mary exclaimed. She turned to Miss Edwards. "What do you think?"

Miss Edwards smiled for the first time since arriving in Mary's sitting room. And then she spoke up, her attention exclusively on Miss Poole. "I do believe Mr. Grier will return from London as soon as he learns of Miss Chadwick's dismissal. And when he does, I shall recommend you to him as my new governess."

CHAPTER THREE

As had become tradition, Grayson Grier met his friends, James Dale and Colin West, in a quiet corner of White's. James did the honors and poured the brandy from the decanter the servant had brought. His dark blonde hair looked almost brown in the dim evening light as a few stray locks fell over his brow.

Today, Friday, March 21, 1820, marked the nineteenth anniversary of the death of their comrade, Richard Hughes, at the battle of Aboukir. And so they'd come, as they always did, for a commemorative drink.

Grayson raised his glass in salute and took a swig of his brandy. Even after all these years he still recalled with perfect accuracy the blistering heat and the sand beneath his boots. The stench of smoke, blood, and gunpowder swiftly returned while screams of agony echoed in his memory. Before the war, he'd believed it his duty to serve king and country. Now, he thought it a barbaric waste of life.

"He would have been four and forty years old by now, had he lived," Colin muttered morosely. His ginger hair gleamed in response to the light spilling from a suspended oil lamp. The scar he'd received at the hands of an enemy soldier puckered his right cheek as he spoke.

Far from home, Egypt had served as hell on earth for them all, but at least Richard hadn't been one of the wretched souls forced to writhe in the sand while he suffered. His death had been swift. One shot and he'd been gone, like a flame snuffed out in an instant.

"Do you suppose he would have married?" Grayson asked, willing himself to recall Richard during happier times, when they'd been at Eton and Cambridge together. Before their decision to buy commissions.

James scoffed. "Only a fool would tie himself to a woman for any duration of time. You're lucky you managed to avoid the parson's mousetrap, Grayson. And at least you realized your mistake quick enough to get an annulment, Colin. I wish I'd been as wise."

"You wouldn't have Michael then," Grayson pointed out. He knew how much James loved his son.

"But you could have divorced your wife once you realized what she was up to," Colin said, "as Mr. Hewitt is doing."

Grayson studied James, whose expression had hardened. Discussing his late wife was never easy. She'd cuckolded him, made a mockery of their marriage, yet had been a loving mother to Michael, who would have suffered the consequence of a separation, never mind an ugly divorce. Grayson knew James would rather sacrifice himself a thousand times over than see his son hurt. But eventually, fate had taken Clara from them both. She'd died, quite suddenly, a few years ago.

The pain James suffered because of her had soured his interest in women. Until Mrs. Hewitt swept into his life during a ball they'd all attended. While Grayson knew his friend would never seduce another man's wife, he'd clearly been smitten by her. The spark between them was evident when James introduced her to Grayson and Colin. Had she been free, there was no doubt in Grayson's mind that James would have pursued her.

Unfortunately, she had since revealed herself to be a much bigger adulteress than Clara. So much so, her husband was determined to pay the expense and suffer the scandal of cutting all ties with her in court.

As expected, Colin's remark led to a charged conversation with James strongly opposed to the idea of being publically scrutinized and risking his reputation for any reason.

"Let's speak of something else," James suggested once Colin was done pointing out how much worse a divorce would be for a woman. "How is your ward, Juliana, faring, Grayson?"

Discomfited by the question, Grayson dropped his

gaze and studied the contents of his glass. Juliana's parents had died in a horrible carriage crash when she was four. She'd been their only child and as their good friend, his father had been named in their will. He'd been Juliana's guardian for two years before Grayson inherited all responsibility for her.

"The last report I received informed me that her French is improving."

"And?" Colin pressed when he said nothing more.

Grayson frowned, took a deep breath, and slowly raised his gaze. He supposed he might as well confess his predicament. "She sacked her governess."

Stunned laughter exploded from James and Colin, causing them to choke on their drinks. Coughing fits followed while Grayson glared at each in turn. When James eventually managed to catch his breath, he said, "Please don't tell me you gave her permission to do so?"

"Of course not." Grayson said, annoyed with the suggestion. "There's a good chance she did it to get my attention and force me back to Sutton Hall. I'll have to give her a lecture and hire another governess. Damned nuisance."

He instantly regretted the words. Juliana would have needed support from his housekeeper and butler to dismiss a servant, which meant it must have been done with good reason. But the letter Dover had sent him was vague at best, increasing Grayson's worries and his frustration.

"When did you see her last?" James quietly asked.

Grayson knit his brow. "It was before Christmas, so…four months ago, perhaps a bit more."

Colin gave a low whistle, to which Grayson responded with a glower.

"Forgive me if I'm overstepping," James said, "but that does seem unusually negligent of you."

Grayson sighed. James wasn't wrong, and yet remaining at Sutton Hall had become difficult. "Juliana is to have her coming out next year. Her governess had a plan which involved an endless amount of lessons in etiquette, conversational skills, dancing, and so on. I believed I'd get in the way, so I chose to stay in Town a bit longer than usual."

More to the point, he'd feared Juliana might ask for his opinion regarding her efforts. Better the whole debacle be taken care of in his absence, without his interference. He was known for blunt speaking. He'd hate to upset the girl in some way with an ill-timed comment.

"You are all she has left, Grayson," said James, who could be equally frank. "And she is a child, stuck in a great big manor with only servants for company. I believe she'll be happy to see you."

"I've no idea what to say to a sixteen-year-old girl," Grayson grumbled. "It was easier when she was younger and I could give her a doll or buy her a pony. Now she's at that awkward stage between child and woman. It's perplexing."

"I'm sure her interests aren't much different from those of women." Colin saluted Grayson with his glass.

"The latest fashion and London gossip ought to make excellent topics."

"As you are the only one among us who has zero experience with children, I'm not sure you should be the first to offer advice," James said. He shifted his gaze back to Grayson. "Do not share any gossip with her. Most of it will be unsuitable for her young ears, and the rest will just make her stupid. Instead, I would suggest you try and get to know the young woman she's growing into. Find out what her new interests are and cater to those."

"I'll think on it," Grayson muttered. One thing was certain. He had to return to Sutton Hall soon.

"You're not entirely correct," Colin said, distracting Grayson from his thoughts.

"About what?" James asked.

Colin raised an arrogant brow. "I do have some experience with children. Isabella Bankroft has two."

James groaned while Grayson rolled his eyes. Isabella Bankroft was Colin's latest mistress.

"I'm not sure that signifies," James remarked, "unless you've actually met them."

"I can't say I have, but she speaks of them a great deal."

"That doesn't count," Grayson and James told him at the same time. Both men chuckled while Colin merely shrugged.

"Will you break things off with her when you return to Woodstone Park?" Grayson asked. Colin, being the enterprising landowner he was, had promised his steward he would be back next week to help oversee the planting.

"Why?" Colin asked with a sly smirk. "You interested?"

"God no," Grayson said. It was bad enough feeling as though he might have failed Juliana without throwing a new paramour into the mix. "I've enough to worry about right now."

"Have you heard the latest news?" someone across the room asked in a loud voice. It only took Grayson a second to recognize the speaker as the Earl of Everton. "She's free, my dear fellows. The divorce is final."

Other men jumped in to voice their opinions and since there could be no doubt as to whom they referred, Grayson shot James a look. Hopefully this gossip pertaining to Mrs. Hewitt wouldn't affect his friend. A tense moment followed a particularly demeaning remark before James thankfully blew out a breath and downed the rest of his drink. He stood. "Forgive me, but I must be off. Perhaps we can meet for dinner before you leave Town?"

"I plan to be on my way tomorrow morning," Grayson said. "I'm afraid dinner will have to wait."

James voiced his regrets but wished him safe travels before he took his leave. Colin gave Grayson a pensive look – the sort that warned an uncomfortable comment was imminent. Grayson braced himself as his friend proceeded to point out, "If you married, your wife would take charge of Juliana's coming out, and you would be free from that concern."

"Acquiring a wife requires careful consideration plus time spent on courtship. And this is supposing I have an interest in getting myself leg shackled, which I assure you I've no desire to do. Not after witnessing your and James's botched attempts at wedded bliss."

"Just because *we've* had particularly bad luck, doesn't mean *you* couldn't be happy."

Grayson was well aware of this fact. His parents had proved wedded bliss existed, but considering his own past experiences with the fairer sex, he'd stopped believing he would marry for love a long time ago.

"Or wretchedly miserable," he remarked. Being cynical in this instance was so much simpler. "And since I'm not a gambling man I'd rather not take the risk. Least of all when my brother has two sons and there's no need for me to produce an heir. No, what I require is a governess who can match Juliana's spirit – someone who'll take the time to understand her, to advise and listen to her while offering sound guidance and a useful education. A friend as well as a mentor."

"That's quite an impressive list of requirements," Colin said with a wry smile. "Does such a creature even exist?"

"She has to," Grayson said. He shook his head and polished off the last of his drink. "Juliana must be ready to face the London Season when the time comes."

With this in mind, Grayson promised Colin he'd be in touch and went to find his coachman. Grosvenor Square wasn't far. Less than a fifteen minute drive.

"I need your help," he informed his mother as soon

as Wensley, her butler, showed him into her parlor a short while later.

Mama greeted him with a smile, the gesture creasing her eyes at the corners. Approaching her seventieth year, she'd lost her youthful glow long ago, but Grayson still considered her a striking woman, though he knew he might be biased.

"Please have a plate of sandwiches delivered along with a fresh pot of tea," Mama told Wensley. Her kind eyes settled on Grayson as soon as the butler was gone. "It's lovely to see you too."

Grayson kissed her cheek. "Forgive me. I fear I'm not quite myself at the moment. How are you?"

"Better than you from the looks of it." Mama kept a steady gaze on him as he took his seat. Despite her advancing years, only a few scattered strands of grey threaded her auburn hair. "What has happened?"

Grayson shifted in his seat. It was impossible to relax into a comfortable position when there were problems to attend to. "A letter arrived from Dover this morning. Apparently Juliana's had enough of Miss Chadwick."

Mama tilted her head as if in thought. "As I recall, she's the governess you hired shortly before returning to London."

"Correct. Dover informs me that Juliana has sacked her."

Mama's expression grew serious. "Juliana has always been a well-behaved girl. Studious albeit with a fondness for the outdoors, but she's never struck me as difficult or rebellious. Since she would have needed Dover's and Mrs. Hodgins's blessing, something must have occurred. Did Dover not specify?"

Grayson shook his head. "He just mentioned having a possible replacement ready for me to consider."

"Well, that certainly makes everything a lot simpler."

Did it? Grayson wasn't so sure. Hiring a decent governess took time. It wasn't the sort of thing one did on a whim. He'd always taken great care when interviewing candidates for that important position, and finding a woman who spoke French like a native was nearly impossible when most were already engaged by the aristocracy.

"Miss Chadwick's credentials were excellent."

"Pftt..." Mama waved a dismissive hand. "Let us forget about her and focus on what you intend to do next."

This was the simplest part of all. "I'm returning to Sutton Hall tomorrow so I can give Juliana my full attention."

"Good." A firm nod underscored her approval.

Grayson took a deep breath before daring to make his request. "I'd like for you to come with me, to help assess Juliana's preparedness and to advise me on how to make sure she reaches her potential."

A maid arrived at that moment, allowing his mother to consider her answer. Grayson watched with impatience as the maid placed a tray on the table and arranged the tea things. She finally finished, bobbing a curtsey on her way out the door.

Mama reached for the teapot and proceeded to pour. "You know I can't leave London during the Season. My charities depend on my presence."

"You have a team of capable people who can manage them for you just as easily as my agent oversees all estate matters when I'm away from Sutton Hall."

"It's not the same."

The whispered words cut Grayson's heart. He bit his tongue to keep from pressing the issue. Of course it wasn't the same. Mama hadn't been to Sutton Hall since Papa's heart had failed him while he'd been walking with her in the gardens.

"I'm sorry. I'm just a bit overwhelmed by all the responsibility." And he desperately needed someone to share his thoughts and ideas with. In London, he had his friends and his mother, but at Sutton Hall, he would be alone with his concerns for Juliana's future.

"How are your investments doing?" Mama asked after taking a sip of her tea.

Grayson blinked in response to the jarring change of subject. "Very well. I'm making excellent returns."

"And Sutton Hall?" Mama queried with a suspicious degree of feigned curiosity.

"According to the weekly report I receive, all is running smoothly if one discounts the issue regarding Miss Chadwick."

Mama set her teacup aside and folded her hands in her lap. "And yet you wear the gravity of a man who's been tasked with preventing the world from falling apart. Isn't it past time you relaxed a little, set your sights on starting a family of your own?"

"I can't relax until I've seen Juliana settled," Grayson told her, deliberately choosing not to engage in the subject of his marriage.

"This isn't what your father intended for you." She sighed, filling the silence left by Grayson's lack of response. "I'll have Nathan join you in a few weeks when he gets back from Italy. He's more than capable of providing you with the company and the advice you desire. Plus, it will be good for the two of you to reconnect. I'm sure you must have a lot to discuss since the last time you met."

Grayson realized Mama had other reasons for wanting his youngest brother gone from London during the Season. Reasons they never discussed. But that didn't mean she wasn't right about what she'd said. Recalling Nathan's charm and good cheer along with his excellent sense of style, Grayson decided he would in fact be a great help when it came to advising Juliana on the latest fashion and how to conduct herself socially.

Warming to the idea of having him visit, Grayson thanked his mother for her suggestion and reached for a sandwich. Tomorrow he'd set off for Sutton Hall. Once there, he'd get to the bottom of Juliana's quarrel with Miss Chadwick and meet the woman Dover had mentioned. His butler and housekeeper meant well, but neither was qualified to judge foreign language skills or teaching abilities. Given the haste with which they'd found this person, Grayson was sure she wouldn't suit. As regrettable as it was, he'd have to turn her away. And once that was done, he'd set his mind to finding Miss Chadwick's permanent replacement.

CHAPTER FOUR

The afternoon sunlight spilled through the tall corner windows of Miss Edwards's bedchamber, illuminating the spacious room as Olivia entered with a tray. Since she'd defended the girl against Miss Chadwick the previous week, Miss Edwards had summoned Olivia daily. And while Olivia knew she shouldn't consider herself hired until she had Mr. Grier's approval, she couldn't quite stop herself from pretending otherwise when Miss Edwards insisted Olivia teach her something new every day.

"Bonjour," Olivia told Miss Edwards before setting her tray on a table that stood between two armchairs. "Which book are you reading today?"

"The same as yesterday," Miss Edwards answered in French as she went to return the book to a shelf, prompting Daphne, the girl's poodle, to raise her head. "It's absolutely riveting. I cannot seem to get enough."

Olivia corrected a small grammatical error, then asked Miss Edwards to repeat the sentence, which she did while Olivia poured the tea.

She wasn't sure whether or not Mr. Grier wanted his young ward studying Johannis Gottlieb Walter's English edition of *Plates of the Thoracic and Abdominal Nerves,* which contained the most graphic illustrations from the physician's many dissections.

She also had no idea where the girl had managed to find such a book. Only the frog Miss Chadwick had mentioned before her dismissal had not been alive or whole when Betsy had gone to clean it away. It had been cut open for Miss Edwards's inspection.

Olivia wasn't sure what to make of this or if Mr. Grier would approve.

"I've taken some notes," Miss Edwards added with unmistakable pride as she returned to her seat. "When I do my next dissection, I'll have a better procedure in place. I also intend to document my findings with sketches, just like Mr. Walter. If I'm lucky, I'll even discern the cause of death."

This comment gave Olivia pause.

"I would imagine it to be poisoning or suffocation," she said, recalling the frog.

Juliana, who'd been in the process of sipping her tea, froze. She blinked over the rim of her cup. "You think me capable of killing an innocent creature so I can better myself?"

"Well I..." Olivia considered the perfectly poised young lady who sat before her. While her interests might make most people squirm, she did not possess the hoydenish nature one might expect from a girl who collected amphibians and rodents. Instead, Miss Edwards was gentle by nature and didn't appear the least bit capable of causing harm to anyone.

"Probably not."

"Herbert wasn't murdered," Miss Edwards said. When Olivia raised her eyebrows she added, "Everyone deserves a name. Don't you think?"

"I suppose."

"It means they'll be remembered as individuals rather than simply a frog or a mouse. You'll probably think this silly of me, but I feel as though I owe them that dignity."

"There's nothing silly about it at all," Olivia told her. "On the contrary, I would consider it proof of your kindness. But if Herbert wasn't...um...encouraged to meet his maker, then how did he die, if you don't mind me asking?"

"Old age, I'd imagine." Miss Edwards gave her a deadpan look. "After all, he was fully grown when I found him, and I'd had him for almost a year before he died. Unfortunately, I never discovered the exact reason for his demise – whether it was his heart that failed him or bleeding in his brain or something else entirely. Miss Chadwick prevented me from doing so."

The former governess's name was bitterly spoken, which wasn't surprising when she'd singlehandedly stopped Miss Edwards from pursuing her passion. As someone who'd loved being outside in the garden while growing up, Olivia could relate. Reading about plants wasn't the same as actually sowing seeds, feeling the soil between your fingers, or nurturing each little seedling until it grew to maturity. Nor could any book about food convey the pleasure of digging up potatoes. It had been like hunting for nuggets of gold in the vegetable bed.

"Since you're not the murdering sort," Olivia said, sending Miss Edwards a pensive look, "it could be a while before you're able to dissect another frog. Until then, I would suggest a fish since those are often available in the kitchen."

"I've thought of that myself," Miss Edwards said, "but every piece of food that arrives is accounted for by Mrs. Hodgins and Cook. "If any item were to go missing, questions would be raised. I fear there would be an investigation and that an innocent servant would take the blame."

Olivia marveled at Miss Edwards's forethought. "In that case, you may want to consider sending me into town. I'll visit the butcher and see if he has something you would be able to use."

Miss Edwards straightened in her seat. "You would do that for me?"

Her mixture of delight and surprise was a pang to Olivia's heart. She knew what it meant to be restrained, to feel as though one's future depended upon the mercy of others, and as if one's full potential was being squandered.

"Absolutely," Olivia told her.

"Why?"

"Because I was once given the tools required to obtain the life I dreamed of. Only to realize I'd never be able to use those tools, and my dreams would remain unfulfilled." She offered Miss Edwards a smile born from newfound hope. "If I can help you realize your dreams and find the happiness you deserve, then I would consider that to be a wonderful achievement."

"I'm awfully glad to have you here." Miss Edwards picked up the plate filled with lemon squares and held it toward Olivia. "Won't you have one?"

Daphne sat up, tail wagging as she eyed the plate.

Feeling as though that would be overstepping, Olivia declined the offer and went to pick up a discarded shawl from the bench at the foot of the bed. She folded it neatly before removing a few fallen rose petals near the base of a vase on the windowsill. Miss Edwards broke off a piece of lemon square and fed it to Daphne.

A movement caught the corner of Olivia's eye and she instinctively looked outside at the drive where a gleaming black carriage, pulled by a team of four, was presently rolling in. Olivia pinched the petals between her fingers and watched as the carriage drew to a halt. One of the Sutton Hall footmen approached with Mr. Dover in his wake. The door opened, the steps were set down, and then...

Olivia leaned forward in expectation.

A man dressed in various shades of brown alit, and although her elevated position prevented her from seeing his face, Olivia knew by his bearing that this must be Mr. Grier. He seemed to be taller than Mr. Dover, who stood a good inch taller than she. And there was a stiffness about him – the sort that suggested the same stern disposition her father had been prone to.

Olivia drew back with immediate dislike. Which was very unfair since she'd not yet made the man's acquaintance. But there was a certain aloofness to the way he moved. Add to that the length of time he'd stayed away from Miss Edwards – the fact that he'd left her in Miss Chadwick's care – and Olivia found it impossible to set aside her preconceived notions.

She turned to Miss Edwards. "I believe your guardian has returned."

The girl stilled. She gulped down the bite she'd just taken from a lemon square and chased it down with some tea before dabbing her fingers on a napkin. Rising, she smoothed her skirts and tucked a stray lock of hair behind one ear. "How do I look?"

"Perfectly presentable," Olivia assured her.

Miss Edwards took a deep breath. "I should go greet him."

"And I should return that tray to the kitchen so Betsy and Fiona can be saved an additional trip." Olivia went to collect it but a sudden thought caused her to hesitate. She turned to Miss Edwards. "Where is your English–French pocket dictionary?"

"In my desk drawer."

"I would recommend taking it with you."

"Whatever for?"

Without answering her, Olivia retrieved the book and opened it to a random page. "Do you know the meaning of the word, *jonquille?*" When Miss Edwards shook her head, Olivia told her, "It's a daffodil. And *joufflu* means chubby."

When Miss Edwards continued to stare at Olivia as though she were a riddle she couldn't quite solve, Olivia said, "Should Mr. Grier wish to know what you have been doing today, as I expect he shall, you can now honestly tell him you've been increasing your French vocabulary. Which I dare say is better than mentioning the book you've been reading."

Miss Edwards's lips twitched, then she laughed suddenly, and the unabashed joy in it filled Olivia's heart to overflowing. She genuinely liked the girl whom she believed to be utterly misunderstood and underappreciated by the man who was meant to be raising her as his own. Olivia knew she was wholly unqualified to help an upper-class lady prepare for her presentation at court. Still, she hoped Miss Edwards could convince her guardian that Olivia was the right woman for the position.

CHAPTER FIVE

Grayson had dreaded his return to Sutton Hall, but the familiarity of his childhood home welcomed him with the warmth of a grandparent's loving embrace. Although he regretted not being here when his father had died, his absence had spared him the unpleasant memory keeping Mama away. Instead of loss, a slew of fond memories assailed him as the carriage turned onto the driveway. Visions filled his head of his first ride, of welcoming James and Colin when they'd come to visit, of family outings and boyish pranks he'd played with Matthew and Nathan.

Upon stepping down from the carriage, he inhaled the fresh countryside air – the scent of primroses, newly cut grass, and sunshine.

"Welcome home, sir," Dover said. The butler took Grayson's satchel and handed it off to the footman who'd opened the carriage door, then issued instructions pertaining to the remainder of Grayson's luggage.

"I trust all is well, despite the recent change in circumstance," Grayson said as he started up the front steps with Dover keeping pace.

"Indeed. As you already know, Mrs. Hodgins and I supported Miss Edwards's dismissal of Miss Chadwick." When Grayson glanced at Dover he said, "Forgive me, but I did not believe you would want your charge to suffer ill treatment from anyone. From what I gather, Miss Chadwick locked Miss Edwards in the dining room where she remained until Roger found her. And once she had finally been released and came to find me, Miss Chadwick threatened her with corporal punishment. We did not want to take the risk of her following through."

Grayson bit back a curse and gave a stiff nod. "Of course. You did the right thing."

At the front door, the butler stepped aside for Grayson to enter. He crossed the threshold and instantly stopped to stare at a large bouquet of daffodils mixed with accents of green. Placed on an oval entryway table, it was impossible to miss.

"Is Mama in residence?" Grayson stupidly asked. He knew his mother to be in London; he'd parted ways with her yesterday evening. He shook his head. She was the only person who valued such displays. Knowing this, the servants never bothered with flowers unless she was present.

"No, sir." The butler had the good grace to say this

with a straight face and without sounding as though he believed his master was daft. "The daffodils are Miss Edwards's doing. I believe Miss Poole helped her select them."

Grayson frowned and turned to his butler in question. "Miss Poole?"

"The woman I mentioned to you in my letter. Miss Chadwick's potential replacement? She's a good sort – a spinster who's had a rough go of it lately, which is why she came here." When Grayson raised an eyebrow Dover explained, "She hoped to acquire the housemaid position, but it was already taken by the time she arrived. But with Miss Chadwick gone, there's a new opening. I would recommend meeting with her as soon as you have a free moment."

Grayson didn't care whether he met Olivia Poole today or tomorrow or never, now that he knew she lacked credentials. He shook his head and made a mental note of the advertisement he'd have to write once he'd spoken with Juliana. His ward ought to be focusing on her lessons, not running around with a stranger who'd soon be sent packing.

Removing his hat and gloves, Grayson handed them over to Dover. "I'm going to my study. Please ask Miss Edwards to come and see me at once."

He'd barely managed to pour himself a brandy and take a sip before the girl arrived. She seemed taller than when he'd last seen her, which wasn't surprising given her age and the fact that he'd been away since early December.

More noticeable were her curves, which definitely hadn't been there before. Indeed, there was no denying that Juliana was rapidly leaving her childhood behind, which not only reminded him of his responsibility toward her but also the importance of preparing her for courtship.

"Are you very angry with me?" she asked as soon as the door closed behind her.

Grayson blinked in response to the direct question. "No. According to what Dover told me, Miss Chadwick deserved the boot."

Juliana's expression, which had been tight thus far, relaxed. She didn't quite smile but the wariness about her eyes faded. She stepped farther into the room. "I've dreaded the scolding I feared you might give me."

"Oh, there will still be a scolding," he assured her. "You stepped out of line."

"But—"

"Miss Chadwick did not become a monster overnight. There would have been signs and rather than write me directly to inform me of your concerns, you undermined my authority. And if that weren't enough, you made Dover and Mrs. Hodgins your accomplices."

"She locked me up," Juliana hissed. "In the dining room. By myself. With a full bladder, I might add. If you ask me, it's a miracle I did not ruin your rug."

Grayson turned to face the windows in order to hide his smile. The truth was he was proud of Juliana for standing up for herself. Still, he feared the repercussion of showing even the slightest hint of approval lest she make a habit of taking charge.

Schooling his features, he glanced at her, considered her stiff posture and blank stare. If one didn't know any better one might think she faced a firing squad instead of the family friend whose duty it was to raise her.

A thought struck. "What did you do?"

"I beg your pardon?"

"Miss Chadwick must have punished you for a reason. Dover didn't say what that reason was." Which meant either the butler had no idea or his loyalties had shifted. Grayson dearly hoped it wasn't the latter.

"She did not appreciate my quarreling with her or the fact that I called her an overstuffed petticoat thief."

Grayson's jaw dropped. "You…"

"I don't regret the insult for a moment. She deserved it."

"Be that as it may," Grayson said once he'd managed to gather his wits, "ladies do not say such things. If you must know, they steer clear of heated altercations. For God's sake, Juliana, you have a reputation to think of, and while you're at it, I wouldn't mind your showing some consideration for mine as well. The household will think I've lost my grip."

"Not an outlandish conclusion to reach considering your lengthy absence."

The remark was more artless than bitter. It felt like a punch to Grayson's gut. He winced. "Forgive me, Juliana. There were matters I had to attend to in London, and besides, I believed you would be too occupied with your lessons to notice if I wasn't here." An abysmal excuse considering he had deliberately stayed away for the sake of avoiding all things related to Juliana's debut preparations. He took a sip of his drink in a futile effort to squash the guilt.

The pained look in her eyes only made him feel worse.

"I needed you, Grayson, but you weren't here. Not even for Christmas."

The guilt tightened its grip.

"You're right. And I'm sorry. But I'm here now." He'd stay as long as he needed in order to make sure his duty toward Juliana was properly fulfilled.

"Promise?"

"I promise," he assured her.

The smile she gave him lifted his spirits. As if every disagreement they'd ever had was suddenly washed away, she crossed to where he stood and brazenly hugged him. "It's good to have you home."

"It's good to be home." He gently set her back on her feet, adding appropriate distance. He noted the book she was holding. "I gather you were reading when Dover asked you to join me?"

"I've been practicing my French." A pensive gleam lit up her eyes. "Miss Poole suggested I find five new words to work on each day. Hence the dictionary."

Grayson frowned. "It would appear as though Miss Poole can do more than pick daffodils then." When Juliana gave him a look of surprise, he explained, "Dover said the vase in the foyer was your doing."

"It was actually Miss Poole's idea."

"I see." Grayson held Juliana's gaze while coming to terms with the fact that somehow, against all odds, a stranger was making decisions regarding décor. "What does Mrs. Hodgins think of all this?"

"Daffodils happen to be her favorite flowers."

"Of course they do," Grayson grumbled. He downed the remainder of his brandy and went to re-fill his glass.

"In fact, she agreed Sutton Hall could do with some sprucing up."

Grayson stared at Juliana. "Flowers last longer outside in the garden. *Un*-picked."

"I suppose that's true," she agreed with a twitch of her nose.

"And can you please explain to me how a woman who came to seek work as a housemaid is offering you advice on how to learn French?" The very idea was absurd. Laughable, in fact. Grayson stilled. If his mother ever learned about this or God forbid, his friends, he'd never live it down.

"She's fluent," Juliana said.

Grayson nearly bit his tongue. "I beg your pardon?"

"In fact, she's surprisingly well educated."

"She's a would-be housemaid," Grayson said. How well educated could she possibly be?

"In fact, I'll wager her French is better than yours." When Grayson laughed Juliana quietly added, "Her German and Latin too, I imagine."

He shook his head. "Impossible. If that were the case

she would have a better position. Unless she's the troublesome sort who keeps getting sacked without reference."

"Let's put your preconceived notions to the test. If you're right and I'm wrong, I promise I'll let Miss Poole go without pouting."

Grayson laughed. "That doesn't sound like much of a threat."

"You've no idea how long I can pout," Juliana informed him before quickly saying, "but if the reverse is the case, you'll hire her as my governess."

"Absolutely not."

"You'll at the very least consider doing so."

Grayson crossed his arms. "No."

Juliana made a show of glancing around. "Forgive me, but do you have someone else in mind?"

Her age and the newfound boldness that came with it were truly starting to grate. He gritted his teeth. "I mean to place an advertisement in the local paper as soon as this conversation is over."

"I see." She seemed to think on that for a moment. "You certainly have the right to do so."

"I'm glad you realize as much," he told her dryly.

"However, if I am to truly forgive your absence these past four months, you'll interview Miss Poole first. Without bias." She gave him the most imploring look – the sort that threatened to bring a man to his knees. "It would mean a great deal to me, Grayson, if you would grant me this simple request."

Grayson took a deep breath and expelled it. *Damn.*

There was no denying the girl had somehow managed to stack all the cards in her favor. One second she'd been suggesting a wager and when he'd denied her, she'd appealed to his conscience and the fact that she probably knew he wanted to see her happy.

"Fine. But if I find her unfit, you'll accept my decision to send her away without any fuss. Is that understood?"

Juliana's eyes lit up. "Absolutely."

The glee with which she spoke that word and the bounce in her stride as she took her leave left Grayson with the sinking feeling that he'd just been duped. Was it really possible for a would-be housemaid to be as highly educated as Juliana suggested? And if so, then where was the catch? If Grayson had learned one thing from life, it was that if something appeared too good to be true, it probably was.

So when Miss Poole was shown into his study a few minutes later, Juliana's request for a lack of bias went straight out the window. Instead, he instinctively focused on finding the fault that had to be there.

Petite, with raven black hair pulled into a tight knot at the back of her head and with piercing green eyes, Olivia Poole carried herself with the sort of dignified solemnity that demanded respect. Her posture was perfectly straight, her chin slightly raised, and rather than glance away, she met his gaze directly.

A frisson of awareness stole its way up Grayson's spine. She wasn't the sort of woman he would consider attractive, and her black gown did little to improve upon this, but he had to admit that she had an uncommon amount of presence.

"You wished to see me, Mr. Grier?"

The question came as a jolt, alerting Grayson to the fact that he'd not yet uttered a word. Instead, he'd been staring at her, taking her measure as it were, and probably looking completely daft in the process.

He cleared his throat. "Please have a seat, Miss Poole."

She considered the chair he indicated, one of a pair that stood directly opposite his with his desk placed firmly between them, and gradually made her way to it. Grayson waited for her to claim her seat before assuming his own.

"My ward has asked me to interview you. For the position of governess." He watched her closely in order to gauge her response. "So tell me about yourself, Miss Poole. Who are you, exactly?"

Her eyes widened a fraction, as though with surprise, but Grayson held firm. He would not apologize for his bluntness. On the contrary, he was very determined to test Miss Poole's mettle.

CHAPTER SIX

The ill-at-ease feeling that filled Olivia's stomach the moment she'd been told to meet Mr. Grier in his study had since expanded. It was only made worse when she finally stood before him and realized he wasn't the sort of man one could choose to ignore.

He was, to put it mildly, dauntingly handsome. A good head taller than she with coffee-colored hair trimmed short and a pair of intense brown eyes, Mr. Grier was also the most imposing man she'd ever encountered. With his grave expression, aided by a slight crease at the bridge of his nose and a sharply defined jawline, he almost looked angry. Nevertheless, she did not find in him the same sort of brutal indifference she'd known in her father. On the contrary, Mr. Grier's gaze, while piercing, contained vast amounts of interest.

His question, however, caught her completely off guard.

She folded her hands in her lap, took a deep breath, and prayed he'd not realize how flustered he'd made her.

Who was she?

It was perhaps the most demanding question she'd ever been asked. Because it wasn't something she'd ever given much thought. She'd been too busy caring for others and since then, too preoccupied with work and figuring out how to honor her sister.

"I cannot give you a ready answer."

He stared at her, his jaw tight with the sort of assessing scrutiny that would make the bravest person squirm. Olivia clasped her hands tighter and forced herself to hold his gaze. To look away now would only show weakness.

"Cannot or will not?" he asked with an edge of rigidity as he leaned forward, his posture stiff.

"I beg your pardon, sir, if my statement sounded defiant. The truth is I've yet to figure it out."

"Hmm…"

Olivia wanted to smack herself. Here she was with a once in a lifetime opportunity to acquire the perfect position. All she had to do was answer a simple question about herself to some degree of satisfaction, and yet she'd failed abysmally.

Noting the flash of disappointment in Mr. Grier's eyes and the manner in which he moved to rise, as if preparing to end the interview before it had begun,

Olivia straightened in her seat and said the first thing that came to mind.

"Superficially speaking, I am a vicar's daughter. My father was pious and strict, but he believed in education for boys and girls alike. More specifically, he did not want it said that his children were stupid. So he taught me my numbers and letters, made sure I knew my history and geography, and imparted to me a knowledge of French, German, and Latin. I speak all three, though I've no idea how good my pronunciation might be since I've never encountered a native speaker."

"Your father did you a great service," Mr. Grier said, relaxing back into his seat.

"I am aware." She didn't add anything more. Her upbringing wasn't his business. He had no need to know the pain with which she'd acquired her learning or what her father's true motivation had been.

"And how well versed are you with regard to upper–class etiquette?" he asked, switching to French.

"If I'm to be honest," she replied, noting the flash of surprise in his eyes when she changed language too, "I know the basics but worry I may have a great deal to learn if I am to teach Miss Edwards. If it eases your mind, I have begun reading up on *The Mirror of the Graces* which I found in your library."

"What about all the details pertaining to a debut?" he asked in German, revealing he lacked proficiency in this language. "A lady of Miss Edwards's standing will have to be presented at court. She'll need to know how to appeal – to attract attention of the right kind."

Olivia knew she was out of her depth in this regard, but she also believed in the positive outcome of hard work and dedication. As long as she applied herself to making Juliana's debut a success, she was confident it would be. Nevertheless, she had to be honest. "I can only teach what I know. And I'll grant you, Mr. Grier, there's a risk that won't be enough. However, you may rest assured I have Miss Edwards's best interests at heart and shall do my utmost not to disappoint either of you."

Mr. Grier narrowed his gaze. An uncomfortably long silence followed until he finally said, "I'll give you a three-week trial as governess, at the end of which we'll evaluate your progress."

Olivia nearly sagged with relief. She'd been given the chance to prove herself worthy and to follow through on her promise to Agnes.

"Thank you, Mr. Grier." Olivia stood, as did he, forcing her to acknowledge his striking size. She swallowed and tried to ignore the nerves that once again tangled inside her stomach. Stepping back, she told him hoarsely, "If you will excuse me, I'd like to begin right away."

"By all means, Miss Poole."

Olivia's heart skipped a beat on account of his tone, which promised he would be watching and assessing. She retreated another step while those dark eyes of his remained upon her, following her every move. It made her feel horribly vulnerable – naked, despite her demure attire and the fichu she deliberately wore to preserve her dignity. Her skin began to prickle and for some inexplicable reason she grew slight of breath.

Unnerved, Olivia turned and strode from the room more rapidly than she'd have liked.

When Grayson woke the next morning, he dressed and went down to breakfast. It had taken him longer than usual to fall asleep last night, and once he had drifted off, he'd been plagued by restless slumber. Probably because of the guilt he continued to feel on account of Juliana.

Well, at least he'd let her have her way with regard to Miss Poole. The woman had surprised him, no doubt about that. He'd appreciated her forthright manner and also found it downright impressive, given the fact that she'd risked not getting the job by admitting a lack of experience. She'd been bold too.

I can only teach what I know.

The blunt remark, so poignantly honest, had set him back on his heels. Miss Poole might appear prim and proper, but with those words and the ones that followed, she'd practically begged to be challenged. And he'd decided to give her that chance.

He shook his head, ridding himself of the memory so he could focus on more important matters. Employing a new governess didn't come close to making up for his lack of presence. Last night, he'd sat down to dinner with Juliana, which was a good start even though their conversation had been slightly awkward. Hopefully with time, this would change and she'd open up to him more and trust that he wanted to help her reach her full potential.

He entered the dining room. And stopped. "One of the place settings is missing."

"Sir?" queried Charles, the attending footman.

"There ought to be two settings. One for myself and one for Miss Edwards."

"Miss Edwards finished her breakfast an hour ago," Dover said, announcing his presence as he arrived with a freshly ironed copy of the local paper. He set the paper next to the singular plate. "I believe she's having her first official lesson with Miss Poole as we speak."

It took some effort for Grayson not to gape at his butler. "Juliana has already risen?"

He'd never known her to get up before nine o'clock in the morning, or for her to meet with her governess prior to ten. He glanced at the clock that sat on the sideboard, convinced he must have mistaken the hour.

"She has," Dover said while Grayson noted that it was indeed just a little past eight. "She came down at seven, exactly as Miss Poole had informed us she would. And she was in excellent spirits too."

Grayson wasn't sure what to make of this remark. He'd been rather looking forward to having his coffee and reading the paper while waiting for Juliana to join him. Now he supposed he'd have to wait until luncheon before he saw her again. And found the opportunity to inquire about any newly acquired interests she might have. As Colin had suggested he do.

Feeling a little deflated, Grayson settled into his seat at the table. There were plenty of things he could do to keep busy in the meantime. Surveying his property and checking up on his tenants would be excellent starts.

With this in mind, he savored his meal, enjoyed the update on current events he received from the paper, and set off for his ride.

Standing by the schoolroom window, Olivia stifled a yawn. She'd been up late last night, outlining a lesson plan for Miss Edwards. Thankfully the girl had accepted Olivia's decision to commence with mathematics without the slightest complaint. On the contrary, she'd shown an impressive amount of focus and keenness to learn how to solve the problems that gave her trouble.

Olivia had deliberately given her a variety of sums to assess her knowledge. As it turned out, they had a great deal of ground to cover if Juliana were to reach a level of acumen Olivia found satisfactory. Her understanding of fractions and how to multiply and divide them was practically nonexistent. Hopefully the girl would prove more capable in other subjects.

She sent Miss Edwards a glance, unsurprised to find her poring over a book outlining the pulmonary system. In five minutes they would begin reviewing her knowledge of history. Until then, they enjoyed a cup of tea which Olivia preferred to take while standing.

Returning her attention to the garden, she sipped the hot beverage and admired the crisp green colors spring had brought – all the fresh buds beginning to bloom. A colorful mixture of purple, yellow, and white crocuses dotted the lawn while clusters of tulips, hyacinths, and daffodils lined every path. Soon blossoms would start to appear on the fruit trees.

The sight and the memories it evoked sent a pang through her heart. It was more than a decade since she'd sat beneath such a tree with Agnes, making promises she'd not yet managed to keep. As beautiful as the season was and as much as she loved it, she no longer faced it with the same hopeful happiness she once had. How could she when it reminded her of impending death?

A movement caught her attention and Olivia shifted her gaze to the rider who now filled her vision. Clad in a perfectly tailored frock–coat that accentuated the breadth of his shoulders, matching waistcoat, and fawn–colored breeches, Mr. Grier commanded a powerful seat in the saddle. The beast he rode was a marvelous complement to the image of strength he evoked, the fluid grace with which the pair moved a splendor to behold.

Olivia watched utterly motionless and, she acknowledged, breathless too, as Mr. Grier turned toward a well–trodden path. He leaned forward slightly, flicked his whip against his horse's flank, and launched into a gallop. Olivia's heart raced along with him.

"Miss Poole?"

She started, gulped down a lungful of air, and turned to Miss Edwards.

"Yes?" Her cheeks felt horribly flushed.

"It's half past nine. Should we not be commencing the history lesson?"

Somehow, Olivia managed a smile. "Of course. I hope you'll forgive my woolgathering. It shan't happen again."

"I understand. The scenery is stunning this time of year." She nodded toward the window through which Olivia had been gazing.

"Isn't it just," Olivia murmured, her thoughts on a certain gentleman rider instead of the foliage Miss Edwards referred to. She cleared her throat and set her teacup aside. "Let's start with the basics. Can you name the order of the British monarchs?"

Much to Olivia's relief, Miss Edwards possessed more historical knowledge than she'd expected. The girl knew the basic details pertaining to major English wars and even important events that had taken place within England's borders. However she faltered with regard to the rest of the world, so Olivia made a mental note to incorporate a bit of history in her geography lessons.

They moved on to science next, a subject at which Miss Edwards excelled. Olivia wasn't surprised. Indeed, it was likely Miss Edwards's knowledge in this particular field exceeded her own.

"I think that's enough academics for one morning," Olivia told Miss Edwards when they finished reviewing a simple text in Latin. "Let's get some fresh air and exercise before luncheon, and then we'll address your social skills."

"I've enjoyed today's lessons," Miss Edwards remarked while they strolled. "They were much more interesting than usual. When Miss Chadwick taught me there was never a back and forth repartee between us. She would simply demand I learn a series of facts by heart and then she would ask me to recite them."

"While such technique might work for multiplication tables or certain poems, I doubt it would work well in general since it prevents the student from understanding the how and the why."

Miss Edwards kicked at a small pebble, sending it bouncing along the path. "I must confess I envy the extent of your knowledge."

"There's a chance you wouldn't do so if you knew how I acquired it," Olivia told her. As much as she appreciated her father's harsh tutelage now, she'd hated every second of it at the time. "My goal is to make sure you've got a good foundation on which to keep building. As longs as that is the case and you have developed a love of learning, there's no limit to the amount of knowledge you yourself may acquire."

Miss Edwards sighed. "I feel as though it would take an eternity for me to know half as much as you do."

Olivia chuckled. "I'm also two decades older."

"I suppose that…" Miss Edwards raised one hand to shield her eyes from the sun while glancing beyond Olivia's shoulder. "Oh look. It appears Mr. Grier is returning from his ride. I'd not even realized he had gone out."

To her complete and utter mortification, Olivia's heart gave a joyful thump. She turned, and her otherwise languid nerves started hopping about the moment her gaze collided with his. Mouth dry, Olivia held her ground while praying that no one would suspect the effect he was starting to have upon her.

It was worse than inappropriate. It defied all reason in light of his curt manner toward her the previous evening. And the lack of interest he'd shown toward his ward through his lengthy absence. Indeed, there was little to recommend him thus far. Yet there was no denying the pleasure she secretly found in admiring her employer's good looks.

Her pulse quickened as he drew within speaking distance. He tipped his hat in greeting and finally shifted his gaze to Miss Edwards, allowing Olivia some reprieve. "Juliana and Miss Poole. From what I gather, you've had a busy morning. As sorry as I was to miss you at breakfast, Juliana, I'm pleased to see you taking your education seriously."

"Rising at seven so I could commence class at eight was not my idea," Miss Edwards informed him. "It was Miss Poole's. Indeed, she forced me from my bed without pity."

"Is that so?" Mr. Grier asked, returning his attention to Olivia, who instantly felt as though she'd been caught in a hunter's snare.

Noting the hint of respect in his voice, however, she relaxed to some degree and gave a swift nod. "Discipline and consistency lead to accomplishment. By getting an early start and keeping fixed hours, Miss Edwards will make the most of each day while still having time for leisurely pursuits and relaxation."

He tilted his head. "I trust you've created a schedule for her?"

"Of course." How could the man think otherwise?

Mr. Grier's lips twitched as though with a hint of humor, but before Olivia had the chance to analyze the expression further, he swung from his saddle and landed directly before her.

A shiver swept over her shoulders and the pit of her stomach tightened. Lord help her, he was tall – more noticeably so than when he'd been sitting upon his horse. The added proximity and bright sunshine allowed her to better observe every nuance of his appearance. The hair peeking out from beneath the brim of his hat was not the flat brown it had seemed yesterday in his study. There were hints of gold and bronze amid those locks. She had the most outrageous temptation to knock his hat off so she'd be allowed a proper look.

His eyes too, though no less intense, revealed the occasional swirls of copper. Most notably when he looked in Olivia's direction and the light caught him at just the right angle, adding a level of heat that threatened to weaken her knees.

With the reins clasped loosely in one hand, he said, "I hope you will both join me for luncheon."

"Of course," said Miss Edwards.

"I, um..." Olivia swallowed. She was the governess. Was it even proper for her to sit down to eat with the lord of the manor? She didn't know the answer any more than she understood why Mr. Grier's proximity managed to tie her in knots. Besides the fact that she'd little experience with men in general and he happened to be a remarkably fine example. What she did know was that she'd no desire to spend an entire hour feeling feverish while butterflies swarmed around in her stomach. "If you'll both excuse me, I'd like to return to my quarters. I'll see you at two, Miss Edwards. In the parlor."

Before either one could remark on her swift retreat, Olivia turned and hastened away, recalling too late that a woman in her position had to be given permission to take her leave.

CHAPTER SEVEN

"My spine is beginning to hurt," Miss Edwards complained that afternoon while practicing her comportment. She had a bad habit of slouching, so Olivia had strapped a ruler to her spine which forced her to sit up straight. As expected, it wasn't the least bit comfortable. Olivia knew this because she too had worn a ruler until a few moments ago, for the sake of solidarity.

Daphne, who'd been curled into a ball at Miss Edwards's feet for the past fifteen minutes or so, rolled onto her back, wiggling a little as if to draw attention. A few playful yaps followed before she leapt to her feet and gave herself a good shake.

"I'll remove the ruler," Olivia said, giving the poodle a quick scratch behind one ear. She straightened. "And if you are able to keep from slouching for half an hour,

I'll agree to let you study one of your science books later instead of Debrett's."

Miss Edwards's eyes lit up. "Then I shall do my best not to disappoint you, Miss Poole."

"Allow me to give you another lesson." Olivia said. She offered Miss Edwards a gentle smile and began undoing the ties that held the ruler in place. "It is not me you must fail to disappoint. It's not even Mr. Grier, but rather yourself."

"How do you mean?"

"When you make your debut next Season, you will draw attention, and people will form an opinion based solely on what they see. It is this first impression that will determine whether or not they choose to make your acquaintance, after which they will judge what you say. If being lauded as a diamond of the first water is your dream, if being popular enough to have your pick of suitors and gaining Lady Jersey's approval matters to you, then—"

"I believe I get the point," Miss Edwards grumbled as the ruler was pulled away. She rolled her shoulders a couple of times, then turned to face Olivia. "It's up to me and me alone to put in the work required so I can live the life I want."

"Precisely." Olivia gestured toward the tea set. "Please set the table for six, arrange the napkins, and show me how you would pour."

Miss Edwards went to collect the saucers first. "May I ask you a personal question?"

"Certainly, though I cannot promise an answer if it's too prying."

"Is this the life *you* want?" Miss Edwards asked. Her posture, Olivia noted, remained perfect as she proceeded to add the cups.

"I'm glad to have this position," Olivia said after some consideration. "And for the first time, I feel as though I am where I am meant to be."

"So you're not disappointed with yourself?"

"How can I be when coming here gave me the chance to meet you?" Olivia asked with a smile.

Miss Edwards grinned. "Now you're just trying to flatter me."

"Not in the least. You're a lovely young woman, Miss Edwards, with great potential. I'm honored to have made your acquaintance."

"Thank you, Miss Poole. I'm terribly glad to have met you as well."

The words were spoken with such sincerity, Olivia found herself blinking rapidly. She cleared her throat. "I've been trying to come up with a discreet location for your experiments," she said, deciding to change the subject before she got too emotional. "My bedchamber would be an excellent spot. It's close to yours, allowing you access to it when you wish without much risk of discovery from anyone."

Miss Edwards, who'd begun folding napkins, paused in the middle of setting one next to a plate. "Are you certain?"

"I believe it to be the best option."

"Thank you, Miss Poole. I scarcely know what to say or how to thank you."

Olivia sent her a no-nonsense look. "Apply yourself to becoming the lady Mr. Grier *expects* you to be, and I shall endeavor to help you become the woman you *want* to be."

CHAPTER EIGHT

Two weeks had passed since Grayson's return, since he'd met Miss Poole for the very first time and allowed her to teach Juliana. A household routine had been established since then. One which encouraged him to rise earlier as well and get through his correspondence, his ledgers, and overall estate matters in a timely fashion. It also allowed him to meet Juliana for an additional meal, during which he was able to quiz her on her progress.

But when he inquired about Miss Poole, Juliana had little to say, besides the fact that she liked her. Which did little to satisfy Grayson's curiosity.

For reasons he could not explain, the governess intrigued him beyond all reason, and drat it all, he wanted to know more. Not an impossible task, had she simply agreed to dine with him and Juliana. Instead, she'd turned him down every time he'd asked, for which he knew he could take her to task. He could in fact force her to sit down to breakfast, luncheon, and dinner, if he so desired.

But he didn't. And with this realization came a far more startling one: when it came to Miss Poole, he wanted her to accept his company because she *wished* to, not because she *had* to.

He pushed back from his desk, stood, and crossed to the window overlooking the rose garden where blooms would start to appear in another month's time. Until then, patches of bluebells brightened the scenery.

So did Miss Poole, Grayson mused as he watched her stroll along one of the paths with Juliana. Unaware of his observation, the governess stooped to pick something up from the ground. When she straightened again and showed her find to Juliana, the governess, who'd always been stiff and serious in his presence, produced a smile so radiant it completely transformed her features. And left Grayson rather unsteady.

In this moment Miss Poole looked...radiant.

It was the most incredible thing Grayson had ever witnessed. So much so, he'd forgotten to breathe. He took a deep lungful of air and expelled it, only to realize he clutched the curtain with rigid fingers. Stunned, he relaxed his hold and dropped his hand to his side. It wasn't like him to lose his head. He'd always been in control, but that smile...

As if sensing his presence, Miss Poole turned more fully toward him. Even though he felt like a lad who'd just been caught sneaking a biscuit from one of Cook's tins, he shoved his hands into his pockets and forced himself to ignore the urge to pretend he hadn't been watching.

Her smile immediately faded, like sunshine hindered by clouds. She gave a curt nod to acknowledge she'd seen him and urged Juliana to keep on walking. The pair disappeared from Grayson's view within seconds, leaving him with the most unpleasant sensation of envying Juliana's ability to put Miss Poole at ease.

It ought not vex him, but damn it all, the fact that he now knew the woman could smile so openly – except when facing him apparently – bothered Grayson to no end. And left him mulling over the matter for the remainder of the day. Because of what it said about him. Apparently, the prim and proper governess did not think him worthy of her smiles. Or maybe she didn't believe he'd approve of her looking as though she enjoyed her work. Either way, it made him feel like a three–headed monster.

By the time he sat down to supper that evening, he had convinced himself that somehow, some way, he had to win Miss Poole over. For his own peace of mind.

He considered Juliana, who ate her serving of salmon with the gusto of someone who'd had a full day. Attempting to ease into the subject he wanted to broach, he carefully asked, "How are your lessons coming along?"

"Brilliantly." This was said with a beaming smile and followed by, "Miss Poole is well–read in all areas, and if there happens to be something she doesn't know, she won't pretend an understanding of the subject. Instead she'll tell me she needs to read up on it in order to answer my questions correctly."

Grayson wasn't surprised. One of the things that had made the biggest impression upon him when he'd interviewed Miss Poole had been her artless honesty. He speared a potato with his fork and casually said, "I realize it's only been a couple of weeks, but do you feel as though you're making progress?"

"Certainly. I no longer struggle with fractions or with solving algebraic equations. Speaking French feels more natural due to the conversational style of the lessons, and did you know there were female gladiators in Ancient Rome?"

Grayson coughed to prevent a green been from going down the wrong way. "No."

"They were called gladiatrices. Isn't that food for thought when considering England's lack of equality?"

"Indeed," he told her dryly, setting his knife aside so he could take a sip of his wine. "I believe all women ought to be given the right to suffer the same gruesome deaths as men."

Juliana scowled at him, though with a hint of humor. "Say what you will but I think it's utterly marvelous."

"I doubt you'd agree if you were the one facing down an opponent who meant to kill you." Every muscle in Grayson's body drew tight. "I've been to war, Juliana. I've shot enemy soldiers without second thought, watched a dear friend felled before my eyes, and I can assure you it was not the least bit marvelous. Twenty years may have passed, but I can still smell the stench of death from that battlefield."

"I'm sorry," she whispered, the words catching in her throat. "I didn't mean to upset you. I merely thought it an interesting fact."

Grayson shoved some more food in his mouth and proceeded to chew. The effort allowed him to focus on something besides the awful memories of that long–ago day in Aboukir. He took a deep breath. Expelled it. And managed to ask, "What else has Miss Poole been teaching?"

"She started me on German yesterday, so I've been practicing basic greetings. And we've been studying the atlas and discussing the difference in food, culture, and climate between different countries. My least favorite part of the day pertains to social skills and accomplishments, but Miss Poole somehow manages to make those classes fun as well."

"In what way?" he asked, genuinely curious.

Juliana shrugged. "By explaining the necessity, I suppose. And by competing against me."

This had Grayson sitting up straighter. "I beg your pardon?"

"Whatever task she gives me, whether it be to list the most relevant peers, curtsey while balancing books on my head, or draft a pretend menu for a fictional dinner party, she always completes the task as well, after which she and I compare notes."

"Does she have any accomplishments?" Grayson asked. When Juliana gave him an odd look, he hastily told her, "She claimed she can only teach what she herself knows, but I'm not entirely sure how much that is."

"I could ask her, if you like." Juliana took another bite of her food.

Grayson studied her while she ate. Having Juliana ferret the information out of Miss Poole would certainly be the simplest solution, but it wouldn't accomplish his goal of smoothing things over with her. In order for him to do that, he'd have to speak with the woman himself, preferably in a casual setting where his authority wouldn't contrast her servitude so damn much. Which naturally ruled out his study.

"You mentioned lessons in crafting a menu," he murmured, an idea forming as he spoke. "I think I'd like to see the result of said lesson by having you plan tomorrow's dinner."

"Do you mean it?" Excitement lit Juliana's eyes just as he'd hoped.

"I'll give you a three pound budget and challenge you to spend as little of it as possible on a meal worthy of royalty." Returning his attention to his food, Grayson said the next part as though it were an afterthought. "Ask Miss Poole to join us so she too can assess your skill."

. . .

"Hasn't she turned down all of the previous invitations?" Juliana asked while Grayson savored the creamy sauce drizzled over his salmon.

"Yes, but I'm sure she'll accept this one for academic reasons." He gave a nonchalant shrug intended to banish any suspicion of an ulterior motive. The last thing he wanted was for Juliana to know just how important Miss Poole's attendance was to him. "If not, I'll write a report."

Juliana's eyebrows shot toward the ceiling. "A report?"

"So Miss Poole will know how you fared." It wouldn't come to that, he was certain. Considering the resolve with which Miss Poole approached her teaching, he was sure she'd want to see the results first hand.

Juliana raised her chin and sent him a confident smile. "I look forward to proving myself to you both."

And he, Grayson mused, looked forward to picking apart Miss Olivia Poole and discovering all of her deeply held secrets.

CHAPTER NINE

T he only downside to being a governess was the
solitude.

Olivia missed engaging with the rest of the servants
as she'd been comfortable doing when she'd first
arrived. Before she'd been hired as governess. With her
position within the household changed, she'd lost her
sense of belonging. Her rank, now somewhere above
Mrs. Hodgkins and Mr. Dover, felt undeserved. So she
retreated to her bedchamber for supper alone, rather
than dine bellow stairs. It wasn't so very different from
the meals at home. Even when Papa had lived they'd
eaten most meals in silence.

Her first days at Sutton Hall had served as a breath
of fresh air. She'd enjoyed the companionship, and
regretted having to give it up.

Choosing to focus on something else, she set her
tray aside and collected the list she and Agnes had

made. Now that Miss Edwards's lessons were running smoothly with a two–hour break for luncheon and the assurance that Olivia would have her evenings to herself, she'd find the time to work her way through it. At last.

Satisfaction poured through her veins as her gaze swept over the neatly penned lines. It made most sense to start at the top and work her way through every item in sequence. Some things were definitely easier to accomplish than others, however, like tasting champagne, which was second to last.

She scanned the other items.

Sail a boat
Wear something scandalous
Learn to ride a horse
Sleep outside under the stars
Go for a late night swim
Have a snowball fight
Get foxed
Stay up all night and watch the sun rise
Visit another country
Gamble
Read a forbidden book
Act in a play
Visit the theatre
Host a dinner party
Send a message in a bottle
Learn to fence
Learn to ice skate
See the ocean

Experience kissing

With a well–placed comment to Miss Edwards, the girl might even help her accomplish a couple of things. Olivia bit her lip. Regardless of how she went about it, she'd have to avoid getting caught. Because if there was one thing she believed would get her sacked without notice, it would be Mr. Grier's discovering she posed a risk – if even the slightest – to his ward's reputation.

And frankly, Olivia would not blame him.

The mere thought of his penetrating gaze, his unnerving scowl, and unyielding mouth caused her gaze to slide over the final escapade listed.

Experience kissing.

Her heart gave a hard thump. The very idea of him and her…

She quickly laughed and shook her head. How preposterous to even wonder when she'd have more luck being kissed by just about anyone else. And besides, she'd want her first kiss to be memorable, not stiff and awkward as it would undoubtedly be with him.

Annoyed to have even allowed the idea, she returned her attention to the first three items: *sail a boat, wear something scandalous,* and *learn to ride a horse.* She tapped her chin while considering each individually. Agnes had probably had a schooner or some equivalent in mind, but Sutton Hall's property did have a lake where two rowboats were anchored to a small jetty. It wasn't ideal, but it was better than no boat at all.

As for wearing something scandalous…

Considering her position, the item would have to be a risqué undergarment. Of which Olivia owned none. She pursed her lips. Her skill with a needle and thread were adequate at best. Nevertheless, she might be able to put together a simple piece of clothing if she had the right materials. Perhaps a visit to the local haberdasher would help in that regard?

Receiving horse riding lessons would definitely be trickier.

So she'd begin with the boat since that was readily available. She'd have to ask Mr. Grier for permission of course, but she saw no reason for him to deny her as long as she and Miss Edwards took the boat out together. As part of a lesson.

Satisfied with her plan, Olivia re–folded her list and slipped it back inside her notebook. She then collected the copy of *Pride and Prejudice* she'd borrowed from the Sutton Hall library. Having reached the midway point, it was hard not to compare Mr. Grier to Mr. Darcy, whom the author described as being tall, handsome, and noble, though also proud, above his company, and above being pleased.

The similarities were so glaring to Olivia's mind, Mr. Grier's was the face she pictured whenever Darcy made an appearance on the page. And it was his voice she heard when he pompously asked for Elizabeth Bennet's hand in marriage.

"Well done," Olivia murmured while reading the set down and refusal Elizabeth gave him. She chuckled, set the book aside on her nightstand, and turned down the light before drifting off to sleep.

She woke with a start in the morning, panting for breath. Her body was overheated, her mind reeling as she recalled the specifics. She'd been in Mr. Grier's study and he'd…

Heaven help her.

She bolted upright and dabbed at her cheeks. As a vicar's daughter who'd been raised with the utmost of piety, one would think her incapable of having such wicked imaginings. And yet, she could still feel the touch of his hands upon her flushed skin.

Olivia closed her eyes briefly and took a deep breath. There was only one thing for it. She'd have to avoid Mr. Grier completely and hope the effect he was having on her would pass.

Which was easier said than done, she realized that afternoon when she was called to his study. Initially, she thought to excuse herself by claiming malaise, only to decide against such an act of deceit. She'd always prided herself on being honest and wasn't about to let a frustrating man alter her moral compass. Even if he did manage to play havoc with her nerves.

So she squared her shoulders and gave his door a quick rap.

"Enter."

Olivia took a deep breath, released it, and pushed the door open.

When she'd last entered this room, she hadn't noticed much besides the man who occupied the space.

Now, during her second visit, she acknowledged the dark wood paneling, the tall bookcases lining one wall, the narrow sideboard, and the painting above it. The image depicted a fashionable man and a woman during a countryside outing with three young boys. The vibrancy of the leaves on an elm in the distance and the way the sun brightened clusters of wildflowers suggested early summer.

"A childhood memory," Mr. Grier murmured, drawing her attention. The barest hint of a smile touched his lips as he regarded the painting. A fleeting spark of regret caught his eyes.

Olivia could not help but stare. This man, who always seemed so composed, to the point of appearing severe, was made vulnerable by the past in much the same way as she. She doubted he realized he'd let down his guard. Or that she had noticed.

Feeling like an intruder, Olivia turned to look at the painting once more, offering Mr. Grier the privacy he deserved. The man and woman were strolling along a grassy meadow while the boys chased after each other in the foreground. A spaniel pranced about to one side and a blue tit watched the group from a treetop.

What struck Olivia most was the gaiety depicted. "Which one are you?"

"I'm farthest to the right. Matthew's all the way to the left, and that's Nathaniel, my youngest brother, in the middle. You might meet him in a couple of weeks when he comes to visit. If you're still here."

The thought of encountering one of Mr. Grier's

relatives piqued Olivia's curiosity. She wondered if his brother would be as sober as he, or if he'd be different.

She studied the joyous expressions the artist had given Mr. Grier's boyish self. "You look so happy." *Uncharacteristically so.*

"I was a child," he said, his voice a touch sharper. He cleared his throat. "Unburdened by the hardships that come with adulthood."

When she looked at him next, his customary scowl had been restored. In fact, he was almost glaring at her, as if permitting himself to be sentimental was not only inconvenient, but also her fault.

She'd no idea why he felt this way or what might have happened to make him so grave, but it did compel her to say, "My sister died when I was two and twenty. I lost Mama a couple of years later and spent the next eleven looking after Papa. A day doesn't pass without my wishing I could return to my childhood. Not because it was easier, for it most certainly wasn't, but because I'd at least have my sister then. I'd not have to face life's troubles alone."

"You have no other family?" His voice was firm, but the sympathy in his eyes allowed Olivia another glimpse of his softer side.

"Papa had a sister, but since he disapproved of the man she married, the connection was severed before I was born."

"I'm sorry." A furrow appeared on his brow. He gestured toward the chair she'd occupied when she was last here and waited for her to sit before he followed suit. "Considering all you have lost and the strength with which you are carrying on, I must appear horribly self-pitying."

His words, or rather the impression they painted of her, bolstered her soul. "It's not for me to judge your situation, Mr. Grier. How can I when I know next to nothing about you?"

He leaned forward slightly, pinning her with his sharp gaze. "Is that an invitation for me to pour my heart out to you?"

Good lord. Was that how it sounded?

"No," she hastily informed him. "I simply meant to say that I lack the information required for me to think poorly of you."

When he dropped his gaze to her lap, Olivia realized to her horror she was wringing her hands. She unclasped them right away and moved them to the armrests. Which only made matters worse when, in the next instant, he slid his penetrating gaze back to her face. It was done with such disturbing slowness, Olivia feared she'd burn to a crisp. With her arms and hands out of the way, she was completely exposed to his perusal. Especially when he reached the vicinity of her breasts.

Olivia's stomach tightened. Her heart began flapping about with a mad sort of alertness. A new sensation – one she could only describe as pleasure – settled at her core.

Heat rushed to her cheeks.

It took monumental effort to keep still and, she

hoped, to appear unaffected while mortification poured through her. What seemed like endless torture was probably over in under one second. His eyes met hers and Olivia breathed a sigh of relief.

"And yet," he said, his low murmur vibrating through her, "I have the distinct impression that you dislike me. That you *have* judged me, and that you have done so harshly."

He wasn't completely mistaken.

"May I speak freely, Mr. Grier?" Thankfully her voice did not sound as weak as her body felt.

"By all means."

Olivia cleared her throat, resisted the urge to clasp her hands together once more, and said, "There is a terseness about you that doesn't allow much room for affability. Add to that the neglect you've shown toward Miss Edwards and—"

"I made certain she had what she needed," he clipped.

"Did you really?" When all he did was glare at her, she said, "Did it ever occur to you that what she might need most of all was you?"

"I'm a man of four and forty while she's a young girl of no more than sixteen." His voice grew increasingly hard.

"While that may well be true," Olivia said, deliberately keeping her voice as gentle and, she hoped, as non–accusatory as possible, "you're also the closest thing to family Miss Edwards has. Yet you did not even bother to visit her during Christmas."

"I sent a gift," he remarked.

"Well then," Olivia said, abandoning all attempt to hide her displeasure, even though she very much feared her blunt manner would have her packing her bags before the day was done. "I suppose that does make up for time spent together. How naïve of me to think otherwise."

"I do not care for your tone, Miss Poole."

"Forgive me," Olivia said, doing her best to revert into the role of obedient servant and failing miserably. The man had a way of touching her every nerve, either with delicious awareness or with a flare of annoyance. "I am simply a woman in your employ, Mr. Grier. I cannot see how my opinion of you should matter one way or the other."

Without bothering to wait for him to give her leave, she stood. He'd asked to speak with her, though she'd no idea why and at this point she'd really no interest in finding out. All she wanted to do was take a brisk walk. Fresh air and exercise were required if she was to banish the deep frustration vibrating in her bones.

"I'll expect to see you at dinner this evening," he told her sharply, rising as well.

She gritted her teeth and prayed she'd resist the urge to strangle him where he stood. "Is that an order?"

"You may consider it in whichever manner you choose, Miss Poole, but since the purpose is for Miss Edwards to show off her hostess abilities, I believe you ought to be there." His gaze was level and utterly unyielding. "Do you have an appropriate gown?"

Honestly, strangulation was too good for him.

"If you expect me to show up in silk, I fear you'll be disappointed." Hands balled at her sides, Olivia turned and quit the room before she did something truly stupid, like tell the blasted man to go to hell.

CHAPTER TEN

G rayson arrived in the parlor at five minutes to six, allowing time to enjoy a drink before the ladies arrived. The amicable conversation he'd intended to have with Miss Poole earlier had turned into a disaster the moment he'd mentioned her seeming displeasure with him. After he gave her leave to speak freely, the woman had launched into an attack on his person that left his ears ringing.

Most puzzling of all, however, was his physical response to her heated words. Frowning, he poured himself a measure of brandy and took a long sip, then topped up the glass. There was no denying the spike of arousal Miss Poole had stirred in his blood while brazenly speaking her mind or the fierce desire he'd had to pull her into his arms and silence her with a kiss.

The unbridled passion she'd shown in anger...

Grayson crossed to the fireplace and watched as orange flames greedily licked at a pair of logs.

What would it be like to harness all of that fervor and redirect it toward more ardent pursuits? His muscles clenched in response to the very forbidden need she'd stoked in both body and mind. She was in his employ for God's sake. Besides, he had Juliana to think of. Lusting after the governess and, even worse, taking the risk of overstepping his bounds where Miss Poole was concerned was utterly unacceptable.

Somehow, he had to get his baser instincts under control.

Footsteps in the hallway sent a shiver of anticipation across his shoulders, and then he heard Juliana's voice. But it was his innate awareness of Miss Poole's presence that made his pulse leap.

He turned. And was somehow not the least bit surprised to find the tiny governess looking as though she'd rather walk a pirate ship's plank than suffer his presence.

What did surprise him, however, was the rest of her appearance. Not her gown, which was just as drab as ever, but her hair. Grayson stared at her in admiration. Instead of the tight knot she usually wore, the silky black tresses were loosely woven into an elegant twist at the nape of her neck with a few strands framing her face.

The effect was beyond charming. More so on account of her disgruntled demeanor which served to accentuate the fine lines at the corners of her eyes.

Grayson suppressed a smile and approached the ladies. What a fool he'd been to dismiss Miss Poole's appearance as unremarkable when they'd first met. But the way she dressed and did her hair had prevented him from seeing how pretty she truly was.

He bowed toward Juliana first and was pleased to note the grace with which she curtseyed.

He met her gaze. "You used to extend one foot too far. I see that error has been corrected."

Pleasure appeared on Juliana's face. "Miss Poole made me practice until I got it just right."

Grayson slid his gaze toward the governess. "Did she also teach you that sometimes, when a man is particularly taken with a lady, he might convey his high regard with more than a bow?"

Miss Poole's eyes widened with what could only be construed as shock and, he surmised with a touch of humor, pure terror.

Grayson suppressed a chuckle. Apparently he'd found a way under the prim and proper governess's skin. And as diabolical as it might be, he relished the satisfaction.

"Indeed she has not," Juliana exclaimed, her voice bright with excitement. "In what way do you refer? Will you show me?"

"Certainly," he said, while Miss Poole stared daggers at him. "Every young lady should know what to expect when she makes her debut."

Deliberately drawing out the moment for the sole purpose of torturing Miss Poole, Grayson set his brandy aside and slowly reached for her hand. It was a known fact that gentlemen only kissed the hands of ladies who were of higher or equal social rank.

For him to give such attention to any servant was beyond improper. Despite the pretense of its being done for educational purposes. In fact, he was fairly sure he'd later ask himself what the hell he'd been thinking. In the meantime, however...

Every muscle inside him contracted the moment his fingers touched hers. There was the slightest gasp – hers, not his – accompanied by an electrical charge so strong he felt like he'd just been struck by lightning.

The urge to leap away from her was as instinctive as the need for added closeness. He took a breath, closed his fingers around her delicate hand, and prepared to drop a quick kiss upon her un–gloved knuckles.

Which was precisely when the devil within decided to make him forget his manners completely. His grip on her hand tightened. His mouth made contact. And then, with a boldness he'd never believed himself capable of, he prolonged the kiss for one second longer than what was deemed proper.

It wasn't the sort of thing Juliana would notice. He hoped. But he knew without doubt that Miss Poole did so when she stiffened beneath his touch. For a second he actually feared she might smack him.

But when he withdrew, he was stunned to find her cheeks flushed with color. Rather than livid, she looked...affected. Good God. Was it possible the governess wasn't as immune to him as she tried to appear? And if that were the case, then what exactly was he expected to do with such information?

Ignore it, you cad.

Leave the poor woman alone.

Relenting, Grayson withdrew his hand completely and gave his attention to Juliana. "Some words of flattery will likely follow, to which you will be expected to say..."

"You're much too kind, Your Grace."

Miss Poole made a choked sort of sound while Grayson raised an eyebrow. "A duke, I see."

Juliana grinned. "I might as well set my cap for the best."

"I completely agree," Grayson said. He turned to Miss Poole. "I trust she's as fond of reading Debrett's now as she was the last time I came to visit?"

"On the contrary, Mr. Grier. Miss Edwards is now well acquainted with all of the British peers." The slightest frown appeared upon Miss Poole's brow as she added, "On paper, that is."

"If that's the case she ought to know that there are no dukes of marital age," Grayson told her, a touch sterner than he'd intended.

"Perhaps it is your knowledge that's lacking," Juliana said, voicing her opinion with the sort of brazen boldness Grayson was certain she must have learned from Miss Poole.

He sighed. "I can assure you I am well versed where Debrett's is concerned."

"Not if you fail to recall the Duke of Cloverfield, who is young, unmarried, and undoubtedly wealthy."

It was one of those moments, much like that long ago day in Aboukir, when Grayson had watched Richard die. His own life had flashed before his eyes a split second later when an explosion had sent him flying headlong into the sand. Except this time it wasn't his life that was doing the flashing. It was Juliana's.

He stared at the innocent girl for whom he'd been made responsible and considered all the dangers awaiting her in the world. His cravat grew uncomfortably tight. Heat gathered upon his brow. Dear God. She wasn't ready. Worst of all, he feared she never would be with her bright and cheerful disposition. A man like Cloverfield would eat her alive and spit out her bones.

He shuddered. "Over my dead body."

"Sir?" Miss Poole queried with concern.

He looked her squarely in the eye. "Forget Debrett's."

"But, Grayson," Juliana said, "you have always insisted I—"

"Yes, yes. I know what I told you." Irritated, though mostly with himself, he forced out the necessary words. "There's a good chance I may have been wrong."

"What?" Juliana squeaked while Miss Poole blinked in rapid succession.

"I want you to be happy beyond all else," he told Juliana. "If you should find such happiness with a peer, then so be it, but there are plenty of perfectly eligible untitled bachelors for you to consider. Promise me you won't go after a title for only the title's sake. And trust me when I tell you that while Cloverfield may be as you described, he will undoubtedly make you regret speaking your vows."

Juliana gave Grayson a wary look filled with confusion. "But he's a member of the nobility, which by its very definition makes him a high ranking gentleman. I doubt he can be as bad as you're trying to make him seem."

"Unfortunately, I am prevented from giving you an accurate description of the man since doing so would require the use of words I'd never permit myself to utter in the presence of ladies."

Juliana's eyes widened. "I don't—"

"Miss Edwards," Miss Poole said with a gentle sort of firmness that demanded both attention and consideration. "Your guardian loves you. He has your best interests at heart. He would not warn you away from any person you wish to form an acquaintance with unless he had good reason to do so."

"I suppose you make a valid point," Juliana muttered. "It's just incredibly disappointing."

"Besides," Miss Poole added, "if the Duke of Cloverfield is as horrid as Mr. Grier claims him to be, the ugliness of his heart and soul will surely show in his features, leaving him with little to recommend him besides his fortune. If that."

Grayson had to bite his lip. Of all the convincing arguments to encourage a sixteen–year–old girl to give up on her supposed prince charming, suggesting he might be hard on her eyes was certainly inspired. Especially if Juliana's expression was any indication. The poor girl looked as though she'd taken a bite from an orange only to realize it was a lemon.

A knock at the door signaled Dover's arrival. "Dinner is served."

Grayson wished he might escort Miss Poole so he could thank her for helping him steer Juliana's thoughts away from Cloverfield. But since Juliana ranked higher, Grayson had no choice but to guide her to the table instead while Miss Poole followed behind. Nevertheless, he could sense her presence, the warmth of her gaze searing the skin at the nape of his neck.

He helped Juliana into her seat, rushing slightly so he could repeat the courtesy for Miss Poole. With a discreet jut of his chin, he motioned away the approaching footman and pulled out her chair. She gave him the barest hint of a smile – the grateful sort that didn't quite reach her eyes.

Dissatisfied with her muted reaction and desperate for more, he helped push her chair close to the table, then deliberately scraped her back with his knuckles as he stepped away. Moving briskly so as not to raise attention, he went to sit between Juliana and Miss Poole at the head of the table. The footmen proceeded to fill their glasses, the first dish arrived, and only then did Grayson risk a glance in Miss Poole's direction.

The lady did not look his way. Instead, she sent her gaze in every other possible direction. Hell, even Dover received more attention from her than did Grayson. A slight that pricked at his nerves.

He reached for his wine, took a long sip, and said, "Miss Edwards and I were talking about you last night, Miss Poole."

An almost imperceptible flinch caused her soup spoon to clang against her dish.

Grayson stifled a grin. He always played to win. Although the game he played with Miss Poole had not yet been defined, it seemed only fair he should put her on just as much edge as she did him.

"We were discussing your accomplishments," Juliana supplied. "If you have any, that is. And what they might be."

Miss Poole kept her gaze firmly trained upon Juliana, but there was no hiding the rapid beat of her pulse at the base of her throat or the blush peeking out from behind her fichu.

Lord, how he longed to whisk away that piece of obscuring lace so he could admire the swell of her breasts without hindrance.

He dragged his gaze back to his plate.

"I fear I do not have many," Miss Poole informed them. She ate some more of her soup before adding, "My skill with needle and thread is not the best. My sister, Agnes, had a talent for painting I never could match. I suppose, if I had to pick something, it would be singing."

"Then you must perform for us," Grayson said, speaking before his brain had a chance to think matters through. Had he taken a moment to do so, it would have occurred to him that putting Miss Poole on the spot was not the gentlemanly thing to do.

Before he could correct his error, however, Juliana jumped in. "Oh yes. I quite agree. It will be such good practice for me to accompany someone with the piano."

Rather than resist, as Grayson believed she would, Miss Poole said, "There's a rowboat down by the lake. I wonder if Juliana and I might use it tomorrow. Weather permitting, of course."

Taken aback by the swift change in subject, Grayson scowled at the footman who came to collect his half-eaten soup. He considered her request and decided it might allow him to spend additional time with her, provided he played his cards right.

"Have you ever handled a row boat before?" he asked, aiming for a casual tone.

"No," Miss Poole admitted, "but I cannot imagine it being too hard."

"It isn't," Juliana said, not helping his plan at all. "I've taken the boats out plenty of times, so I can show you how it's done."

Grayson decided to change tactic. "Your intention will be to..."

"To fish," Miss Poole said, her voice so inspired there was no doubt in his mind she'd come up with that explanation right on the spot.

Interesting.

Juliana of course was practically bouncing with all

the joy of a young woman looking to try something new.

"Really?" Grayson pretended to give Miss Poole's comment a great deal of thought before saying, "I'm surprised you didn't mention your skill with a line and hook when we spoke of your accomplishments."

"Ah..." Miss Poole pinched her lips together and looked at him as though intent on reading his mind. He merely raised an eyebrow and waited. Until she confessed, "I'm not familiar with the sport but I doubt it's overly complicated."

"A certain skill is required if one desires to catch something." He reached for his wine. "I'm happy to offer instruction."

"That really isn't—"

"Oh yes," Juliana exclaimed. "Do say you'll join us."

He'd counted on the girl's desire for him to spend more time with her and turned to her now with a grateful nod. "Of course. I have no objection to your taking a boat and fishing, provided I come with you."

A plate filled with thinly sliced veal and roasted vegetables was placed before him.

"Then I'll not object to singing," Miss Poole informed him.

Grayson stared at her. It hadn't occurred to him until that second that she'd have the gumption to bargain with favors, even though she was in his employ and he could technically order her to do his bidding. Nevertheless, there was no denying the determined gleam in her moss–green eyes or the challenging twitch of her lips.

Whatever game they were playing, whatever the rules and eventual outcome, Miss Poole was fully engaged. She was the governess. He was lord of the manor. And yet, he could sense something vital between them – a connection as dangerous as it was intriguing.

"I've also been considering a visit to the shops," Miss Poole added as if she'd not just swept the rug out from under his feet. "It will do Miss Edwards good to get out more. And every young lady deserves to purchase new ribbons from time to time."

"I suppose," Grayson hedged. It struck him as odd that the woman was suddenly voicing all these ideas. He studied the gentle curve of her cheek and her otherwise guileless expression, searching for some ulterior motive to her requests. Finding none, yet choosing to err on the side of caution he said, "I shall accompany you. We'll take the carriage whenever you choose."

CHAPTER ELEVEN

The brief look of displeasure on Miss Poole's face confirmed Grayson's instinct. Miss Poole had a goal that required the use of a boat and a visit to town. Well, perhaps the boat was incidental, but the visit to town sure as hell smelled suspicious.

"Can we go tomorrow afternoon?" Juliana suggested with bright-eyed enthusiasm. "After fishing?"

Grayson's heart gave a painful squeeze. The fact that such a simple outing excited her so was testament to the solitude she had been made to suffer. He did not hesitate in his answer. "If Miss Poole agrees."

The governess blinked, then gave a slow nod. "Tomorrow afternoon will suit me well."

Silence followed as they continued eating. The veal was incredibly tender, melting in Grayson's mouth and exploding with decadent flavor. He took several bites before saying, "This is remarkably good, Juliana. The soup too."

"Just wait until the dessert arrives." Juliana grinned, her eyes sparkling with the knowledge of what was to come. "And I didn't spend more than two pounds."

"I commend you," he told her sincerely and turned to Miss Poole. "You've taught her well."

She dipped her chin, appreciation pulling the edge of her mouth into a soft smile. Grayson's chest tightened. *Finally.* This was for him. It might not be as bright as the one he'd seen her give Juliana, but it was warm enough to comfort his soul.

"Miss Edwards had a lengthy discussion with Mrs. Bradley, who kindly permitted her to browse through her recipe books."

Grayson froze in stupefaction. "You found the recipes for these dishes?"

"And made the shopping list with Mrs. Bradley's assistance." Juliana practically glowed with pride. And for good reason. She'd not only taken on Grayson's challenge, she'd found a way to surprise and impress him.

He stared at his food, then at Miss Poole, and finally at Juliana once more. "But I only gave you one day's notice."

"Yes, but if one applies oneself, as Miss Poole so often says, one can accomplish a great many things within a short time."

Laughter stole its way up Grayson's throat, the

unfamiliar sound filling the air as he grinned at them both. "Astonishing. Absolutely and undeniably—"

"Good lord," Juliana murmured. "He's—"

"Laughing," Miss Poole said, the wonder in her voice reflected in the studious tilt of her head and wide–eyed expression. She and Juliana were both gaping at him as though he were some curiosity in a museum.

The sensation – a long forgotten vibration of tendons and muscle – was equally strenuous and liberating. Odd but good at the same time. He finished with a throaty grunt, picked up his glass, and took a long sip. "I'm proud of you, Juliana. Well done."

"Thank you, Grayson."

Their plates were removed and small porcelain bowls were brought in, one for each of them, while bubbly liquid was poured into three clean glasses.

"Is that..." Miss Poole's voice betrayed a hint of uncontained excitement, prompting Grayson to glance at her.

"Champagne," Juliana said. "I thought it a good accompaniment to the ices."

Grayson's attention remained on Miss Poole, on the eager spark in her eyes, the way her lips parted ever so slightly in anticipation of trying the wine. It was breathtaking to watch, but also humbling to realize how much something he took for granted mattered to her. Without giving the ice in her bowl much more than a passing glance, she reached for her drink as though it were the Holy Grail, and set the glass to her lips.

What followed was not only mesmerizing, but totally and utterly seductive.

Everything around Grayson slowed as he watched the governess close her eyes and tilt her head back. Her dark eyelashes fluttered against her creamy white skin as the fragrant wine slid over her tongue, causing her throat to work as she swallowed. Traces of liquid, glistening on her lower lip, had him gripping the edge of the table, his muscles coiled in tight knots with the effort it took to maintain his composure.

And then came the sigh, a sensual expression of undeniable pleasure that told him exactly what this woman would sound like during the throes of passion. It was without a doubt the most erotic thing he'd ever seen.

Bloody hell.

Grayson darted a look toward Juliana, fearful she might have witnessed the unacceptable focus with which he'd watched Miss Poole drink. Or worse, the fact that he probably looked like he'd happily haul her off to his room to taste the champagne that still clung to her lips.

Thankfully, Juliana's attention was on her dessert, and since he could do with some cooling down, Grayson picked up his own spoon and let himself taste it. The distraction it offered was just what he needed as minty goodness mixed with chocolate and cream filled his mouth.

"Do you like it?" Juliana asked, eyeing him with unvarnished interest.

Grayson expelled a breath, forcing the tension out of his body. "It's delicious."

Miss Poole voiced her agreement while Grayson returned his attention to his bowl. Despite the change in subject, his lust hadn't fully abated. As such, he very much feared it might spike if he caught Miss Poole licking her spoon. So he kept his gaze averted and focused on eating his food. It wouldn't do to embarrass himself or anyone else when he rose from the table. And as things stood at the moment, doing so was a very real possibility unless he managed to get himself under control.

Olivia felt as though some giant creature had picked up her world and given it a tremendous shake. Her nerves were on edge, her thoughts in a muddle, and her stomach a flip–floppy mess. It was, in short, an insufferable state of being.

And it was all thanks to one blasted man.

Steeling herself, she prepared to sing the first verse of the song Miss Edwards had picked while doing her utmost to ignore Mr. Grier's imposing presence. He lounged on the sofa almost directly opposite where she stood. To avoid making eye contact, she raised her chin and fixed her gaze on a painting above him. To look directly at him threatened more than her tightly held composure. It threatened her sanity.

A series of notes leapt happily into the air when

Miss Edwards began to play. Olivia took a deep breath. And sang.

If she could only get through this.

The bargain she'd made with Mr. Grier certainly made her performance worthwhile. But she'd be dishonest in claiming she'd only had Agnes's list in mind when she'd done it. The truth was she'd savored the chance to turn the tables a little on her frustrating employer.

Heat swamped her once more. His kiss to her hand provoked a series of new sensations. Intense, sinful, and wildly inappropriate were but a few words with which to describe what had taken no more than a couple of seconds. The problem was it had taken one second too long. And yet, in her bewilderment, she'd not been certain that it was deliberate. Indeed, she'd convinced herself if wasn't.

Because the alternative...

Oh, the alternative...

Olivia's voice faltered on that earth-shattering thought. Despite her better judgment, she lowered her gaze to Mr. Grier. Only to find herself more confused than ever by his schooled expression. The man showed no hint of having lascivious thoughts where she was concerned. Which had to mean she was the only one with the wicked ideas.

She took a sharp breath, losing a note in the process, and did her best to recover.

Heat burned her cheeks and panic set in. She could not under any circumstances permit herself to yearn for Mr. Grier. Especially not when she barely liked the man. It was madness. Nothing would come of such folly.

"Are you all right, Miss Poole?"

Olivia started. How had she missed his approach? And the fact the song had ended?

She gave a dishonest nod and glanced at Miss Edwards. The girl was giving her a quizzical look – the sort that made Olivia wonder if she'd somehow managed to sing in Chinese.

"I'm just a bit tired, I'm afraid." Desperate for a reprieve, she forced her attention back to Mr. Grier. "If you'll permit, I'd like to retire for the evening."

He stared at her for a long, unbearable moment, those dark eyes of his locked with hers before finally shifting away. "Of course. Good night, Miss Poole."

"Good night, Mr. Grier. Miss Edwards." Never before had Olivia practiced the sort of restraint required to walk from that parlor rather than run.

And to think she'd have to face him again tomorrow.

She quickened her stride as soon as she reached the hallway and hastened upstairs to the confines of her bedchamber. Once inside, she sank against the door and expelled a tortured breath. If Mr. Grier ever learned of the manner in which he affected her, she'd probably kill herself and take her chances with St. Peter. But at least, despite all of that, she was finally making headway with her list, and with honoring Agnes.

CHAPTER TWELVE

Excitement bubbled inside Olivia the following day when she and Juliana set off for the lake. Not even the promise of Mr. Grier's presence could dampen her mood. She was far too keen to get onto the water to worry about the butterflies taking flight in her stomach when he came to join them. Or to consider how good he looked with his hair slightly mussed by the breeze. His confident stride did not bear mentioning any more than the snug fit of his fawn–colored breeches.

No. Olivia was far more interested in the fishing rods under his arm and the basket he carried. Or so she told herself since she could not afford to admire his virile physique lest she be reduced to a simpering fool. Which was out of the question.

Determined to maintain her equilibrium, she drew back her shoulders and greeted him with the deference he deserved as her employer. "Good morning, sir. I see you've come fully equipped for our outing."

Something dark and dangerous flashed in his eyes, so swiftly Olivia wondered if she'd imagined it.

His gaze brightened with enthusiasm. The edge of his mouth twitched, not quite giving way to a smile. "I could find only two rods so we'll have to share. There's bait in the basket along with some lemonade and a few sandwiches so we won't have to rush back for luncheon."

His thoughtfulness was somewhat surprising. It contradicted the indifference he'd shown Miss Edwards through his extensive absence and seeming lack of knowledge regarding her ill-treatment by Miss Chadwick. Then again, he did appear to be trying to make up for this mistake, first by granting Miss Edwards the chance to host a dinner and now by choosing to spend the day fishing and shopping with her. Even though he surely had business to attend to. An estate like Sutton Hall did not run itself.

Olivia considered this as she watched him load the boat with all the supplies. Concentration strained his features as he arranged the fishing rods to the side and set the basket on one of the benches. Was it possible she'd misjudged him?

Undoubtedly. Though she chose not to dwell any more on the question at present. For if he could leave her flustered despite her low regard, she worried what he'd have the power to do if she actually started to like him. She tightened her hold on the book she'd brought, annoyed with herself for having such thoughts when she ought not be thinking about him at all.

"Are you all right?" Miss Edwards whispered.

Olivia flinched and pasted a hasty smile on her face. "Yes. Yes, of course."

"Because you look a little unwell." Miss Edwards studied her with an alarming degree of interest. "As though you've eaten something that doesn't agree with your stomach."

"I was merely thinking of my late sister," Olivia lied, the guilt that accompanied it a heavy weight on her heart. "She would have loved to experience this."

"I'm sorry," Miss Edwards said. "I didn't realize…"

"It's no matter really." She'd no desire to talk about Agnes now lest she ruin the mood.

To her everlasting relief, Mr. Grier finished getting the boat ready in the next instant and offered Miss Edwards his hand. "Ready?"

The girl hurried toward him so he could help her embark. He waited until she was safely seated before extending his hand toward Olivia. Keeping her gaze averted from his, she moved toward him with every intention of proving herself immune to his touch. Last night, he'd caught her by surprise when he'd kissed her hand. That was all.

Resolved, she sucked in a breath and thought of James 1:14–16 as she placed her hand in Mr. Grier's. *Choosing sin will only destroy me.*

His fingers closed around hers and Olivia instinctively shuddered as every fiber of her being sprang to life with eager awareness.

"Watch your step," he murmured, his hold on her strengthening to keep her steady as she climbed inside.

He didn't release her until she was sitting opposite Miss Edwards, which was when she realized the only remaining space wide enough to accommodate him was at her side. Olivia leaned forward, prepared to switch places with the basket next to Miss Edwards while Mr. Grier unfastened the boat from the jetty. But she'd barely gotten her bottom up off the bench when the boat suddenly rocked to one side as he clambered on board, the sudden motion knocking her back.

His large body settled beside her, pressing along hers from shoulder to hip. This was what she'd meant to avoid by squeezing in beside Mrs. Brennent when she'd departed Treadmire – this close proximity to a man with whom she wasn't related.

Panic had filled her then at the thought of having Mr. Marsh and a stranger pushed up against her. To her shame, she did not share the same aversion toward Mr. Grier.

On the contrary, she welcomed the contact – the prickly heat creeping over her skin where his body touched hers, the secret thrill of feeling his muscles move as he shifted, of being able to map the contours of his arm and thigh through pure sensation. It was wicked. *She* was wicked. But heaven help her, she was also completely lost to the potent effect of his much-too-close proximity.

"You said you've never rowed before." His knee bumped hers as he turned to meet her gaze.

"Correct." How she managed to speak when it felt like her throat was made of sandpaper, she'd no idea.

"Then I would suggest you learn." He dropped his gaze. "What's that for?"

"Hmm?" He'd done it again – muddled her mind with his touch and abrupt change of topic.

"The book. I noticed it before."

"Oh. Um…" Olivia shook her head, desperate to return to her usual sensible self.

"It's a copy of Schiller's play, *Kabale Und Lieber*. I thought Miss Edwards might be able to read from it while we wait for our catch."

He frowned. "She just started learning German recently."

"I realize it will test her limited knowledge, but it was the only German language book I was able to find in the library."

"Well, I suggest you hand it to her now so you can grab the end of that oar." He waited until Olivia had complied before pushing away from the jetty. Water rippled around them as they slid further out onto the lake. Olivia tightened her grip on the oar handle and tried to move it against the water. It rose from the lake and slapped back down, sending a spray of water into the air.

"It's kind of like swimming," Mr. Grier said. "You need to use the broad part of the oar to push against the water. Like this." He placed one hand on top of Olivia's and proceeded to row. "Don't angle the oar too much one way or the other. Lift up and rotate. Dive under the surface and pull back. See? Now you try."

Olivia did her best to copy his demonstration. It took a bit of coordination but it helped when she matched his movements, and after a few failed attempts she finally figured it out. Delighted, she laughed as the boat glided smoothly across the lake. Goodness gracious this was invigorating. It filled her with an uncommon sense of accomplishment and made her feel like she'd just conquered the world.

"Well done, Miss Poole," Miss Edwards exclaimed with the same amount of praise Olivia offered when her charge did something correctly.

"We'd best start turning before we hit the embankment," Mr. Grier said. "Stop rowing, Miss Poole, and let me do the work."

She did as he asked, stilling her movements while he kept on rowing. The boat rocked gently as it came about, and then Mr. Grier moved the handle of his oar toward her. "Would you care to try on your own?"

Olivia glanced at him in surprise. "You wouldn't mind?"

"Not if it's something you'd like to attempt."

The warm sincerity in his gaze was so apart from the sharp intensity she was accustomed to from him, she scarcely knew how to respond. But there could be no denying her bone–deep desire to take him up on his offer. So she gave a quick nod. "It is."

Approval showed in the briefest of smiles. And then

he was helping Olivia take the oars. His arm reached behind her, caging her in as he placed his hands on the oar handles right next to hers. Applying a gentle touch, he guided her into an even rhythm, counting the beats before letting go. A gasp of elation sprang from Olivia's throat as she rowed the boat forward unaided.

"Well done." Mr. Grier's praise made her feel as though she could do anything in the world – take on any task she desired. "You're doing superbly."

Olivia grinned. "Had I known this would be such fun I'd have found a boat for myself years ago."

"I'm rather glad you didn't," Mr. Grier murmured, so low Olivia doubted Miss Edwards could hear.

She wondered at his remark and what he might mean and eventually gave up trying in favor of offering thanks. Being here, doing this, meant more to her than he or Miss Edwards would ever know, for it had enabled her to live out yet another of Agnes's dreams.

Pride bloomed deep within Grayson's chest as Miss Poole took charge of the rowing. Not because her task was especially difficult, because it wasn't, but because he'd sensed a deep yearning within her. And rather than ignore it in favor of social strictures and proper conduct and whatever rules might bind her and keep her from living a little, she'd chosen to dismiss them all in favor of taking something for herself.

It was evident in the way her eyes sparkled and how

her lips stretched until she was openly laughing. The joy on her face was infectious. Hell, it not only made Juliana laugh too but him as well. He could scarcely believe it. First last night and now today. Miss Poole had singlehandedly managed to distract him from the relentless burden of guilt and responsibility weighing upon his shoulders. For the first time since his father's passing, Grayson was able to breathe, to ignore the troubles constantly lingering at the back of his mind and simply relax.

The moment would without doubt be fleeting, but that didn't make it any less meaningful.

He helped her steer away from the opposite embankment and back toward the middle of the lake. "I believe this might be a good spot for fishing. Reverse your movements Miss Poole to halt the forward motion. That's it. Perfect."

"I'll find the bait," Juliana said and promptly turned to the basket beside her.

Grayson watched her with interest, certain she'd balk at the sight of live worms wriggling about in a jar. Instead, he was stunned by her lack of fussiness as she picked up one wriggling worm between her fingers and raised her gaze to his. "What comes next?"

"Um…" He sent Miss Poole a hasty glance to gauge her reaction, but she merely shrugged one shoulder and pressed her curving lips together, which wasn't the least bit helpful. Shouldn't Juliana's lack of squeamishness shock her as much as it did him? "I cannot believe you're holding a worm."

It was the first thing that came to mind and thus the first thing he thought of saying.

Juliana knit her brow. "How else is it supposed to get out of the jar and onto the hook?"

"I rather imagined I'd do the hooking," he told her.

"Why?" Juliana asked with confusion.

"Because ladies don't usually care to deal with slimy creatures." He couldn't believe he had to explain this as though he were the one acting against social norms.

Juliana considered the worm. "I don't see why when it's totally harmless."

Good Lord.

Grayson had always known Juliana favored the outdoors. He'd watched her stroll around the garden, pick flowers, take rides without ever seeing a hint of hoydenish behavior. But what if he hadn't been paying proper attention?

He quickly reached forward and snatched the worm from between her fingers. "I'll see to the baiting while you prepare the lemonade for us."

"Unfair," Juliana replied with a glare and a pout.

"Young ladies don't handle worms," he informed her. "They host teas, picnics, and dinner parties."

"But I—"

"Miss Edwards." Miss Poole's placating voice stopped Juliana from further complaints. "Remember what we discussed."

Grayson raised an eyebrow and glanced at Miss Poole. He'd rather like to know what she might be referring to. More so when Juliana gave a quick nod of agreement and started unpacking the lemonade. He made a mental note to quiz the governess later without Juliana present.

In the meantime...

He grabbed one of the fishing rods, baited the hook, and dropped the line in the water before repeating the process for the other rod. As soon as Juliana was done handing out glasses, he offered her one of the rods and showed her how to wedge it against a block of wood attached to the floor frame so she wouldn't have to keep holding it steady. He did the same for Miss Poole, his hand brushing hers to allow for the briefest of contact.

It was enough to make his heart pound in response to the sparks she so guilelessly scattered across his skin. He took a deep breath and slowly expelled it. Sitting beside her, feeling the warmth of her supple body moving against him as she rowed, had tested his sanity and his resolve. But in his desire for added closeness – the knowledge that this was all he could hope for with her – he had accepted the torture in exchange for the pleasure of having her near.

Bloody hell, she smelled delicious, like ripe citrus mixed with fresh honey.

"Mr. Grier?"

The sound of her voice cleared the fog in his brain. "I beg your pardon?"

A humorous smile curved her lips. "I do believe I can manage."

Realizing he was leaning toward her, his hand still

on the rod, he jerked himself back and let go. "Right. Of course you can."

Averting her gaze, she secured her fishing rod as Juliana had done, though not before he managed to see the deep shade of red sweeping her cheeks. Grayson smothered a triumphant smile and sent Juliana a hasty glance. Thankfully, his ward's attention was fixed on the book Miss Poole had brought with her.

"*Einmal für allemal,*" Juliana attempted, taking great care to sound out the words as she read them. "*Der hand–el wird ern...ernft—*"

"*Ernfthaft,*" Miss Poole supplied. "It means serious."

"And the rest of it?" Juliana bit her lip and mouthed the words again. "I'm guessing the first part is 'once for...all'? Once and for all?"

"Correct. *Handel* means trade," Miss Poole informed her without adding anything further.

When Grayson opened his mouth to elaborate, Miss Poole placed a staying hand on his arm. Which naturally sent his mind reeling, because how the devil had she known he'd interfere without looking at him? Was she even aware that she'd touched him and did she know that the press of her hand was enough to make him go mad?

"So then the trade is serious?" Juliana asked while Grayson struggled to get a grip on himself.

He'd forgotten what they were talking about and tried to focus on figuring it out.

"The trade is getting serious," Olivia corrected, withdrawing her hand from his arm. "Try reading it again now that you understand the meaning."

Right. The German.

Grayson turned his attention toward the embankment, deliberately training is gaze on anything *not* Olivia Poole. The loss of her touch, the bereft feeling itching his skin, made him want to press his own palm to the spot where her hand had been. Disturbed by the power she seemed to wield with so little effort, he fought the urge and resisted.

Meanwhile, Juliana and Miss Poole continued discussing the text while drinking lemonade and eating biscuits. "It's not fair," Juliana said a bit later, pulling Grayson back to the subject of *Kabale Und Lieber.* "If Louise and Ferdinand love each other, they ought to be able to marry."

"If only life were so easy," Miss Poole mused. "But you see, Ferdinand is a high ranking member of society and Louise is just a musician's daughter."

"So what?" Juliana asked as she snapped the book shut and set it aside.

Grayson's jaw dropped. "Do you not see the problem?"

"Marrying would lead to scandal," Miss Poole explained, her voice a bit tighter than before. Gentling her tone she softly added, "Life is often unfair and as such, Ferdinand and Louise are doomed to be star–crossed lovers. Much like Romeo and Juliette."

"Another ridiculous story," Juliana muttered.

"It certainly doesn't have the happy ending one might wish for," Miss Poole said.

Grayson wasn't sure why this comment annoyed him. Maybe it had something to do with the melancholic sigh that followed, or maybe it was because the entire discussion revealed a flaw in Juliana's way of thinking.

Either way, he found himself increasingly tense and quite unable to stop from suddenly asking, "Is that why you never married, Miss Poole? Because you were denied the husband you wanted?"

CHAPTER THIRTEEN

As part of her daily housekeeping duties, Mary was doing her late-morning rounds when a movement beyond one of the music room windows caught her attention. Turning more fully toward the view she spotted the boat on the water. And stopped to stare. Was that Mr. Grier? With Miss Edwards and Miss Poole?

Surprise came first, followed by satisfaction. He should be spending more time with his ward. Miss Edwards deserved his attention and guidance. And it wouldn't hurt for him to chat with a woman of Miss Poole's character.

Mary smiled at that thought. Miss Poole might have been at her wits end when she'd first arrived, but she had since proven herself resilient and principled, worthy of anyone's admiration.

She flinched at the sound of the door swinging open behind her.

"I was wondering where I might find you." Mr. Dover's voice, so wonderfully familiar, warmed her to the tips of her toes. She turned toward him as he crossed to where she stood. A look of interest shone in his eyes. "What's got your attention?"

She tilted her head toward the window. "Have a look for yourself."

Mr. Dover drew closer until he stood by her side. He looked through the window. A twitch at the edge of his lips accompanied by a sigh of contentment conveyed the pleasure he found in the view.

"He looks so relaxed." His voice caught with a hint of emotion. "It's good to see him enjoying himself for a change."

Mary agreed. She'd not seen Mr. Grier smile since his father's passing, a shame since he'd once had a wonderful smile and laughter. "Miss Edwards will surely benefit from his increased attention."

Mr. Dover was silent a moment and then, "They almost look like a…"

"What?" Mary prompted when he let the thought trail off.

He shook his head and glanced at her with a hint of sentimentality. "I was going to say family."

Surprised by the notion, Mary returned her attention to the scene on the lake. Mr. Grier wasn't related to Miss Edwards or to Miss Poole, but upon further reflection, Mary could see Mr. Dover's point. It didn't look like Miss Edwards was Mr. Grier's burden or as if Miss Poole were intruding on their time together. If anything, it looked as though they welcomed each other's company and as if they...belonged together.

"It reminds me of when his father would take him and his brothers fishing," Mr. Dover said. "The pleasure they found in spending the day together was as unmistakable as it is now."

"You don't suppose...that is to say..." Mary bit her lip, unsure if voicing her thought would be wise.

"You're wondering if Miss Poole might be the woman Mr. Grier needs." He dropped his gaze, his eyes meeting Mary's until heat crept into her cheeks. "There's no denying she's good for our lad. Taking the boat out was her idea, in case you were wondering."

"Really?"

"Roger told me about it. Said Miss Poole asked for permission to take Miss Edwards fishing."

"And Mr. Grier agreed to accompany them without protest?"

Mr. Dover's eyebrows rose toward his thinning hairline. "On the contrary, Mr. Grier insisted he go with them."

Mary paused on a sharp inhalation and glanced outside once more. "Do you know what this means?"

"That Miss Poole has managed to do the impossible?"

"Quite so." The thought that followed prompted her to give Mr. Dover her full attention. "What if this is Mr. Grier's chance at a love match?"

Mr. Dover laughed with surprise. "My dear Mrs. Hodgins, I wasn't aware you were such a romantic."

Self-awareness prompted her to fiddle with the curtain tie. "I have my moments."

A comfortable silence settled between them before he eventually said, "Although it's not unheard of for a governess to become lady of the manor, I believe she'd have to be upper class in order to aspire to such a position. Miss Poole isn't any such thing."

"Perhaps not, but Mr. Grier isn't a peer either, which technically leaves him free to do as he wishes as long as he's willing to withstand social disapproval." Mary released the curtain tie and turned more fully toward Mr. Dover. She gave him an imploring look. "We must honor his father's will."

Mr. Dover gave a slow and thoughtful nod. "Steer his son in the right direction. Be supportive and help him recognize love when he finds it."

The request had come as a shock at first. With time, Mary had seen the desperation in it. Her former master had known his son well. He'd realized his death would not make it easier for him to think of himself and that he might require assistance.

"I suppose that's true." Mr. Dover scratched his head, displacing some neatly combed strands of his silver-streaked hair before dropping his hand. "But you and I are just servants, Mrs. Hodgins. I'm not sure what we can do to help."

"Neither am I," Mary admitted, "besides making sure there's plenty of opportunity for them to form an attachment – that they are not interrupted for any reason when they are together."

"Your plan is to give them the chance they need to get to know one another?"

"They can hardly fall in love otherwise."

Amusement danced in the butler's eyes. His expression eased into smoother lines. "You make an excellent point. Perhaps we can discuss the matter at greater length this evening, over a glass of wine in your sitting room?"

There was no denying the flicker of hope in his caramel–colored eyes or the joy his suggestion stirred in her breast. "I'd like that, Mr. Dover."

He held her gaze a moment longer before stepping back. "Mrs. Bradley asked me to tell you that this week's supplies have arrived from Varney."

"In that case I'd best return to the kitchen." The food would have to be weighed to make sure it matched the order and the expenditure listed in her ledger. "I'll see you later, Mr. Dover."

"I shall look forward to it," he told her as she took her leave with a lighter tread than usual. Drinks with Mr. Dover was certainly progress. A happy smile caught her lips as she looked forward to seeing where it might lead.

CHAPTER FOURTEEN

"Grayson."

Rather than acknowledge the accusation in Miss Edwards's voice, Mr. Grier kept his gaze firmly on Olivia while she did her best to refrain from squirming.

Is that why you never married? Because you were denied the husband you wanted?

The question, though calmly spoken, was without doubt the most shocking one she'd ever received. It wasn't the sort of thing a gentleman asked a woman in his employ. Not in a million years.

Still, now that he'd done so, Olivia was determined to answer with matching boldness. She would not quiver before him or shy away, despite the temptation to leap from the boat and escape his piercing scrutiny.

Instead, she'd bloody well stand her ground regardless of how exposed and unsettled he made her feel.

With this in mind, she took a deep breath and gave her response. "No."

She said nothing further and prayed he'd refrain from pressing the issue. The last thing she wanted to tell him was that she'd never been courted, that she'd been stuck without hope of starting a family of her own, that there had been no opportunity for her to fall in love. This would only reveal how deprived she'd been and worse, lead to pity.

Unfortunately, she underestimated his desire to learn more about her. For rather than let the matter rest, he casually asked, "Why then, Miss Poole?"

"You are too forward, Mr. Grier, but since you've clearly set your mind on appeasing your curiosity where I'm concerned, I shall tell you why I've never married." Frustrated by his insistence, she squared her shoulders and told him bluntly, "It is because my father wouldn't permit it."

There was no denying the pleasure with which she watched Mr. Grier's eyebrows rise toward his hairline. Surprise was evident in his features. Whatever he'd thought she might say, it hadn't been this.

"I don't understand," he muttered just as her fishing line started to move. "I'm—"

"What's your excuse?" she asked, taking the chance to turn the tables. If he thought to bother her, she'd gladly return the favor. She even smiled at his wide-eyed expression and chose to press her advantage. "As your father's heir, it is your duty to marry and secure the family lineage. Is it not? Yet here you are, well past your prime, without so much as a hint of settling down."

To her everlasting satisfaction, the pompous man's mouth fell open. He gaped at her. "Did you just call me old?"

Miss Edwards snorted with poorly concealed amusement while Olivia held herself perfectly still. Her heart bounced about as if it were unhinged. Good grief. The blasted man had made her forget herself completely, and now she'd insulted him and there was a very good chance he'd not stand for it.

If she were wise, she'd apologize to him immediately, before he decided she was a bad influence on Miss Edwards.

Doing her best to squash her pride, she prepared to do what she had to in order to save her position only to be denied the chance when he said, "And while it is none of your business, I'll have you know that I do have a lady in mind for Sutton Hall's future mistress."

It was Olivia's turn to be stumped. She'd not expected this.

"Who?" Miss Edwards demanded. It seemed she was just as surprised by this news as Olivia.

"Miss Howell," he said, the name rushing past his lips as though shot from a cannon. A sharp intake of breath was followed by a slow exhale as he crossed his arms and sent Olivia a challenging look.

"Oh." Miss Edwards seemed to consider this information and finally shrugged one shoulder before informing Olivia. "She's very nice."

"Young, too, and quite pretty," Mr. Grier added, his posture stiffer than usual.

Olivia glared at him, at his smug smile and the arrogant gleam in his eyes. She had the strongest urge to shove him overboard right now, which wasn't like her at all.

Irritated with him and with herself for letting him rile her, Olivia twisted away, intent on blocking him from her mind. Of course he was looking to marry. And of course the woman he took to wife would be young and healthy, capable of producing as many children as he desired. It ought not bother her in the slightest.

And yet, there was no denying the niggling disappointment deep in her breast. Due to what? The fact that he'd flirted with her a little? If that was indeed what he'd been doing. Now that she knew his interests lay elsewhere, she wasn't so sure.

Her fishing line jerked, alerting her to a possible catch. She picked up her fishing rod with both hands at the same time as loud yapping reached them from the front lawn.

"Daphne?" Miss Edwards spoke to Mr. Grier. "Can you see what's happening?"

Distracted by the weight tugging hard at the end of the line, Olivia ignored her companions. She needed to focus on something else – something besides the image of Mr. Grier speaking his vows to the lovely Miss Howell.

"It looks as though one of the maids is chasing her,"

Mr. Grier muttered.

A hard pull on the end of the line forced Olivia up off the bench. The motion sent the boat rocking, putting her slightly off balance.

Quacking ensued and Miss Edwards gasped. "Daphne! No!"

"Miss Poole," Mr. Grier said as she tried to lean back, bracing one foot against the side of the boat for purchase. "Please sit down."

Not yet. Not when she was finally pulling the fish – a perch from the looks of it – from the water. The yapping increased, as did the quacking. Miss Edwards insisted Mr. Grier row them back to shore. Olivia shifted her feet and the boat dipped to one side.

A hand – *his* hand – settled firmly against her back, no doubt in an effort to keep her steady. "Allow me to help while—"

Whatever else he'd meant to say was lost to her as she whipped around, intent on insisting he leave her alone. But the words she meant to say caught in her throat as the boat plunged to one side, then jolted back in the other direction, pitching her forward and sending her over the side.

She hit the water with a splash and a most undignified squeal before sinking under the surface. Instinct took over and she began fighting the weight of her waterlogged gown, but as she attempted to swim, her progress was halted by something anchoring her in place.

Fearful of submitting to panic, Olivia opened her eyes to try and see what the hindrance could be. It looked like the twigs from a branch resting upon the lakebed had caught the back of her skirt. Olivia tried to dive deeper so she could untangle herself, but no matter how much she twisted and turned, the area where the twigs snagged her gown remained out of reach.

Perfect.

She would obviously drown now and her epitaph would likely read:

Here lies the fool, Olivia Pool. Although she could swim, a branch did her in.

Annoyed by her own stupidity, by the manner in which she'd gotten herself into this situation – because of a man who would never consider her more than a servant – she yanked her gown harder. She could not die like this. It was far too humiliating.

The water suddenly shifted around her and then a large body brushed up against her, pushing her sideways. Her lungs started to burn with the effort it took to keep holding her breath. Rough movements tugged on her body, easing the tension that held her in place until she was suddenly being pushed upward.

Relief poured through her when she broke the surface one second later. She coughed and sputtered, gasping as air was forced into her lungs.

"Good heavens." Miss Edwards's voice came from somewhere overhead. "Is she all right?"

Tendrils of hair plastered over Olivia's face

obscured her vision as strong arms grabbed her, hauling her against a solid frame.

"I've got you," Mr. Grier murmured close to her ear, his voice rough and shaky as he pushed her hair from her eyes. "Tell me you're well. Please say something to me. Anything at all. Just—"

"Thank you." The words were more of a wheeze than anything else.

He emitted a ragged breath as he hugged her to him and, she'd later recall, pressed a kiss to her brow. Treading water, he guided her back to the boat and helped her climb in. She landed in an awkward sprawl in the bottom, her head resting heavily on the bench where she'd been sitting a short while before. Eyes closed, she savored the warmth of the sun on her face, the breeze gently tickling her skin, the pleasure of being alive.

The boat rocked sharply to the right as Mr. Grier hauled himself over the side. A thud followed when his feet landed beside Olivia.

A brief silence followed and then, "Miss Poole?"

Olivia opened her eyes and met Mr. Grier's assessing gaze. He was leaning over her, studying her with a complex emotion that made him look less like the bastion he always appeared and more like a terrified man in desperate need of more reassurance.

For the second time, Mr. Grier had let down his guard in her presence and shown Olivia that he was not made of stone. She blinked up at him while doing her best to squash a sudden and most inappropriate urge to wrap her arms around him, to hold him close, and to ease his concerns.

"I am well," she said instead. "I am unharmed."

He took a sharp breath and expelled it. The hard lines on his forehead faded and then his shoulders sagged. A hand, large and strong, clasped hers, infusing her with a sense of rightness – of belonging – that was so out of place she nearly gasped.

"Thank God." His gravelly voice conveyed a depth of emotion that shot through Olivia's veins and straight to her heart. To her dismay, he sank down beside her instead of taking a seat on the bench, and drew her against his side.

"Can you row us back to shore?" he asked Miss Edwards.

"Of course." Miss Edwards grabbed the oar handles and quickly set the boat in motion.

"We'll get you dried off soon enough," Mr. Grier promised. "You'll be fine. Just fine."

The warmth in his voice chased away the wet chill seeping into Olivia's bones. Soft but firm, it offered an endless amount of comfort.

When they returned to the jetty, he was the first to disembark.

Betsy, who'd picked up Daphne, was there to greet them, an anxious expression straining her features. "I saw what happened. What can I do to help?"

"You can lock up that dog," Mr. Grier told her, his movements efficient as he proceeded to dock the boat.

"It wasn't Daphne's fault," Miss Edwards protested.

"No," Olivia agreed. "If anything I am the one to blame. Had it not been for me, we'd not have been on the lake in the first place."

Mr. Grier stared at her, his dark eyes holding her captive while making her very aware of the way her gown clung to her body. Gone was the terror he'd revealed just moments before, replaced by the piercing sort of intensity that would turn the most pious nun's knees to jelly. It didn't help that his shirt and breeches were pasted to his body, revealing contours that ought to remain hidden.

Heat flooded Olivia's cheeks and the edge of Mr. Grier's mouth twitched, informing her that he'd noted the blush, but before she could think of how to react or what she might say to explain away her response, he'd returned his attention to Betsy.

"Go back to the house and have a hot bath prepared for Miss Poole straight away. The last thing we want is for her to catch a cold."

"And for you, sir?" Betsy asked.

"I can wait," he said. Betsy didn't hesitate further, hurrying off with Daphne in her arms.

"Do you mind if we head into town a bit later than planned?" Olivia asked Miss Edwards and Mr. Grier while the three of them walked back to the house. It was slow going due to the sodden skirts wrapped around Olivia's legs. Her wet shoes didn't help. "My bath can be quick but it will take time for my hair to fully dry."

.　.　.

"We're staying home for the rest of the day," Mr. Grier informed her. He gave her a sardonic look before adding, "So you can rest."

"I'm fine," Olivia told him. "I've already said so."

"We can easily postpone our outing until tomorrow," Miss Edwards said, the smile she gave Olivia assuring her of her sincerity.

"You'll have your bath and then you will climb into bed," Mr. Grier said while the squelch of his boots added weight to each word.

"But it's—"

He rounded on her then, his eyes hard as flint while his lips pressed together in a grim line. "You very nearly died today while in my care. So don't argue with me further. Not when there's still a chance of your coming down with a fever."

Olivia didn't think she was at greater risk of falling ill than he was, but chose to keep that thought to herself. Instead she told him, "I was just going to say that it's only mid–day. I'm not sure staying in bed until tomorrow is feasible."

He held her gaze for another second, then turned away with a muttered remark she couldn't make out, and continued his progress toward the house while she and Miss Edwards followed behind.

CHAPTER FIFTEEN

T he sun shone brightly from behind a few scattered clouds the following afternoon as Grayson, Juliana, and Miss Poole set off for town in his carriage. He'd paced the foyer while waiting for them, his patience slipping a little more each time he glanced at the clock. They'd been late. By five long minutes. But at least Miss Poole had been bright and composed, such a difference from her shaky condition after the accident.

Yesterday he'd faced the same slowing of time he'd experienced in Aboukir when he'd watched Richard die. A similar sense of helplessness had gripped him while he'd fought to free Miss Poole, painfully aware of how easily he might lose her. And then the aggravating woman had suggested they stick to their plan and go shopping. Honestly, it was a miracle he hadn't strangled her right there on the spot.

Agitated, he glared at the passing scenery. She'd tested his patience and his pride with her comment about his age, prompting him to be dishonest, which didn't bode well for his own peace of mind. Because he'd always spoken the truth. Until he'd mentioned Miss Howell.

It was so unlike him.

Hell, he'd no interest in the girl or in marriage. It had been a spur of the moment remark – an impulsive response to Miss Poole's critical comment. The carriage bounced over a pothole, jostling him. He kept his gaze firmly on the freshly ploughed fields while trying to figure out why he'd done it.

Because you like her, you fool. Because her opinion of you matters. Because you don't want her thinking you're well past your prime. Because that hurt.

It was a jarring realization to make, because it meant she'd begun to matter.

Of course she had. When he'd thought he might lose her...

Good God. His heart still hurt just thinking about it.

"Damned nuisance."

"I beg your pardon?" Juliana queried.

Grayson started. He turned to see that both ladies were staring at him, unblinking.

"Forgive me," he said, his tone dry. "I was contemplating the Scottish Insurrection and the result it may have on one of my investments."

"Ah," said Miss Poole with an irritating degree of suspicion.

Grayson clenched his jaw and returned his gaze to the view outside. If only he'd chosen to stay home and do some woodwork. The craft his father had taught him and which he had since turned into a lucrative business would surely have helped him expel some of the tension pulling at every muscle. Instead, he would be keeping company with a woman who promised to drive him mad. Partly because of the ghastly black dress she'd again chosen to wear and partly because of the terrible thoughts the despicable garment led to.

Like the urge to rip it away from her body and burn it.

He closed his eyes and thanked the Lord when the carriage finally drew to a halt.

"If you like, Miss Poole and I can visit the haberdashery while you visit the cobbler next door," Juliana said once they'd all alit from the carriage. "We can reconvene at the coffee shop later."

Her hopeful expression informed him that she did not want him tagging along on her shopping expedition. And who could blame her when he was in this rotten mood?

"Very well." He retrieved his pocket watch and gave it a quick glance. "Will an hour suffice?"

"I'm sure we can manage our errands in less," Miss Poole quipped.

Recalling her and Juliana's tardiness when he'd been waiting for them in the foyer, he muttered, "I doubt it. We'll reconvene at ten after three, which will give you the extra five minutes I'm certain you'll need."

Mr. Grier was clearly in a snit, most likely because of the previous day's events. He'd been shaken, that much was clear to Olivia. But given the fact that she was fine – that they both were – his fears should have been put to rest. Yet he remained brooding and surly. He clearly wasn't enjoying their outing.

She watched him walk away while reminding herself not to care if he treated her with indifference. Which was easier said than done. Especially after the deep concern he'd shown after he'd saved her. There was no forgetting the sweet caress of his lips as he'd braced her against him. But maybe she put too much weight on the gesture. Maybe he'd simply acted in shock. After all, he had said he planned on taking Miss Howell – whoever she was – to wife.

A pang of jealousy struck her heart, prompting her to wince.

"Don't mind him," Miss Edwards said. "He's obviously got his unmentionables in a twist."

Olivia gave a startled laugh. "You really shouldn't say such things, Miss Edwards."

"And you really ought to start calling me Juliana."

The suggestion caught Olivia by surprise. "I'm not sure that would be very appropriate."

"It is if you think me your friend." The girl fiddled with the beadwork on her reticule. "Unless, of course, you don't."

"Oh, but I do." Olivia exclaimed, prompting a wide smile from her young charge.

"Then we're in agreement?" They stepped aside to give way to a man with a crate wedged on one shoulder.

"Only if you will call me Olivia in return."

Juliana grinned as a carriage rattled past. "I'd be happy to."

Olivia took the girl's arm as a testament to their agreement. "Come on then. Let's purchase some ribbons."

They entered the haberdashery to the sound of a tinkling bell. The smell of newly oiled wood hung in the air. The shop was mostly empty, save for an older woman conversing with the clerk, who welcomed Olivia and Juliana with a nod of acknowledgement. Tall glossy shelving units and cabinets lined the walls, filled with neatly arranged assortments of boxes, yarns, stacked trimmings, and bolts of fabric.

"Are you looking for anything in particular?" the clerk asked once she'd finished attending to the other customer. A lean woman with spectacles perched on a pointy nose, thin lips, and deep grooves set in her cheeks, she'd left her youth behind a long time ago.

"I'd like to purchase some blue ribbon and crystal beads, if you have them," Juliana said. To Olivia she added, "I'm going to make a pretty bow for Daphne to wear around her neck."

"You'll find various shades in this box," the clerk said, pulling the container from one of the shelves behind the counter. "The beads are in the small drawers over there."

The clerk looked at Olivia next. "And for you?"

Olivia bit her lip. She glanced at Juliana, who was now fully occupied by the blue ribbons. Although yesterday's rowing experience had ended in disaster, it had allowed Olivia to strike *sail a boat* from her list and move on to the next item.

"May I see your collection of lace and red ribbon?"

The clerk didn't even blink, for which Olivia was grateful. "Of course."

Additional boxes were retrieved and set on the well-used counter, their lids removed to reveal the most beautiful trimmings Olivia had ever seen. She stared at the lace in wonder, stunned by the intricate craftsmanship. And the ribbons were gorgeous too.

Olivia traced one fingertip carefully over a slippery length of satin.

"That's a beautiful color," Juliana said.

Olivia nodded. "It's my favorite."

"Then you must buy some."

"I'll certainly consider it." Olivia gave her attention to the lace and quickly found a piece to suit her needs. She addressed the clerk. "I'd like half a yard of this along with another half a yard of the ribbon. Some thread to match too. And a needle with which to sew."

The clerk retrieved a pair of scissors and started preparing her order along with the items Juliana wanted.

"Might we visit the butcher next?" Juliana asked.

"It's what we agreed," Olivia said. Their plan to catch a fish for Juliana to dissect had failed because of Olivia. As a result, she'd promised to help the girl acquire another specimen during their trip to Varney.

Olivia paid the clerk and took her brown paper parcel while Juliana added a few more items to her order. Leaving her to it, Olivia went to peruse some buttons and hair combs displayed on a table near the front window. The delicately carved teeth and mother of pearl inlays on each comb, along with the sleekly polished surface, turned the wood into works of art.

"They're made by a local craftsman," the clerk informed Olivia while wrapping up Juliana's order.

"They're exquisite," Olivia murmured, picking one up and turning it over between her fingers.

"Would you like to try one?"

Olivia shook her head and returned the comb. "Thank you, but no. At five shillings a piece I'm afraid I cannot afford to."

"I could purchase one for you as a gift," Juliana said.

"Absolutely not," Olivia told her, horrified by the idea that the girl she was hired to teach would consider spending her pin money in such a way. Noting the disheartened look on her face, however, Olivia hastened to add, "I appreciate the generous offer, but it would be wrong of me to accept."

She prepared to turn for the door as they were now ready to leave, when a movement outside drew her attention. Mr. Grier was in the process of raising his hat in greeting.

This caused Olivia's gaze to slide sideways, until she spotted a lovely young woman with endless blonde curls tucked under the brim of a fashionable bonnet.

With a creamy complexion tinged with a perfect amount of blush in her cheeks, deep rosy lips, and eyes that matched the bluest of skies, she was everything Olivia wasn't.

"Who is that?" she asked and immediately regretted posing the question since she ought not care about the identity of the woman Mr. Grier spoke with. Unless she herself had an interest in him. Which she most certainly did not.

She sent Juliana a swift glance to gauge her reaction. Thankfully she did not appear to have noticed anything wrong with Olivia's curiosity or the slight clip to her tone when she'd spoken.

"Miss Edwina Howell," Juliana supplied as the shop door opened to admit a new customer.

The name stabbed at Olivia's breast. "She's the lady Mr. Grier means to marry."

"I suppose, though I must confess I'm surprised." Juliana frowned before adding, "Her parents, Viscount and Viscountess Oldbridge, own Oldbridge House a few miles north of here. She's their only child. Based on my previous interactions with her, I believe she's intent on catching Grayson, though his interest in her never struck me as more than polite at best."

"She's very pretty," Olivia remarked since there was no denying the fact.

"I've always considered her unremarkable."

Olivia snorted. Miss Howell was literally the furthest thing from unremarkable Olivia had ever seen. The woman looked like a princess who'd just stepped out of a fairytale. "You don't like her."

"Not true," Juliana said while they watched Mr. Grier exchange pleasantries with Miss Howell. "She's perfectly lovely, good natured, and kind."

An awful sensation began taking root in Olivia's stomach. She did her best to squash it. Jealousy had no place here. Not with regard to herself and a man she had no business wanting.

"She sounds rather perfect." It was impossible not to come across as bitter while acknowledging the fact that Miss Howell might one day be mistress of Sutton Hall. Unlike Olivia, who would remain beneath Mr. Grier's notice forever.

She shook her head. What perfectly asinine musings.

So he'd made her heart flutter a couple of times and had caused her to blush on occasion. All of that was probably perfectly normal given her limited experience with men. In time, such reactions would surely dissipate, and she would no longer have him intruding upon her dreams.

Yes. That was it. She was the piously raised daughter of a vicar. It was only natural for her carnal desires to be tested the moment she ventured out into the world. Her job was to resist it.

With this in mind, she hardened her heart and told

Juliana, "We cannot remain here forever. If we're to visit the butcher before reconvening with Mr. Grier for tea, we probably ought to be on our way."

Even if leaving the shop would involve crossing paths with Miss Howell.

CHAPTER SIXTEEN

G rayson had hoped to avoid Miss Howell the moment he'd seen her turn the street corner. Having just left the cobbler, he'd taken a hasty step back in a desperate move to retreat inside before she saw him. Alas, he'd not been swift enough and was now forced to suffer her hopeful gaze and that genteel way of hers that prevented him from excusing himself from her company without exchanging pleasantries.

What the hell had he been thinking, telling Miss Poole and Juliana he meant to marry the chit when he'd always sought to avoid her? Not because there was anything unlikeable about her *per se*. He'd simply never felt anything for her besides indifference. Indeed, he believed he'd have a more interesting conversation with a fashion plate than with Miss Howell. Not to mention her age. She was much too young for his taste.

"I'm so incredibly glad to see you again, Mr. Grier."

Miss Howell smiled at him, not with the coyness so often witnessed among London ladies, but with genuine appreciation. "Now that you have returned, you simply must make good on that invitation Mama and Papa issued when you were last here. If you'll recall, you had to decline on account of a cold, from which you appear to have since recovered."

He attempted a smile which felt strained and ill-fitting. "Indeed. Colds do tend to come and go in the space of one week. It would be worrisome if mine were still with me more than four months later."

"How right you are." She angled her head while peering at him with the sort of owlish interest that made him feel as if a noose had been dropped around his neck. "When would you like to stop by for dinner? My parents and I will be traveling next week."

"Oh?" This was excellent news though he did his best not to look too pleased. "Where to?"

"We're heading to Scotland for my aunt and uncle's silver wedding anniversary."

Grayson did a quick calculation. He'd never been to Scotland, but he'd been to Manchester, which was roughly half way. Getting there had taken a couple of weeks so… "You'll be gone a while then, I suspect."

"Until early July." She hesitated, as if hoping he'd say something more. When he didn't she told him, "I'd dearly love to see you before I go. Shall we say Friday? Six o'clock?"

"I…ah…" Grayson cleared his throat while trying to think up a reasonable excuse.

The door to the haberdashery shop opened in the next instant, and Juliana exited onto the pavement, followed by the delectable Miss Poole.

Delectable?

Grayson considered the woman and realized the word suited her to perfection. However ill–advised it might be for him to think of an employee in such terms.

"Good day, Miss Howell," said Juliana. "May I present my governess, Miss Olivia Poole?"

Miss Howell smiled sweetly. She did not turn her nose up at the idea of being introduced to a servant as her mother would likely do. Instead she said, "It's a pleasure to make your acquaintance."

To be fair, there was nothing disagreeable about the lady. She always looked lovely in her smart dresses and with her hair perfectly coiffed. Most importantly, she possessed what most would describe as a very likeable character.

Unfortunately, Grayson found her remarkably boring.

He glanced at Miss Poole and felt an immediate spark of…something…when she gave him a combative stare in return. Unlike Miss Howell, this woman was brimming with passion and knowledge and something else – a secret element begging to be uncovered. The interest he saw in her eyes combined with her seeming wish to avoid him were like a lure with which to catch the biggest, baddest, fish in the sea.

If she were present, supper with Miss Howell and her parents might be tolerable.

Straightening, he turned to Miss Howell. "That supper you mentioned. Why not take it at Sutton Hall instead of Oldbridge House?"

"Well I–"

"You've never dined there before so it ought to be a novel experience, I'd imagine." He said this with every intention of appealing to the part of her that craved agreeability beyond all else.

As expected, she smiled. "Thank you, Mr. Grier. I shall tell Mama and Papa the good news. Is Friday still a good day?"

"It is."

"And the hour?"

"Six o' clock suits me well."

"Excellent." Miss Howell looked as though she'd just been handed the keys to the city. "If you'll excuse me, I'd best get on with my purchases, but I shall look forward to seeing you again soon, Mr. Grier. Miss Edwards. Miss Poole."

Grayson gave her a parting nod while Miss Edwards and Miss Poole bid her a good day.

"Miss Poole and I have one more purchase to make before we have tea," Juliana informed him as soon as Miss Howell was gone.

"I'll accompany you," Grayson said. Although he dreaded Miss Poole's proximity and the effect it would have upon him, he was equally loath to part with her. Which put him in a bit of a bind.

"That's awfully good of you," Juliana said while eyeing her governess with what appeared to be marked desperation. "We would certainly be honored by your company although we...um..."

"Our business pertains to a feminine matter," Miss Poole informed him, her tone so curt he felt as though he'd insulted them by daring to offer his escort.

The remark bristled, though it had the effect they no doubt desired. The very last thing he wanted was to be present while his ward shopped for stays or, God forbid, sanitary cloths for her courses.

"Very well. I'll see to procuring a table for us at the teashop. You may join me there when you're ready." He tipped his hat and strode off, choosing to take the long route for the purpose of banishing some pent-up tension. It had subsided to some degree while he'd been at the cobblers but was now back in full force.

At least he'd be getting a new pair of boots out of this, he mused while cursing the predicament Miss Poole posed. He was clearly attracted to her, but was prevented from acting upon it due to his code of honor. He wanted her company, which promised thought, discourse, and conflict – things he'd not realized he lacked or needed until she'd swept into his life.

Honestly, the simplest course of action was to leave, head back to London, and forget Miss Poole altogether. Or sack her and hire another governess.

Grayson sighed. Either of those solutions would disappoint Juliana, which was something he could not do after his latest blunder. No. He'd simply have to pull himself together, avoid temptation, and focus on what truly mattered right now – Juliana's happiness and social launch. He was a grown man, for God's sake. He'd figure it out somehow.

Or so he thought until Friday when Miss Howell arrived with her parents. Funny how fast five days could go by when a dreaded event awaited. Since his excursion to Varney, Grayson had seen very little of Miss Poole. She seemed content keeping to the schoolroom and parlor, two rooms he'd avoided for the purpose of self–preservation. And she had not dined with him or Juliana since that one evening when he had insisted she join them.

But he could sense her presence whenever he entered Sutton Hall thanks to the constant appearance of fresh bouquets in the foyer. The first peonies of the season had filled the space with their sweet fragrance when he'd returned from his ride that morning. Of course, they'd also filled his mind with visions of *her*.

"Please make sure Miss Poole is reminded of this evening's dinner," he told Juliana during luncheon. "I expect her to be there."

Juliana raised her chin and proceeded to study him with an unnerving degree of interest. "While I'm happy to have her counterbalance Miss Howell's disinteresting discourse, won't Miss Howell and her parents consider Miss Poole's attendance a bit unorthodox?"

"Possibly, but since this will be your first social dinner, I think it will benefit you and Miss Poole if she is there to judge your performance. And offer guidance, should it be necessary."

It had absolutely nothing to do with the fact that he

found Miss Poole riveting or that he hoped she might add some flavorful comments to spice things up.

This hope, however, had withered by the time the third course arrived. Miss Poole, who'd been seated so far from him she might as well be on an entirely different planet, had said no more than two words since she'd arrived in the parlor a couple of hours earlier. *Good evening.* That was it. Hardly the sort of conversational morsel a man could sink his teeth into.

Grayson reached for his wine with every hope of becoming numb to Lady Oldbridge's shrill voice, her husband's flat tone, and their daughter's soft-spoken words. Each one irritated him for different reasons while poor Juliana, who always carried a conversation with flair when they were alone, had not been allowed the chance to shine.

Enough was enough.

"Juliana," he said, ignoring Lord Oldbridge's third mention of a hunting party he kept insisting Grayson attend toward the end of August. "Why don't you tell us about your studies?"

"Education is so important for young ladies and gentlemen alike," Lady Oldbridge said before Juliana managed to open her mouth. "Naturally, the subject matter is different for women, as it should be. His lordship and I made certain Edwina's governess taught her French. She speaks the language like a native."

"I'm sure she does," Grayson said, "but I was asking Ju—"

"Her knowledge of art is also most impressive," the

viscountess continued. "She can match every painting in the National Gallery with the correct artist. And she can also identify any piece of music after hearing only the first few notes. It's quite extraordinary."

"I'm sure it is," Grayson said while staring back at Miss Howell's eager mama. "Your daughter is sure to do well in life with such useful skills."

Lady Oldbridge tilted her head and blinked a few times while her husband coughed into his napkin. "I'm not sure I like what you're implying, Mr. Grier. Edwina has worked extremely hard on her accomplishments. So much so, she left a lasting impression upon my good friend, Lady Cowper."

Grayson narrowed his eyes. Dropping the name of one of Almack's most influential patronesses like that and linking it to her own was no accident.

"He meant no offense." This from the person who'd said the least all evening – the one person no one expected to have an opinion, never mind voice it.

All gazes shifted toward Miss Poole, who sat as though she'd been cast from plaster.

Silence. And then…

"You presume to know the mind of your employer?" Lady Oldbridge inquired.

"Of course not." Miss Poole's cheeks, which had been pale before, were now blindingly red. She took a few breaths and appeared to clench her jaw. Her posture grew increasingly rigid. "Forgive me for speaking out of turn, my lady, and for overstepping."

Grayson frowned. Having witnessed Miss Poole's

strength of character for himself, the meekness she showed his guests grated, even though his rational mind told him it was normal.

Heedless of this fact, he told her plainly, "I invited you to join us because I value your opinion, Miss Poole. You need not apologize for having one or for making it heard."

"She is the governess," Lady Oldbridge hissed while her husband gulped down a full glass of wine.

"I am aware," Grayson said dryly.

"Her presence here is highly irregular," Lady Oldbridge added while glaring at Miss Poole as though she were dirt beneath her slippers.

"It is necessary," he told her bluntly. "For the purpose of gauging Juliana's social skills and her accomplishments, which I'm sure you'll agree to be as impressive as your lovely daughter's."

"Well, I suppose—"

"Why don't you demonstrate," he suggested to Juliana in French.

"I'm not sure what to say," Juliana responded in German.

"What's that?" asked Lady Oldbridge. "I don't understand."

"How about you?" Grayson asked Miss Howell, reverting to French. "Do you speak German?"

"I'm afraid not," Miss Howell replied, her cheeks flushing with color.

"What about Latin or some other language?" When Miss Howell shook her head, Grayson shifted his gaze to Miss Poole and told her in German, "Her governess clearly wasn't as clever as you."

Miss Poole did not smile in response to the compliment. Indeed, her expression was so stern it bordered on mutinous. Rather than answer him, she gave her attention to Miss Howell instead. "May I ask you a question?"

Although both her parents frowned in response, Miss Howell lit up. "Certainly."

"Considering your extensive knowledge of music, I trust you also play?"

"Of course she plays," Lady Oldbridge exclaimed.

Miss Poole offered the woman a smile Grayson did not believe she deserved. Worst of all, it was handed out to someone other than him. He gnashed his teeth and reached for his wine while Miss Poole said, "In that case, I'm sure we should all enjoy hearing her play. If she is amenable, that is."

"She'd be delighted," Lady Oldbridge declared.

Plates were whisked away and dessert brought in while Grayson adjusted his brain to the idea of having to sit through Miss Howell's piano recital instead of Juliana's. He glared at Miss Poole, who seemed to pay him no mind. Why had she done it? Why had she interfered? Most pressing of all, why had she been so unbearably nice to a woman who'd scolded her seconds before?

He did not know, but it bothered the hell out of him. Especially since he knew Miss Poole had the gumption required to give as good as she got. She'd put him in his place, after all. Yet here she was, bowing her head to Lady Oldbridge, *smiling* at her, and inviting her insipid daughter to play his pianoforte when he'd had every intention of having Juliana perform with Miss Poole.

He snatched up his spoon and shoved some pudding into his mouth. His thinking had nothing to do with how much he enjoyed the sound of Miss Poole's voice or the fact that his boyish self wished to pull her proverbial pigtails. It wasn't because he liked her more than he ought or because he simply wanted the chance to gaze at her unhindered.

Of course not. That would be mad.

And his reasoning was perfectly sound.

Juliana needed the practice more than Miss Howell, and Miss Poole would help her keep pace. That was all there was to it.

He huffed a breath and told himself the situation was not as bad as all that. Miss Howell would play one piece, after which Juliana could take a turn. He'd make certain of it.

As luck would have it, however, the piece Miss Howell selected was longer than any other. It went on and on and…

Finally the notes began to fade. Grayson, who'd been sitting beside Juliana on the sofa, proceeded to clap. "Well done, Miss Howell. You do play remarkably well."

Miss Howell blushed. "Thank you, Mr. Grier."

"Once married, she shall delight her husbands' guests without fail," Lady Oldbridge declared.

"Undoubtedly," Grayson replied, his attention already moving toward the back of the room where Miss Poole was sitting. Except she wasn't.

He stared at the empty chair, no longer occupied by the governess. Somehow, at some point during Miss Howell's playing or the ensuing conversation, Miss Poole had departed without begging her leave. Without him being the wiser. And that was not to be borne.

CHAPTER SEVENTEEN

Olivia knew she'd overstepped and that she deserved to be admonished. She didn't consider herself the cowardly sort, having faced her father's reprimands often, but she still prayed she would not be summoned to Mr. Grier's study the following day. He would have nothing good to say. After all, she had spoken on his behalf *and* taken her leave without being excused.

Her heart flapped about from the moment she woke until she'd concluded her afternoon lessons with Juliana. Only then, with no hint of stormy weather upon the horizon, did she permit herself to relax.

"May I use your bedchamber later this evening?" Juliana asked before heading off to prepare for supper. Since their outing to Varney, she'd made a study of the rabbit they'd managed to purchase.

"Of course." Olivia wanted to ask her a number of

questions in return. *Did anyone notice my absence last night? Did Mr. Grier?* Juliana herself had not said a word. It was maddening. As though the evening had never happened.

Equally maddening had been her knowledge of Mr. Grier's plan to offer for Miss Howell. She fleetingly wondered if he'd told her father of his intentions last night while enjoying a drink with the man after dinner.

Giving herself a mental kick for permitting herself to ponder matters that didn't concern her, Olivia parted ways with Juliana and returned to her own bedchamber for the evening. She would read a book, relax as best as she could. *Not* think of her handsome employer or how much he'd vexed her last night. Eat supper alone.

Her heart gave an unhappy sigh at that thought. It was as it should be, she told herself. She did not belong below stairs anymore and attending supper with Mr. Grier and Juliana had been excruciatingly uncomfortable on the two occasions she'd done so. It certainly wasn't something she wished to repeat. Was it?

She shook her head and entered her room, nearly missing a folded piece of paper which lay on the floor. Olivia stared at it. Someone must have slipped it under her door.

Her pulse kicked into a faster rhythm as she shut the door and bent to retrieve the missive. Already her skin was heating, her stomach turning as though doing cartwheels.

For reasons she could not explain, she knew before she saw the bold script that it was from him.

Meet me in my study at ten. There are matters we need to discuss.

Olivia's fingers trembled. She forced air into her lungs and slumped onto her bed. So much for avoiding a set–down. So much for avoiding the havoc Mr. Grier wrought on her nerves with his steely dark gaze and powerful presence. She would face him tonight, after Juliana retired. *Don't worry. All will be well. You've faced far worse in the past.*

A hot, prickly flush said otherwise.

Setting the paper on her bedside table, Olivia pressed her cool palms to her heated cheeks. It was important she remember her place and his. He was a wealthy landowner – a gentleman for heaven's sake – while she was no more than a vicar's daughter. Allowing herself to be flustered by him was silly. Especially since there was little for her to like about him in the first place.

Besides the fact that he seemed to care for Juliana's well–being.

And his offer to teach Olivia how to row.

Never mind the concern he'd shown toward her when he'd saved her from drowning.

Or the way his features softened whenever he smiled.

Olivia shook her head in annoyance. To suppose a man as handsome as Mr. Grier might think her pretty was not only ludicrous but impossible. She was odd–

looking at best with her black hair, pale skin, plump lips, and sharp nose.

Rising, she went to prepare her desk for Juliana's arrival later. Her list lay there now with *sail a boat* crossed out.

Wear something scandalous was next – a task Olivia had embarked upon last week when she'd purchased the red satin ribbon and lace.

Since then, she'd worked on creating the item she had in mind. Needlework had never been her strong suit so the project had taken longer than expected. More so because she could work on it only when she was completely alone and knew she'd not be disturbed.

Olivia's fingers slid over the frothy white lace, skimming the intricate edging before sliding over the slippery satin. She studied her creation, which she'd completed last night after managing to escape the music room during Miss Howell's recital.

Time to try it on.

She sank to the edge of her bed and took a deep breath. Having lived all her life without frilly garments, embellished bonnets, jewelry, or anything meant to make a girl feel pretty, Olivia hesitated. Her heart beat forcefully in her breast. This had been Agnes's silly idea, intended no doubt as a protest against Papa's stringent rules.

"Such things can only lead to sin," Papa had informed his daughters when they'd once asked if they might each have a colorful ribbon for their hair. "Boys will take notice and trouble will follow. Besides, charm

SOPHIE BARNES

172

is deceitful and beauty is vain, but a woman who fears the Lord, she shall be praised."

Olivia clutched the ribbon while warring against three decades of virtuous rigor. Her childhood home had contained no mirrors since such could too easily lead to idolatry and the polluting of the soul.

She glanced at the empty spot on the wall where a mirror had hung upon her arrival. The looking glass lay in one of the dresser drawers now, though not so much because she feared it might lead to conceit. Rather, it was because she wasn't accustomed to seeing herself and because doing so whenever she turned toward the mirror unnerved her.

Setting her jaw, Olivia reached for the hem of her skirt and pulled it up over her knees. Papa was gone. So were Mama and Agnes. All Olivia had left was a promise she'd made. The duty compelling her to follow through on it trumped her father's preaching, because it was born from love. Agnes had dreamed, she'd longed for more than what she'd been granted, and it was up to Olivia now to live the life she'd been denied.

Deliberately, Olivia pushed Papa from her mind and removed the plain cotton garter that held her coarse woolen stocking in place on her left leg. In its stead, she tied the lace-trimmed ribbon around the top of her calf, just below her knee, and lowered her skirts.

A curious sensation swept through her. It wasn't shame or guilt as she'd half expected, but...pleasant. Her lips quirked. Outwardly, she appeared the same – unchanged and plain. But beneath her skirts she carried a secret which most surprising of all made her feel pretty. Olivia grinned. Who would have thought that a scandalous underthing, invisible to the world, would have such power?

She shook her head, befuddled. Had she known, she might have taken to wearing such things a long time ago. *Thank you, Agnes, for giving me this.* She prepared to cross out *wear something scandalous* from her list before removing the garter once more.

Only to pause.

The garter bolstered her spirit and quieted her nerves. It made her feel not only pretty but stronger than ever before.

By putting it on she'd pushed past her fears in a way that rowing a boat had failed to achieve. This was daring and thrilling and...

She bit her lip. Her pencil hovered over the list. Could she really claim to have worn something scandalous if she'd only done so briefly, in the privacy of her bedchamber? Not really, she decided, her pulse quickening. She leaned back, set the pencil aside, folded the list, and returned it to her notebook.

Inhaling deeply, Olivia made her decision. She would wear the garter for the remainder of the evening in order to fully satisfy Agnes's wish. And possibly also to savor the thrill.

∾

"There's something different about you tonight," Betsy declared when Olivia came to collect her tray from the kitchen. "I can't put my finger on it, but you look changed."

"It's the sparkle in her eyes," said Mrs. Bradley, who was filling Olivia's plate with fragrant roast lamb and mushroom pie.

"You've come alive, Miss Poole," Roger said with lighthearted cheer. He winked at Olivia and while it did not affect her in the same way Mr. Grier's attention might have, it still made her flush from self-awareness.

"What is it?" Betsy pressed. A saucy smile tugged at her lips as she leaned in closer, her voice when she spoke a near whisper. "Have you received attention from a man you fancy?"

Olivia nearly choked. She stared at Betsy and wondered how the maid might think it possible for her to not only meet such a man but find the time to engage in flirtation. She shook her head. "It's nothing like that. I simply came to a realization."

"Well, it must have been a good one," Mrs. Bradley said. She set the plate on Olivia's tray and wiped her hands on a cloth. "A woman your age oughtn't look as though she's constantly off to a funeral."

Olivia gave her a smile, one of the few she'd managed to produce since that long ago spring day with Agnes under the cherry tree. For the longest time, smiling had made her more hollow inside. It hadn't felt natural either. But then she'd met Juliana and the girl's lively spirit had warmed a spot in Olivia's heart, thawing the frozen layers around it until it beat with renewed vigor.

"You should join us," Roger said. "Unless you prefer dining alone."

Olivia stared at him – at the kindness in his eyes. It wasn't a preference for solitude that had caused her to take her meals upstairs by herself, but rather the worry these people resented her for rising up through the ranks so quickly. As a result, she'd felt out of place.

"I don't prefer it," she confessed. "I simply believed my position demanded I keep to myself."

"Nonsense," said Betsy.

"We might not have welcomed Miss Chadwick." Mrs. Bradley removed a tray filled with bread rolls from the oven. A warm, yeasty aroma filled the kitchen. "But you're nothing like her."

"Besides, self–isolation can only lead to misery," Betsy said. "I'll set a spot for you at the table right next to me, so I can make sure you're informed of the latest gossip."

The maid and cook both laughed while Roger groaned and told Olivia not to pay Betsy any mind. "If she tells you I fancy Fiona, you're not to believe her."

Olivia grinned in response to his teasing tone and the lively comments that followed.

"According to Mr. Dover," Betsy whispered an hour later while giving the butler a hasty look, "Mr. Grier was never the same after returning from war. I'd not be surprised if it's the reason behind his stern demeanor."

"I suppose war would change a man," Olivia mused before taking a sip of water.

"What changed you?" Betsy asked.

Olivia blinked and set her glass aside. "How do you mean?"

"You were glum when you came here but no one is born that way." She took a bite of food and gave Olivia a curious look. "What happened?"

"I suppose I stopped enjoying life when I realized my sister was dying." Olivia shrugged one shoulder and studied her plate while trying to recall the last time she'd known true happiness. "When I think of my childhood, I see it in shades of brown and grey. Agnes, with her bright personality, offered the only splash of color in that dreary world."

"How long has it been since her death?"

"Thirteen years."

A brief moment of silence followed before Betsy said, "Well, you've got us now, Miss Poole. We'll make sure you don't lose your smile again."

The conversation bubbling around her, and the laughter and joy lending warmth to the room lifted the weight that had dragged down her heart for so long.

It was no different than it had been when she'd first arrived here, but *she* was different, Olivia realized. Finally, after suffering from a hollowed-out heart for thirteen years and feeling as though her life were a chore she simply had to get through, she was ready to put the past behind her and take charge of her future.

Meeting Juliana and having the girl remind her how

to smile again helped. So did the list from Agnes. It wasn't a series of duties to be carried out, but rather a gift to be cherished. Each experience posed a challenge that, if completed, would lead to accomplishments filled with memorable moments.

Olivia stilled on that thought as all became clear. Working her way through the list would not only force her to live the life her sister had dreamed of, but to have an extraordinary one of her own. Provided Mr. Grier allowed her to stay on as governess after her recent blunders.

If he didn't, if he decided she was better suited to being a maid or worse, to seeking employment elsewhere, she'd lose the opportunities offered by Sutton Hall. And the chance to complete her list any time soon.

With this in mind she arrived at his study at ten o'clock sharp, prepared to face his censure.

"Enter."

His bold voice answered her knock. She took a deep breath to bolster her nerves and stepped inside the masculine room. For reasons she could not explain, her gaze went straight to the family portrait that hung on the wall.

Seeing Mr. Grier as a child surrounded by parents and siblings, recalling the vulnerability he'd made her privy to while he'd spoken of them, humanized him. It made it easier to face him when she considered him as a loving son and brother instead of the powerful man who invaded her dreams more frequently than she dared to consider.

"Miss Poole."

Olivia's stomach tightened in response to her name, spoken with velvety smoothness. Like a magnet, it drew her attention away from the portrait and to the spot where he stood. Their eyes met and held, fanning that all too familiar desire he stoked in her with his mere existence.

She'd denied it for so long, but what was the use? All she accomplished was lying to herself.

"Mr. Grier," she said, relieved by the strength in her voice even as the heat in her cheeks made her cringe. Hopefully the dim light from a couple of oil lamps would not let him notice her blush.

He gestured to one of the chairs standing opposite his. "Please have a seat. Would you care for a drink? A sherry, perhaps?"

Caught off guard by the offer yet glad to be given the means for additional fortification, she gave a swift nod. "A sherry would be appreciated. Thank you."

She took a seat on one of the proffered chairs while he moved to the sideboard, presenting her with his back. Unable to resist, Olivia stole a glance at him. It was impossible not to admire his broad shoulders or the way his hair teased the edge of his jacket collar. Her fingers twitched with the uncanny urge to touch him right there. Perhaps while he held her close. Perhaps while they...

No.

Stop it.

Good lord. What was wrong with her?

Embarrassed, she tore her gaze away and devoted her full attention to the desk before her. It was built from dark wood, mahogany perhaps, and was intricately carved. The items on its surface – a silver tray holding an inkwell and quill, a couple of leather bound books, and a stack of papers – were also neatly organized she noted with approval.

"Here you are."

Olivia flinched. She'd not heard him approach.

Spotting the glass he held toward her, she raised her hand, prepared to take it, but its small size made it impossible for her to do so without touching him. Her fingers brushed his and everything stilled except for the beat of her heart.

Fearing she would reveal the potent effect he had upon her, she accepted the glass without looking directly at him and took an immediate sip. Just as the door she'd left open closed with a snick.

CHAPTER EIGHTEEN

"I'd rather no one overhear us," Mr. Grier explained in a low rumble.

Olivia took another sip of her drink and did her best to ignore the rapid beat of her pulse. Heat streaked through her limbs before coming to rest below her left knee where she'd tied her scarlet garter.

Unexpected excitement filled her as she acknowledged its snugness. Secretly wearing an item so daring beneath her otherwise drab attire was rousing. It made her feel powerful and alluring.

"About last night," he said, fixing his gaze upon her once he'd taken a seat in his chair. "I believe you owe me an explanation."

That brought her back to solid ground with a thump.

Olivia set her glass on the desk before her and straightened her spine. "For speaking out of turn?"

"No." His irritation was undeniable. "I take no issue with that. Even though you were wrong to suggest I made no attempt at causing offense when I can assure you I absolutely meant to do precisely that. Lady Oldbridge is an insufferable snob. However, I do appreciate your diplomatic interference since nothing good will come from making an enemy of her.

"I am referring to your inviting Miss Howell to play in Juliana's stead – something you had no right to do since you are not mistress of Sutton Hall."

Olivia gritted her teeth. She knew why she'd done it, but did she dare be honest with him? If she told him the truth, would he punish her for it?

She closed her eyes briefly before she proceeded. "You treated Miss Howell badly. It was unkind, Mr. Grier. *You* were unkind toward a good–natured woman who did not deserve being made to feel empty–headed or foolish. Least of all by the man who plans to make her his wife."

"I didn't—"

"Yes you did," Olivia pressed, her anger rising in the face of his denial. "You may not have seen the pained look in her eyes when you suggested her accomplishments were useless, but I did."

"You're mistaken," he said, his voice tight.

"I can assure you I am not," she insisted. "Perhaps if you'd spent less time feeling sorry for yourself because you were made to suffer an evening with her parents – an evening you arranged, I might add – you'd have noticed how much your opinion mattered and how deeply your words cut. Honestly, I hope she refuses when you ask for her hand."

Mr. Grier stared at her, his chest rising and falling as though he'd been the one to deliver the set–down she'd unceremoniously thrown in his face.

So much for avoiding his ire.

And yet, she didn't regret a single word. Still, in an attempt at self–preservation, she could not help but open her mouth once more. "For—"

"Do *not* beg my forgiveness for that." His expression was stonier than ever before, his eyes hard as flint. "You'll simply risk ruining the intended effect, which I assume is to make me feel like an ass."

Olivia's lips twitched. She couldn't help it and before she knew it, she was openly grinning at him while he looked at her as though she'd sprouted horns. His features gradually softened and the tension Olivia so often felt in his presence eased into something more comfortable.

"I dare say I've waited forever for this," he told her quietly.

"For me to give you another set–down?" she asked, puzzled.

He shook his head and instead of enlightening her, he said, "Your honesty is invaluable, Miss Poole. I appreciate it more than you know, regardless of how hard it may be to hear. I'm sorry for being a beast to Miss Howell. You're right. She did not deserve it."

"She is the one to whom you ought to apologize, not me."

"I'll do so, I assure you." His expression turned pensive. "My reason for summoning you this evening was not solely to admonish you for the liberty you took last night, but also to get a sense of how things are going with Juliana. You've been teaching her for three weeks now. As initially agreed, we're supposed to decide if you will stay on as her governess."

"I would like to," Olivia said without the least bit of hesitation. "I believe she's happy with my instruction and that her improvement is noticeable."

"I agree, although I do have one question."

"Yes?"

"When we went boating, you said something to Juliana. Something about remembering what you discussed. I've been meaning to ask what you meant."

Olivia stared at him for a moment while trying to think of how best to answer his question. Eventually she told him, "I was referring to some advice I gave her on how important it is to behave like a lady whenever witnesses are present."

"She should do so even when there aren't."

"Of course. But girls her age will often try to rebel."

"Is that why she wanted to handle the worms?"

"Possibly."

He gave her a thoughtful look before finally nodding and reaching for some sort of notebook in which he proceeded to write.

Olivia's head spun. That was it? She did not have to fear further reprimand or demotion?

Blinking, she considered Mr. Grier's strained

posture as he wrote. Perhaps he was more forgiving than she'd believed? Perhaps he was kinder, despite the way he'd treated Miss Howell? Everyone made mistakes, after all. She'd certainly made her own fair share. And he had told her he'd ask Miss Howell's forgiveness.

"If that is all," she said, suddenly eager to be alone with her thoughts, "I should like to retire for the evening."

He raised his gaze to hers and pushed the notebook aside. "You do not care for my company, do you?"

Olivia's heart began prancing about once more. It was that intensely dark gaze – that devilish half smile that singed her skin and turned her stupid. "I'm supposed to meet Miss Edwards in the schoolroom tomorrow morning."

It didn't quite answer his question. She dared not do so since she was bound to reveal the truth. *Your company terrifies me.*

Additional questions would follow. She couldn't allow that to happen.

"Of course." He did not move to rise. Instead he asked, "Why did you sneak off last night?"

"Miss Howell was playing," she said, folding her hands in her lap while he took a sip of his brandy. "It would have been rude to interrupt."

"You could have waited for her to finish."

"I know."

That statement and all the unspoken thoughts it provoked hung in the air between them until he finally told her, "In future, I'd appreciate it if you would bid me goodnight first."

With that, he picked up his quill, reached for his notebook, and resumed writing.

All she could do was nod. If she spoke at that moment she feared she'd reveal every shameless thought she'd had about him since her arrival. So she took a deep breath to calm her nerves before saying, "Then I shall do so now if there's nothing else. Good night, Mr. Grier."

He did not bother looking at her. "Good night, Miss Poole."

Officially dismissed, Olivia fled the room. She'd never been more eager to leave his presence or more desperate to hide the longing he stirred in her breast.

Grayson raised his head as soon as he heard the door close and stared at it for a good long moment. Frowning, he leaned back in his chair and went over their meeting in his head. He'd only pretended to have more important things to attend to for the sake of maintaining control. Indeed, when she'd railed at him for his rudeness toward poor Miss Howell, it had taken extreme restraint on his part to hide the effect her biting words had upon him.

Hell, his body still hummed with desire, a desire he'd done his best to conceal by attempting humor. Which wasn't like him at all. Despite the happy family he'd been raised in, his life had always been serious. He'd been his father's heir. Responsibility had been placed upon his shoulders at birth.

Later, he'd gone off to war where he'd not just witnessed an overwhelming amount of anguish and death, but where he'd watched his friend die. There one moment, gone the next. Utterly pointless. And for what?

He glanced at his family portrait and thought back on all the years that had followed. He'd done his best to bury those awful wartime memories by cavorting with friends and enjoying his mistresses. When Papa had asked him to come home to Sutton Hall so he could prepare him to manage the estate, Grayson had brushed him off.

There would be plenty of time for that later.

Except there wasn't.

Papa's heart had given out one Saturday morning while he'd been walking with Mama in the garden, leaving Grayson with an estate and a ward that depended upon him pulling himself together.

With a sigh he reached for his brandy. Staying away for four months had been wrong. He'd known it in his gut but he'd done it anyway. And if it hadn't been for Juliana sacking Miss Chadwick, he'd probably still be in London. Because he'd needed a break from all the responsibility resting upon his shoulders. He'd needed to think of something besides Juliana's debut and how important it was to make sure her launch was a smashing success. He owed it to his father and to Juliana's parents. He owed it to her.

So making light of a situation – any situation – did not come naturally. Not with the burden of duty a constant millstone about his neck. And yet he'd attempted and Miss Poole had laughed.

Chest tight with a strange new emotion he couldn't quite place, Grayson closed his eyes and thought of his prim and proper governess. She'd blushed profusely when she'd accepted the sherry from him and his fingers brushed hers. His pulse quickened at the memory.

Submitting to temptation, he permitted himself for the very first time to let his mind linger on how she'd felt when he'd held her in the water and to imagine what she would look like beneath the dull layers of grey she insisted on wearing.

Her waist would be slim, her hips flared, and...

God help him she'd be divine. And he wanted her, he acknowledged. With the desperation of a man who'd lived his entire life in a state of starvation only to be presented with an exquisite iced pudding he could not have.

Miss Poole was the governess.

She was a vicar's daughter.

Ruining her would not only hurt her. It might hurt Juliana as well if word got out.

He muttered a curse and downed the rest of his brandy, then stood. Miss Poole deserved better than to be the fodder for his wicked imaginings. She was a good woman, a dedicated teacher. And he was a beast for letting her fuel his desires.

Disgusted, he left his study and headed outside. A cold swim in the lake would set him to rights. Tomorrow he'd write the Howells and beg their forgiveness. And then he'd prepare for Nathaniel's arrival, which would, he hoped, provide him with a much needed distraction.

Olivia stared out at the garden, absently listening to Juliana read from Moliere's *The Flying Doctor*. It was time to reevaluate the list.

Riding had been one of the things Agnes dreamed about more than anything else. She'd watched with breathless admiration whenever she spotted someone on a horse. Of course Papa had owned one. His name had been Moses, but he'd been meant for Papa's cabriolet, not for riding.

Once when Olivia and Agnes had climbed onto a stool beside Moses with the intention of trying to sit upon him, Papa had arrived. A lecture on disobedience had followed along with five strokes across each of their palms with the switch.

They'd never gone near Moses again.

And after her recent boating accident, Olivia didn't dare go near a horse. Thankfully there were other items on the list that were easier and safer to accomplish.

Olivia considered them. Having memorized the list

from start to finish, she knew each item on it. Getting foxed, learning how to gamble, and reading a shocking book were options to consider. And then there were the more challenging ones, like seeing the ocean, attending the theatre, and visiting another country.

Somehow, Olivia would have to find the means to accomplish those once she left Sutton Hall. Until then...

She turned to Juliana. "Would you be willing to teach me how to play chess?"

CHAPTER NINETEEN

Grayson dipped his quill in the inkwell on his desk and continued to write. A letter had arrived from his solicitor, Mr. Tomkins, that morning, requesting permission to hire additional craftsmen for Grayson's growing venture so product demand could be met. With Mr. Tomkins serving as a middleman while assuring discretion, Grayson had managed to hire a few select artisans who replicated his woodwork designs to perfection.

He'd spent several hours revising the budget in order to realize Mr. Tomkins's wish without cutting wages for the other employees.

The obvious answer had been for him to front the cost himself until profits began to cover it. He could afford to do so easily enough, but he believed his hobby–turned–business should stand on its own two feet. If it required additional funds from the private

Grier coffers, then there was something wrong with the way things were being managed.

A knock at the door announced Dover's arrival. The butler stepped into the room just as Grayson was signing his name to the letter. "Yes?"

"Viscount and Viscountess Oldbridge have come to call," Dover announced while Grayson blotted the page.

Frustration licked at Grayson's spine. He'd been hoping to head back into his workshop now that his correspondence for the day had been dealt with. So much for spending some time alone with his new project.

He glanced at Dover. "Is Miss Howell with them?"

"She is not," Dover said.

Grayson blew out a breath. "Please show my guests to the parlor and make sure tea is served. I'll join them shortly."

"Very good, sir."

Dover departed and Grayson muttered a curse. He had no desire to meet with the Oldbridges. Least of all when he suspected they'd want something from him. Why else would they show up unannounced on his doorstep?

He finished preparing his letter for Mr. Tomkins, folding it and sealing it, then marking the address. Apologizing to the Howells had been a mistake, the sort that made him look weak and approachable. He ought not have done it, no matter how much he'd wanted to please Miss Poole.

Damn it.

He shoved his chair back and stood. He could not blame her. Had it not been for his own stupidity, the Oldbridges would not have taken offense. Miss Poole had merely advised him on how to correct the situation and she'd been right to do so.

And now they'd returned, uninvited.

Jaw clenched with annoyance, Grayson strode from his study and made his way to the parlor.

"Please have this dispatched straight away," he told Dover, whom he met in the hallway. He handed him the letter to Mr. Tomkins and took a deep breath before going to greet his guests.

He drew to a halt when he found them. Instead of sitting still in anticipation of his arrival, they were strolling about the room, peering at every item upon every surface. Lady Oldbridge reached for a porcelain figurine Grayson's mother had once received from his father as an anniversary gift.

He cleared his throat. "My lord and lady. What an unexpected surprise."

They turned, their expressions brightening with the sort of glee one might expect from villains who'd just executed a devious plan without anyone being the wiser.

Grayson suppressed a shudder and crossed to the seating arrangement. "Please join me."

He deliberately spoke the words with the same degree of authority he'd been accustomed to in the army. It had the desired effect, preventing Lady Oldbridge from sullying his mother's shepherdess with her touch while turning Lord Oldbridge's attention away from the lovely bouquet of flowers gracing a side table.

The lilacs were also present in the foyer, teasing Grayson with their scent whenever he passed. He glared at the ones that had now appeared in the parlor. Despite his effort to avoid Miss Poole for the past two days, the woman's presence in his home was impossible to ignore.

"Those flowers smell incredible," Lord Oldbridge told his wife, pointing in their general direction as he approached Grayson. "You should procure some for our garden."

"We've got enough lavender as it is," Lady Oldbridge informed her husband while Grayson bit back a comment. She swept toward the sofa and sat. "Shall I serve tea?"

Grayson lowered himself to a vacant armchair with a sigh. "Please do."

"We were very pleased by your letter, Mr. Grier," Lady Oldbridge said once they'd all received a cup of tea. A plate of biscuits sat on the table between them. "It reflects your strength of character and has helped ease some of the concerns we had after dining here."

"Concerns?" Grayson queried and proceeded to take a sip of his tea.

"You did not appear as interested in our daughter as we'd expected. Your comments suggested you disapproved of her accomplishments. But after your letter, it's clear to us all that the two of you shall have a wonderful future together. His lordship and I heartily approve. That's why we're here. To give our blessing."

"Your what?" Grayson sputtered.

"Our blessing." Lady Oldbridge beamed at him. "Regarding your courtship and eventual marriage."

It was difficult not to stare at the woman while wondering where the crack in her head might be. His mind raced. He'd told Juliana and Miss Poole of his intention to take Miss Howell to wife. Was it possible either one had mentioned as much to the girl's parents? If so, when on earth would they have done so? He tried to think but came up blank, which probably meant the Oldbridges' determination to have him for a son-in-law was unrelated.

His heart gave a wild thud. He'd known Miss Howell fancied him, and rather than keep her at a distance, he'd invited her to dinner. How bloody stupid was he?

"I believe you misunderstand my intentions," he said, voicing his thoughts with the utmost of care and making a stoic effort not to do as instinct compelled him, which was to speak his mind. The words, *are you mad*, slid toward the tip of his tongue but he forced them back.

"I'm sure we do not," Lady Oldbridge said while Lord Oldbridge remained mute. There was no doubt as to who overpowered whom in that marriage. "What other reason would a bachelor have for inviting a young unmarried lady to his home for dinner?"

"I invited all of you," Grayson said, desperately grasping at straws. "As a family."

"And then you arranged for her to show off her musical talents."

"I did no such thing. If you will recall, Miss Poole was the one who suggested Miss Howell play for us after supper."

"Ah yes. The governess." Lady Oldbridge's eyes narrowed, alerting Grayson to his mistake. He should not have mentioned Miss Poole. "She has an interesting degree of authority, Mr. Grier."

"She is an intelligent woman," Grayson said. He'd be damned if he was going to let Lady Oldbridge make insinuations without standing his ground. "I value her opinion."

"We are peers, Mr. Grier. We do not appreciate dining with members of the serving class, no matter how much you may value their opinion."

"While I appreciate your honesty, my lady, this is my home," Grayson told the blasted woman. "Should I desire my footmen to sit down at table with me, then that is my prerogative."

"Really, Mr. Grier. You cannot be serious. But even if you are, it is Miss Poole we are discussing." Lady Oldbridge raised her chin just enough to stare down her nose. "She spoke on your behalf."

"For which she apologized." Grayson drummed his fingers on the armrest and glanced at the sideboard. Perhaps it was time to pour himself a brandy.

"My point is," Lady Oldbridge said once she'd

finished eating the biscuit she'd recently bitten into, "it's a known fact that men have their needs."

"I beg your pardon?" Grayson knew he was gaping. He could not believe Lady Oldbridge would dare to broach such a matter. He glanced at her husband, who seemed to be admiring the ceiling. Good God.

"Mistresses are to be expected," Lady Oldbridge went on as if they were discussing the weather. "But taking up with your ward's governess is unacceptable due to the scandal that's likely to follow. So while I recognize the appeal, Lord Oldbridge and I would ask you to be more discreet."

The temptation to stand up and tell the Oldbridges to get the hell out of his house was too bloody tempting. How dare they come here and insinuate he and Miss Poole were lovers?

It's no less than what you yourself have imagined.

Perhaps not, but there was a big difference between imagination and reality.

With self–restraint stiffening his spine, Grayson leaned forward so he could stare directly into Lady Oldbridge's accusing eyes. "I would never cross the boundary that lies between a master and his servant."

"You did so the moment you invited her to join us for supper," Lady Oldbridge replied. She raised an eyebrow as if challenging him to deny this.

"Please be advised that your insinuation offends me greatly, my lady. You may rest assured that Miss Poole is a respectable woman and an excellent governess to

Miss Edwards. I'll not let you or anyone else sully her name without any basis."

"There was also the way in which you regarded her," Lady Oldbridge said, blithely ignoring his statements. "You may deny your interest as much as you like, but it did not escape my notice."

Grayson stared at her. "What are you talking about?"

Lady Oldbridge sighed. "You looked as though you were parched and she were a pitcher of water."

"I most certainly did not," Grayson said, intent on denying every accusation the woman threw at him.

"Hmm. Well I would certainly hate for Lady Cowper to hear of your indiscretions."

Grayson clenched his fists and tried to think. Lady Cowper was one of London's most influential women. If Lady Oldbridge convinced her to bar Juliana from Almack's or worse, suggested to her that Juliana might be connected to scandal, her debut would suffer.

Of course, there was a chance the viscountess was bluffing for the sole purpose of adding pressure.

But what if she wasn't? Rumor had it she'd ruined Miss Adeline Evert's debut so the promising beauty wouldn't distract from her daughter. Miss Howell had been the center of attention when she'd made her come out while poor Miss Evert had been reduced to a wallflower.

Doing his best to hide his rising panic, Grayson calmly asked, "Is that a threat?"

"I'd rather you think of it as encouragement." Lady

Oldbridge stirred her tea with irritating slowness. She pursed her lips. "Naturally, I shall do my utmost to help Miss Edwards once you and Edwina are married."

"Married?" A startled laugh escaped him. When neither of his guests expressed an ounce of humor, he instantly hardened his features. "I believe I made myself perfectly clear. I've no intention of courting your daughter, never mind marrying her."

"Have you no consideration for your ward's future, Mr. Grier?"

Heat shot to the top of Grayson's head. He narrowed his gaze on the awful woman seated before him. "Miss Edwards's future is my primary concern at present."

"Good." Lady Oldbridge dabbed her mouth with a napkin. "Edwina understands the ways of the world, Mr. Grier. She has no illusions pertaining to marriage. We are simply asking you to be less blatant with regard to your affairs."

"There is no affair," Grayson clipped. "It's a false-hood you've dreamed up."

"That's the spirit," Lady Oldbridge said. She stood, prompting her husband to rush to his feet. "As you know, we're departing for Inverness tomorrow morning and shan't return until the first week of July. We shall expect you to call on Edwina then. Take her for a walk or a ride. She'll like that."

Grayson got up too. He had every intention of hurrying the couple toward the exit.

"I only want Edwina's happiness," Lady Oldbridge

MR. GRIER AND THE GOVERNESS   199

told him seriously. "And I shall do what I must to secure it."

"I'd heed her words," Lord Oldbridge murmured as soon as his wife was headed toward the foyer. "She's always liked getting her way and giving Edwina whatever her heart desires."

Grayson silently thanked the man for the warning while he envisioned a dozen ways in which to wring Lady Oldbridge's neck. Gritting his teeth, he remained on the front steps until the Oldbridge carriage had vanished from sight. Only then did he allow himself to relax a little. Thankfully, they would be gone for the next several weeks, which was plenty of time for him to find a way out of this muddle. One thing was certain. He would *not* be wedding Miss Howell.

"Make sure no one disturbs me," he told Dover before he retreated to his study. He needed time to process the last half hour and promptly poured himself the glass of brandy he'd considered having earlier.

He took a sip and savored the heat coating his throat as the liquid slid into his stomach. Crossing to the window, he looked out upon the garden where Miss Poole and Juliana were... He frowned. He wasn't quite sure what they were doing besides making peculiar gestures while talking.

A smile tugged at his lips. Whatever activity they were engaged in both appeared to be having fun. Grayson's heart swelled. He'd never seen Juliana so animated before. The same could be said of Miss Poole who was presently hopping about while making a face.

Juliana proceeded to laugh, and so did he.

The temptation to join them and find out what they were up to was fierce, but he would resist. He had to.

So he turned away from the window and from the woman who haunted his dreams. She had to remain untouched, if for no other reason than to make sure there would be no substance to Lady Oldbridge's words.

CHAPTER TWENTY

"How are you doing with your project?" Olivia asked Juliana one evening. After taking supper in the kitchen as had become her habit of late, she'd returned to her bedchamber where Juliana was in the process of sketching an eyeball she'd been preserving in a jar of alcohol beneath Olivia's bed. It had come from the rabbit they'd purchased at the butcher's. No part of that animal had gone to waste. As soon as the main dissection was over, Juliana had placed every organ in its own container.

"I'm having trouble differentiating between the central retinal artery and the central retinal vein. Come have a look."

Olivia watched Juliana pick up a long spindly tool. With the desk pushed up against the opposite wall, Juliana sat with her back to the room, shielding Olivia from the specimen she was exploring.

"I'd rather not," Olivia said. In her opinion eyes belonged in heads, not on desks, no matter how willing she was to encourage the girl's learning. To Olivia's way of thinking, it was not her job to prevent her student from studying a subject of interest, but to facilitate such study to the best of her abilities.

After all, the world was evolving, so who knew? Maybe Juliana would become England's first female physician. She certainly had the interest. Whether or not she would manage to find a husband who'd lend support to such a pursuit was a different matter. And that was without considering Mr. Grier's potential protestations. Recalling his reaction to Juliana's handling of worms when they'd gone fishing, Olivia feared he'd be very opposed to her dissecting anything other than Debrett's.

"And it's getting late," Olivia said, suddenly worried they'd be discovered by Mrs. Hodgins when she made her rounds. As she tended to do at roughly this hour. "Put the eye back in the jar and get to bed, Juliana. We cannot risk word of your late night activities reaching Mr. Grier."

Juliana sighed. "I suppose not. Thank you for helping me do this without his knowledge."

Olivia frowned. She did not like the way that comment was phrased. It made her feel like a liar and a sneak, which wasn't like her at all. But since she strongly believed girls ought to be given the same opportunities boys received with regard to their education, she had little choice. After all, Mr. Grier had made his position abundantly clear. He wanted Juliana to focus on taking the London ballrooms by storm and on making a magnificent match.

Considering Society's judgmental views of a woman's place in the world, Olivia did not believe it would go over well if it became known that Juliana found cadavers more compelling than fashion plates.

Grayson avoided Miss Poole for the next two weeks. She was too great a temptation and distraction from the estate work he ought to be focusing on. Disgruntled, he closed himself away in his study each morning where he forced himself to concentrate on his ledgers and correspondence until noon. After luncheon the first day, he rode out to check on his tenants, who were all doing splendidly thanks to Grayson's excellent steward, Mr. Brummel.

It would have been useful if there'd been a need for Grayson to help fix a roof or a fence, but there wasn't. Everything was running smoothly, however, leaving him with plenty of spare time to ponder his forthright governess.

Would she be as bold in the bedroom as she'd been while facing him in his study?

With a curse, he returned from his ride and handed his horse to one of the grooms, then walked the short distance to the workshop his father had built. Taught by his father, who'd been schooled in woodworking by

Grayson's great grandfather, Papa had handed down the knowledge of craftsmanship the Grier men prided themselves on. It was the sort of useful hobby that brought satisfaction and would have enabled them all to become successful tradesmen, should the need have arisen.

After retrieving a key from his pocket, Grayson unlocked the wooden door to the building and pushed it open. He knew how to fashion an ornate pediment on a case piece and how to create a flawless pedestal base for a table. But his interest wasn't in the production of furniture, as it had been for his father and grandfather.

A smile pulled at the edge of his lips as he stepped inside the workshop and closed the door. The space was kept clean by Mrs. Hodgins personally since Grayson was wary of trusting anyone else with his secret.

He crossed to his work bench, pulled out a stool and sat before opening up the large wooden box he'd built as a youth. This was his favorite possession – the first piece he'd completed without his father's aid. He'd been so proud of himself for getting it to open and close without a hitch. He still was, but it was the look of approval in Papa's eyes when Grayson had presented the box to him that had made him feel ten feet tall.

His throat tightened at the memory. He'd been four and thirty years old when Papa's heart stopped ticking – a man who should have been able to carry on as expected. But the truth was the loss had crippled him.

He'd not been prepared. Looking back, he realized age made no difference. He'd still been a child who'd lost a parent. Being an adult did not make it any easier to bear.

Inhaling deeply, Grayson slid his fingers across the box's smooth rosewood lid. He'd carved an image in the center of it to depict a deer among a cluster of trees. It was not his best work, but it was by far the most important.

He flipped the metal latch and opened the lid, revealing a wide assortment of intricate pieces he'd worked on over the years – delicate hair combs, bracelets, and brooches, all with mother of pearl inlays. Some were more complete than others but each one mattered because it portrayed an idea.

Dipping his hand inside the box, Grayson retrieved a comb and turned it between his fingers. After careful placement at a few specialty shops, his accessories had become so popular he'd soon received orders for more.

He set the comb aside and grabbed a piece of paper and a pencil. With a few swift strokes he'd created a female profile with hair done up in a knot at the nape of the neck. He drew the top edge of a comb securing the hair and sloped the edges as though they were part of an unfinished heart, squared off at each end.

Elaborating on this idea he began drawing the comb by itself. He sketched the outline of it and added the teeth. Flowers set between swirling leaves were added and shaded. This would form the basis for the mother-of-pearl inlay. He'd finish the wood off with black lacquer to give it the bold effect he saw in the woman who'd served as inspiration.

Grayson set his pencil aside and studied the profile. He'd meant to keep his mind off Miss Poole, yet there was no denying the striking resemblance.

Good God. If his friends learned he'd not only taken to designing hair combs but that he was doing so because he fancied a servant, they'd never let him live it down. He'd be teased about it until kingdom come.

Heart aching, he pushed the sketch aside and stood. It didn't take long for him to find the correct piece of wood or his favorite tools. Determined to keep his thoughts from lingering on Miss Poole and the magical sparkle he'd seen in her eyes when he'd made her laugh, Grayson started to carve a rough shape. In the coming days he would transform the angular block into an intricate hair–ornament with curves to match the lady for whom it would be intended.

When Olivia picked *Twelfth Night* as the play she wished to perform, Juliana had argued that they would need a much bigger cast. She'd claimed it would be impossible for just the two of them to act out the entire play on their own. But she'd eventually discovered the fun in playing the part of multiple characters by changing her voice and tone. When Olivia switched from Viola, the heroine, to Feste, the fool, with exag-gerated flair, Juliana had howled with laughter.

Between Juliana's lessons, practicing the play, and learning basic chess, Olivia had little time to ponder the man who employed her. Which was just as well, she decided while making her way to her bedchamber one afternoon. She did not wish for complications. Rather, she wanted to help Juliana make a successful debut next Season while keeping her promise to Agnes.

That was all.

She reached the foyer and turned for the stairs at the same exact moment the front door opened.

A man with a riding crop clasped in one hand, whom she judged to be roughly the same age as she, entered. His features resembled Mr. Grier's though his expression was softer and his hair a touch lighter. Dressed in a green frock coat, brown breeches, dusty boots, and a black top hat, he stood in the open doorway, staring at Olivia.

"And who might you be?" he asked with a grin, giving her a full head–to–toe perusal. A mischievous sparkle lit his eyes. "Surely not the governess. You're much too pretty to hold such a serious position."

"I am indeed the governess," Olivia said with an answering smile. "And you must be my employer's brother."

The man removed his hat and swept an elegant bow. "Mr. Nathaniel Grier at your service." He straightened and glanced around. "Where's Dover? He's usually here to greet me and to make sure my horse gets unloaded."

"You came on horseback?" Olivia asked and immediately felt like an imbecile. Of course he'd come on horseback. He'd not be holding a riding crop if he hadn't.

He laughed. "Indeed. A carriage will arrive later with my traveling trunks and the lovely Mrs. Newhurst."

"I see." Olivia had no idea who Mrs. Newhurst might be and it wasn't her place to ask. A moment of silence followed before she thought to say, "I'll go and find Dover so he may assist you."

She'd barely turned before the man in question appeared, striding toward them from the opposite end of the house.

"Forgive me, sir," said Mr. Dover. "I was not aware of your arrival. Please, allow me to take your hat and gloves."

"Where will I find my brother?" Mr. Nathaniel Grier inquired.

"I believe he's in his study," Dover said.

As if summoned, the door to the study opened and Mr. Grier appeared, offering Olivia the first look she'd had of him in several long days. He was handsomer than she'd permitted herself to remember, his arresting dark gaze sending her poor heart into a frantic rhythm.

"Grayson," his brother exclaimed with a bright burst of cheerfulness.

Pleasure warmed Mr. Grier's expression though he didn't exhibit the same degree of humor. "It's good to see you, Nathan. Thank you for coming."

"Ordinarily, I would complain at the lack of a welcoming party. On second thought, I rather appreciate being greeted by the loveliest creature in England instead of you and Dover." He winked at Olivia, causing her cheeks to heat. "Wherever did you find her, Grayson?"

Mr. Grier frowned. "I believe she found us. Let's remove ourselves to my study, Nathan. We've much to discuss."

Olivia's insides contracted as he disappeared back inside the room. She knew it was stupid of her to be disappointed by the lack of attention he'd paid her. By contrast, his brother sent her a devilish smile. "If you'll excuse me, Miss..."

"Poole," she informed him.

He held her gaze for the briefest moment, then strode off after his brother. The door closed and Olivia nearly sagged against the wall as she expelled a breath she'd not even known she was holding. With a nervous glance at Mr. Dover to make sure he'd not taken note of her jittery nerves, she hastened up the stairs with every intention of closing herself away in her bedchamber for the rest of the day.

CHAPTER TWENTY-ONE

Grayson poured two glasses of brandy and handed one to Nathan. "You look well. I trust you had an enjoyable time in Italy?"

"I did, but I'm glad to be back. Specifically here at Sutton Hall." Nathan sipped his drink and sank onto a chair. "It grounds me."

It was impossible for Grayson not to smile just a little. While he'd taken over their father's duties, Matthew had married and produced heirs. But Nathan remained the carefree soul who lived every day as though it were his last.

"That's actually something I'd like to address," Grayson murmured. He moved to the desk and perched on the edge of it, his legs stretched out and crossed at the ankles. "Perhaps, if you were to settle down, you could lead a normal life."

Nathan froze mid sip. He lowered his glass and

stared at Grayson, his eyes uncharacteristically serious. "You know that's out of the question."

"But maybe with the right woman you could—"

"Settling down is for serious people like you and Matthew. He's done his part but you are the eldest – the one who ought to lead by example – and I don't see you hastening to the altar."

"You're right. Matthew made certain I wouldn't have to, but unlike you *I* have a purpose."

Nathan set his glass to his lips and gave a lazy shrug. "My purpose is to have fun. Lord knows someone in this family needs to."

The comment struck Grayson squarely across his chest. His brother wasn't wrong. It had been years since Grayson had found true joy in anything. While in London with his friends, he savored their company, but he never truly relaxed. The burden of responsibility wouldn't allow it. Still, he missed those years before the war, when life had lacked the pain of loss and the seriousness that came from constantly worrying over others.

"I have to see Juliana properly settled," he said. "I must ensure Mama is well cared for, that you are provided for, and that Sutton Hall thrives. Tenant families rely upon me, Nathan."

"I'm sorry." Nathan frowned into his glass before returning his gaze to Grayson. "I know life hasn't been easy for you, but I am here now, ready to offer support. Mama said you need help with Juliana. Mrs. Newhurst might be useful in that regard too, I should think."

Grayson's muscles tightened until he felt like a statue. He couldn't move, could scarcely breathe, and it took every piece of effort he possessed to make himself ask, "Mrs. Newhurst?"

"I happened upon her in Paris while on my way to London. We decided to accompany one another the rest of the way. She was very friendly when we first met – stopped by for tea one afternoon. When I mentioned my plan to visit you, she asked if she might join me."

Cold dread seeped through Grayson's veins. A shiver stole over his shoulders. "And you agreed to let her?"

"I saw no reason not to," Nathan said. He gave Grayson a quizzical look. "Is there something I should know?"

Grayson hesitated. Should he reveal the source of his guilt and heartache to Nathan? No. Not yet. He'd rather avoid speaking of Delilah for as long as possible, even though he already hated having to face her.

He shook his head. "It doesn't signify." Hopefully that was true. "Let's return to the subject of Juliana. I need someone with whom to discuss her progress."

"You worry she won't be ready?"

"I did, but I'm no longer sure. She's made a lot of progress since my return from London and with another year left for her to prepare, I do believe she'll manage. But there's been a complication." Confessing his faux pas to Nathan would hopefully lead to productive conversation and, he hoped, a solution. "I may have told Juliana that I intend to marry Miss Howell. And since the Oldbridges themselves are very set on this idea, I find myself in a bit of a muddle."

"You're getting married?" Nathan sat up straighter.

"Not if I can help it, but Lady Oldbridge has threatened to hurt Juliana's prospects unless I agree to do as she wants."

"Which is to marry her daughter."

"Miss Howell is an only child. More to the point, she has developed a tendre for me, though I can't imagine why. In any event her mother is quite determined to make her daughter happy by getting me leg-shackled to her. I've no idea how to extricate myself from the mess without causing more damage."

Nathan scoffed. "Lady Oldbridge is an insufferable woman. Her daughter, however, is awfully sweet."

"Precisely." He fixed his brother with his most serious gaze.

Understanding dawned in Nathan's eyes. His mouth dropped open. "Miss Howell is the 'right woman' you want *me* to marry? Are you out of your bloody mind, Grayson?"

"You'll get the townhouse in London, which has an attractive address considering its location on Grosvenor Square. I'll also increase your monthly allowance."

"Hypothetically speaking, what the hell makes you think the Oldbridges will agree if they've got their minds set on you?"

Grayson narrowed his gaze on his brother. "I trust you to charm you way into their hearts, brother."

Nathan choked on a laugh. "Absolutely not."

"Why?"

"Because I actually happen to like Miss Howell, and she deserves better. You know she does."

Grayson scrubbed one hand across his face. "Forgive me. You're absolutely right. I just…I need to think of something."

Nathan tossed back the remainder of his drink and went to refill his glass. "You've always done the honorable thing, so why not marry the chit yourself if doing so will secure Juliana's future?"

"I've told you why."

"No. You have not." Nathan turned to face him. "All you've said is that you don't need a wife or children because dear Matthew has taken care of that for you. But it would seem you're in a pickle now, and rather than crossing the Rubicon yourself, you're trying to get me do it for you."

An ache began growing behind Grayson's heart. He nodded. "The thing of it is…"

"Yes?" Nathan prompted.

Grayson took a deep breath. "I want what Mama and Papa had."

"What's that?"

"I want a love match or no match at all." Embarrassed by the confession, he dropped his gaze to the floor.

"Are you serious?" Nathan asked. Rather than laughing at him as Grayson had feared, his brother showed strong disbelief. "You're four and forty years old and as far as I know, you've made no effort to meet a woman for whom you might one day harbor such deep affection. You don't frequent ballrooms or attend house parties. When in London, you only see the family and your friends, Dale and West."

"True." Grayson pushed away from the desk and sighed. "Marriage was always something I hoped would come naturally, if it were meant to happen for me, that is."

"Well, maybe the time has come," Nathan said. "Miss Howell is kind. Even a heart as somber as yours will surely be inspired to develop tender feelings for her." When Grayson didn't respond right away, Nathan asked, "What are the Oldbridges holding over you to force your hand thus?"

For a second, Grayson considered dismissing the question, but that wasn't fair to Nathan. If he was going to try and help him out of this mess, he deserved no less than the truth. "Her ladyship threatened to let it be known that I'm bedding Miss Poole."

Nathan's eyes grew to the size of saucers. "You're shagging Juliana's governess?"

"Good God." Grayson glanced at the door to make sure it was firmly shut. "Be quiet, would you."

"Hats off to you," Nathan whispered. "That one's a looker."

Grayson rolled his eyes. "She and I are not involved. Lady Oldbridge has simply chosen to exaggerate reality for the purpose of adding pressure."

"What on earth would inspire her to create such a

threat?" Nathan asked with interest. He leaned forward, watching Grayson until Grayson felt the urge to tug at his cravat. It was damned humiliating, having to explain oneself to one's youngest sibling.

Relenting, Grayson told his brother about the dinner, about Miss Poole's comment on his behalf, her inviting Miss Howell to play the piano, and how she'd elected to leave without being dismissed. "As you can see, Lady Oldbridge has pulled a lie from thin air. Miss Poole was there to oversee Juliana's comportment and—"

"Did you invite past governesses to do so, Grayson?"

"It wasn't necessary before."

"I'd say," Nathan said with a smile too smug for Grayson's liking.

"Miss Poole is a respectable woman," Grayson insisted. "A vicar's daughter, just so you know. I would never ever consider—"

"But you'd like to," Nathan said. He waggled his eyebrows. "And unfortunately for you, I believe Lady Oldbridge, being the perceptive busybody we know her to be, realized as much. That is why her insinuation's a threat. Because you've acknowledged the seed of truth there is to it."

Grayson shook his head. "No. I—"

"Don't worry, brother. Worse things have happened than this. Take the Battle of Waterloo for instance." He stood and set his glass aside. "When you're ready to talk about it, let me know. I'm happy to help you enjoy a bit of reckless behavior for a change. And considering

Miss Poole's age, which is surely somewhere close to mine, I'm sure she'd welcome your lusty advances with breathless moans and—"

"For the love of God," Grayson growled.

Pretending to swoon against a nearby bookcase, Nathan gave a loud sigh. "Oh, Grayson. Please, Grayson. Yes, Grayson."

"Stop it this instant," Grayson warned, but the truth was his brother's playacting had made him laugh. "You're being an idiot."

"Fine." Nathan straightened himself. "Just remember, you're both adults. There's no reason why you can't carry on as you please behind closed doors, provided Miss Poole is willing. No one need know. In the meantime, I shall endeavor to think of a way for you to avoid the parson's mousetrap. How long before the Oldbridges expect you to call?"

"They've actually gone to Scotland and shan't be back until July."

Nathan stared at Grayson and blinked a few times in slow succession. "I sometimes wonder how you manage to make as much as you do out of nothing at all."

"Being threatened by Lady Oldbridge is not nothing due to the impact her effort may have upon Juliana."

"Perhaps not," Nathan allowed, "but a month and a half is plenty of time to figure things out. So don't worry. Enjoy the rest of your brandy while I take a bath. I'm sure there must be a dozen ways out of this for you. Including one that involves Miss Poole."

SOPHIE BARNES

He strode from the room with a bounce to his step and a whistle.

Grayson lowered himself to a chair with a groan. He was beginning to fear he'd regret involving his brother.

～

"What do you think of Mrs. Newhurst?" Juliana asked.

The question came as a surprise, right on the heels of a math lesson Juliana had been working on most of the morning. Olivia allowed herself a moment to consider the pretty blonde who'd arrived the previous afternoon. Dressed in a smart forget–me–not blue travelling dress with matching jacket, she'd looked like a fashion plate brought to life. Her wispy curls framed her delicate features as though designed to do so by Michelangelo himself.

"She's beautiful," Olivia said.

"She's also a widow," Juliana said. She handed her math pages to Olivia for inspection. "Which does make one wonder about her relationship with Nathan. Do you suppose she might be his mistress?"

Olivia coughed. She'd not really taken the time to consider if that were the case. "I'm really not sure. Anyway, it would be wrong to speculate about a subject that doesn't concern us. Besides, this isn't the sort of thing a young lady should think of, never mind discuss."

"I am a scientist," Juliana said as though Olivia were daft. "It's in my nature to question everything. It's also normal for me to have a basic understanding of adult relations."

"Right," Olivia muttered. She cleared her throat and gave her attention to Juliana's worksheets, desperate to put an end to the subject. "I'll review these while you read from your history book. We'll go outside afterward and stretch our legs."

"And check on the mouse traps?"

Olivia chuckled. It was curious what excited the girl. "Of course."

They set off one hour later. Much to Olivia's relief, Juliana had finally grasped the concept of algebraic equations and had only gotten one sum wrong because she'd skipped a step. When Olivia asked her to make the calculation again, she arrived at the correct answer.

"Do you think we might have caught more than one?" Juliana asked as they approached the spot in the garden where the traps lay.

"I've no idea. We'll simply have to see."

Quickening her steps, Juliana hastened toward the first trap and flipped the see–saw lid to peek inside. She scrunched her nose. "There's only a beetle, which ought not be heavy enough to fall through."

"It's still something for you to study," Olivia told her in an attempt to ease her disappointment. "Beetles can be interesting creatures, can they not?"

"I suppose so, but it's not the same as a mouse." Miss Edwards retrieved the beetle which she placed in her pocket, despite Olivia's insisting she ought to put it in one of the small linen pouches she carried. "That is reserved for the mice. I'll not waste it on an insect."

"But won't the beetle escape?" Olivia asked as they went to check the next trap.

Juliana merely shrugged. She clearly didn't care about the poor beetle.

Unfortunately, the next trap did not contain even that much. It was entirely empty and the bait Juliana had laid out was gone. She stared at the trap. "Why isn't this working?"

"Maybe a bird stole the cheese," Olivia suggested. "Or one of the cats?"

"I suppose." Juliana stood, gave a big huff, and marched off.

Olivia wished there were more she could do to help, but catching mice wasn't her forté and asking someone else to do it would only alert others to Juliana's hobby. But as Olivia crossed the graveled pathway to the hedgerow beneath which the last trap was placed, Juliana, who'd lowered herself to a crouched position, leapt to her feet. She turned to face Olivia with a wide grin, her eyes shining brighter than the afternoon sun.

"I've got one! Come see."

Struck by the girl's infectious good cheer, Olivia hastened her steps. She did not care for rodents of any kind, but it was impossible not to share in Juliana's keen excitement. Reaching her, Olivia peered down into the small wooden box from which a tiny brown mouse with enormous black eyes stared back at them in what appeared to be absolute terror.

"Can you believe Miss Chadwick would feed such a poor creature to one of the cats?" Juliana asked.

Olivia shook her head. "It's hard to imagine anyone doing so."

"There's only the one for now, but it's a good start." She carefully transferred the trembling mouse to one of the pouches and put the trap back beneath the hedge. When she stood, her expression changed to one of concern as she glanced past Olivia's shoulder. "Nathan and Mrs. Newhurst are coming this way. Quick. Put the pouch in your skirt pocket."

Olivia drew back. "I am not putting a mouse in my pocket. Why not put it in yours?"

"I've a beetle in mine, in case you'd forgotten."

"Then take the beetle out and replace it with the mouse."

Panic settled in Juliana's eyes. "Please. It won't bite you. It can't while it's in the pouch."

"I believe mice can chew their way through most things," Olivia argued.

"Eventually, but this is just for a moment. If Nathan sees the pouches he will want to know what's inside and I risk losing another mouse. Not to mention the freedom to catch another."

The agonized look in Juliana's eyes was enough to melt lead. With a sigh, Olivia opened her skirt pocket wide so Juliana could drop the pouch inside. She shuddered in response to the wriggly movement against her thigh.

"Juliana and Miss Poole," Mr. Grier said in a bubbly

voice as he and Mrs. Newhurst came within speaking distance. "How delightful to find the two of you here. Perhaps you'll be able to help us convince my stubborn brother to spend time away from his study."

"We wanted him to come riding with us," Mrs. Newhurst said, her sky blue eyes assessing Olivia in a manner that made her feel blander than unflavored porridge. "It's a beautiful day after all."

"Do you ride, Miss Poole?" the gentleman asked.

Olivia shook her head. "I'm afraid not."

"Then we must remedy that," he declared.

"Oh yes," Juliana exclaimed. She clapped her hands together. "I heartily agree."

"Everyone ought to know how to ride in this day and age," Mrs. Newhurst said as though the idea of anyone not being able to handle a horse was inconceivable.

"It wouldn't be appropriate," Olivia said. Unable to help herself, she glanced toward the stables. Of course she wanted to learn. Not only because it was on the list but because her sister had not been the only one who'd yearned for the freedom of racing across an open field.

But the boating incident urged her to be more cautious. And besides, it wasn't right for a servant to engage in such sport.

"Nonsense, Miss Poole." Mr. Grier grabbed Olivia's arm and proceeded to steer her along the path that led to the stables. "You are a governess, not a scullery maid. Your job is to teach Juliana, to prepare her for her coming out, and to serve as her companion. Letting her ride unchaperoned with a groomsman, now that would be inappropriate, Miss Poole."

"I suppose," Olivia conceded while dragging her feet. She glanced over her shoulder at Juliana who trailed after her with Mrs. Newhurst by her side.

Mr. Grier leaned a bit closer. "Once you learn how to ride, you'll never want to stop. It's unlike anything else, I can assure you."

Olivia swallowed. "I'm not sure your brother will approve."

"Of you, Miss Poole?" He laughed as though she'd made a fantastic joke. "I highly doubt it."

His manner, while friendly and charming, was much too forceful for Olivia's comfort. She worried he would lead her straight into trouble if she weren't careful. For although her employer would not be able to punish his brother with anything much, the same could not be said of Olivia. She had to conduct herself in a manner appropriate to a governess, not let herself be carried away by what appeared to be a reckless scoundrel.

So she withdrew her arm and stepped sideways, adding distance between herself and Mr. Grier. "Miss Edwards and I ought to return indoors and resume our lessons."

"Must we?" Juliana asked, her whole body slumping. "Riding would be much more fun."

"It will have to wait." As if in agreement, the mouse in Olivia's pocket moved, which nearly caused her to jump. She forced a smile. "Enjoy the rest of your walk, sir. Mrs. Newhurst. Come along, Miss Edwards, we've yet to cover the habits of rodents."

"Oh yes." Juliana's eyes widened. "I'd quite forgotten."

"I can assure you I had not," Olivia told her firmly as she set off with every expectation of Juliana following.

CHAPTER TWENTY-TWO

A growl of frustration rose from somewhere deep inside Grayson. Standing by his study window, too irritated by his brother's attempt at convincing him work didn't matter and that he should drop everything to entertain Delilah – a woman he not only hadn't invited but could not stand – he'd watched Nathan speak with Miss Poole. He'd seen the way in which he'd cozied up to her, linking arms to draw her close and dipping his head while he chatted away.

He'd also seen the tense look on her face, the way she leaned away from Nathan while he dragged her along.

What the hell was he playing at? Miss Poole wasn't his type, yet if he didn't know any better, he'd say his brother was keen on the woman.

Damn it.

He'd planned to keep avoiding her. And stay as far

away from Delilah as possible while she remained beneath his roof. But interference was clearly necessary. Whatever his game, Nathan was unsettling Miss Poole, and Grayson wouldn't tolerate that.

With a disgruntled sigh, he marched outside and took in the scene before him. Miss Poole, who'd been striding toward the door, drew to a sudden halt when she saw him. So did Juliana, who'd been hurrying after her. Farther along, Nathan appeared deep in thought while Mrs. Newhurst looked strangely abandoned.

Miss Poole stared at Grayson, who blocked her path, her expression tight. Juliana on the other hand broke into a wide smile as soon as she spotted him. She called his name, which drew Nathan's attention. And Delilah's.

Nathan immediately grinned. "I see you've chosen to join us after all. I wonder what made you change your mind."

"Will you walk with me, Mr. Grier?" Delilah called, a pleasant smile crinkling her otherwise perfect porcelain features.

It would be rude to refuse her, and yet, Grayson sensed that refusing Delilah right now was critical in setting the tone for her stay. "Perhaps a bit later. To start, I wanted to ask if there might be an interest in taking tea on the terrace."

"I'd love that," Juliana said.

"I didn't think you had the time," Nathan teased. He glanced at Miss Poole. "Apparently someone has caused you to find it."

Delilah, clearly imagining this remark pertained to her, tittered like a shy debutante even though she was anything but. Grayson groaned.

"I do hope you'll ask the governess to join us," Nathan added with laughter in his voice.

Grayson made a mental note to put him in his place later, and nodded. "Of course. She's welcome to do so if she wishes."

"Thank you," Miss Poole said, her voice a touch faint. "But I've work to attend to. Miss Edwards's math assignment needs to be graded."

"Surely that can wait," Nathan said.

"I really don't think—"

"Miss Poole," Grayson said, firming his voice as much as possible. "I'd appreciate your presence. If it's not too much trouble."

It had been days – weeks – since he'd been so near her, and now that he was, he dreaded the thought of her leaving his side. He needed to bask in the pleasure that coursed through his veins whenever she met his gaze.

"But I…" She gave him a helpless look that made his heart dip.

She did not want to remain. Not even when he requested her to.

"If you have more pressing matters to attend to, Miss Poole," Delilah said as though she were mistress of Sutton Hall, "you must not let us keep you."

Something in Miss Poole's expression changed. A hardening of resolve was the best way to describe it. Miss Poole raised her chin and directed her gaze at

Delilah. "The grading can wait. I'd be honored to join you for tea."

Delilah glanced at Grayson and promptly smiled, even wider than before. The expression did not reach her eyes, nor did it suit her.

Fearing the lady might insist he be the one to escort her, Grayson called to Nathan, "Will you please show Mrs. Newhurst the way? I'll ask one of the maids to attend us."

"I can do so," Miss Poole suggested.

"Or I can," Juliana said.

"Thank you, Juliana," Grayson managed, just as Miss Poole opened her mouth to add something further. "We'll meet you on the terrace."

The governess gave a dissatisfied huff and crossed her arms as if in protest. Grayson scowled at her. Was being left alone with him really so bad?

"Can I please have my coin collection back?" Juliana asked Miss Poole. "You took it for safekeeping if you'll recall."

A pouch was quickly retrieved from Miss Poole's pocket and then Juliana was gone. Grayson knit his brow. Since when had Juliana collected coins? And shouldn't such a collection jangle somewhat?

He shook his head and offered Miss Poole his arm. "Shall we?"

Her touch was hesitant and slight, as though she were a deer invited to stroll with a hungry wolf. Grayson hated that. He didn't want her to fear him. The notion that she might brought his thoughts back to

Nathan and Miss Poole's rapid retreat from his company.

"If I may make an observation," he began, choosing his words with care as they started forward, "you looked distressed when I arrived. Did my brother say something to upset you?"

"He was friendly," she replied after a moment's hesitation.

"That doesn't answer my question." When she said nothing further, Grayson told her, "I want you to know you can come to me with any issue, knowing I'll listen and lend my support. It's no secret Nathaniel can be a bit forward at times, so if he overstepped in some way..."

"He wanted me to do something I feared you'd disapprove of." Miss Poole frowned at the ground while they walked a bit further. When he drew her to a halt, she glanced at him and confessed, "I found him pushy and while I'm sure his intentions were good, I didn't like it."

Grayson's facial muscles tightened. He tried to relax. Getting angry on Miss Poole's behalf and letting that anger show was unlikely to put her at ease. He placed his hand over hers, hoping to offer comfort while doing his best to ignore the electrical spark the simple touch produced. It shot through his veins and brought his attention straight to her lips, which parted as though by surprise.

God, how he wanted to kiss her, to hold her and

taste her and make her crave him with as much ardor as he'd begun craving her.

"What did he want you to do?" Grayson spoke the question as though his voice were detached from his body. Part of him dreaded her answer, but then again, they were discussing Nathan. While he knew he could be an incorrigible flirt, whispering wicked suggestions in ladies ears, he would never proposition Miss Poole.

"To ride," she said.

Grayson nearly choked. "I beg your pardon?"

"He and Mrs. Newhurst were talking of going, of how they'd tried to convince you to join them. Your brother asked if I knew how to ride and when I told him I did not, he insisted I try right away."

"Horses," Grayson managed. "You're speaking of horses."

She gave him an odd look. "Of course. What else would I be referring to?"

"What indeed?" He took a deep breath and expelled it. Drawing her closer, he resumed their walk. "And you feared I'd be opposed?"

"Heading off to the stables and asking one of the grooms to saddle a horse – requesting he teach me how to ride it – would be incredibly arrogant given my position. Even if your brother were to make the request on my behalf."

"I suppose." He gave her a sideways glance and saw the agitated look in her eyes.

"I am a servant," she pressed, as though he needed reminding. "Not a family member nor even a guest.

For me to indulge in such sport would surely be unseemly."

"What if I gave you permission?" He noted her surprise and bit back a curse. Ignoring the negative light in which she obviously viewed him as some sort of authoritarian ogre, he said, "If you wish to learn, I can make arrangements."

"But..." She gazed at him as though his head were on backward. "Why would you do such a thing?"

A rough smile tugged at the edge of his lips. "Consider it a reward for getting Juliana to enjoy her lessons rather than loathe them. She's made great progress during the brief time you've been instructing her."

"I scarcely know what to say. Learning how to ride would probably take up a great deal of time. I'm sure you wouldn't want that."

The terrace appeared as they turned a corner. Nathan and Delilah were already taking their seats at the black wrought iron table that stood there. He and Miss Poole would join them soon, but before they did, he had to persuade her to let him help since it was clear she wanted to learn. She just didn't dare take the leap.

Choosing a decisive approach, he said, "I'll speak to the head groom today and make arrangements for you to start lessons tomorrow."

She shook her head. Despite the look of yearning that shone in her eyes, there was also desperation. Dropping her voice to a near whisper, she asked, "What will the rest of the servants think?"

Her worry was clear. She feared they would believe

she'd won his favor by welcoming him to her bed. As much as he'd like such an arrangement, he knew it could never be. Not that this mattered if it was what people believed. Care had to be taken. Not only for Miss Poole's sake but for his and Juliana's as well. It would not do to provide Lady Oldbridge with more ammunition.

"I shall make it clear to everyone that this request comes directly from Juliana. She loves to ride and it makes sense that she should be able to have her governess join her on occasion." He dipped his head and softly murmured, "Will that do?"

Miss Poole nodded. "Yes, Mr. Grier. Thank you."

Her lips twitched with an effort to restrain the smile that threatened to spread across her entire face. Grayson's chest filled with warmth. He wanted to make her happy, whether because he sensed she'd had little joy in her life or because of the deep attraction he harbored, he wasn't sure. But when it came to Miss Poole, making her smile was akin to holding the keys to the kingdom.

"She's absolutely delightful," Nathan said that evening while he and Grayson enjoyed a moment of brotherly solitude in the library. Thankfully, Delilah had chosen to retire immediately after supper, saving Grayson from having to entertain her.

"Her innocence is intoxicating," Nathan went on. "The ease with which she blushes is so refreshing. You'll not find that in London these days, certainly not from a

MR. GRIER AND THE GOVERNESS

woman her age. A pity she's hidden away here. I'm sure many men would like to—"

Grayson's snifter shattered, sending a spray of crystal and brandy across the floor. His shoulders shook with a new sort of rage. It was unlike anything he had experienced before – it was dark and possessive and would surely see Nathan into an early grave if he kept on speaking of Miss Poole in such a manner.

"Stay away from her," he growled, his posture tense as he leaned forward in his seat. If need be, he'd beat all indecent thoughts of Miss Poole from Nathan's head with his fists. Even though he knew this was irrational, that Nathan posed no threat whatsoever, that he was all pretense, a lamb in wolf's clothing. It made no difference in the moment.

"Bloody hell, Grayson. You're bleeding."

"I said—"

"Here." Nathan shoved a handkerchief into his hand and went to the bell pull.

"So help me God," Grayson said. He added a wince when a shard of crystal dug into his flesh and he swiftly removed it. "You may be my brother, but I'll toss you out on your ass if you so much as look at Miss Poole in a manner I disapprove of."

"Grayson, I—"

"You will not speak with her in private or press her to walk with you against her will. You will not flirt with her or encourage her to ignore her conscience. Instead, you will treat her with the respect she deserves. Is that clear?"

"Good lord." Nathan had never appeared more shocked. The recently used bell pull swayed gently against the wall behind him. "I didn't think I'd see the day."

Irritation roughened Grayson's voice. "What day?"

"The one where the mighty Grayson Grier would fall, slayed by the charms of a virtuous governess."

"What?"

Nathan chuckled. An annoying degree of humor flashed in his schoolboy eyes. He shoved his hands in his pockets and rocked on his heels. "You not only want Miss Poole. You're smitten by her."

"Don't be absurd," Grayson grumbled, but the words lacked conviction. He shifted in his seat and scowled at Nathan who looked tremendously pleased. "As her employer it is my duty to make sure she's happy and that my idiot brother doesn't cross any lines. She's an excellent governess to Juliana. I'd hate for her to go because you've made her uncomfortable. Especially since it'll be a nuisance having to hire someone else."

"I can think of numerous ways for you to make Miss Poole tremendously happy," Nathan said with a wicked smirk.

Grayson was prevented from lunging at him and swiping it from his face due to Dover's arrival. The butler assessed the scene and ordered one of the maids to clean up the mess.

CHAPTER TWENTY-THREE

Olivia stared at the horse she was meant to ride. It was magnificent, with gleaming black flanks, long legs and flexing muscles. The beast's size was impressive. It caught her gaze and held it while being led toward her, its hooves clapping the ground. A shiver raked Olivia's spine. If she fell from that height it would hurt like the devil. She'd be lucky if she escaped uninjured.

"Are you certain that's the horse Mr. Grier recommended for me?" Olivia asked Mr. Andrews, the head groom. As much as she'd been looking forward to the experience, she was starting to doubt the wisdom in the activity.

"Midnight is Mr. Grier's own personal horse." Mr. Andrews spoke calmly, as if Olivia were an anxious filly in need of soothing. "He's a large beast to be sure, but he's gentle, wise, and very experienced."

"He won't throw you," Juliana said. The girl had insisted on accompanying Olivia to the stables in order to oversee her first ride.

Olivia knit her brow while studying Midnight with trepidation. "Isn't there a smaller horse I could use? One where I wouldn't be quite so high off the ground?"

"None will be as easygoing as Midnight." The horse gave a soft whinny as if to agree. The scent of hay and manure hung thick in the air. "Trust me on this, Miss Poole. As you're a beginner, he'll make certain you have a safe ride. And besides, you're not heading off on your own. I'll be leading you on a walk of the property, that's all."

"And I am supposed to perch on that?" Olivia asked with a nod toward the side saddle. It looked like an awkward way of riding, but of course it was what was expected of her. She could hardly hitch up her skirts and sit astride.

"It's not as hard as it looks," Juliana assured her.

"If you'd be so good as to come over here to this stool, I'll help you mount," Mr. Andrews told her.

Uncertain yet determined, not only because Mr. Grier was offering her the chance of a lifetime but also because this was one of the things Agnes had wished for most, Olivia approached the stool. She placed her right foot upon it like the groom instructed, reached up to grab the saddle for support, and hoisted herself upward.

"Ah. Miss Poole."

Olivia swept her gaze toward the stable doors

through which Mr. Nathanial Grier strode. Eyes sparkling and with a boyish grin lending a touch of carefreeness Olivia envied, he reached her side in a few long paces.

"Allow me, Andrews," he remarked.

"Mr. Grier specifically told me to—"

"Yes, yes. I'm sure he did. But I'm here now and ready to offer assistance."

Olivia glanced over her shoulder at the two men. Mr. Andrews did not look remotely pleased with this turn of events while Mr. Grier's brother seemed unwilling to let that affect him. He simply nudged the groom out of the way and stepped into his place.

"Nathaniel," Juliana warned, but it was too late. The man's hands settled firmly upon Olivia's hips.

"Mr. Grier," Olivia gasped.

"Do call me Nathaniel," he said, his grip tightening. "It avoids confusion."

"This really isn't—"

"Up you go."

Olivia squealed as her body was lifted. The stool disappeared from beneath her feet. She grabbed the saddle and tried to turn, to land upon the blasted contraption of a side saddle in some dignified manner. But everything happened so fast and she'd not been instructed on where each leg was meant to go. So to her absolute mortification, she ended up dangling across Midnight's back with her bottom straight up in the air.

"Well done, sir," Mr. Andrews muttered.

"You shouldn't have interfered," Juliana chastised.

"I'm sorry, Miss Poole," Nathaniel spoke with what sounded like poorly suppressed laughter. "Are you all right?"

"What do you think?" Olivia grumbled. The raised parts of the saddle were digging into her stomach.

"Well, I—"

"What the hell is this?" The angry click of approaching footsteps accompanied the tersely spoken question.

Olivia groaned. Perfect. Her employer was here now as well, just in time to see her make a cake of herself.

"I was trying to help her mount," his brother said. "I didn't expect her to land in a heap."

"You should have let Andrews handle it, Nathan. I gave him clear instructions on how to proceed."

"Forgive me, Mr. Grier," said Mr. Andrews. "I should have insisted."

"Yes. You should have," Mr. Grier told him.

"It's not his fault," Juliana said while Olivia's ears began to burn with humiliation.

"Of that I have no doubt," Mr. Grier replied. He cleared his throat. "Miss Poole, we must get you into the proper position."

"All right," was all she could manage while praying all three men would suffer memory lapses as soon as this ordeal was over.

"Here we go," Mr. Grier said. A large pair of hands encased her waist, infusing her body with a comforting sense of security. Gently, those hands pulled her backward, away from Midnight and down onto solid ground.

Instinctively, Olivia sought support and reached out, her palms coming to rest upon Mr. Grier's chest. She took a sharp breath as she registered not only firmness but steady heartbeats. Her own pulse leapt in response and her mouth went dry.

Glancing up, she met his dark gaze. For the briefest of seconds she fancied he tightened his hold on her waist, that he drew her slightly closer while struggling to catch his own breath.

The spell broke as soon as he spoke. "Let's try that again, Miss Poole. Just place your hands on my shoulders, step onto the stool, and I'll hoist you into the saddle on the count of three."

This time, with Mr. Grier's guidance, Olivia managed to find her way into the saddle. She instinctively leaned forward, however, attempting to hold her balance by keeping her body as close to Midnight as possible.

"You need to reposition your legs," Mr. Grier informed her.

"Perhaps if she—"

"Stay out of this," Mr. Grier told his brother sharply. "You've meddled enough for one day."

"Fine," Nathaniel grumbled. He'd never looked more put out, though his expression changed soon enough in response to Mrs. Newhurst's arrival.

Olivia stared at the lady as she sauntered closer. Dressed in a splendid emerald green riding habit trimmed with black cording, she looked like she belonged in the Royal Gallery. Her blonde curls were neatly coiled so they peeked out beneath the brim of her elegant hat. Next to her, Olivia felt like a lackluster piece of coal.

"I thought I'd lend Miss Poole assistance," Mrs. Newhurst announced, in response to which Juliana rolled her eyes. "After all, I am more adept at side saddle than any of you."

"She's right about that," Nathaniel said with a chuckle.

Mr. Grier muttered something beneath his breath before addressing Mr. Andrews with greater force. "Please ready Stardust for Mrs. Newhurst and Comet for Miss Edwards." He glanced at his ward. "Provided you're also riding?"

"Of course I am." Juliana raised her chin and sent him a challenging look.

"I'll take Cassiopeia then," Nathaniel said. "Unless you fancy her yourself, Grayson?"

"I'm not riding," Mr. Grier said. The remark, spoken with a hint of irritation, caused Olivia's stomach to clench in the most inexplicable way. Before she had time to address the feeling, he grabbed her thigh and began repositioning her leg.

Olivia stilled in response to his touch. It was firm and decisive. Raising her knee slightly, he hooked it over the pommel and...kept his hand there, resting upon her shin, immediately on top of the red satin garter she wore beneath her skirts.

His thumb moved over it with lazy movements. "Miss Poole?"

Heart dancing about in her breast, Olivia glanced at him while attempting to breathe. "Yes?"

His features softened and something resembling a smile, albeit a faint one, tugged at his lips. "You need to straighten your posture. Here, take the reins."

Swallowing, she did as he instructed while he offered guidance. As soon as she was properly seated, he helped her position her fingers, weaving the reins between them until she held them correctly. Olivia's heart bounced when his hand returned to her thigh. It was wholly improper, never mind the fact that he appeared to be making sure her leg wouldn't slip.

Still, she glanced in the direction of the others, just to make sure no one was watching, and caught Mrs. Newhurst's sharp gaze. The lady immediately turned as if to feign ignorance of Mr. Grier's inappropriate attention toward her.

Embarrassed and worried that Mrs. Newhurst might misconstrue the situation, Olivia forced a loud, "Thank you, Mr. Grier. That will do."

He glanced up sharply and snared her with his dark eyes. Holding firm, she steeled herself against the powerful yearning his nearness stirred. She could not afford to want him. Or for anyone to suspect he might want her in return.

What a fanciful notion that was.

And yet, she could not continue making excuses, explaining away what she already knew to be true. It was in the way he looked at her, the way he touched her. Although it defied all logical reasoning, Olivia sensed a burning desire between them that threatened to ruin everything of importance – Juliana's reputation, Mr. Grier's standing within society, her own future happiness.

She could not allow that.

So she tore her gaze away from his and gave her attention to Mr. Andrews when he returned. Head held high while she clasped the reins tightly and did her best not to look down at the ground, she allowed the groom to lead her out onto the path that would take her on a tour of the garden.

Grayson watched Miss Poole's retreating form until she turned the corner. Juliana soon followed with Nathan not far behind. "Keep an eye on her, will you?"

"Are you certain you'd not rather do so yourself?" Nathan asked with a smirk.

"Positive," Grayson said and wished his brother a pleasant ride.

"Would you mind helping me out?" Delilah asked when she rode up beside him next. "I fear the lace of my half–boot has come undone."

Sure enough, the lace had completely unraveled. Grayson took a step closer and started doing it up with swift movements, adding a double knot for good measure. "There. That ought to hold."

Before he could move away she leaned toward him, forcing him to reach up and steady her body before she fell. A pretty smile captured her lips. "I'd almost forgotten how good it feels to have you hold me."

With a wince, Grayson pushed her back into an upright position. "You cannot fool me, Delilah. Not anymore."

"Let's take tea together when I return," she said, completely ignoring his comment. "Give me the chance to remind you of just how good we were together."

"I'd rather eat glass," Grayson muttered, upon which he slapped Cassiopeia's flank, urging her into a forward trot and taking Delilah away from his presence.

He blew out a breath and ran his hands through his hair. It was time for him to encourage her hasty departure.

Leaving the stables, he strode toward his workshop, eating up the ground with angry strides. To think he'd once craved Delilah's attention and basked in her company. The bitter memories stirred by her presence filled him with self–loathing.

Breathing hard, he thrust his workshop door open. The smell of sawdust slowed his pulse and calmed his spirit. He crossed to the workbench and found his latest project. The comb was exquisite – his best design yet with its intricate lace–work and mother of pearl inlays.

He turned it over between his fingers. Envisioning it in Miss Poole's black hair wasn't hard, but would she allow him to gift it to her? Would she wear it if he did?

With a sigh, he went back to work, polishing the

wood until the surface was almost glassy. Using a stencil he'd made a few days earlier, he marked the mother–of–pearl and cut it to size. The rough edges would need filing. And there was some adjustment required on one corner. It didn't lie as flush with the surface of the comb as he wanted, after fitting it into the matching indentation he'd carved. The mother of pearl would also have to be glued, so there was plenty of work left before the comb was completely finished.

He set it aside and took out his pocket watch to gauge the hour. It always surprised him how swiftly time flew when he worked on these projects. A little over three hours in this case. Miss Poole's ride should be long over by now.

Curious to learn how it had gone, he left the workshop and returned to the house. A hot cup of tea would suit him well. Perhaps a sandwich or two to go along with it and he'd be all right until supper.

"Where is everyone?" Grayson asked Dover when he met him in the hallway.

"Miss Edwards and Miss Poole are enjoying tea in the parlor with your brother," Dover informed him. "If you wish to join them, I'll send for another cup."

"Please do," Grayson said. "And something to eat. I'm famished."

"Very good, sir."

Dover headed toward the kitchen stairs and Grayson prepared to join the rest of the party, only to pause. His trousers were covered in fine wood filings, and since he'd been working with his hands, he really ought to wash them before he sat down to tea.

Deciding to change his clothes and freshen up, he passed the parlor and climbed the stairs. Turning right, he strode toward his bedchamber door, opened it and entered his room. Only to come to a jarring halt.

Delilah, dressed in a sheer barely–there–at–all chemise, lounged in his bed as though she lived to serve him.

"What the hell are you doing here?" he demanded.

She gave him a saucy grin. "Waiting for you, of course."

"You need to leave," he told her gruffly. "Right now."

"Don't be so stuffy, Grayson. Don't you remember the fun we used to have together?"

"What I remember is that you lied."

"Semantics," she murmured with a tiny shrug that made him want to haul her from the bed and toss her out the nearest window.

"Fact," he countered, with a grimace.

"Very well," she agreed, much to his surprise before adding a quietly spoken, "I'm sorry. I should have told you I was married."

Grayson stared at her. "You turned me into the sort of man I despise."

"Like I said, I'm sorry. I didn't mean to hurt you in any way, but Edward was old and I was stuck. You offered the passion I craved."

"It was wrong."

"But wonderful." She rose up onto her elbows, positioning herself so the afternoon sunlight that spilled through the windows turned her chemise translucent.

Had she planned it that way as part of her obvious ploy to seduce him? He'd not put it past her. The awful fact was it seemed to be working. To his total and utter shame, the need building inside him these past few weeks because of Miss Poole roared to life at the sight of what Delilah offered.

Worst of all, he couldn't hide it.

She seemed to delight in this as she gave a low chuckle. "Your body clearly agrees. And besides, Edward's gone now, which means we're free to enjoy each other as much as we like."

"No." It was all he could manage right now. He forced the word out between gritted teeth in an effort to retain control – to stop himself from crossing the floor and doing something he knew he'd regret as soon as it was over.

She patted the bed. "Come on. It's obvious you want me."

"You're wrong." He told himself to leave, to quit his room and not return until he knew she was gone. But what if a servant found her here? What sort of conclusions would they draw? He fisted his hands at his sides and told her bluntly, "I need a change of clothes, so please get out of my room. We can discuss this at greater length later."

She produced a long suffering sigh. "Very well."

Relief poured through Grayson even as his impatience with Delilah grew when she took her sweet time climbing off the bed. Bending in a way that ensured him a clear view down the front of her chemise, she retrieved the wrapper she'd dropped on the floor. Grayson rolled his eyes and prayed for strength. It was the middle of the afternoon for God's sake. What the hell was she thinking, coming here like this?

Having straightened and put the wrapper on, she moved toward the door, but paused when she reached his side. Her hand rose, winding around the back of his neck as she brazenly pressed herself to him.

"Don't," he muttered.

"Are you quite certain?" Her hold on him tightened, forcing him to grab her so he could dislodge her from his person.

A sharp inhale of breath filled the air around him. Delilah flashed a grin as she glanced past his shoulder. And then came the sound of retreating footsteps hastening off to some other location.

"What the..." Grayson tried to turn but Delilah hindered his movements. He muttered a curse. "Get off me."

She stumbled back a step as he shoved her aside. "You needn't worry, my darling. It was only the governess."

"The governess," Grayson repeated, the words sounding hollow.

"Too bad you insisted on cutting things short. I rather imagine it might have been fun to give her a little show, teach her a thing or two about what she's obviously missing."

Grayson stared at the door which he, being the massive idiot he was, had forgotten to close when he'd seen Delilah. He shook his head and glanced at the woman who'd clearly made it her mission in life to pursue him until he went mad. "What did you say?"

"No woman looks as tightly trussed as that without having needs that aren't being met."

"How long was she there?" How much did she see and what had she made of it all? Grayson's heart beat with aching regret. Whether because she prided herself on being forthright or because of her broad education which seemed to rival his own, Miss Poole's opinion of him mattered.

And Grayson feared he'd fallen in that regard after what she'd just witnessed.

"I didn't spot her until we embraced."

Unwilling to argue the honesty of that comment, Grayson stepped aside and pointed at the door. "Out. Now."

Delilah raised her chin and met his gaze directly. Gone was her alluring seductiveness of earlier, replaced now by hardened determination. "If you're thinking of sending me away, I would suggest you reconsider. After all, I rather enjoy being here with you and your brother, away from all the hustle and bustle of London, and have no qualms with staying for good. Besides, we wouldn't want anyone else to learn about Nathaniel's secret."

"What the hell are you saying?"

She offered a careless shrug. "Merely that I would be less inclined to gossip if I were your wife."

It took every bit of self–restraint Grayson possessed not to strike the blasted woman. He was a gentleman after all and gentlemen did not resort to violence, least of all against the fairer sex.

So he resigned himself to glaring at her as she swept from the room. As soon as she crossed the threshold he slammed the door and turned the key in the lock, ensuring she wouldn't return. He took a few steadying breaths and tried to expel the tightly coiled tension within, but it was no use. Delilah had effectively ruined his day, perhaps even his life if he did not find the means by which to dispel her threat, which was so much worse than Lady Oldbridge's.

If she chose, Delilah could ruin the Grier name and everyone associated with it forever. She could see Nathan hanged.

Horrified, Grayson changed his clothes quickly and left his room, intent on telling his brother what had transpired.

CHAPTER TWENTY-FOUR

For two days Olivia worried Mr. Grier might send for her, that he might demand a meeting in his study so he could quiz her on what she'd seen and persuade her not to speak of it to anyone. When he didn't, it occurred to her he might not know she'd been passing his bedchamber while he'd been pressing attentions upon Mrs. Newhurst.

Pressing attentions?

Olivia stifled a miserable laugh while recalling the woman's state of undress at the time. No, she might as well think of the incident in correct terms. Mrs. Newhurst had clearly delighted in Mr. Grier's embrace. Her eyes had sparkled while her scantily clad body pressed into his with enthusiastic fervor.

The two were obviously more than acquaintances. They were lovers. Mrs. Newhurst was Mr. Grier's mistress, and while it bothered Olivia that he allowed such a shameful woman to stay beneath the same roof as his ward, she had no right to demand he send her packing.

Her desire to have Mrs. Newhurst gone had nothing to do with the sharp pang of envy that pierced her heart the moment she'd seen them together. What a fool she'd been, imagining some sort of romance between herself and Mr. Grier of all people. It was clear now that the only reason he'd shown some interest was because she was a woman and she'd been available, should he choose to cross the boundary between master and servant.

But Mrs. Newhurst was here now, and it was a great deal easier for him to lure a seasoned widow into his bed.

Idiot.

She had to put Mr. Grier from her mind. She had to stop craving his notice and wishing for more than what was proper. She would not allow herself to remember the way he'd looked at her in the stables or how his hand had lingered upon her leg. None of that mattered. Not when he was having relations with Mrs. Newhurst. And maybe she wasn't the only one. Maybe Mr. Grier was the sort of philanderer who prided himself on his numerous conquests.

Mama had warned her of such men once. They spoke pretty words and could coax the most pious woman into submission, but at the end of the day, they only wanted one thing. And it wasn't forever.

Stomach tight with the sort of disappointment that

made no logical sense, Olivia straightened her spine and squared her shoulders. She was here to work, not to embroil herself in affairs of the heart. There were lessons to be taught. It was high time she stopped acting the coward by hiding up here in her room.

"You can do this. You can bury your feelings and be the governess Juliana needs."

Bolstered by her own firm voice, Olivia left her room and went to find Mr. Dover. She would request his help instead of involving Mr. Grier, whom she planned on steering clear of to the best of her ability.

"Do you know of a suitable dance instructor whose services we might enlist?"

Mr. Dover raised his chin and seemed to consider. "Miss Chadwick used Mr. Roberts until he moved to London. I'm not sure if there's anyone else nearby."

It wasn't the answer Olivia hoped for. "I suppose I should place an advertisement in the paper then."

"That's certainly an option and I'm more than happy to help you with it if the master agrees. However, it might be prudent of you to enlist his brother's assistance since he's in residence. I doubt you'll find a superior dancer in anyone else."

Grateful for that piece of information, Olivia thanked Mr. Dover and went in search of Nathaniel. He'd been extremely attentive toward her during her first riding lesson, and she'd since warmed to him. Although he was a self–proclaimed rogue who took great pleasure in teasing others and often said the most shocking things, she no longer felt the need to escape him.

However unwise that might be.

Moving briskly through the house, she eventually found him in the conservatory. Thankfully he was alone, allowing Olivia to approach him and make her request without having to suffer Mrs. Newhurst's inquisitive looks or Mr. Grier's penetrating gaze.

She cleared her throat to announce her presence and draw Nathaniel's attention from the newspaper he was hiding behind.

He lowered it and immediately smiled. "Miss Poole. What an absolute delight."

"Forgive my intrusion. This won't take long, I promise."

He folded the paper and set it aside. He then stood, despite their difference in status. Hands clasped behind his back he gently said, "Don't trouble yourself. Just tell me how I may be of assistance."

Olivia gave a quick nod. "While I am able to improve upon Miss Edwards's knowledge of most things and ensure her social etiquette is up to par, there are areas in which I find myself out of my depth."

"Go on." Nathaniel's voice held a great deal of interest.

"Her musical ability is commendable. She's been well trained from a young age, so I don't see her failing in that regard. And besides, it's not as though she'll be called upon to play a public concerto or—"

"Miss Poole."

"Yes?"

"You're dissimulating. You're also wringing your hands." A smile touched his lips. He leaned forward, lowering his head just enough to meet her at eye level. "Just spit it out."

An involuntary laugh escaped her. "Very well. The thing of it is, Miss Edwards needs instruction on how to dance, and since I was never taught, she'll require someone else to assist her. Mr. Dover tells me you are proficient."

Nathaniel's mouth stretched into a wide grin. "My dear Miss Poole. I am the best." He straightened and studied her for a moment. Curiosity filled his gaze. "My brother isn't bad either. I wonder why you didn't ask him for assistance. After all, he is your employer and Juliana's guardian. It would have been the most appropriate course of action, I should think."

Olivia swallowed. She'd hoped he would not question her motive for trying to enlist his help instead of Mr. Grier's. "I'm sure your brother has more important matters to attend to."

"Nothing is more important to him than Juliana's debut, I assure you."

"Then maybe he should—" She clamped her mouth shut, biting off the angry words and leaving the rest of her thoughts unspoken.

"What?" he asked with a slight tilt of his head.

"Nothing. It's no business of mine." She forced an uncomfortable smile. "If you would, please come find me when you are ready to give the first lesson."

"No better time than the present, I say. Provided Juliana is free for the next hour, that is."

"She is. I'll fetch her straight away."

They reconvened in the Sutton Hall ballroom ten minutes later.

"I know how to dance," Juliana complained.

Olivia knew she hated the exercise, but she also knew it was necessary for Juliana to be good at it. Since she'd no idea how adept the girl was at dancing, she intended to find out so there would be time for any necessary improvements.

"When you make your debut," Olivia told Juliana gently, "all eyes will be upon you."

"I am aware," Juliana said with a sigh of exasperation. "Everyone has been telling me so for years."

"You will be watched and assessed," Olivia pressed, determined to make the girl aware of how important this was. "Judgment will be passed and based upon this, your options for the future will be laid out before you. If you fail to excel, you may not be able to marry the man of your choosing. Do you understand? Your ability to dance with grace, to comport yourself with perfection, to speak sensibly and show yourself to your best advantage, could decide your fate. Remember, in many cases it's not just up to the gentleman in question. His parents' opinion will matter too, so you have to impress. You must be the best option on the marriage mart if you're to ensure the choice remains in your hands. Otherwise, you could be forced to settle."

"When you put it like that," Juliana grumbled, "I

suppose there is some sense to it all."

"I would never insist you learn something you've no interest in unless I believed it necessary." Olivia glanced at their companion, who waited patiently. "And Mr. Grier is a charming, good natured man. I'm sure you'll find the lesson more fun than you did with Mr. Roberts."

"You're probably right," Juliana agreed. She managed a smile and stepped toward her would-be instructor. "Let us proceed then. Shall we?"

Grayson stared at the open ledger before him. He'd spent the last two days moving between his workshop, his bedchamber, and his study. Hiding from Delilah and from Miss Poole.

The only other person he'd spoken to lately was Nathan, who'd apologized profusely for his lack of discretion. In hindsight, he'd taken Grayson's angry set-down and ensuing tirade with admirable restraint, considering some of the words Grayson had let fly.

He drummed his fingers on the armrest and frowned at the door. Enough was enough. This was his home. He should not have to sneak about in fear of whom he'd encounter. At least Delilah had not hunted him down since their exchange in his bedchamber. For this, he was grateful, though he still feared she'd press her advances again the moment they crossed paths.

With a sigh, he stood. It was time for him to stop

being a coward.

Grayson unlocked the door and stepped into the hallway. He went to the parlor, but found it empty. A little odd given the hour. He would have expected Miss Poole to be here, instructing Juliana on her social etiquette. It would make it easier for him if they were together – if he did not have to face Miss Poole alone.

On a positive note, Delilah wasn't here either.

Relieved, Grayson went to the music room next. This too was empty. As were the schoolroom, the library, the dining room, and the conservatory.

"Where is everyone?" Grayson asked Dover when he found him in a sitting room off to one side. He was overseeing the polishing of the Sutton Hall silver.

"Mrs. Newhurst took the carriage to town after luncheon," Dover informed him. "Everyone else was in the ballroom, last I checked."

"The ballroom?"

"Indeed. Miss Edwards is receiving lessons from your brother."

Grayson blinked, thanked the butler, and turned on his heel. Of course Juliana required dance lessons. She needed to know the reel, the quadrille, the waltz, and the traditional country dances. How could he have forgotten? And why on earth had Miss Poole not mentioned this to him?

Instead, she'd gone to his brother.

It bothered him that she'd asked Nathan for help instead of coming to him. He was her employer, after all. Not Nathan.

Irritated, he was prepared to inform Miss Poole that if dance lessons were required, he would be happy to hire a skilled instructor. He could bring one from London if need be. To ask Nathan, an upper–class gentleman of leisure, to teach Juliana was not to be borne. It simply wasn't.

But when Grayson entered the ballroom and took in the scene before him, the stern words he'd been prepared to deliver abandoned him. He stared, mute and with a rising sense of aggression pulsing through his veins. Because it wasn't Juliana Nathan held in his arms. It was Miss Poole.

Grayson's heart gave a forceful thud of objection.

Miss Poole, damn her, was twirling about the dance floor while grinning at Nathan with sparkling eyes. And damn Nathan too, for holding her inappropriately close.

It didn't matter that Nathan would not want her. *She* didn't know that.

Grayson clenched his jaw. The irritation born from the idea of being bypassed sparked and transformed to anger. His muscles flexed as he fisted his hands, his every instinct urging him to cross the floor and haul Miss Poole away from his brother.

For the first time in his life, the idea of punching Nathan entered his head. Miss Poole did not belong in his arms, she belonged...she...

He shook his head in an effort to silence the blood roaring in his ears. Chest tight, he managed to breathe even though it required tremendous effort.

Nathan guided Miss Poole toward the side of the ballroom where Grayson stood. Of course his dastardly brother had chosen the waltz, the most intimate of all dances. Which begged the question: what the devil was he playing at?

Unable to stand it a moment longer, Grayson stepped forward. "What the hell is going on?"

Miss Poole tripped the moment he spoke and made a grab for Nathan, who wound his arm more securely around her while coming to a clumsy halt.

"They're obviously dancing," came Juliana's voice from somewhere to Grayson's left. He glanced at her in surprise, having not even noticed her presence.

"Perfect timing as always, Grayson," Nathan said with uncharacteristic annoyance. "You startled the poor woman."

Grayson swung his attention back to Nathan and Miss Poole. He narrowed his gaze while observing the slowness with which she released her hold on his brother and withdrew. "I was under the impression you were teaching Juliana."

"And so I was," Nathan said. He crossed his arms and glared at Grayson, all evidence of his usual care-freeness lacking. "We decided to take a break and show Miss Poole a few steps since she's never danced before."

"Well, you were doing it wrong," Grayson said, his frustration prompting him to lash out in a way he knew he'd later regret. It couldn't be helped. Coming on the heels of Delilah's advances, which wouldn't have happened had Nathan not brought her into his home, seeing the woman he wanted in the arms of his brother had unleashed something dangerous inside Grayson.

He hated it, but there was no avoiding it now. Jealousy was a beast that wouldn't be easily slayed.

"We weren't aiming for perfection," Nathan told Grayson, "merely at having some fun."

"You're not setting a good example for Juliana," Grayson argued.

"My apologies," Miss Poole said, her posture and voice equally stiff. "I made an error in judgment by agreeing to dance with your brother. It shan't happen again."

"What the..." Nathan gave her a swift look before returning his gaze to Grayson. "Don't listen to my halfwit brother. You're not a slave, Miss Poole. You're entitled to enjoy yourself on occasion."

"Not like this," Miss Poole said with an edge of defiance that cut Grayson straight to the bone. "I'm a servant. Heaven only knows what I was thinking."

She stepped away from Nathan and moved toward the edge of the room. Nathan sent Grayson an angry scowl. "If you're wise, I would suggest you—"

"Miss Poole," Grayson said, effectively silencing Nathan as he drew Miss Poole's attention. She froze in mid stride and turned toward him, ready to follow his orders. Swallowing a bitter curse, he aimed for an even tone while saying, "Everyone ought to know how to dance, but Juliana's education must take priority. Since Nathan is an exemplary dancer, it does make sense that he should instruct her. While I instruct you."

CHAPTER TWENTY-FIVE

Olivia wasn't sure what to think, much less what to say or how to react. After seeing Mrs. Newhurst wrapped in Mr. Grier's arms while scantily clad, she had no desire for increased contact with him. Never mind the impropriety of the master partnering with a servant. And yet, to refuse the hand he extended toward her while Nathaniel and Juliana bore witness would be like a slap to his face.

Perhaps he deserved it?

No. He owed her nothing. Not even an explanation. If she'd allowed her heart to get carried away with fanciful notions, that was her fault, not his. He had every right to dally with Mrs. Newhurst if he desired. Even though he meant to marry Miss Howell. Good lord, the man was a scoundrel.

And now he was asking Olivia to dance. Despite her reservations, Olivia walked toward him and placed her hand in his. Those confident fingers that had lingered upon her leg the other day when she'd had her first riding lesson closed around hers. A gentle tug followed, distracting her briefly from the hot sparks that shot up her arm.

Her body responded as though by command, turning more fully toward his until it felt as though he encased her. It was just a dance, she reminded herself while trying to catch her breath. Yet the moment she raised her gaze to his, she understood it was so much more. She could see it in his eyes – the powerful need for control.

It rattled her nerves even as her heart leapt in anticipation of what would come next.

His palm settled firmly against her back.

The hand holding hers tightened as he drew her nearer, into a world where only he existed. The scent of him – a mixture of sandalwood, coffee, and something uniquely him – surrounded her.

"Follow my lead," he murmured, the gruffness in his voice raking her skin to produce a delicious shiver.

Olivia's pulse quickened as they began to move, slower than she'd done with Nathaniel, and with more meticulous movements. Clearly Mr. Grier intended for her to learn correct form while his brother had merely striven to give her some fun.

This – what she experienced now – wasn't fun. It was physically overwhelming, the sort of experience destined to make her miserable once it was over.

Because it would leave her longing and desperate for more. But this was all there could be.

"I'm sorry," she whispered before she thought better of it, but the air between them had to be cleared. She could not go on as though they were enemies waging war against each other. Not when he made her feel as he did. "I'm sure Mrs. Newhurst must have told you that I—"

"It's not what you think." He spun her a little too roughly, making it hard for her to keep up. Slowing, she heard him swallow. "My apology—ah."

"Forgive me." She'd stepped forward with the wrong foot, straight onto his.

"It's fine. You will improve with practice." He guided her toward the opposite end of the room, away from where Juliana danced with Nathaniel. "What I wish to tell you, Miss Poole, is that my relationship with Mrs. Newhurst is not what you likely believe it to be after what you witnessed."

Uncomfortable with the subject, Olivia glanced away from him. "I'm sure it's none of my business. You are unmarried and she is a widow. You're free to do as you please without censure, least of all from someone like me."

"Someone like you?" he queried.

"A sheltered woman with no worldly experience, who also happens to be in your employ. I've no right to judge you. Or Mrs. Newhurst for that matter. My only suggestion would be for you to keep your affair discreet and as far away from Miss Edwards as possible."

"Miss Poole, I am not—" He must have realized he'd spoken too loudly, for he instantly dropped his tone. "I am not having an affair with Mrs. Newhurst."

Oh, how she wished to believe him, but there was no denying what she'd seen with her own eyes. "As I said, it's not for me to judge."

"Good lord." He pulled her closer – scandalously so – and spoke right next to her ear. "There's only one woman I want, Miss Poole, and it's not her or Miss Howell."

Despite her best effort to fight the searing effect he had upon her, heat flooded her veins and skittered along her spine. Drawn to him like a moth to a flame, she met his dark gaze and forced herself to hold it, to snare him with equal prowess and to make herself say, "They're the only ones you can have."

It was her last resort, the final shield she could wield against him now that he'd made himself clear. If she revealed her own wants and desires, she feared he'd take advantage and break her heart in the process.

"I wasn't suggesting otherwise." Jaw set as though with displeasure, he guided her along the periphery of the ballroom, back toward the others. "Still, I'd like you to understand the situation I'm faced with. It's…it's important to me that you do so."

Baffled by the need he seemed to have for her approval, Olivia stared at him while trying to make heads and tales of his startling confession. "I am merely the governess, sir. My opinion shouldn't matter."

"Yet it does. More so than anyone else's."

A nervous laugh escaped her. This new, open, and vulnerable side to him was almost more distressing than the hardened man who tempted her with sinful thoughts. "I'm sure that's not true. Your brother for instance—"

"Is hardly ever serious and when he is he often tells me what he thinks I want to hear as opposed to the unvarnished truth." He turned her in a wide arc while guiding her to a slow halt. "Allow me the chance to explain myself without the risk of others overhearing. We can meet in my study as we've done before. Tonight, at ten o'clock."

Olivia shook her head. "Mr. Grier, I really don't think that's wise."

"Please. I beg you."

He released her in the next instant and took a step back. A bow followed and Olivia somehow remembered she ought to curtsey in response. The dance had greatly disturbed her senses and left her feeling as though she risked falling into a void from which there could be no escape. The desperate look in Mr. Grier's eyes reached inside her to clutch at her heart.

As hard as it was, she resisted and gave a quick shake of her head.

"I can't." And because she couldn't stand his look of disappointment or the hurt in his eyes, she turned away, praying she'd made the right decision.

CHAPTER TWENTY-SIX

"Shall we check on the traps again and see if we've caught additional mice for me to study?" Juliana asked once she and Olivia left the ballroom a few minutes later.

Somehow, they'd reached the terrace doors without Olivia's realizing it. She blinked. "Of course. That's a good idea."

Fresh air would do her a world of good at the moment.

They followed the path toward the nearest trap. Finding it empty, they went to inspect the next one. Juliana bent to look inside.

"Look." She leapt to her feet and thrust the box in Olivia's direction. "Tiger won't be alone anymore."

"You named the other mouse Tiger?" Olivia asked, the oddity momentarily distracting her from her private concerns.

"I believe in the power of names," Juliana informed her. "This one will be called Lion. What do you think of that?"

"It's perfect," Olivia said with a chuckle.

Juliana grinned and together they went to check on the final trap. Finding no mouse, they left it under the hedge and started back inside.

"If one is male and the other female," Juliana said as they walked, gravel crunching beneath their feet, "I'll be able to follow the course of a pregnancy and the subsequent birth of a litter. Just imagine!"

Olivia scarcely dared do so. After all, one single mouse could easily produce five to seven pups at a time, possibly double that number. "I think we'll have to reevaluate the mouse situation if Tiger or Lion begins increasing."

"I hope you're not suggesting we send a pregnant mother mouse off on her own," Juliana said.

"Um…"

"Doing so would make us no better than Miss Chadwick."

"Setting a mouse loose in the garden is hardly the same as feeding it to a cat," Olivia pointed out though she sensed she would lose this argument.

"Considering all the Sutton Hall cats roam free, I disagree." Juliana raised her chin and told Olivia, "Come what may, Lion and Tiger will stay with me. I won't have them murdered."

Good grief. What had she done? If Juliana stuck to her guns Sutton Hall might have a future infestation on its hands. Just as Miss Chadwick had warned. All because Olivia had been trying to cheer up an unhappy girl.

Although she decided to let the subject rest for the moment, Olivia knew she'd have to bring it up later if it looked as though additional mice might arrive. She'd have to convince Juliana to be reasonable.

Returning to her room that evening after supper, she took a seat at her desk where Juliana's science books lay.

Opening the desk drawer, she withdrew her notebook and pulled her list from between the pages. She stared at it a moment before allowing her fingers to trace Agnes's writing, as though by doing so she could reach across time and touch her beloved sister.

Her fingers swept across *Go for a late night swim* before coming to rest on the final challenge. *Experience kissing.*

Slumping in her seat, she expelled a weary breath and stared at the page. Her thoughts went directly to Mr. Grier and without really thinking, she picked up her quill and wrote his name. Right next to kissing.

An unhappy laugh escaped her. She truly was a fool.

Annoyed with herself, she crossed out his name, re-folded the paper and placed it in her notebook for safe-keeping.

A knock sounded at her door a few moments later. It was Juliana who'd come to continue her anatomical studies.

"How are your new friends faring?" Olivia asked in

French while helping Juliana collect the right jar from under her bed.

"They seem to be getting on well with each other." Juliana set the appropriate jar on the desk. "I'm concerned about you, however."

"Me?"

"You've not been yourself this afternoon, and when I met Grayson for supper he specifically asked me to make sure you were all right."

"I'm sure his concern must have thrilled Mrs. Newhurst." Lord, she hated how bitter she sounded.

Juliana didn't appear to notice. "I think she was too busy telling Nathaniel about a new gown she intends to order. In any case, she didn't voice an opinion."

Which was just as well. Olivia did not want Mrs. Newhurst's attention upon her. Or Nathaniel's or Mr. Grier's.

"I'm perfectly fine," she told Juliana while snatching up one of the science books the girl had been using. Settling onto the bed, she propped herself against her pillow and gave her undivided attention to the study of cross pollination. But rather than focus on the text, her mind lingered on her handsome employer and then, to stop thinking of him, she thought of that late night swim.

She'd told him she wouldn't come, and she hadn't. Yet for some stupid reason Grayson had hoped and prayed she'd dare to confront him. The compulsion to tell her everything and ask her for guidance was overwhelming, but alas, there was no confession to make. Not as long as she remained absent.

Unhappy with the situation, he rather felt like heading toward the stables right now and taking off to some faraway place where no one would find him. He could visit James or Colin. But damn it all, he couldn't abandon Juliana. And to be honest, leaving Miss Poole wasn't right either.

Deciding to go to bed in the hope that sleep would offer a welcome reprieve, he left his study. As he approached the stairs, feminine laughter sounded from the parlor – not Miss Poole's warm tone but rather the overdone shrillness belonging to Delilah. Grayson groaned. He had to pass the parlor in order to get upstairs, and with the door wide open, he was certain he would be spotted.

Still, he tried to slip past silently, only to be halted by a vibrantly spoken, "There you are, Grayson. We've missed you this evening. Please come join us."

Unable to ignore Delilah's comment, Grayson turned toward the room where she and Nathan occupied themselves with a game of cards.

"Thank you, but I'm exhausted," Grayson told them. "It's been a long day."

"A long few days," Delilah said with marked disapproval. Smiling at him she added, "As a gentleman you ought not ignore your guests so."

Grayson hardened his features. "As far as I am

concerned there is only one guest here and you arrived without warning, thus preventing me from making changes to my busy schedule. I apologize if you find my ability to entertain you lacking. Perhaps you would prefer to seek diversion elsewhere?"

On the moon would suit him splendidly.

Delilah set her chin at a stubborn angle. "Not at all. I am quite content being here."

Grayson stared at her, puzzled by her motive. Considering he'd foiled her attempt to reignite what they'd once had and his obvious lack of interest in her since, he couldn't comprehend why the annoying woman wouldn't just leave and try her luck elsewhere. It was bloody frustrating. Especially since he couldn't just toss her out. Doing that would surely incur her wrath, and Lord knew what trouble she could create.

He suppressed a series of uncouth expletives even as he envisioned a number of ways in which to strangle her. As long as she continued holding his brother's indiscretions over Grayson's head, she could remain at Sutton Hall forever if she so desired.

"And we are very content having you," Nathan said with a beaming smile. To Grayson he said, "Don't keep us from our card play any longer, and we'll not keep you from your rest. Be off with you, Grayson, so I may proceed to trounce Mrs. Newhurst with my next move."

"Trounce me?" Delilah turned her attention toward the cards in her hand while Nathan gave a quick jerk of his head, suggesting Grayson should take his leave now.

Grayson mouthed words of thanks to his brother and fled, taking the stairs while Delilah said, "Ha. I beat you again." Immediately followed by, "Oh. Where did he go?"

Hastening his steps, Grayson reached the landing and strode to his bedchamber. The fire a maid had lit earlier in the evening offered a welcome glow.

Relieved to be alone, Grayson struck a flint and held it to a nearby oil lamp. He'd need the light if he was to read the book he'd been looking forward to settling in with.

With deft movements he shrugged his arms from the sleeves of his jacket and flung the garment across the back of a chair. Next, he undid his cravat while wondering why some gentlemen felt it necessary to employ a servant whose sole responsibility it was to help them dress and undress.

Unlike his brothers, who never went anywhere without their valets, Grayson had never hired one. Neither had Papa, who'd always insisted that any man who couldn't manage the simple task of dressing himself without assistance didn't deserve to leave the house.

Grayson stilled for a moment, his heart made heavy by sentimentality. God, how he missed his father and his words of advice, those firm nods of approval.

A lump formed in his throat as he recalled the moment he'd been informed of his passing. Grayson had been with Delilah, determined to cast aside unpleasant memories, too busy to notice his father's declining health or to make good on the request he'd made during the last two years of his life.

Papa had never asked Grayson for anything except to come home and learn how to manage estate matters and Juliana's continued education. But Grayson had put it off. He'd had more important things to do, like finding bliss in the arms of a beautiful woman so he could escape the nightmares he'd had since the war.

With a heavy sigh, Grayson pulled his cravat from around his neck and dropped it on top of his jacket. A glass of brandy should help soothe his spirit, so he crossed to the sideboard and poured himself a generous measure. He took a sip and savored the heat sliding down his throat. It spread through his chest and allowed him to cast off some of the guilt.

Finally.

He snatched up his book and took a seat in the armchair before the fire. Stretching out his legs, he crossed his ankles and placed his glass of brandy on the table beside him. On a deep inhale, he opened the book – the copy of *Pride and Prejudice* Juliana had told him Miss Poole was reading a few weeks ago.

He'd never read it himself and was surprised to discover how much he enjoyed it. The language was witty, the plot captivating, though perhaps a bit unrealistic. After all, Mr. Darcy was far above Miss Elizabeth Bennett in station. To suppose the two would end up together was something of a stretch. Especially when her sister appeared intent on creating a scandal.

Well, it was fiction, he supposed, as he commenced

reading. The nearby clock on the fireplace mantle ticked away the seconds and chimed the hour. Twice.

Grayson glanced up from the book, surprised at the time. It was one in the morning. How on earth could that be? And how was it that he had begun envisioning himself as the arrogant Mr. Darcy while picturing Miss Poole as the kindly Elizabeth Bennett? Perhaps because she'd given Darcy a piece of her mind rather than accept his offer of marriage?

Grayson blinked. It was precisely the sort of thing he imagined Miss Poole might do were he to propose. Which he wouldn't.

Instead, he'd drive himself insane with thoughts of what if…

Annoyed and increasingly tired, he set the book aside and went to close the curtains. His hand caught the heavy jacquard and was just about to pull it shut when a movement outside drew his attention. He stilled, trying to make sense of what he was seeing. It couldn't be. Not at this hour. And yet there was no denying the fact that Miss Poole was striding across the lawn, hurrying away from the house while wearing a… dressing gown?

She glanced back at the house and Grayson instinctively sucked in a breath and stepped to one side, hiding behind the curtain like a fool. He scowled. What the hell was she doing? Miss Poole should not be roaming the grounds at this hour. He should have made it clear to her that he'd taken note so she would return indoors straight away.

Giving his head a quick shake, he glanced back outside just as she disappeared into the darkness. He muttered a curse. Wonderful. Instead of climbing into bed and getting a good night's rest, he now had to go and find out what she was up to and make sure no harm befell her.

A thought struck.

Grayson went utterly still. Was it possible she was going to a secret liaison? She'd said no to meeting him, but that did not prevent her from making arrangements with someone else.

He considered the idea, however distasteful, taking a moment to ponder the rest of his servants. One of his footmen was young and handsome. And Andrews wasn't bad either. More to the point, both men were unmarried, as was Miss Poole.

Grayson snatched up his jacket and marched to the door. If Miss Poole had decided to take either man as her lover, he'd have to put an end to the matter. She was Juliana's governess for God's sake. One of the reason's he'd let her have the position was because he'd thought her beyond reproach. As a vicar's daughter, she ought to have the highest moral standards. He'd been certain she did but perhaps he'd been wrong. Hell, it wouldn't be the first time he'd misjudged a woman. Just look at Miss Chadwick and Delilah.

Increasingly angry with himself and with Miss Poole, he returned downstairs and cut a path straight toward the terrace door. He unlocked it, stepped out into the chill evening air, and shut the door securely.

With only the light from the moon to guide him, he followed the path Miss Poole had taken across the lawn toward the lake.

His heart jolted as he recalled her near–death experience. No one should go near that lake alone. He'd made that clear. Hadn't he?

Unable to remember if he'd done so or not, Grayson quickened his stride. What if the foolish woman wasn't having a scandalous rendezvous after all? Deep down inside he knew he'd made a preposterous assumption, which meant she was up to something else. She'd gone to the lake. By herself. At night. With no one to rescue her if the worst happened.

What was her plan?

What was she thinking?

What…

He drew a sharp breath and nearly stumbled while every heartbeat became a gallop, racing in opposite directions. For there she was, standing at the edge of the lake without a stitch on. Bathed in moonlight.

CHAPTER TWENTY-SEVEN

Somehow, Grayson had the forethought to dart behind the nearest tree before she saw him. Everything inside him tensed as his brain began to acknowledge what his eyes had actually witnessed. Miss Poole, the woman who made him crave the forbidden, was but a few yards away. Naked.

He shook his head, attempted to dislodge his riotous thoughts and cool the forceful ardor that had assailed him the instant he'd caught a glimpse of her well-rounded bottom. She was alone. By the lake. Waiting for someone? No, he'd already dismissed that option. So then...

He peeked out from behind the tree. She was knee deep in the water now, her fingers trailing across the surface as she moved farther into the lake.

Everything within Grayson drew into a tight knot. He held his breath, fighting the instinct to make his presence known, while willing her from the water. He'd gone for the occasional swim himself in this lake over the years. But he'd grown up here, was familiar with the depth and with the spot where the lakebed suddenly dropped.

Dear God. Miss Poole was a smart woman who ought to know better than to come here alone.

Or so he'd believed until now.

Heaven help him, he couldn't believe she would be so reckless with her own safety.

The water reached the middle of her back now. She stopped her progress and Grayson breathed a sigh of relief. She would turn back, return to shore, and dry off. He prepared to leave, to give her the privacy she deserved. Only to freeze as she raised her arms above her head and dove straight forward, under the surface, leaving behind no more than a ripple.

Grayson's heart stopped dead in his chest. A croaking sound lodged itself in his throat. Unable to breathe he stared at the inky black water. *Come on. Resurface.* His pulse shot back to life as panic rushed through him. He scanned the water. The ripples had stilled, leaving behind a glassy surface.

Terrified, Grayson tore off his boots and his jacket, prepared to dive in and save her. He'd almost reached the spot where she'd left her clothes when she suddenly reemerged. A victorious laugh filled the air. It was cut short the moment she saw him. Surprise widened her eyes, followed by what appeared to be mortification, no doubt on account of getting caught.

He stared, taking an almost perverse amount of pleasure in watching her squirm beneath the weight of his gaze. Served her right for making him fear for her safety. He crossed his arms. "What are you doing?"

She glanced around, almost as though she hoped he was speaking to somebody else. "Swimming."

Her voice was low, hesitant, like that of a child who knew they'd done wrong and expected to get a scolding.

Grayson's jaw tightened. "I can see that. What I cannot comprehend is what might have possessed you."

"I'm sorry. I thought I—"

"What if something happened to you? What if you drowned?" His voice rose with renewed anger. "Did you ever consider the impact such a tragedy would have upon Juliana or me for that matter? Devil take it, Miss Poole, you are under my protection."

"Nothing would have happened," Miss Poole countered. "I'm a strong swimmer."

"As you proved when you fell from the boat," he shot back with irritation. Lord have mercy, women could be stubborn creatures.

"What happened then would not happen now."

"Why the hell not?"

She was silent a moment before she said, "If you'll recall, my gown got caught on a branch beneath the surface. As a result, I took the precaution of taking my clothes off tonight."

Grayson stared at her. In the heat of his panic and ensuing anger, he'd forgotten she was undressed. The reminder licked at the nape of his neck, causing his skin to tingle with hot awareness. So she'd considered the risk. But that didn't mean she'd been any less careless.

He cleared his throat. "Get out of the water."

She glared at him as though he were mad. "I most certainly shan't. Not while you're watching."

The devil within made him speak without thinking. "Would you rather I come in and fetch you?"

Her eyes went impossibly wide. She gaped at him. "You wouldn't."

Of course not, but there was some satisfaction in pressing her boundaries. He took a deep breath and turned. "I promise not to look." When she didn't respond he said, "Please, Miss Poole. Before you catch a chill."

It took a moment for Olivia to gather her courage. Trust Mr. Grier of all people to be the one person to spot her during her swim. He'd put an abrupt end to it too, but at least she could say she'd done it. At least she could strike late night swim from her list.

"I'm not a reckless idiot," she said as she strode from the water. Somehow, despite his threat to haul her from the lake himself, she trusted him not to look. Because even though he'd just acted the rogue, she knew him to be a gentleman at his core. "I wasn't going to venture far from the shore."

He made a gruff non-committal sound at the back of his throat.

Olivia sighed. No one was meant to find out. Least of all him. But since he had, she was forced to consider his feelings on the matter. She reached for the towel she'd brought with her and dried herself off with efficient movements before putting her nightgown back on.

After brushing her feet off with the towel she toed on her slippers and picked up her dressing gown. While pulling it tight and tying the belt, she pondered Mr. Grier's stiff posture. His boots remained in a heap on the ground not far from his discarded jacket, allowing her a rare view of his back. The waistcoat he wore was stretched taut, accentuating his width and strength while the lack of cravat allowed her to see the nape of his neck.

Olivia's fingers twitched with a near-painful urge to reach out and touch him, right there where his thick dark hair brushed his skin. Swallowing, she permitted her gaze to drop lower, to admire his sturdy build and…

Her heart did a jittery dance when she dared a glimpse of what looked like a perfectly toned backside. The snug fit of his breeches accentuated a pair of muscular thighs while the lower part of his legs were hugged by a pair of hose so white they stood out against the surrounding darkness.

"Well?" he prompted, making her jump.

She sucked in a breath. "Ready."

He turned, his expression completely devoid of emotion while he fixed her with a level gaze. "Don't ever do this again. If you want to go for a swim, you may do so during the day. Just let it be known so no one disturbs you, and have one of the maids accompany you for safety."

"Thank you, but I shan't venture near the lake again," Olivia told him. She bit her lip without even thinking and noted the way Mr. Grier's eyes gleamed in response to the moonlight. A shiver raced down her spine. They were alone. Utterly and completely. Both in some state of undress. She more than he.

Awareness unfurled deep within her. If he desired, he could seduce her right here, right now. She wouldn't resist. Not as long as the night offered refuge. But she would regret it come morning. They both would. He more than she, she wagered.

"Miss Poole…" The rawness of his voice suggested his thoughts had turned in the same direction as hers. Olivia's pulse quickened. Would he close the distance between them or not – press his mouth to hers for that kiss she sensed they both craved in equal measure?

"Yes?" she managed, her voice breathy while every cell in her body went on full alert. She was especially conscious of the fact that she had no confining stays to dispense with should he decide to…

"We ought to return indoors."

Olivia blinked. "Yes. Yes of course."

He took a deep breath and let it out slowly. Then, as though it took every ounce of strength he possessed, he collected his jacket and boots. Olivia watched while he put them on, savoring the intimacy the act allowed her to share with him.

Once properly attired, he swept his arm toward the house, indicating that they should proceed. Olivia started forward while he kept pace by her side. Neither said anything more, but she sensed something had changed. It was as if they'd agreed it was only a matter of time now before they both surrendered.

Grayson glared at his bedchamber door. He'd told the maid who'd brought up breakfast that no one was to disturb him, yet someone had chosen to do so. The individual knocked for the third time, paused, and tried the handle.

"Grayson?" Nathan's cheery voice made Grayson's teeth gnash.

Exasperated, Grayson hauled himself out of bed, crossed the floor, and opened the door. "What?"

Nathan blinked. And then he stared. His eyes widened. "Good lord. You look like death."

"What. Do. You. Want?" After his run–in with Miss Poole last night, he'd not slept a wink. His mind had been in turmoil, his thoughts too numerous to count, and his body too bloody wound up to let him rest.

"It's almost noon," Nathan noted. "You're usually up by this hour."

"Your point?"

Nathan gave him a hesitant look. "To make sure you were all right. Dover did say you'd rather be left alone, which in and of itself raised my concern. Did something else happen last night? With Delilah?"

Grayson snorted. Something absolutely had happened last night, though not with Delilah. He scrubbed a hand across his face. The late morning bristle abraded his skin. They'd shared a moment, he and Miss Poole. He'd felt it with an undeniable certainty.

For the very first time since suspecting the raw desire he harbored wasn't one-sided, he'd sensed a welcoming need in her, a silent call for him to act on their mutual yearning. And he, gentleman idiot that he was, had turned down the offer.

"No." Grayson eyed his brother. "Shut the door, will you?"

"I've been pondering your predicament," Nathan said while doing as Grayson asked. "If you were to become engaged to Miss Howell, perhaps Delilah would—"

"Don't," Grayson warned. "Just help me find some clothes."

Nathan sighed. He crossed to the dresser and opened a drawer while Grayson went to the wash stand. He'd need a quick shave before he showed himself downstairs.

"You've got two determined women trying to trap you into marriage." Nathan pulled a shirt from the dresser and turned to Grayson, who was busy lathering his jaw. "The easiest thing to do would be to pick one in order to rid yourself of the other."

"Or," Grayson said, "I could make it abundantly clear that they're both wasting their time."

Nathan stilled. "I realize this is my fault but—"

"Relax. I've no intention of letting Delilah hurt you or this family." Grayson frowned as he picked up his blade. Taking care not to nick himself, he scraped it across his soapy cheek. "I'll have to find a solution. As loath as I am to resort to her methods, I may have no choice."

"I've never taken you for the blackmailing sort," Nathan murmured.

"Me neither," Grayson confessed. He shot his brother a look while rinsing his blade. "She's maneuvered me into a corner though. I fear she won't let up unless she feels threatened."

"There is another solution," Nathan said once Grayson had set his blade to his other cheek. "You could wed Miss Poole."

Grayson froze, meeting Nathan's gaze in the mirror. His heart beat an unsteady rhythm.

"You know that's impossible." Breaking eye contact with his brother, Grayson finished his shave.

"Because it's unheard of for a man of your rank to marry a servant?"

Grayson wiped his face with a towel and turned. "You know my position on marriage, Nathan. I'll only ever marry for love and I don't love Miss Poole. It's just desire."

"Are you certain of that?" Nathan tilted his head, studying Grayson. "Because if your lack of sleep, the state of disarray you're in, and your grumpiness aren't related to Delilah then…"

Grayson swallowed. Last night, when Miss Poole had vanished into the water, there'd been a moment – a horrifyingly bone–numbing one in which he'd experienced an end to his own existence.

Tamping down the memory, he squared his shoulders.

"It's not love." It couldn't be. He shook his head. "Besides, we've been over this. Marrying the governess is out of the question."

"But—"

"Don't be naïve, Nathan. My marrying Miss Poole would hardly stop Delilah from revealing your secret. And why the devil are we discussing this anyway. It's fantasy, Nathan, and it will never be anything more."

CHAPTER TWENTY-EIGHT

When Olivia woke and glanced at the clock, she shot out of bed. Good Lord. She'd slept through breakfast and luncheon. Whatever would everyone think? More to the point, why hadn't anyone fetched her?

Moving swiftly, she washed herself at her washstand, dried off, and put on her chemise and front-tying stays. With brisk movements she knotted her hair and pinned it in place, then put on her dreary gown and began doing up the front fastenings. She'd have to apologize to Juliana for rising so late. Hopefully the other servants hadn't taken much note and—

A loud thump stopped her movements. A series of barks followed.

Olivia rushed from her room, concern nipping at her heels. Daphne was always so quiet and well behaved, which meant something must have happened.

Juliana's ensuing shouts increased her concern. She hurried across the hallway to Juliana's door and flung it wide just in time to watch a vase topple over. It crashed to the floor in a sparkly explosion of glass that left a bouquet of flowers lying upon the floor in a puddle.

"Shut the door," Juliana yelled.

Olivia stepped inside, prepared to do precisely that, when something fast brushed her feet, making her jump.

Juliana leapt toward her. "No!"

Before Olivia managed to get her bearings and do as Juliana had asked, Daphne raced past her, into the hallway and...

Olivia turned as the dog disappeared into her room. Concerned by the noise she'd heard, she hadn't considered closing the door. She prepared to go and retrieve the dog.

"We've got to catch her," Juliana insisted. "Before she kills Tiger."

"Your mouse?" Everything suddenly made perfect sense, but at the same time, it was as if Juliana's comment presented a number of terrible outcomes. Worst of all was the possibility of the mouse running loose in the rest of the house. And of Mr. Grier finding out.

Unwilling to explain herself to him, as she'd have to do if he learned she'd helped Juliana set up a mouse habitat in her room, Olivia raced after Daphne. "We'll trap them both in my bedchamber."

But before they arrived, the mouse reemerged.

Olivia moved with lightning speed, determined to cut off its path toward the stairs. It turned with a squeak and darted toward a corner where Juliana managed to trap it.

She scooped the terrified creature into her hands. "Where's Daphne?"

Olivia spun, her searching gaze landing upon the tiny dog just as she vanished around a corner, yapping away with the misplaced belief that she still chased a mouse. "I'll fetch her while you take care of Tiger."

"Thank you for your help," Juliana called as Olivia went in pursuit of the poodle. She'd have to speak to the girl later about not letting the mice out of the box in which she kept them. For now, she resigned herself to catching Daphne before...

Too late. She'd already reached the foyer.

"Daphne," Olivia hissed. At almost one o'clock in the afternoon there was every possibility she'd be spotted by someone. And she wasn't even wearing stockings or shoes.

But leaving Daphne be wasn't an option. What if the dog decided to chew up a book or scratch at a piece of expensive furniture or, heaven forbid, wet the carpet?

The door to the servants' stairs opened, nearly knocking her onto her bottom. With perfect timing she dodged the obstacle, narrowly missing whoever it was who'd arrived in the hallway.

"Miss Poole?" Betsy's voice sounded behind her. "Where on earth are your shoes?"

Olivia waved her off without a backward glance and

continued on her way, barely catching a glimpse of Daphne's tail before she disappeared into the library. Olivia entered and closed the door, then took a moment to catch her breath before approaching a green velvet sofa.

With a sigh, she lowered herself to her hands and knees and peered underneath it. Dark eyes set in a toffee–colored fuzz–ball stared back at her with unde-niable self–satisfaction. Olivia stared at Daphne as real-ization swooped in, scalding her from head to toe. Because there the puppy was, nibbling away on Olivia's scandalous garter.

"Daphne." Olivia reached under the sofa and tried to grab the dog. "Come here."

Instead of complying, Daphne turned, dragging the garter away from Olivia's line of vision.

"Drat." She'd have to move the sofa in order to reach her.

Olivia bit her lip and prepared to rise, but then the door opened behind her and she instinctively froze. Squeezing her eyes shut, she muttered a curse while wishing the ground would swallow her up.

Sadly, she wasn't so lucky.

"Do I even dare demand an explanation?" Mr. Grier asked in a velvety voice that sent shivers cascading down her spine.

Olivia swallowed and pushed herself into a standing position. She took a deep breath and smoothed her skirts before turning to face him. "I was, um…"

He raised an eyebrow. "Yes?"

She frowned. Did he have to look so handsome? It wasn't fair. Not when she wasn't even wearing stockings. Heat flooded her cheeks. "I..."

"Your feet are bare," Mr. Grier informed her. His gaze had dropped to the floor. He seemed to be staring at her toes with an almost pained sort of expression.

"I overslept," she blurted. "I'm so terribly sorry. Please forgive me."

"It would be hypocritical of me not to do so, seeing as I too have risen quite late. Apparently nocturnal swims have that effect."

The gravity with which he said this made Olivia want to shrink from existence as she recalled her nudity and his presence. "It won't happen again. I swear it."

He stared at her for a moment before shifting his gaze to one side. His features suddenly brightened. "Daphne. What on earth are you doing here?"

"She got away from us," Olivia said, finding her tongue and promptly wishing she hadn't since all she seemed able to use it for now was stating the obvious. "I'm sorry. I know she shouldn't be down here without supervision, which is why I was trying to get her out from under the sofa."

Ignoring her comment, Mr. Grier dropped to a crouch and extended one hand toward Daphne who happily approached. A grin spread across Mr. Grier's handsome face as he scooped the boisterous dog into his arms and proceeded to scratch her behind one ear.

Olivia watched in dismay as the weight he always

seemed to carry slipped from his shoulders, allowing a hint of the carefree boy she'd seen in the family portrait in his study. And just like that her heart melted.

Oh, how she longed to be the woman who eased his daily concerns, who helped him face his burden of duty and gave him reason to smile. Because that smile – the one he'd saved for Daphne – was absolutely divine.

With a grin that made Olivia realize she actually envied a dog, Mr. Grier stood while allowing Daphne to lick at his jaw. This prompted a chuckle until he caught Olivia's gaze.

Sobering slightly, he cleared his throat and held Daphne toward her. "I believe this is what you were seeking."

Olivia nodded and stepped toward him, ready to accept the puppy. Daphne kicked one leg and shifted her weight as she slid into Olivia's arms, causing her to not only lean into Mr. Grier's solid body, but also to set her hand over his.

An electric spark snapped at her veins, strumming her pulse and sending it racing. She sucked in a breath and looked up to find herself snared by Mr. Grier's gaze. His eyes crinkled slightly at the corners due to the humor he'd recently been conveying. But there was something else in his expression besides his carefree abandon of moments ago – an acute awareness that matched her own.

The heat from his hand spilled through her, warming her insides. Between them Daphne made an impatient sound. She licked at Olivia's collar bone as if attempting to gain some attention. And as she did so Mr. Grier stroked one finger across the length of Olivia's hand, and it was as if her insides collided in one gigantic shiver.

Unnerved and unsure of how to respond, frightened by her sudden desire to rise onto her toes and kiss him, she leapt away, taking Daphne with her. Whatever this was, this thing that kept happening between them, it wasn't right and it had to stop.

With unsteady breaths, Olivia stared at him while he stared back. "Thank you, Mr. Grier, for helping me collect Daphne."

"It was my pleasure, Miss Poole."

Olivia hugged Daphne to her as if the dog could somehow shield her from the overwhelming emotions Mr. Grier stirred in her. He had no business touching her in such a suggestive manner. Not when he went around embracing Mrs. Newhurst while planning his nuptials to Miss Howell.

She had to make her position clear. She would not be degraded to being his mistress. The temptation he posed, however, terrified her. Because she feared that if he chose to pursue her in earnest, she'd lack the strength to resist.

With this in mind, she took a step back. "I ought to return upstairs. Thank you again. For...for everything."

She glanced at the sofa, aware her garter was still underneath it. The fact did not sit well with her at all, but collecting it now while Mr. Grier watched was out of the question. As inconvenient as it was, she'd have to come back and fetch it later.

Forcing herself to accept this, she started toward the door.

"I've been meaning to ask," Mr. Grier said, halting her after a couple of paces.

She turned to face him. "Yes?"

"Andrews tells me you're making progress with the riding, but how are you liking it?"

"Very well, sir."

A frown appeared upon his brow. He almost looked on the verge of chastising her. Instead he gave a quick nod. "Glad to hear it."

"If that is all, I really ought to prepare myself for Juliana's first lesson of the day. It's very late already."

"Of course. I shouldn't have kept you."

Deciding not to comment, Olivia glanced at the sofa one last time before fleeing his presence.

Grayson stared at the door through which Miss Poole had departed. Finding her here had been a welcome surprise. Although he had to admit, his initial view of her bottom sticking up in the air had done little to soothe the tense state he'd been in since last night's adventure.

Daphne had offered a brief and necessary distraction.

Until he'd attempted handing her to Miss Poole.

He sucked in a breath, recalling the spike of arousal he'd felt when their hands had touched, the over-whelming need to dip his head and taste her. And her response, that tiny gasp she'd emitted before going utterly still, had made him bolder. Stupidly so, he acknowledged now.

Caught up in the moment he'd crossed the line.

But it was as though every instance they shared with each other, from her first interview in his study, to their waltz, to seeing her naked at the lake, to this, served as fuel for what promised to be an explosive surrender on both parts.

They could resist it as much as they chose – hell, he was doing his best – but he was starting to think their coming together was merely a matter of time. A fated inevitability, regardless of how unwise.

Shifting, he prepared to collect the book he'd initially come for. Instead, he glanced at the sofa. Miss Poole had directed a longing glance toward it before she'd left the room. Why?

She'd already retrieved Daphne, but maybe there was something else?

Curious, Grayson lowered himself to the floor. He was probably being silly. If there had been something else besides Daphne under the sofa, surely Miss Poole would have said so.

He glanced underneath, his pulse kicking when he saw there was indeed something there. It looked like a bunched up piece of fabric. Stretching his arm as far as he could, he caught hold of what felt like fine lace.

Hmm...

Grayson pulled his arm back and stared at the tangled piece of red ribbon he held in his hand. He'd been right about the lace. The ribbon was trimmed with it on both sides. Puzzled, he started unraveling it, muttering slightly when he touched a wet spot Daphne must surely have had in her mouth.

So the dog had carried it off, hidden under the sofa with it, and prompted Miss Poole to look at the sofa with deep regret before leaving.

Intrigued and increasingly puzzled, he smoothed out the article, laid it across his bent knee, and blinked. The lace did not extend along the entire length of ribbon. Instead, the ribbon ends were unadorned, each one long enough to be tied in a bow.

Grayson's pulse leapt. It might have been a while since he'd last been with a woman, but he was well enough acquainted with their underthings to know what this was. A garter. Fashioned from scarlet silk ribbon and edged with exquisite lace.

Could it be Juliana's?

Anxious this might be the case, Grayson studied the craftsmanship. No, the stitching was slightly uneven in places, clearly made by someone who lacked Juliana's skill. Which had to mean...

It belonged to Miss Poole.

Heat flashed across Grayson's skin. He took a series of steadying breaths in an effort to calm his initial response.

The very idea of his prim and proper governess

dressed in that boring gown of hers while secretly wearing this underneath was positively seductive. It suggested a level of daring he desperately longed to explore. However ill–advised.

He swallowed, sliding his fingertip over the lace, imagining it tied snuggly around Miss Poole's leg. A groan rose from somewhere so deep within it actually pained him. With a curse, he snatched up the garter and stood, adjusted his trousers, and tried to think of something less arousing, like Delilah's threat to reveal Nathan's secret.

With a disgruntled huff, Grayson looked at the garter. He ought to put it back under the sofa for Miss Poole to find. Or return it to her in person. Instead he allowed the devil encamped on his shoulder to have his say and stuffed the scandalous article into his pocket.

CHAPTER TWENTY-NINE

I t was impossible for Olivia to focus on the text Juliana was reading out loud, a piece by Voltaire. Or was it Rousseau? She'd mindlessly picked up a book and handed it to her.

"Shall I continue?" Juliana asked, jostling Olivia's thoughts.

"Please do," Olivia said, briefly averting her gaze from the view of the garden. "You're doing remarkably well."

Juliana smiled, clearly pleased by the compliment. Her French had improved dramatically since Olivia started instructing her. It helped to speak the language daily, not just in class but outside of it too.

Dipping her head, she resumed reading, which allowed Olivia to return her attention to the tulips and delphiniums on the opposite side of the window. The flowers had a soothing effect upon her nerves, which had been in chaos since her return to the library half an hour earlier.

A nervous quiver twisted her insides. She crossed her arms and hugged herself tightly. The garter she'd been expecting to find beneath the sofa hadn't been there, which meant someone else had retrieved it before she'd gotten the chance. Closing her eyes, she prayed for the hundredth time it was one of the maids who'd done so.

The jittery beat of her heart reminded her it was more likely done by the man who'd found her rummaging under the sofa. She did her best to take steady breaths while wondering what Mr. Grier must think of her now. Not only of her misplacing such an item in the library of all places, but of its...its...appearance. Scarlet and lace. She imagined it was the sort of thing Mrs. Newhurst would wear.

Expelling a dismal groan, Olivia pinched the bridge of her nose. He'd consider her wanton, no doubt, unless she explained what she'd been up to. But doing so would not paint her in a better light. If anything, it would only prove she wasn't as straitlaced or sensible as she'd been letting on. And hadn't he made it clear from the very beginning that these were characteristics he valued in a governess?

If he were to learn she'd been taking advantage of her position, he'd surely sack her on the spot. And where would she be then?

Back where she'd started, more or less, though no doubt worse after growing fond of Sutton Hall. She'd

made friends for the first time in her life, not just with
the staff but with Juliana as well. She cared for the girl,
was genuinely invested in her future. To walk away
from her would be horribly hard.

Not nearly as hard as walking away from him.

She swallowed that thought, clenched her jaw and
stiffened her spine. Foolish fancy. What did it matter
when he was to marry Miss Howell?

Grayson knew he was being the worst sort of cad.
Which was unlike him. A gentleman would have
returned Miss Poole's garter to her hours ago. Seated at
the dining room table, he reached for his glass of wine
and took a long sip while Delilah prattled on about
gowns and bonnets.

He wasn't a gentleman, he decided as one of the
footmen served some roast veal, creamed potatoes, and
stewed mushrooms. Gentlemen didn't have wicked
ideas regarding their governesses. And when it came to
Miss Poole, his thoughts had been growing increasingly
heated since they'd first met. Hell, he couldn't get a
decent night's sleep anymore without waking in a
sweaty state of unfulfilled need.

It was becoming a physical problem at this point, a
mental one too since it practically rendered him useless
with regard to running estate matters. A man could
only distract himself for so long. Especially when the
source of his lust was constantly present in some form

or other, like in the fresh flowers that kept appearing or in conversations he had with Nathan and Juliana.

Ignoring Miss Poole was impossible.

Especially with her garter tucked away in his pocket. The thought alone was thrilling – scandalous – improper. As for the act itself…

There was something so wonderfully intimate in it, like having her close at all times and sharing a secret. He frowned while chewing a piece of veal. It was unlikely Miss Poole felt the same. Indeed, if he were to hazard a guess, she was probably fretting about the garter's mysterious disappearance and worrying over who'd found it.

He had to return it tonight.

Intent on doing the right thing, he headed upstairs after sharing an after dinner drink with Nathan. Reaching the landing, he paused before turning left rather than right. His heart gave an uneven knock of anticipation. He swallowed, attempting to think up a plan – what to say and how to react.

I found this and wondered if it might be yours.

Here's your garter, Miss Poole. I'd like to commend you on the craftsmanship.

My apologies for not handing this over to you sooner.

God help him. At this rate he'd be lucky if she didn't snatch the garter out of his hand and slam the door in his face. He reached said door and retrieved the garter, standing there like an imbecile in the hallway. This was without a doubt the stupidest thing he'd ever done.

He glanced toward Juliana's room across the hallway. What the hell was he thinking? He ought not be here. If he were caught sneaking about outside Miss Poole's bedchamber door she'd be ruined.

And yet he had to return the garter.

Which he could do by calling her to his study tomorrow.

He knit his brow, and gave the door a gentle knock.

Nobody answered – a bit of a letdown that. Perhaps Miss Poole was already asleep? Or maybe she hadn't heard him. She'd better not have gone swimming again.

He gave the door another rap, a little harder this time. Still no answer.

Grayson turned, prepared to leave when approaching footsteps made his heart lurch. Someone was coming, no doubt Mrs. Hodgins making her rounds before bed. Good God, if she found him here, lurching about, what the hell would he say?

Panicking, Grayson opened the door to Miss Poole's room and...froze. "What the hell?"

He stared at Juliana's stricken expression, then quickly stepped inside and shut the door to avoid having to face Mrs. Hodgins. He glanced around the cramped space. No sign of Miss Poole. Instead, there were books scattered about. And jars.

Grayson frowned.

"I don't think you should be here," Juliana said.

"I came to return something to Miss Poole, an item of hers I believe she misplaced." He narrowed his gaze while considering Juliana's tense posture. "What are *you* doing here?"

Juliana said nothing while holding his gaze, and it occurred to Grayson he'd caught her. Doing what exactly, he wasn't quite sure. He crossed the short distance to where she sat. She stiffened and moved her hands, flattening them on the desk as if to cover up something.

Grayson paused behind her shoulder. He hated intruding on people's privacy, but he also despised secrets. Reaching down, he took hold of Juliana's wrist and moved it aside. For a second he'd no clue what he was looking at, until he shifted his gaze to the left and saw...

He wasn't sure what it was precisely, but he knew it didn't belong on a desk in Miss Poole's bedchamber. "What on earth is that?"

"It's a...um...a stomach," Juliana whispered, her voice so low Grayson had to strain in order to hear her.

"A stomach?"

"From a rabbit," Juliana clarified.

Grayson stared at the stomach, then at the piece of paper Juliana had tried to hide. It contained a detailed sketch of the organ along with a series of notes.

Still grappling with his discovery, not just of Juliana being in Miss Poole's quarters but of what he considered a most bizarre interest for a young lady, he drew the only logical conclusion he could think of. "You're studying it?"

"Yes," she admitted.

"And you're doing it here so you won't be found out." He wasn't exactly angered by it, but he certainly wasn't pleased either. Setting his jaw he told Juliana, "Return to your room at once and prepare for bed."

"But it's not even—"

"Now, Juliana."

She hesitated just long enough to put her stubbornness on display before pushing her chair back and rising. Moving swiftly she tidied her things, placed the glass jar with the stomach inside under the bed, and went to the door. She paused there, a pained look in her eyes. "Please don't sack her for this. She was only trying to help me."

Somehow, those words made everything worse. "Help you how, exactly? In deceiving me? In smuggling animal parts behind my back?"

Her expression tightened. "I knew you wouldn't understand."

Before Grayson could come to terms with that statement and form a response, she'd gone. Her bedchamber door slammed shut seconds later leaving Grayson alone in Miss Poole's room. Still standing by the desk, he returned his attention to the stack of books piled in one corner. *Plates of the Thoracic and Abdominal Nerves, Tabulae Anatomicae, Anatomisches Handbuch, De Humani Corporis Fabrica.*

There were several notebooks as well.

He picked one up and leafed through it, astonished to find not only detailed diagrams of various body parts, but notes pertaining to how they worked, their significance for the creature to whom they belonged, and even measurements.

A hollow sensation filled his chest.

Juliana was wrong. It wasn't so much his lack of understanding that made him lash out but rather the hurt and disappointment over her lack of faith in him. Over Miss Poole's not confiding something of this importance in him.

It made him wonder what else the seemingly virtuous governess might be hiding. Virtuous. Ha! Virtuous women did not swim naked at night. They did not leave scandalous underthings lying about for men to find, and they certainly didn't help young ladies dissect God's creatures.

The more Grayson thought about it – thought about her – the more his anger grew in direct proportion with his disappointment. She'd claimed a pious upbringing and he had taken her at her word.

Maybe she'd been lying all along. Maybe Miss Poole wasn't what she seemed.

Good God. What if she were on the run? Perhaps from a husband she didn't care for? Or from the authorities. Anything was possible given the fact she'd misled him.

Increasingly concerned, Grayson reached for the desk drawer. If she were hiding something else from him, something that could have a negative impact upon him and his family, he needed to know about it right now.

The drawer opened without a hitch to reveal a leather-bound notebook.

Logic told him Miss Poole was a decent woman. Her

behavior toward Juliana, the fact she'd intervened on her behalf with Miss Chadwick, was but one piece of evidence of this. Logic also told him that if Miss Poole had a damning secret, she probably would not have left any evidence of it in a spot where Juliana might easily find it.

But it gave him the excuse to learn more about her.

Ignoring his voice of reason and the warning that he was about to breach Miss Poole's privacy, he reached inside the drawer and retrieved the notebook.

Grayson slid his thumb over the smooth leather binding, briefly fighting the urge to return the book to the drawer and leave. Reminding himself that Miss Poole had neglected to tell him about Juliana's extra–curricular studies – that she'd helped her hide them from him, no less – he flipped the book open.

A worn piece of paper, folded in quarters, came into view.

He dismissed it for the moment, his interest on the diary entries filling the pages. They went back years, all the way to Miss Poole's childhood, and consisted mostly of one line comments like, *Agnes and I went swimming today. Papa was furious*, or, *Mama's sight is getting worse. She can no longer do her knitting*, and then, *Agnes's coughing persists. I wish there were more I could do.*

Grayson swallowed. He had no business intruding like this. What the hell had he been thinking?

You had to make sure Miss Poole wasn't hiding anything else, he reminded himself, not that it made him feel any better.

For a moment, he considered reading what she'd written since arriving at Sutton Hall. Did she mention him in her diary? And if so, what did she say? He stood stock still for a second before he gave his head a good shake and prepared to put the book back, only to have the folded piece of paper slip to the floor.

Grayson stooped to pick it up. He caught it between his fingers and paused. The creases suggested it had been folded and unfolded dozens of times, perhaps hundreds, so it was clearly of great importance.

Unable to resist, Grayson unfolded the paper. He knit his brow as he began reading. *Sail a boat, wear something scandalous, learn to ride a horse, learn how to dance, go for a late night swim, sleep beneath the stars...*

What the devil?

It looked like a list of things to be carried out. Considering some of the items, most notably the ones he knew Miss Poole had accomplished were marked by tiny x's, he had to assume this was the case. Which meant what exactly?

That she'd been taking advantage of her position? That rather than teach Juliana she'd been trying to fulfill some girlish dreams?

Not exactly. Miss Poole was an excellent tutor. If she'd made a list of things she'd like to experience and being at Sutton Hall gave her the chance to do so, he had no qualms with it. What bothered him was the lack of transparency, the fact that he'd thought he'd known her only to learn there was so much more – a secret side she'd been hiding.

He considered the rest of the items the list had to offer only to pause on the final one. His heart gave a swift beat and his hold on the paper tightened.

Experience kissing.

It was right there in bold ink and, lord help him, with his name directly beside it.

Grayson swallowed. Yes, his name was crossed out, as if Miss Poole had considered him for the experience only to doubt if he were the right choice.

He was. No other man would take his place. Of that he was damn sure.

Marriage is out of the question.

Was it? Nathan didn't think so. And besides, it would just be a kiss, nothing more. A kiss did not have to lead to the altar, but at least it would help quench his thirst. Hers too, he imagined, since there was no longer any doubt about whether or not the attraction he felt was mutual.

It was. His name in that exact spot proved it.

Rising, Grayson folded the paper and placed it inside the book. An explanation was in order. And he'd get it from her now that he knew she was open to his advances. What better way to pry information from her than through seduction?

His anger abated, allowing excitement to take its place. He'd be firm with her, might even make her squirm a little, but only because he knew the buildup of tension would increase the pleasure of her surrender.

Chest tight and with anticipation pulsing through him, he had put the book back in the drawer, closed it and prepared to go find Miss Poole, when the woman in question stepped through the door. She stopped, utterly frozen, her lips slightly parted.

Grayson watched her, acknowledged the series of thoughts that flickered behind her eyes – the doubt and apprehension, the need she had for answers, her wish to flee.

Her gaze left his, darting about the room as if attempting to work out what he'd been up to. Eventually, she glanced at the desk, specifically at the drawer.

She stared at it, swallowed and took a deep breath. "Wha...what are you doing here, Mr. Grier?"

Enjoying her state of confusion, relishing the chance he had to punish her for her secrecy, if only a little, he dipped his hand inside his pocket and pulled out the garter. Her eyes widened and her cheeks turned a deep shade of red.

Grayson fought the urge to laugh, choosing instead to school his features. "Returning this."

"I...um...that is." She sent him a panicked look. "I can explain."

"And I look forward to it." He moved toward her, stepping so close there could be no question about him invading her space. At this proximity she was forced to tilt her head back in order to meet his gaze while he, the scoundrel she'd turned him into, envisioned her wrapped in his arms.

Soon. Once they were safely ensconced in his study where no one would hear them.

CHAPTER THIRTY

Olivia's heart flapped about like an anxious bird. Once, when she'd been roughly nine years old, she'd snuck some drawing supplies in her pocket when she'd gone to church. As Vicar Poole's daughter, her presence at the weekly service was expected, no matter what.

The lecture she'd received by Papa later had smarted. She recalled in vivid detail that feeling of her face heating, the tips of her ears burning while he delivered his scolding.

This was worse.

It was as though her insides were knotted together, strangling her while her stomach turned inside out. She tried to think of something to say, but Mr. Grier was too close, so close she could no longer think let alone speak. All she could do was feel, that coiled up tension she'd sensed between them before somehow stronger and fiercer – ready to snap – an underlying hint of inescapable certainty.

"I..." she tried again, but it was no use. Her throat had gone dry and her tongue wouldn't work as it was supposed to.

His hand grasped her elbow, the spark of awareness the simple touch caused jolting her nerves and making her flinch.

"Steady," he murmured, tightening his grip.

Olivia's breath caught in her throat.

The edge of his mouth quirked as though with a hint of amusement. Over what, she'd no idea.

"Mr. Grier." To her eternal mortification his name didn't carry the confident tone she'd hoped for. Instead, it sounded more like a sigh.

His dark eyes bore into hers, the intensity in his gaze increasing the beat of her pulse. Olivia's knees grew weak. She wasn't sure what was happening here, but she sensed her life was about to change, and she wasn't sure whether she ought to embrace it or run from it as fast as she could.

"It's time we talked." He nudged her sideways and then, before Olivia managed to put her thoughts in order, to give him the explanation he deserved, she was being led from her room like a naughty child.

His comment served as a welcome distraction. "You make it sound as though it's a rare activity you and I never engage in."

Not responding, he marched her toward the stairs while she did her best to keep up with his longer strides. His fingers dug into her arm, holding her upright while urging her onward as they descended the stairs together. Olivia stumbled off the last step but Mr. Grier's grip stopped her from falling. She recovered with relative ease, only tripping a little as they proceeded toward his study.

Mr. Grier entered the room, bringing Olivia with him. The door closed with a loud click and then he released her. "Don't move."

Olivia didn't dare. Feeling as though she'd been turned upside down and dropped on her head, she feared she'd collapse if she tried. Instead she watched as Mr. Grier set down the oil lamp he'd brought from her room and began rebuilding the fire from earlier. She rubbed her arm, not so much because it was sore but because she felt the absence of his hand now as keenly as she did the cool evening air.

"I've got some questions for you, Miss Poole," he told her when eager flames licked at the log in the grate. A smoky scent filled the air. He rose to his full height and crossed to the sideboard where he selected a crystal decanter. "I advise you to answer them honestly. Drink?"

"I, um…"

He filled two glasses before she decided whether or not she wished to accept.

After crossing to his desk, he set both glasses down then pulled out a chair, turning it slightly. Olivia moved toward it, her steps a little unsteady without his assistance, and possibly due to her nerves being once more on edge. She dreaded the conversation they were about to have.

Taking a deep breath she lowered herself to the proffered seat. Her stomach trembled when he also sat, not with his massive desk wedged between them as she had hoped, but in the chair adjacent to hers.

He angled it so he faced her and nodded toward her glass. "Have some brandy, Miss Poole. You look as though you could do with the fortification."

She heartily agreed and picked up the glass, her fingers shaking as she set it to her lips and drank. She winced in response to the sharp bite that greeted her tongue, but forced the liquid down her throat, surprised by its soothing effect.

"Now then," Mr. Grier said, his eyes watching her every move with unsettling focus, "why was Juliana studying the insides of a rabbit in your bedchamber this evening?"

Olivia gulped. She'd expected him to address her misplaced garter. Instead, he'd surprised her by revealing something she'd not been aware he knew until this moment. Readjusting her thoughts, she braced herself for conflict and told him plainly, "She wishes to understand how the body works."

"I'm certain such information can be found in a book," Mr. Grier said, his voice tight. "Imagine my surprise when I tried to return your belonging to you and found Juliana with a jar containing a stomach."

Heat enveloped Olivia's face. "She has expressed an interest in acquiring firsthand knowledge, Mr. Grier.

She's actually quite astute with regard to such matters and I—"

"Miss Poole." Her name was spoken with firmness. "Juliana is an upper-class lady in my care. She is my responsibility. I owe it to her parents, God rest their souls, to make sure her life is as bright as they would have wanted. To this end, it is imperative for her to have a successful debut, which is what you have been hired to ensure."

"I agree. A successful debut is important." Ignoring the urge to leave it at that Olivia said, "But so is happiness, sir. Please don't deprive her of what she enjoys most in life."

His expression hardened. "You don't believe I care for her happiness?"

"That's not what I...um..." She'd not explained herself clearly and he'd decided to twist her words. "I think her happiness matters to you a great deal."

"Honesty, Miss Poole. If you recall, I insist upon it."

Right.

Olivia knit her brow. "Very well. If you must know, I think your bull-headed need for approval from those who are no longer with us have made you ignore what truly matters."

"And what would that be?" Something dark flashed in his gaze, hinting at tightly controlled anger.

Deciding she had nothing to lose, that he'd probably made up his mind to sack her before she'd found him in her room, she chose to leap to Juliana's defense with all she was worth. "The fact that Miss Edwards excels at everything you've asked of her. She's learned Debrett's by heart, despite it having no practical application. Her French is now fluent and she's making excellent strides in Latin *because* of her interest in science. Her mathematical capabilities are impressive for someone her age, her inclination to slouch has been corrected, and your brother has informed me that her dancing skills are destined to leave the *ton* in awe.

"Never mind the fact that she knows how to keep accounts and—"

"Hold on." Mr. Grier gave her a disbelieving look. "You've taught her how to keep accounts?"

"It seemed like the practical sort of thing that might be of use to her later," Olivia said. "And let's not forget the instruction she has received on how to manage a home, from what to consider when hiring servants to setting the weekly menu and working out how to host a retreat or a ball. We've covered this and more, all so you would never be able to tell her she'd squandered her future on something you don't understand."

He stared at her long and hard while she fought the urge to squirm. It hadn't occurred to her that she'd kept all these thoughts bottled up. Somehow her tongue had been loosened and she'd allowed them to flood the air between them.

Heaven help her.

"Women aren't admitted to universities." He said this without any hint at what he was thinking. "They cannot practice medicine, so if Juliana pursues this interest, it can only lead to disappointment."

"She is perfectly aware of the limitations, Mr. Grier. It is not there she will find disappointment but rather in your lack of support."

He stood, quite suddenly, making her flinch.

Forcing a deep breath into her lungs, she watched as he shoved his hands in his pockets and strode to the fireplace. He stood there for a moment, staring into the flames before he said, "Cutting animals open to study their insides is not the sort of thing young ladies ought to be doing. She should be painting, doing needlework, playing the pianoforte."

"Miss Edwards is able to do all of those things," Olivia murmured. She considered his tall frame for a moment and how alone he looked on the opposite side of the room. It occurred to her that the burden of responsibility must be overwhelming and that he could use some ballast. With this in mind, she rose to her feet and approached him. "Consider the ladies of your acquaintance."

"Hmm?" He flinched as if startled by her proximity, suggesting he'd been lost in thought.

"I doubt if any of them can tell you why the grass is green or how clouds are formed. Miss Edwards can, and while I'll agree that her interest in science extends far beyond this to areas some might deem inappropriate, it would be a shame if she were prevented from reaching her full potential simply because it's not done."

"Miss Poole…"

"We're not discussing her admittance to university, Mr. Grier, even though she would be able to study science at the University of Bologna." He gave her a quelling look prompting her to move on. "All she wants is the freedom to be herself without censure from those closest to her."

"Why would you presume I'd not lend my support?"

She blinked. Was he being serious? "You would not even permit her to bait the hook when we went fishing. Because touching worms is beneath a young lady. I did not think your position on dissection would be much better."

"Nevertheless, you should have been honest with me, even if you thought I'd forbid Juliana from carrying on with her studies. I am her guardian. As such, I had the right to make that decision, not you."

His words made something inside Olivia shrivel. She'd wronged him and in doing so she feared she'd lost his respect. "I'm sorry. It was badly done on my part."

"Agreed." He spoke the word sharply, then gave her an assessing look that seemed to peel away her defenses until her soul was laid bare. "However, I'll admit you may have a point regarding the fear I harbor, the need I have for her to succeed. It isn't easy, bringing up someone else's child, always worrying if I'm fulfilling Mr. and Mrs. Edwards's expectations and raising their daughter as they would have wanted. In my effort to succeed, I realize now I may have failed Juliana."

"Not in the least." Compelled to reassure him, Olivia placed her hand upon his arm. "The skills she's acquired at your insistence will ensure her debut goes well, that she draws the right sort of attention and has her pick of eligible men."

"I hope so," he muttered.

A pensive look entered his eyes. It vanished as he cleared his throat. "There's another matter I'd like to address. Mrs. Newhurst, to be precise. What you saw... it wasn't as it appeared."

"Your relationship with your mistress is none of my concern." It certainly wasn't something she wished to discuss at great length.

He produced a startled sort of laugh. "Mrs. Newhurst isn't my mistress. That is, she used to be some years ago before I found out she was married."

Olivia gaped at him. "You went after another man's wife?"

"No, I...well yes, I suppose..." He firmed his jaw. "She told me she was a widow."

"I see." A deflated feeling came over her as she acknowledged that Mrs. Newhurst had an intimate knowledge of Mr. Grier's body, the sort of knowledge Olivia would never have.

An unpleasant sensation crept through her veins, twisting and expanding until it enveloped her heart. She'd never been jealous of anyone in her life, but in that moment, she hated Mrs. Newhurst.

"What I need you to understand," Mr. Grier said, "is that I did not invite her here. I certainly did not ask her to visit my bedchamber. And I never encouraged her advances."

Olivia stared at him and saw the sincerity in his eyes, that same desperation she'd glimpsed in the ballroom when he'd insisted she hear him out. She'd been too afraid then of accepting his invitation and finding herself alone in his presence. But they were already alone, not by design, but because she'd crossed him.

Listening was the least she could do to apologize for her actions.

"Why then, was she in your arms?"

CHAPTER THIRTY-ONE

"I realize this may seem implausible to you," Grayson said, "but she placed herself there without invitation."

As expected, Miss Poole's eyebrows rose with disbelief. "How exactly does that happen?"

"She's a forward woman who also happens to be extremely determined." He glanced at his brandy, considered taking a sip but changed his mind. He'd have some later once he'd gotten everything out in the open. "After crossing paths with Nathan in Paris, she convinced him to let her accompany him here."

Miss Poole looked dubious. "Wouldn't London hold more interest for her with the Season in full swing?"

"One would think so. Especially for a young widow who's made a name for herself as one of the easiest conquests Town has to offer. She wasted no time replacing me when I dropped her."

Splotches of pink appeared on Miss Poole's cheeks, and Grayson could not help but wonder if it related to the idea of a woman sating her appetites without a care for her reputation or the fact that he himself had been one of her lovers.

Despite this obvious show of discomfort, Miss Poole calmly asked. "Then what is her motive in coming?"

"Blackmail."

Miss Poole's lips parted. Her lovely brown eyes widened. "Blackmail?"

"Exactly so. Apparently, Mrs. Newhurst means to force me into marriage."

"But…" Her brow crumpled with an adorable degree of thoughtfulness, making her look both serious and confused. "Doesn't she know you intend to marry Miss Howell?"

"Another issue in need of clarification." He sent her a wary glance. How would she react to the truth? "I may have exaggerated my intentions."

"What?"

"I've never had matrimonial thoughts with regard to Miss Howell. Only now, Lady Oldbridge is quite determined to have me for her son–in–law and has threatened to hurt Juliana's prospects unless that happens."

"But you said…that is…" She looked at him in an odd way, then suddenly blurted, "Why on earth would you pretend that you planned to marry her if you didn't?"

In hindsight, his reasoning seemed irrational at best.

Embarrassed, he dropped his gaze. "You accused me of being well past my prime."

Silence.

And then, "You cannot be serious."

Needing to move, Grayson grabbed the fireplace poker and nudged the log he'd added earlier. Sparks leapt upward as if attempting to make their escape through the chimney. "Believe it or not, your opinion matters, Miss Poole. It has always mattered. Since the moment you said you could only teach what you know. I realized in that instant that you were honest and that I could trust you."

"Except with regard to Miss Edwards's scientific studies." When he didn't comment she said, "So just to clarify, Miss Howell believes you plan to propose, her mother has threatened to hurt Miss Edwards if you refuse, while Mrs. Newhurst is trying to blackmail you into marrying her."

"That's correct." He set the poker aside and turned to face her.

"Good grief. It's worse than one of Shakespeare's comedies." She slanted a look of concern at him. "Will you tell me what Mrs. Newhurst's leverage is?"

Grayson hesitated. He wanted to discuss it with her, to seek her advice and accept the help he knew she would offer, but Nathan's secret was no small thing. Though he knew he could trust Miss Poole with it, he worried she might choose to quit his employ once she knew what Nathan had done. Hell, he'd had the hardest time coming to terms with it himself, but unlike Miss

Poole, Grayson loved his brother. Who he was would never change that.

"Suffice it to say, Nathan has committed a crime punishable by death."

Instead of the shock he'd expected, Miss Poole laughed. Not a lot, but enough to inform him that she did not believe him for a second. The words that followed confirmed this. "That's impossible. Your brother, though perhaps a bit of a flamboyant dandy, is kind and good natured. He's amusing to be around and a constant source of good cheer. For him to be guilty of murder is simply absurd."

"I couldn't agree more." Choosing to move on swiftly, before she could think on the matter at greater length, he told her, "In any event, I wanted to explain the situation to you so you wouldn't think ill of me. I'm not the sort of man who courts one lady while dallying with another."

Relief poured through her. She swallowed and attempted to gather her wits. "I hope you can forgive the misunderstanding." He made a noncommittal sound deep in his throat.

Uncomfortable with the distance between them, Olivia took a step forward. She pressed her lips together briefly before she made herself say, "Considering what you've just confided in me, I should probably tell you that Miss Edwards has been doing more than dissecting a dead rabbit. She's also been catching mice. Not to kill, mind you, but to study."

"Did she succeed?"

"I…um…"

"Well?" he demanded, his voice hardening.

"Yes. She's caught two."

"And where, pray tell, are these mice now?"

"In her bedchamber."

"Good God. If she's careless about it, we'll have an infestation on our hands." Catching Olivia's gaze he told her sternly, "No more lies or deceptions, Miss Poole. The next time I catch you being dishonest with me, I'll send you packing. Is that understood?"

For some unfathomable reason, she chose to argue. "I didn't exactly lie to you, sir."

"You hid a great deal, wouldn't you agree?" He dropped his chin and looked her squarely in the eye. "I ask you again, Miss Poole. Will you be honest with me from now on, knowing I will dismiss you if you're not?"

"Yes," she answered on a rush of air.

The edge of his mouth twitched. A wicked smile slid into place, transforming his features from stern employer to mischievous rogue. "Then I shall proceed with my next question."

"Your next question," Olivia squeaked, staring at him. Mr. Grier hardly ever smiled and the fact that he did so now, that he was looking at her with wolfish interest, gave her the horrid sensation of having walked into a trap.

Her heart sped up and nearly tripped over when he leaned toward her.

His eyes gleamed in the firelight. And then, like a devil without a conscience, he said, "Tell me about your garter."

Olivia's skin pricked with an almost feverish discomfort. Standing upright became a chore as embarrassment drove through her. She longed to flee, to run from him as fast as she could, to never face him again.

Instead she heard herself say, "That's not a question."

The gleam in his eyes intensified. "Semantics, wouldn't you say?"

He had her there.

"The truth, Miss Poole." His smile became a knowing smirk and it struck her that he was enjoying himself – that he liked her discomfort. Perhaps because he believed she deserved it? Maybe this was his way of punishing her?

Fair enough.

Olivia straightened her spine. "I made it. I obviously didn't mean for it to end up under the sofa, but Daphne ran off with it and then you caught me unawares. It didn't seem fitting for me to retrieve it while you watched, so I left it, hoping to fetch it later, only to find it gone."

"I probably should have returned it sooner." He tilted his head and allowed his gaze to slide over her. "Given your otherwise staid appearance, the scarlet ribbon surprised me, as did the lace trimming. I must confess, I found it quite...provocative."

Olivia couldn't move. She could barely breathe as heat engulfed her. Because the way he'd spoken that word, with a low vibration of decadent sensuality, had the effect of a soft caress.

"It's just a garter," Olivia said, her voice weak.

"If that were true, it would be fashioned from plain white cotton, but it's not. It's made from red silk and white lace. Why so daring?"

Discomfited by his question, Olivia chose to ask one of her own. "Do you press all your employees about their undergarments?"

"Only those who leave them lying about in rooms I frequent."

"I didn't—"

"Please answer the question, Miss Poole."

Frustrated, Olivia clenched her jaw and glared at him. "Just because I wear solemn clothes doesn't mean I don't like feeling…" She waved her hand, desperately seeking the right word. He raised a brow. "Pretty, I suppose."

Irritation flashed across his face, disappearing as swiftly as it had appeared. "Honesty, Miss Poole. I believe we agreed upon it."

Apprehension swept the length of Olivia's spine as understanding dawned.

"You found the list."

"Quite so."

Never before had Olivia felt more cornered. She hated him for it, but a promise was a promise. Refusing to shy away like a coward, she raised her chin. "My sister and I began making it when she became sick. In doing so, she was able to live out each dream in her mind, which helped bring her peace in the end."

"The list is made up of the things your sister wanted to do."

"Exactly. Before she died." Forced to pause on account of the ache in her throat, Olivia took a deep breath and prayed the tears pressing against her eyes wouldn't fall. "She wanted more than the life we knew. She longed for adventure and when she realized she'd never have that, she made me promise to fulfill her dreams on her behalf."

His answering sigh was a mixture of disappointment and compassion. "I'm sorry for the loss you suffered and the life your sister was denied. It was wrong of me to pry. I shouldn't have done it."

"Then why did you?" she asked, surprising herself since she'd not meant to voice the question. It hung between them, demanding he be as honest as she.

"Because I believed the list was your doing. Except it's not, is it? It's not you who want to wear something scandalous, go for a late night swim, sleep beneath the stars, or experience kissing." Pain hardened his eyes. "Those are someone else's dreams, which means my name was only there as a means to an end."

So he'd read the entire thing. Of course he had. It was only one page. Olivia's lips parted in the face of the choice she was being offered. She could agree with him and move on. Or she could pick bravery over cowardice.

"If I let you believe that," Olivia told him, her heart a frantic mess of fearful emotion hammering hard against her breast, "I would be breaking my promise to you by lying."

He went utterly still. The tension between them returned. It grew, alerting her to the precipice on which she stood. Closing her eyes briefly, Olivia took a deep breath. It was time for her to throw caution to the wind, to take something for herself and create a memory she could look back on later with fondness. It was time for her to jump.

CHAPTER THIRTY-TWO

Grayson's world shifted in preparation for something momentous. He stared at Miss Poole, every cell in his body on high alert, and waited for her confession. He'd pressed her hard this evening, demanding answers to difficult questions. Rather than shy away, however, she'd met him head on, had even made him reflect on how he'd been handling Juliana's education.

His anger with Miss Poole hadn't stemmed from learning of Juliana's peculiar interest, but from the fact they'd hidden it from him. But the governess had, as she so often did, impressed him with her explanation. It was hard for him to find fault with it considering how well he liked her. Which was probably why his heart had grown heavy when he'd learned that it wasn't she who'd wanted to live life as though it were some grand adventure.

If I let you believe that, I would be breaking my promise to you by lying.

Renewed hope lifted his spirits. His pulse leapt back into action. "What are you saying?"

She licked her lips, reminding him of how much he longed to taste her. His chest tightened with that ridiculous craving he always experienced when she was near.

"Some of the things on the list were my idea, like sleeping under the stars, hosting a dinner party, and seeing the ocean."

"What about kissing?" he dared to ask, no longer able to stand the anticipation.

"A dream we shared."

Her whispered confession made him move closer. He brought his hand to her cheek, allowed his thumb to trail over her skin, and savored her tremulous breath, her shivery response to his touch.

A hiss stole past his lips, forced from somewhere deep within. "Would you like me to help you fulfill that dream?"

She leaned into his caress, her eyes already glazed with desire. And then, a mere breath of air gave her reply. "Yes."

The distance between them vanished before the next heartbeat, his mouth finding hers while his arms wound around her, pulling her close.

To his immense satisfaction she slid her hands over his shoulders and up into his hair, stirring his blood with a wild hunger that made him crave more.

Intent on coaxing it from her, he licked her lower lip. She shuddered. "Open for me, Miss Poole."

She sucked in a breath and slowly expelled it, her breath gently tickling his mouth as she rose to his challenge.

A growl was ripped from his throat. It was followed by an answering murmur when he began teaching her how bold and daring a kiss could be. How it could make sparks fly across skin, weaken both body and mind, seduce, and most enticing of all, hint at an even greater pleasure.

The mere thought...

Driven by instinct he walked her backward and pressed her against the wall. Her grip on him tightened, holding him to her while she did her best to follow his lead, her fervor igniting him like nothing else. She might be innocent and untrained in the art of kissing, but that only made it better. He loved knowing she'd never done this before, that he was her first. And she was catching on fast, teasing him now in a way that made him fear for his sanity.

She was like springtime after the frost, like a cool sip of fresh lemonade on a hot summer's day, like rays of sunshine bursting between stormy clouds. She smelled divine, of lavender soap and honey. She made him feel young and hopeful again, taking him back to the boyish wonder he'd known before he'd set off for war. It was a feeling he'd forgotten until this moment.

Needing more, he kissed a path along her cheek while sliding one hand to her waist. She whimpered when he flicked his tongue against the edge of her ear, and she clutched at his shoulders for support. Grayson moved his hand lower, exploring the flare of her hip, the lush curve of her bottom.

"You cannot know how long I've dreamt about this." He gave her a squeeze and she tilted her hips, prompting him to lean back a little and lower his gaze, to admire the perfect swell of her bosom as it rose toward him.

Catching her gaze, he acknowledged the need in her eyes. Was she aware of how deep her own desire ran and what it would take to fulfill it? Probably not, he decided, allowing his finger to slide down the side of her neck and along the edge of her delicate collarbone.

"Mr. Grier." Desperation clung to her voice.

"Grayson," he amended, catching the edge of her fichu beneath his finger and drawing it out from beneath her neckline. "I insist."

Her throat worked as though it took great amounts of effort for her to speak. And then...

"Grayson."

His name, a plea that spilled from the tip of her tongue. It increased his arousal tenfold. With a curse born from knowing he couldn't just take her here in his study against the wall, that he would return upstairs unfulfilled yet again, he yanked the fichu from her gown and lowered his head for a taste of perfection.

It wasn't enough.

With her, he worried it never would be. But deep satisfaction still filled him when she sighed with pleasure, when instead of retreating she drew him closer, inviting him to do as he wished.

Olivia was overcome by sensation. She'd never experienced anything like it. Had never felt more alive. Because of this man. Mr. Grier.

Grayson.

He'd kissed her and in so doing, he'd shown her what she'd been missing and made her want more. She gasped in response to his mouth moving over the swell of her breasts and again when he drew her neckline lower.

"I want to know every inch of you," he murmured, the provocative words compelling her body to arch as the heat from his breath sank under her skin. This was by far the wickedest thing she'd ever experienced but also the most delightful.

Needing purchase, she leaned her head back to steady herself, fisting his hair in her hands and holding him to her. He was her master and she was his servant. They shouldn't be doing any of this. It was unspeakably scandalous. They really ought to stop.

Instead, Olivia sighed. She welcomed each touch while secretly hoping for more. And when he returned his mouth to hers a while later, she kissed him back with added fervor, so he'd know the effect he was having on her.

His hands settled boldly upon her thighs, adjusting

her slightly before he pressed closer, and it was as if her world exploded and she was tossed into the air. A wave crashed over her head, sweeping her under and turning her over. Her body shook and a high pitched sound filled her ears, wrought from a place inside her she'd not even know existed.

"My God." Grayson's voice was filled with wonder as he hugged her to him. "I barely touched you."

She trembled in the aftermath and took a shaky breath. "I've never…"

A tender kiss touched her cheek. "You are the most astounding woman I've ever encountered, Olivia. May I call you Olivia?"

Her voice was slightly muffled by his jacket when she told him, "It would be odd if you didn't after what we've just shared."

"Would it shock you to learn that I'd like to share more?"

"No." She leaned back just enough to meet his gaze. "I want the same."

His nostrils flared and his hold on her tightened. For a moment it looked like he struggled to breathe. He finally blew out a raspy breath and loosened his grip. Gently, carefully, he adjusted her bodice and took a step back. "I need for you to think about what that would mean."

"You don't believe I'm clear–headed right now?"

"I know you're not. And I'm not much better off, but I'm trying to do the right thing." He scooped up her fichu and held it toward her. "Please, return upstairs, get some sleep, and consider the implications."

She stared at him. He was right, of course, and far more sensible than she at the moment. Because the truth was she wasn't just thinking of taking a stroll into town. She was planning to hop into bed with her employer and to let him take her innocence. Knowing full well he'd never take her to wife.

"All right," she said. "I will do as you suggest."

He took her hand and pulled her to him, then dipped his head and pressed his lips to hers in a tender kiss. She sagged against him, delighting in the freedom honesty gave them – in the intimate moments it now allowed for.

"Give me a copy of your list," he told her a few seconds later when they parted ways, "and I'll do what I can to help you fulfill it."

It was a promise, she realized as she took her leave. A promise that brought her one step closer to falling in love with a man who could never be hers.

CHAPTER THIRTY-THREE

"I can't believe she told you," Juliana complained. She was scowling at Grayson from across the breakfast table.

He scowled back. "Keeping mice inside the house is reckless, no matter your reasoning."

"It doesn't change the fact that I trusted Miss Poole and that she betrayed me."

"You encouraged her to risk her position for you," Grayson said, irritated by Juliana's thoughtlessness. "Imagine if they'd escaped, burrowed their way inside the wood paneling and made a cozy nest there. Do you have any idea of the speed with which they multiply?"

"Of course I do," Juliana snapped. "It's one of the main reasons I chose to keep mice, so I can study the birth and growth of their pups in a timely fashion."

"Good lord." Grayson wasn't sure what to say to that besides, "You'll have to do so elsewhere, Juliana. Those mice are leaving the house today. As soon as we're done eating."

"You're so—" She cut herself off with a throaty growl of annoyance.

Grayson did his best to reel in his own temper. He thought of what Olivia had said about lending Juliana his support rather than trying to stifle her dreams. Studying the reproduction of mice wasn't exactly the most appropriate pastime activity for a lady, but he'd rather be a part of it than risk her doing something worse behind his back.

"I'll help you set up a makeshift study in my workshop. You can keep the mice and the rest of your curiosities there."

She stared at him as if not daring to believe the offer he'd made. "Truly?"

When he nodded she leapt from her chair, crossed to where he sat, and wound her arms around his neck in an awkward sort of hug. A kiss on the cheek followed. "Thank you, Grayson."

He cleared his throat and managed to disengage himself from her right before Nathan entered the room with Delilah.

"I'll meet you upstairs when you're ready," Juliana told Grayson as soon as she'd finished greeting the new arrivals.

"Give me ten minutes," Grayson said and promptly took a sip of his tea.

"What was that about?" Nathan asked as soon as Juliana was gone.

"A lion and a tiger," Grayson answered.

"For Juliana?" Nathan and Delilah asked in unison and with equal amounts of surprise.

Grayson merely took a bite of his toast. He wasn't in the mood to explain further. Instead, he chose to enjoy the rest of his breakfast while savoring the warm sensation filling his heart to overflowing. Being supportive, abandoning his rigid adherence to protocol for a moment, felt good.

Olivia was right. Juliana had proved herself to be hardworking and willing to meet his expectations – society's expectations. It was time he rewarded her for it.

It was also time to seek out Olivia.

Last night had been extraordinary. She'd proved more passionate than he'd dreamed, more eager and open and utterly perfect. The taste of her, the fact that she'd come undone in his arms with the slightest of ease, had fueled his fantasies later when he'd been alone.

He shifted in his seat and did his best to school his expression. If Nathan caught him grinning at his food, his brother would demand an explanation. So he took another sip of tea

He was desperate to see her again, perhaps sneak a kiss if the chance presented itself – help her fulfill the promise she'd made to her sister. A thought struck and he immediately stood.

"Forgive me, but there's a pressing matter I must attend to at once."

Nathan raised an eyebrow while Delilah narrowed her gaze. Unfortunately, Delilah was the one to speak. "I must confess I'm increasingly disappointed with the lack of attention you've given me since my arrival. If you'll recall, we agreed you would be more obliging."

She gave him a pointed stare while stirring sugar into her tea.

Grayson stilled, his mood slightly dimmed at the unpleasant reminder. "I've already told you, I'm a very busy man and you chose to visit without any warning."

"That excuse will only get you so far."

"I don't have time for picnics or trips into town," Grayson informed her, his irritation rising.

"But I do," Nathan said. He smiled broadly at Delilah. "How about you and I visit Taunton after breakfast? I've heard exemplary things about the French modiste there."

"French, you say?"

"Indeed," Nathan told her and took a slow sip of his tea.

"Well, I suppose it wouldn't hurt to explore other towns in the county. Although I'd much prefer to do so with you, Grayson."

Grayson gave her a tight smile. "Nathan is the better option. He loves fashion while I loathe it. I'll only ruin your visit with my complaints."

"Very well," Delilah muttered. "As long as you agree to go for a walk with me tomorrow."

"Of course," Grayson said, glad to be given the time to think up another excuse to avoid her. Perhaps it was time for him to get sick with influenza? He sent Nathan a look of thanks and wished him and Delilah a pleasant excursion, then quit the room.

Having finished her breakfast, Olivia waited for Juliana to join her while passing the time with a lovely daydream involving herself and Grayson. She started at the sound of footsteps and turned, facing the school-room door as Juliana entered with Grayson directly behind her.

Heat rushed to her cheeks when she met his gaze. The answering gleam in his eyes assured her that he recalled every detail of their encounter the night before – that he'd thought of it too. Her stomach tightened, as did her stays, reminding her of the impropriety they had shared.

"Good morning," she managed, forcing her attention to Juliana before the desire filling Grayson's expression seared her to the bone. She picked up a book, anything to keep her mind focused. "Will you be joining us for mathematics today, Mr. Grier?"

"As enjoyable as that would no doubt be, I'm here for a different reason, Miss Poole."

"Oh?"

"Grayson has offered to let me use his workshop for my scientific studies," Juliana said with excitement. "We're moving Lion and Tiger there, along with the jars from your room."

MR. GRIER AND THE GOVERNESS

"If you'll grant us access," Grayson said.

"Of course." Olivia looked from one to the other. "You wish to do so now?"

"If it isn't any trouble," Grayson said. He was strolling about the room now, picking up the occasional item, turning it over, distracting Olivia to no end.

"Miss Poole?" Juliana prompted.

Olivia flinched and Grayson sent her a smirk – the wicked sort undoubtedly meant to weaken her knees.

Mouth dry, she steadied herself against her desk and turned toward Juliana. "No trouble at all. We'll skip today's mathematics lesson then, shall we?"

Juliana beamed. "Thank you, Miss Poole."

"No thanks needed." She wasn't sure how she managed to walk to the door without stumbling when her legs were clearly made of jelly.

"And if you're able to take tomorrow off too," Grayson said, "it might be nice to visit the seaside."

Olivia drew to a halt. She turned toward him while Juliana expressed a definite interest in such an outing. "The seaside?"

"I'd like to be more supportive of Juliana's interests." But his gaze was fixed upon Olivia while he spoke. "Going to the seaside would give her the chance to collect some shells, perhaps some crabs and jellyfish which she can bring home to study. As her governess, you would have to come too, Miss Poole."

"I can scarcely wait," Juliana said with a beaming smile that lit up her eyes.

Olivia grinned. "Me neither."

"Then it is agreed," Grayson said, his voice firm. He gestured in the direction of the hallway. "After you, Miss Poole."

Olivia led the way to her room where they gathered the jars from under her bed, placing them in a crate for Grayson to carry. Olivia and Juliana collected the mice next and then they were off, heading toward Grayson's workshop. Olivia had been aware of the structure since her arrival at Sutton Hall, but with no reason to venture near it, she hadn't considered its purpose, besides it probably being a shed of some sort.

"I've never been in there either," Juliana informed Olivia as they approached. "Makes one wonder what he's hiding."

Olivia caught Grayson's gaze and was stunned by the flicker of unease she found there. "Everything all right?"

"It's just my hobby, that's all," he answered, his mouth quirking with uncharacteristic bashfulness.

"How intriguing," Olivia murmured, smiling in an attempt to put him at ease. It was clear he worried what she and Juliana might think of whatever it was he chose to pass the time with.

Upon reaching the building, he set the crate down and retrieved a key. He unlocked the door and pushed it open, then stepped aside, granting Juliana and Olivia entry.

Juliana entered, her weight prompting a floorboard to creak, and immediately gasped. Olivia shared a quick look with Grayson before she followed the girl inside. And came to a quick stop beside her. The dry smell of wood shavings thickened the air. She stared at the space, at the various saws hanging on the wall, at the assortment of boxes lined upon shelves, and at the wide workbench where she imagined Grayson crafting... whatever it was the man made. Olivia moved toward it while Grayson directed Juliana toward the other side of the room.

"I realize it's just a couple of sawhorses with a plank of wood on top," Grayson was saying, "but it's spacious and—"

"Perfect," Juliana declared with a laugh.

Olivia glanced at her and noted how pleased she looked with her new workspace before returning her attention to the workbench. A few sheets of paper, abandoned it seemed, drew her attention. She picked one up and sucked in a breath when she realized what she was seeing – a gorgeous design for a lady's comb complete with tortoise shell inlays.

Befuddled, she set the design aside and gave her attention to the most intricately carved box she'd ever laid eyes on. Her fingers trailed over the surface. She glanced at Grayson. "May I?"

He paused only briefly before he gave his consent. Olivia flipped open the lid.

"What do you think?" Grayson asked, his voice slightly edgy as he came to stand beside her.

Olivia trailed one fingertip over the beautifully polished wood of the combs she'd discovered. Some were more complete than others, but all were remark-able works of art. The level of skill required to make these, to not have one of the teeth accidentally break and to avoid cracking the wood when the slots for the inlays were carved, rendered her breathless.

"You're the local craftsman," she said, turning to meet his gaze. "The one the clerk at the haberdashery mentioned."

"Correct."

When he appeared to wait for her verdict she gave her attention back to the combs. "I think you're incred-ibly talented. These combs are exquisite."

He expelled a raspy breath and she realized how much her opinion had actually mattered. "I'm glad."

Reaching forward, he moved as though to retrieve one of the combs, bringing his hand down over Olivia's. She sucked in a breath and instinctively glanced toward Juliana. Thankfully, the girl was much too busy arranging her things to pay attention to what Olivia and Grayson were up to.

His thumb stroked over her knuckles as he sidled closer. So close his arm pressed into hers. And then he was threading their fingers together and all Olivia could do was pray she wouldn't combust on the spot.

"Last night was incredible," he murmured. "I've thought of it countless times since. Tell me I'm not alone."

Her gaze shot toward his. "How can you possibly think you might be?"

A roguish smile caught his lips. Releasing her hand,

he slid it to one side so he could retrieve a comb from the box. "This one's for you. I've been working on it for a while now. It's not quite finished, but it will be soon."

Humbled by the gesture, Olivia took the comb so she could admire it up close. "It's beautiful. So delicate."

"My combs are usually brown, but I was inspired by your hair."

Her lips parted as understanding dawned. "You haven't just been working on this for a while. You've been doing so with me in mind."

He shrugged one shoulder. "I had to do something to chase away all the inappropriate thoughts I had about you."

"Inna—"

"Keeping busy was the only solution." He glanced across the room while Olivia stared at him in dumbfounded silence. "Juliana. I realize I've forgotten to bring the notebook I wanted to gift you. It's on top of my desk in the study, wrapped in parchment. Perhaps you'd like to fetch it?"

Juliana's eyes lit up. "Thank you, Grayson. I shan't be long."

The door closed behind her as she left, leaving Olivia alone with Grayson. He pulled her into his arms and kissed her.

CHAPTER THIRTY-FOUR

"There's been a development," Mary informed Mr. Dover when their paths crossed in the upstairs hallway. She'd been going to check the linen closet when he came toward her from the other direction. Her cheeks warmed in response to the smile he gave her.

It was silly. She knew this. But that didn't keep her from enjoying his company.

His eyes crinkled at the corners. "You look like a young girl who's just had her first piece of chocolate. What is it, Mrs. Hodgins? Something good, I'll wager."

"I hope so," she said and quickly glanced around just to be sure no other servants were lurking nearby. "Miss Poole was in Mr. Grier's study last night. That is to say, I saw her leave as I was finishing my rounds for the evening. Which I ended up doing later than usual because of you."

Mr. Dover grinned. "Distracted you from your duties, did I?"

Mary's pulse quickened as he stepped slightly closer. He was doing it again, saying things that made her giddy. She wasn't sure if he was just being friendly or if it was something more. "I enjoyed our discussion a great deal."

"As did I. Never would have taken you for a fellow mycologist."

"I'd hardly call myself a mycologist." Mary's cheeks heated until she feared she was blushing profusely. She shrugged in an effort to seem less affected. "Mushrooms just interest me, that's all."

"Which is why I'm hoping you'll go for a walk with me one day. There's a spot in the forest, not too far away, where scarlet elf cups seem to flourish."

"Really?" She gazed at him in wonder. "I'd love to see them."

"Then I'll show them to you on your next day off." Pleasure warmed his eyes. "Now, about Miss Poole being in Mr. Grier's study. You mentioned a development?"

"Yes. Right." Lord, she could scarcely think straight now that the promise of taking a stroll with him filled her brain. "I've no desire to make assumptions, but she did look rather rumpled when she left."

Mr. Dover knit his brow. "I'm not sure I like what you're suggesting. Miss Poole is a young woman under Mr. Grier's care. If he's taking liberties with her then—"

"I thought the same at first, but have since had time to reflect."

He drew a bit closer. "And what have you concluded?"

"We are hoping he'll realize how perfect she'd be, not only as his wife but also as a substitute mother for Miss Edwards. Yes?"

"Certainly, but I had imagined more boating or—"

"I very much doubt Miss Poole will be climbing aboard another boat any time soon after what happened. Or that Mr. Grier will let her. The incident shook him. Even Fiona, who's almost always got her head in the clouds, realized he'd had a bad fright."

"Of course. But then he could take Miss Poole for a walk in the garden or arrange for a picnic."

"True. Although…" Mary bit her lip.

"Although?"

"I can't help but think this a good thing. I mean, you've seen the master today."

Mr. Dover held her gaze. "I have."

"Then you will agree Miss Poole makes him happy."

"You know I do. We've already discussed this. But that doesn't mean I approve of him getting up to mischief with her when they're not married."

A smile caught Mary's lips. She placed a gentle hand on Mr. Dover's arm. "Neither do I, but Mr. Grier is a good man. He's kind and thoughtful behind that guarded façade of his – eases the burden for his staff as much as possible by folding his clothes and making his bed, seeing to it that his shoes and boots are always in perfect order."

"The army gave him that discipline. If you'll recall he was as careless as most other boys before he enlisted." This was said with sentimental fondness.

"He deserves to be happy. If a bit of mischief is what it will take for him to wed the right woman, then so be it." Mary lowered her voice. "According to Betsy, Mrs. Newhurst is quite determined to make him hers, and based on what Roger overheard Lady Oldbridge say when she came to dine, Miss Howell's no better. That very evening she was supposed to get Mr. Grier alone so her mother could find them together and force an engagement. Lady Oldbridge wanted it done before they travelled. I worry what she'll get up to when she returns."

She barely managed to say the last part when Miss Edwards came hastening toward them.

"Everything all right?" Mary asked. The girl was breathing hard as though she'd been running.

"Mr. Grier has a gift for me in his study. A notebook he's asked me to fetch and I'm just"—she gulped down a breath—"very excited."

"And where is Mr. Grier now?" Mr. Dover asked.

"In his workshop with Miss Poole. They're waiting for my return."

"Well, we mustn't keep you then," Mary told her, "although I would recommend you slow your pace. Just to be safe."

Miss Edwards promised to do so and continued on

her way. No sooner was she gone than Mrs. Newhurst appeared from the direction of the library.

"I wonder if either of you can tell me where I might find Mr. Grier. I've checked his study and the library, but both were empty."

Mary darted a quick look at Mr. Dover who, contrary to what she'd expected, raised his chin and informed Mrs. Newhurst, "I believe he must have gone out."

"Oh." Exasperation was evident in the widow's pinched expression. "Where to?"

"I really can't say," Dover told her in the driest voice Mary had ever heard him use.

Mrs. Newhurst raised her chin with a little disdainful sniff then swept away, disappearing to some other part of the house.

Mary sighed. "That was very well done of you."

"We must do our part if Mr. Grier is to open his heart to love. Even if it means helping him get up to mischief."

Mary grinned. "You're a good man, Mr. Dover."

He gave her a smile in return before leaning in and quietly asking, "Any chance you might call me Philip?"

The sweet pressure of Grayson's lips, followed by gentle coaxing, silenced the world around Olivia. All she could do was feel– the steady beat of her heart as he drew her closer, the slow slide of his mouth against hers, the strong arms wrapped around her while warm hands supported her back.

A low rumble vibrated through him, a guttural sound of approval as she responded to his caress, casting aside all concern of discovery in favor of simply enjoying the moment. His hand caught her jaw, his thumb gently scraping her skin while he cradled her head. The rich flavor of coffee spilled over her tongue while the scent of musk and sandalwood swirled through the air.

She breathed it in, savoring the masculine fragrance while sagging against him. A sigh, part pleasure part need, flowed from her mouth to his. The edge of the workbench collided with her lower back.

Grayson withdrew his mouth from hers, his chest rising and falling with strenuous movements as he pressed his forehead to hers. His ragged breaths ghosted across her cheek, making her crave so much more than this moment allowed for.

"I hate having to end this, but Juliana will soon return." The sound of regret in his voice echoed the way she felt. With a sigh, he took a step back, the light in his eyes assuring her of the truth in his words. His restraint was fragile and he was doing his best to keep it intact.

"Perhaps later," she suggested.

His gaze darkened and when he spoke next, his words were measured. "Suggesting more when we're both heated up is like playing with fire, Olivia. I'm trying my damnedest to do the right thing here – to make sure you don't lose your innocence due to some mindless moment of passion. But I'm only a man."

She gazed at him, both grateful and frustrated. "You make me want things I've never wanted before."

His answering laugh was gruff. "Don't say things like that. I beg you."

Noting the desperation in his tightly drawn features, she eased away, allowing him space to pull himself together. She needed the same – some means by which to cool her ardor. "I'll give you my answer soon."

He gave her a hard stare before he finally nodded. "In the meantime, we'll work on your list, starting with tomorrow's outing."

"It's incredibly kind of you to help."

The look he gave her was slightly odd. A frown followed. "Do you think I don't care about you? That my only interest where you're concerned is in getting you into my bed?"

"I hadn't really considered," she confessed, taken aback by the sudden edge to his voice.

"Then I would ask you to do so. Because from where I'm standing, there's a hell of a lot more between you and me than the need for a quick tumble." He swallowed with rough movements, then took her mouth once more in a hard, impassioned kiss that threatened to light up his workshop. "I hold you in the highest esteem, Olivia Poole. No matter what happens or where these kisses might take us, I need you to remember that."

She barely managed a nod of agreement before he released her, leaving her slightly off balance when the door opened, admitting Juliana.

Notebook in hand, the girl went straight to Grayson and gave him a hug. "Thank you ever so much. I absolutely love it."

Olivia moved away from them, hiding the flush she could feel in her cheeks while pretending interest in various items on a shelf. Grayson was right to insist she give their new relationship serious thought, because the effect he had on her, this ability of his to make her oblivious to all else, was terrifying.

All her life, she'd employed common sense, yet here she was, ready to leap off a cliff for a man she couldn't marry. It was insane. She'd acknowledged as much when he told her she wasn't clear-headed enough to be making important decisions regarding her virtue. Lord help her, the fire he'd stoked in her yet again had made her incapable of being rational. The only thing on her mind was—she wanted more. Which made her realize the danger such moments posed.

Perplexed by the turn her life had taken, she stared at what appeared to be a collection of samples, an assortment of wood cut into various blocks, each with different surface treatments. She reached for one, turned it over between her fingers, and tried not to worry about the direction in which she was headed. *Impossible.* When he kissed her, he encouraged a primitive need – one which nature compelled her to follow through on. If she wasn't careful, she'd not only let him take her but beg him to do so.

All you can ever be is his mistress.

She knew this, but was she prepared for such a life? It would depend a great deal on how much she was prepared to endure, and on whether or not she was willing to pay for the experience with a broken heart.

CHAPTER THIRTY-FIVE

Excitement rushed through Grayson's veins as he stepped down from the carriage the following day. A salty breeze, pungent from the presence of seaweed, swirled around him. He turned and extended his hand, raising a brow when Juliana looked poised to leap from the conveyance. She froze on the step, appeared to reign in her girlish compulsion to act with a lack of decorum, and allowed him to help her down.

He grinned as he released her. "Go on. I know you want to."

Without hesitation she dashed past the grassy dunes and onto the beach below, Daphne yapping at her side. Warmth filled Grayson's chest. He'd never really considered how important Juliana was to him beyond being a duty he had to oversee. But she was so much more than that. He genuinely liked her and cared for her. Over the years, the imp had become a relation.

Hell, his bond with her was in many ways stronger than with his brother, Matthew, whom he rarely saw.

Returning his attention to the carriage, he offered to help Olivia down. The sparkle of sunshine in her eyes as she leaned through the doorway and took a deep breath created a fuzzy sort of feeling deep in his chest. A wide smile stretched across her face, then she placed her hand in his. And it was as if he'd been struck by lightning, the electrical charge so powerful it nearly knocked him off his feet.

Perhaps because he'd just been confined to a small space with her for over two hours without being able to touch her?

He didn't dare do more than squeeze her hand now. Not with the coachman and two footmen present. Fearing they'd wonder at his delay in letting her go, he dropped her hand and ordered the footmen to set up the picnic for later.

"Shall we proceed?" he asked Olivia, whose gaze was fixed upon the band of blue peeking out from behind the dunes.

She turned to him, a bright smile upon her lips. "Yes."

They set off at a quick pace, pushing past the marram grass, white sand squeaking beneath their feet, until the entire beach came into view and he heard Olivia's intake of breath.

"It's beautiful, Grayson."

She stood in profile, which enabled him to admire her delicate jawline, the rosy fullness of her cheeks, the way her chin jutted forward beneath that full lower lip he liked to nip at, the gentle curve of her nose, and the fringe of black lashes framing her eyes. The soft creases her smile produced both at the edge of her mouth and at the corners of her eyes warmed her features and added distinction.

"Yes. It is."

She turned toward him, revealing the tears that threatened. Grayson's gut clenched in response to the raw emotion, to the open honesty she displayed.

Instead of retreating from him, she allowed him to see how much their coming here meant. "Thank you."

He offered a nod, one he hoped she'd interpret as more than what anyone watching them might. Based on the sweet smile she gave him, she understood without him needing to speak. Which was rare, he realized as they ambled down the dunes together toward Juliana. Finding a person with whom one shared the sort of connection he sensed between them was exceptional. Hell, he'd only ever heard his mother describe it when she'd spoken of Papa after his passing. She'd told him that if he should find such a feeling one day, he should hold onto it with all his might and not let it slip between his fingers for any reason.

He took a deep breath, attempting to calm the sudden mixture of anticipation and panic that threatened to send his heart racing. He could not lose Olivia, but in light of their situations – their different social positions – he couldn't give her the life she deserved either. Not even if he managed to rid himself of Delilah and Miss Howell.

It pained him to acknowledge this, but he had to be realistic. He could not let Nathan fill his head with impossible dreams built from magical rainbows. Not when he had a family name to protect and a ward whose future depended on him avoiding the sort of scandal he would invite if he asked a servant to be his wife.

"I found one."

Juliana's voice broke through his thoughts, offering a welcome reprieve from his self–imposed torture. He strode to where she stood, passing her discarded stockings and shoes on the way. She held out her hand palm up to reveal a small crab.

"Do you think it will survive if I bring it home with us?" she asked.

Grayson stared at the brown creature. "I'm not sure."

Olivia came to stand beside him. He sensed her presence, the pull between them strong despite her keeping some distance and him not looking directly at her.

"You'll need to replicate its natural habitat to the best of your ability," Olivia told Juliana. "And I would bring more than one crab, just in case they favor company."

"Will you help me?" Juliana asked, her eyes on Grayson.

He considered the challenge. "It's no small thing

you're asking. We'd have to provide your new pets with water containing the right amount of salt. They'd also need sand, and some means by which to climb out of the water. Plus, you'd have to feed them. Any idea what they eat?"

"Fish," Juliana informed him without hesitation. "That's the easy part."

She wasn't wrong there. "I need to think about it."

Despite the disappointment dimming her eyes, Juliana nodded and refrained from arguing the point before she strolled off. Her ability to accept this decision revealed a new degree of maturity in her. She was being reasonable for a change, and he was fairly certain he owed that to Olivia.

He glanced at her, a thrill of pleasure enveloping him as he watched the wind pull at her hair, loosening some of those tightly pinned strands. "You should follow her lead, take off your shoes and stockings, let the sand creep between your toes."

"You're just looking for an excuse to see my feet again," she whispered, her voice teasing.

He chuckled. "Guilty, I'm afraid."

She grinned and his heart cracked open, inviting her in. This woman, the one who stood before him with a challenging look of mischief burning bright in her eyes, contrasted the staid one who roamed Sutton Hall. Maybe it was because the rules that ought to govern them both could be tossed aside out here, the fact that he'd undone her with kisses a few days prior, or simply because they'd escaped the daily toil where obligations echoed around them.

He'd like to think it was all three, possibly more, as he watched her kick off her shoes. She reached beneath her gown next, her gaze catching his as she slipped off her bright red garter and placed it on top of her shoes. He didn't bother pretending a lack of interest. He couldn't. Not when he prayed she'd one day allow him to do the honors.

A far more modest white garter slipped from her other leg and then she was rolling down her stockings. "Aren't you going to take off your boots and hose?"

He started at the realization that he was simply standing there, lost in the daydream that was Olivia Poole. "Of course. But I may need your help."

This earned him a look of disbelief. He grinned in response and dropped to a sitting position, then raised one booted foot toward her. "They're pretty snug."

Olivia bit her lip and glanced around as if debating whether or not it was proper for her to do as he asked. Arms crossed, she studied him briefly while he tried to look like an innocent puppy. She wrinkled her nose in the most adorable way, then huffed in resignation and stepped toward him. Her hands gripped his ankle and then she started to pull.

A frown appeared at the bridge of her nose, right between her eyes. She flattened her mouth and appeared to pull harder while he leaned back. The boot slid away and she stumbled backward, gasping slightly beneath her breath.

"Is it always this hard?"

A wicked response came to mind. Grayson cast it aside and lifted his other foot. "For the most part."

"It's a wonder men bother to wear them." She took hold of his ankle and started removing the next boot. "Why not favor shoes?"

"Some men do, I suppose, but boots are more practical. Especially when one is venturing out into nature. And besides" – he waggled his eyebrows – "they do lend a dashing effect to a man's appearance, wouldn't you agree?"

Rather than answer, she sent him a grin as the boot was pulled from his foot. She dropped it next to the other, then turned to admire the view while he set his mind to removing his hose.

"It's so incredibly vast," she remarked, her voice filled with wonder, "with endless possibilities waiting in every direction."

"Do I detect a desire to travel?" He pushed himself to his feet and moved a bit nearer to her. Juliana, he noted, was busy admiring something at the edge of the water, the hem of her white muslin gown flowing in the surf while Daphne danced around her.

"I'd like nothing more." The sad laugh that followed pierced him to his core. "I'm fluent in French and German, yet I've never left England."

He understood, or at least he believed he did. "There's no reason why you can't go abroad one day."

"On the contrary, there's every reason."

He wanted to argue, to promise he'd take her everywhere she wished to go, as long as she became his lover. But that would be cheating, tipping the balance in his favor by meddling with her ability to make a sound decision. Besides, he wanted more from her than bed sport. He wanted to know – *needed* to know – that in the event she should come to his bed, she would do so because of him and not because of what she might gain.

So he kept quiet while letting the breeze toy with his hair. Later, after eating a tasty meal of ham, cheese, roasted chicken, onion pie, and fruit amidst the tall grasses of the dunes, Grayson stretched out on a blanket with one arm lazily draped across his eyes.

Here, sheltered from the wind, he soaked up the sunshine while Juliana chattered away about her plans for a crab sanctuary at Sutton Hall. She exchanged ideas with Olivia, who offered advice and support.

A warm sense of comfort settled behind Grayson's breastbone. Even though neither Juliana nor Olivia were his relations by blood, he couldn't deny the familial bond he felt as he lay here, their voices humming around him, the breeze caressing his skin while the sun soothed his soul.

It was a feeling that took him back to a time when he'd been fearless, when he'd lived in blissful ignorance of the hardships life would bring, when he'd been truly happy and unconcerned. And it occurred to him that he didn't want to lose that feeling again. Somehow, he'd have to find a way of holding on to it, even after they got back to Sutton Hall.

CHAPTER THIRTY-SIX

Olivia snapped to attention at the sound of someone clearing their throat. Abandoning her daydream, which had involved pleasant memories of her recent seaside outing with Grayson and Juliana, she turned toward the drawing room door where the man who filled her thoughts to excess was standing, one shoulder propped against the doorframe, an amused look in his eyes.

"Thinking of me?" he asked.

Heat flooded her cheeks. "Certainly not."

He flashed a roguish smile. "Liar."

Olivia stared at him while attempting to gather her wits, and it occurred to her that he'd undergone an incredible transformation during the past week. Since the first time they'd kissed. He looked happier now, more at ease. His sternness was gone, replaced by a carefree demeanor.

Had anyone else noticed? And if so, had they guessed at the reason behind his dramatic change?

"Now you're frowning," he murmured. "We can't have that."

"I don't want the other servants to find out what's happened between us," she whispered. Never mind his brother, Mrs. Newhurst, or Juliana. She chose to keep that concern to herself.

His expression turned thoughtful as he pushed away from the door and strode farther into the room. "They won't as long as we are discreet."

Olivia wasn't so certain. "I fear we may be more transparent than we believe."

"Even if that is the case, even if they were to have suspicions, my servants are loyal to me. They won't spread gossip about the village." Hands clasped behind his back, he faced her. "Nathan won't say anything either and neither will Mrs. Newhurst, seeing as they've not been here this past week after getting delayed in Taunton."

"It was good of your brother to make that happen."

"Yes. I'll have to thank him when he returns. Even though he does owe me, seeing as I'd not be troubled by Mrs. Newhurst were it not for him. But enough about everyone else, let's return to your earlier musings, the ones I so rudely interrupted a moment ago. The ones that made you blush."

His teasing tone was infectious. She smiled in response. "Your legs, if you truly must know."

He grinned with obvious amusement. "My legs?"

"Your calves, to be precise. I saw them at the beach, if you'll recall."

"And?" His lips twitched with a hint of suppressed humor.

She shrugged and picked at her skirt. "It never occurred to me how shapely they would be or that they'd be dusted by hair. My father's didn't look anything like that, nor did my uncle's."

"Well, mine are an exceptionally fine pair."

She gave him a withering look. "If you're going to mock me then—"

"Mock you?" He strode forward, cutting away the space between them, and dropped to one knee.

Olivia's heart jolted. She darted an anxious look at the door where any number of people might soon appear. "Get up."

"Not before I've made one thing clear." He grabbed her hand and pulled her toward the edge of her seat. "I would never mock you, Olivia. Tease you, yes, but mock you, no. Don't ever think otherwise."

And then, as if her nerves hadn't suffered enough already, he pressed his mouth to hers in a searing kiss that demanded she believe him. She gasped for air when he withdrew and glanced at the door once more, almost certain she'd find someone watching.

"You shouldn't do such things," she chided.

"I couldn't resist." He stood and pulled her to her feet. "Especially since there was no risk of being discovered. Juliana is in the workshop and the servants are busy counting candles, polishing the ballroom mirrors, and waxing the floor. Now, if you are done worrying, please come with me."

Unable to resist and curious to know what he wanted to show her, Olivia followed him. Much to her surprise, they headed toward the stables, where a pair of saddled horses stood waiting.

"Where are the grooms?" Olivia asked, the nervousness she'd experienced in the drawing room returning.

"I sent them to appraise a foal an acquaintance of mine is selling. They shan't return for another two hours at least."

"You planned this diversion?"

"It seemed like an excellent way of ensuring I'd have the opportunity to spend the afternoon alone with you." He drew her into his arms and kissed her again, this time with increased languor, as if they had all the time in the world. It was the sort of kiss that conveyed deep emotion, the sort that said more than words ever would, the sort that threatened to have her believing in dreams coming true.

Olivia fought the sensation with all her might. She couldn't allow it to grow lest it sweep her along in a maelstrom of fanciful notions, each one destined to crush her heart. This was just a bit of fun, a brief experience to be savored, that was all. Eventually she would have to walk away.

She told herself this as he slanted his mouth and deepened the kiss, as he held her tightly while she hugged him back, as every part of her heart and soul expanded with something that would have terrified her had she paused long enough to recognize the emotion growing deep within.

"I could kiss you all day," he confessed, resting his forehead against hers. "But we'd best be off if we're to accomplish what I have planned before anyone is the wiser. Here, allow me to help you."

He caught her by the waist and lifted her into her saddle, then swung himself onto the other mount.

Olivia gripped the reins. "You should know that I've only just started to trot a horse."

"We'll keep an easy gait then." He kicked his animal into motion and hers instinctively followed, walking out onto the path behind the stables and picking up its pace as soon as they reached the tree line.

The weather was cooler today than when they'd gone to the seaside, due in part to the clouds blocking the sun. Olivia didn't mind. How could she when she was with the most wonderful man in the world, riding through the countryside, experiencing life in a way she'd never dreamed possible.

Oh, Agnes, how you would have loved this.

Her heart clenched at the memory of her sister. She would have been thirty years old now, had she lived. A difficult truth to come to grips with, despite having dealt with the grief.

"We'll stop over there by that tree," Grayson said, scattering her musings.

By the time Olivia reached the spot, he had alighted and stood ready to help her dismount. His hands settled firmly against her waist and he slid her toward him, allowing her body to drag against his.

"Scoundrel," she muttered while secretly hoping he'd brought her out here to be ravished.

"Irresistible minx," he answered with wicked amusement flashing in his dark eyes.

To her disappointment, he stepped away, releasing her as he went to fasten the reins of both horses to the tree. Reaching up alongside his saddle, he retrieved something – something Olivia hadn't noticed before. Most likely because she'd been too distracted by Grayson himself.

She sucked in a breath as he turned and extended the hilt of a rapier to her. Her fingers curled around it, testing the new sensation that came with holding a sword. Raising her gaze, she found Grayson studying her with interest.

"*Learn how to fence*," he said. "I might not be the most skilled swordsman in England, but I'm able to teach you the basics."

Completely undone by his thoughtfulness, by the trouble he'd gone to in order to make this lesson possible for her, she simply stared at him, unsure of what to say. A simple, "thank you," would not be enough. She said it anyway, as soon as she got her jaw working.

He held her gaze for a moment, the edge of his mouth drawn into a warm sort of smile that made her feel...

She swallowed, too afraid to think the word because

logic told her it couldn't be real. And she could not afford to mistake desire and whatever companionable friendship he offered as anything more.

"You'll want to hold it like this. Plant your feet apart, knees slightly bent, and extend your arms for balance. Go on. Try it."

Olivia mirrored his stance and held it while he made corrections to her posture and the positioning of her arms. He then showed her how to move, with light and agile steps that were harder to execute than they appeared.

"This is exhausting," she said. She'd followed Grayson's instructions for what must have been at least half an hour, after which he'd suggested some sparing to test her knew skills.

It was difficult, recalling the right footwork, posture, and arm movements all while trying to stop his advance. Her arm grew increasingly tired with each pass he made, her heart bouncing along with exertion as she did her best to keep up.

His rapier connected with hers once more, forcing it to one side. She grabbed the hilt with both hands in a futile attempt to steady the blade. Grayson, no longer the man she wanted to kiss but rather the one she longed to throttle, grinned as though he were having a marvelous time.

"It will get easier with practice," he promised, and promptly disarmed her with an easy flick of his wrist.

Her rapier twirled through the air before landing with a small thud in the nearby grass. Olivia huffed and placed her hands on her hips. "I think it might be too soon to cross learning to fence off the list."

"Did you think you'd turn into Angelo Domenico in the space of one afternoon?"

"I don't know who that is," she said as she collected her weapon. "A famous swordsman, I assume?"

"An Italian fencing master who founded Angelo's School of Arms in London some sixty years ago. He instructed our late king and provided lessons to members of the aristocracy."

"But not to you?"

"No." A faraway look entered his eyes. "I was taught by my father."

"I'm sorry."

His gaze cleared. "Why?"

"Because you clearly miss him."

"Every day. But while I have my regrets where Papa is concerned, I'm glad to have fond memories to look back on. Having him teach me how to fence is one such memory." A sentimental smile tugged at his lips. "He was always so patient. And he knew where our limits were – mine, Matthew's, and Nathan's. He'd push us until we reached them, and then he'd reward us for our efforts, either by taking us swimming or by surprising us with a treat he'd asked Cook to prepare in advance. Because he knew we'd live up to his expectations. He believed in us more than we believed in ourselves."

"It sounds like he was a wonderful man."

"He was."

"And your mother?"

Birds twittered in a nearby tree. Grayson sighed. "The busiest woman in London. She occupies herself with endless projects. It's her way of coping with her loss."

"Does she ever visit?"

"Here?" He picked up his sheath and slid his rapier inside. "The memories are too painful. She doesn't even want to go near the London townhouse where she and Papa spent the social seasons. I suggested she keep using it – that she and I share it – but she refused."

"It must be difficult," Olivia mused, handing her rapier to him when he extended his hand, "to love someone so deeply and then to lose them."

He held her gaze, studying her for a moment before he asked, "What were your parents like?"

She gave a weary laugh. "Papa was very devout and solemn. He considered idleness a sin, but he never complained about having daughters rather than sons because he believed we were delivered to him as part of God's plan. As you know, he provided my sister and me with an education few women have the chance to receive. For this I am grateful, but for the rest..." She shook her head. "There was never a warm embrace or words of encouragement. Only Mama provided those, and only when Papa wouldn't hear. Instead, we received an endless number of scoldings and were forbidden from engaging in any diversions."

"You had no friends?"

"Papa was of the opinion outsiders would lead us astray. The only bit of fun I recall from my childhood was learning how to swim. Papa didn't approve when he realized what we'd been up to, that his daughters had been sneaking away from home for weeks on end so they could float about in a river. He punished us for it."

Grayson's eyes hardened. "How?"

Olivia had no wish to discuss this but neither did she want to lie. Setting her jaw, she told him simply, "We received five lashes each for the transgression."

"He struck you?" His outrage could not be denied.

"Across our knuckles."

"And yet you stayed. Even after your sister and mother were dead."

"Leaving wasn't an option, Grayson. Whatever shortcomings my father had, he raised me. Despite his meager earnings, he provided for his family. So while I can't claim to miss him or even to have loved him, I owed him."

"You sacrificed years of your life." The remark had an angry edge to it.

"Maybe," she agreed. "But if things had gone differently, if I had left sooner, then there's a good chance you and I wouldn't have met."

He dropped her rapier and closed the distance between them in two long strides. And then his arms were around her, hugging her to him so tightly she struggled to breathe. "You are the best person I've ever known."

She smiled against his chest while pressing her

cheek into the brown wool of his jacket. "You're rather wonderful yourself."

A heavy sigh gusted over the top of her head. "You wouldn't say so if you knew how I thanked Papa for all the love and affection he gave me."

Concerned by the bitterness in his voice, Olivia angled her face in an effort to see his expression. All she caught was a stubborn chin. "How can that be when you are the best man I know?"

He grunted slightly and loosened his hold. "We ought to return to Sutton Hall before someone questions our whereabouts."

Olivia nodded. If he didn't want to explain his comment, she wouldn't press him, though she did hope he'd choose to confide in her later. In the meantime, she would regret mentioning her parents. It had been a natural act of reciprocity after he'd spoken of his, but it had been foolish. She'd ruined the mood, dimming the joy they'd found in their outing.

Unsure of how to return to a happier place, she kept silent until they arrived at the stables. Only then, when she dismounted, did she manage to find the words she'd been seeking. "I wasn't witness to what you did, Grayson. I've no idea who you were in your youth. But I know who you are now. Dutiful, kind, understanding, and fair – traits any man would be proud to have in his son."

He dropped his gaze but clasped her hand. "I'm doing my best to make it right."

"It's more than that." She gave his hand a squeeze. "You're doing your best because you care."

He raised his head. A smile fluttered across his lips. "Your faith in me is a bit overwhelming."

"Does it make you uneasy?" She kept her tone light, slightly teasing in an effort to banish the tension completely.

"Quite the opposite."

She smiled, not simply to bolster his spirits or brighten his mood, but because she believed every word she'd just told him. "Good."

He shook his head as if slightly baffled. "You should go to the workshop, check on Juliana before returning to the house. It will make it easier for you to think of an answer, should anyone ask where you've been."

"All right." She withdrew her hand and turned to go. The urge to look back was overwhelming. She resisted and kept moving, adding distance to the man for whom her heart beat with increasing fondness.

CHAPTER THIRTY-SEVEN

I t was nearly impossible for Grayson to keep from smiling these days. Just catching a glimpse of Olivia brightened his mood like nothing else could. Nathan noticed the difference when he and Delilah returned from Taunton, judging from the glint of mischief sparkling in his eyes. Grayson doubted it had anything to do with his spending time alone with Delilah for several days in a row.

He glanced at the clock. It was almost six. He ought to prepare for supper.

Instead, he walked to the back of the house and stepped outside. The sun had been shining all day and the air was still warm. Not a single cloud could be seen in the sky. His pulse leapt with excitement. Although he'd seen Olivia plenty of times since teaching her how to fence, he'd not been able to get her alone, not without the risk of raising suspicion.

But maybe tonight?

With anticipation burning through him he went back indoors. He'd need some blankets, perhaps a pillow or two. Definitely a basket of treats.

He gathered the blankets and pillows before changing into his evening attire. The basket of treats would have to wait until the servants retired, which was something of a nuisance, though one that couldn't be helped if he were to safeguard Olivia's reputation.

In light of what he had planned for later, getting through dinner required a great deal of patience. It seemed to drag on forever.

"You look extremely agitated this evening," Nathan remarked while sharing a drink with him later. "Delilah noticed it too."

Grayson stiffened. "It's nothing."

"Nothing?" Nathan smirked. "If I were a betting man, I would rather suppose you might be romancing a certain governess."

"Nathan." Grayson spoke his brother's name with a note of warning.

"Don't worry. I won't tell anyone. Like I've said, you could do with having a woman of Miss Poole's character in your life. She's as good as they come. Decent. And since she no longer has any relations, I probably ought to warn you, dear brother."

"Warn me?" Grayson wasn't sure what to make of that.

Nathan leaned forward, a dangerous glint in his

eyes. "Hurt her, and you shall have me to deal with. Is that understood?"

Grayson gaped at him. "Are you taking Miss Poole under your wing?"

"I'm making sure you don't do something stupid."

"You're the one who encouraged me to pursue an affair with her."

"Provided you're willing to give her your name."

"You know I—"

"If you're not brave enough to do so, Grayson, then you have no business trying to bed her. Not when it's so bloody obvious how much she cares for you."

Grayson went utterly still. He cared for her too, but was that enough for him to risk scandal? To possibly diminish Juliana's chance at a good match? He shook his head. "Have you forgotten about Miss Howell and Delilah? Even if I were brave enough to thwart the rules of society and marry Miss Poole, I can't until I'm certain they won't pose a threat."

"Lady Oldbridge's threat will come to naught the moment you wed Miss Poole." Nathan shifted in his seat and stretched out his legs. "As for Delilah, just leave her to me."

"Leave her to you?" Grayson straightened with concern. It hadn't escaped his notice that his brother now used the woman's first name. "What the hell does that mean?"

Nathan reached for his glass. "Her involvement is my doing. It therefore goes without saying that I ought to fix it. Suppose she's no longer a threat and you are free to do as you please. Would you marry Miss Poole then?"

"I..."

Nathan emptied his glass and set it aside. He stood and dropped his gaze to Grayson who sat immobile. "I'll leave you to work that out, though instinct tells me you already know the answer."

Grayson's mind reeled as he listened to Nathan's retreating footsteps. He'd not really considered having no obstacles in the way of his happiness. And while he'd always desired a love match, Nathan was right. If he married Olivia, then Lady Oldbridge would not be able to tell anyone that he'd turned Juliana's governess into his mistress, thus voiding her threat. Which left Delilah.

Grayson blinked. What the hell did Nathan intend to do?

Olivia stared at the note she'd found on her bedchamber floor after supper. It was from Grayson, requesting she meet him in the observatory, which sat above the servants' quarters. Curious, she grabbed her shawl and proceeded toward the stairs leading to the third floor. The carpeting muted her footfalls, allowing her to move silently through the house. The light from her oil lamp slid across the wainscoting as she stepped onto the top landing. Here, a narrower set of stairs continued toward the attic.

Instead she turned right, moving through a short

hallway until she reached the only room up here – a large rectangular box of a space, framed by glass on all sides, and placed on the east side of Sutton Hall's roof. Olivia opened the door and entered, her gaze instinctively drawn toward Grayson who stood, his posture slightly bent as he peered through a telescope angled toward the night sky.

Olivia paused, allowing herself the chance to observe him, the way one hand curled around the brass tube, holding it steady while he adjusted the eyepiece. He must have sensed her presence, because he suddenly straightened, his gaze landing on her with so much warmth she almost melted.

"You came," he said, his deep timbre urging her closer.

"How could I not?"

The edge of his mouth lifted. He held out his hand. "Care for a look?"

A spark ignited between them the moment her hand clasped his. She sucked in a breath while adjusting herself to the dizzying swirl in her stomach and the frantic beat of her heart. With careful movements she set her oil lamp aside on a nearby table, then allowed him to guide her into position.

She leaned forward, acutely aware of his thigh pressing into her hip, of his palm spreading over her waist as he held her in place, steadying her while she admired the night sky.

"Astonishing," she murmured, withdrawing slightly to peer through the window before returning her eye to the eyepiece. "The stars seem so close when I look through here, like I can almost reach out and touch them."

"I used to spend hours up here, exploring the cosmos. That's Sirius, the brightest star in the night sky."

She let herself savor the view for a few additional seconds before she stepped back. Straightening, she asked him softly, "What made you stop?"

"Life, I suppose. When Papa died I was suddenly swamped by responsibility – learning how to run an estate and care for a child. I didn't have the same time for leisurely pursuits as I used to."

"And with time, you forgot about the things you once enjoyed."

"Quite so." His hand trailed over her cheek in a gentle caress. "Until I met you."

Olivia wasn't sure what to say. No words seemed to suffice considering what he'd revealed with those simple words. She'd impacted his world – she mattered – and her decision was made. She would give herself to him without reservation. Because she loved him, wholly and completely.

The revelation was equally shocking and expected. As soon as she'd had it, her heart settled into a steadier rhythm, and the jittery nerves she always experienced when they were alone together subsided. Calmness filled her, pushing aside every doubt she'd had about taking this step. With Grayson it would be right. There was no guarantee she would find that with anyone else.

What if he marries Miss Howell or Mrs. Newhurst?

Olivia knew he was caught in a snare he might not escape from. She also knew she wasn't the sort of woman a man like Mr. Grier would take to wife, even if he were free to choose. The only way for her to secure a permanent place in his life then would be as his mistress. And that would mean sentencing any children they might have to illegitimacy.

Unthinkable.

But to walk away from him without experiencing the pleasure she knew she'd find in his arms was impossible. The regret would eat her alive.

"Where have your thoughts wandered off to?" he asked, curiosity etched on his face.

She pushed aside her troubling thoughts of the unhappy future that surely awaited and smiled at him. "You'll find out soon enough."

"I'm intrigued."

"As am I. Why did you ask me up here?"

He held her gaze for a moment as if considering whether to press her further. But then he nodded toward her lantern. "Take that and follow me."

Grayson grabbed his own lantern and crossed toward a glass door leading onto the roof. He pulled it open for Olivia, then followed her into the cool night air. Their lantern light swept through the darkness, falling in soft muted tones on the spot he'd prepared.

Her breath caught as she took in the blankets and pillows laid out before her, the basket strategically placed to one side. "What on earth?"

"Your chance to sleep beneath the stars."

How could she not love this man when he did things like this? When his thoughtfulness brought tears to her eyes? "Thank you."

He took the lantern from her hand and placed it on the ground beside his own. His hand caught hers, drawing her down onto the blankets until she was sitting opposite him with her legs swept to one side. "You deserve to be cherished."

"As do you." She spoke from her heart and in so doing, she caught his attention.

He held her gaze for the longest moment, a hint of wonder in his dark eyes. A gentle smile followed, the warmth behind it enveloping her until she felt like he held her heart in the palm of his hand.

As if he'd felt it too and was slightly undone by the strong connection, he cleared his throat and turned to the basket, from which he withdrew a bottle.

After uncorking it with a pop, he handed it to her. "My favorite wine. It's meant for dessert but I'd just as happily drink it with my main course."

Olivia set the bottle to her mouth and drank, enjoying the sweet flavor as it slid over her tongue.

"I can see why. It's what I imagine nectar must taste like." She handed the bottle back to him and watched him take a sip too. Pleasure lit his face as he drank, allowing her yet another glimpse of the carefree boy he'd once been. If only she could guide him back to that place forever by easing his burdens and helping him win back the joy from his youth.

He wiped his mouth with the back of his hand and set the bottle aside, then began unwrapping the food. A piece of meat pie, cut in half, came into view, followed by two slices of pound cake.

Olivia picked up a piece of pie and bit into the flaky crust. A rich combination of grilled chicken, stewed mushrooms, and fried onions filled her mouth. It tasted divine, despite its being cold.

"I believe the secret to a good pie is in the dough. My mother never quite mastered it. Her pie crusts were always too robust."

"Your mother cooked?" Surprise was evident in the pitch of his voice. "I would have imagined you had a maid–of–all–works at the very least, in light of your social position."

Olivia stifled a groan. This was where the true difference between them would show. She took a deep breath. "Papa may have been considered a gentleman because of his profession, but his parish was poor, his income a paltry amount that dwindled to nothing when Agnes grew ill and Mama began going blind. The medical bills were crippling, not to mention the extra expense when Papa himself began ailing a few years later."

Their only blessing had been the house which came with Papa's employment.

"But there must have been some money somewhere," Grayson muttered. "I mean, in order to become an ordained vicar a man must attend university, which is not free from expense."

"Papa's father covered the cost, but Papa was the youngest of six. His eldest brother was obviously set to inherit most of the family fortune. You know how it is, Grayson. Youngest sons are expected to find respectable work within the law, the army, or the clergy. Having so many siblings before him hardly helped, nor did having two sisters in need of dowries."

"You and your sister would have required the same. I realize your father might have been harsh, but he must have put something aside for you. I mean, it would have been expected and as a vicar's daughter, you shouldn't have lacked suitors." The look he gave her was almost desperate, as if he prayed she'd tell him there had indeed been a young man who'd vied for her hand long ago – a flicker of sunlight in her dark past.

She shook her head. "Papa could not afford the expense, and even if he'd been able to, I'm not sure he'd have done it. You see, while most fathers desire to marry their daughters off as swiftly as possible, mine acknowledged our value."

"You were the maids he couldn't afford."

She forced a smile, hoping to lighten the mood. "I'm extremely skilled with a broom."

"As well as mending, laundering, and scrubbing dishes, I should think." Increased sharpness punctuated each word.

"All necessary tasks," Olivia stated without any shame. Noting the way his gaze hardened, she hastened to intercept his next comment by saying, "There's nothing wrong with doing one's part. My family needed me, Grayson. Papa needed me. And while he may have educated Agnes and me with a mind to the future, ensuring we had the knowledge to help him with his duties in the event he became indisposed, I gained an education I might otherwise have lacked. I'm not sorry for that."

"I just can't stand the thought of your being worked to the point of exhaustion." Unhappiness on her behalf tightened his features. He clenched his jaw while practically glaring. "Of being struck for the slightest offense."

"It seems worse now in hindsight than it actually was at the time. Back then, I didn't have much else to compare with. I wasn't acquainted with men or women of leisure. The people I knew, the villagers I grew up with, toiled every day in order to make ends meet. It was the norm for Agnes and me. Unlike me, who's more of a pragmatist, she would escape to her daydreams whenever the chance arose, which is how the list began."

"With sailing a boat."

Olivia nodded, recalling how Agnes had longed for adventure. "She didn't want to accept the life she'd been given. And then she died, without even knowing what it was like to be kissed."

"I'm so sorry."

His raspy voice accompanied the tears stealing into Olivia's eyes. She took a quick breath. "That was the last thing she asked of me, the final experience she requested, knowing I shared that dream. When I woke the next morning, she was gone."

Without saying a word, Grayson handed her the bottle of wine. She drank from it without hesitation, then picked up a slice of cake and allowed the decadent flavor to soothe her. He ate his cake as well, prolonging the silence while frogs croaked somewhere in the distance.

"Before Papa died," Grayson said finally, "he called me home. His wish, as stated in the letter he sent me, was to make sure I knew how to carry on once he was gone. He wanted to give me an update on estate matters and address Juliana's future."

"You don't have to talk about this just because I spoke about Agnes." When she'd quizzed him about his father after their duel, he'd withdrawn from her, which had to mean it was a subject he struggled to face. She'd no wish to push him.

A ragged breath left him. "I do. It's important to me that you know what I've done – that you see me for who I really am."

"Grayson, I—"

"I was four and thirty years old, Olivia. Papa's request was not unreasonable, but I ignored it, because I had a more pressing matter."

Olivia tensed. She didn't like the self–loathing with which he spoke. Afraid of what he might reveal yet sensing a certain expectancy in him, she quietly asked, "What pressing matter?"

"Delilah Newhurst." The bitterness in his voice

made Olivia's heart clamp together. "I spent over a decade distracting myself with drink and women. Aware of the horrors I'd witnessed, the memories I attempted to block out by drowning myself in drink and having a good time in bed, my parents allowed me more slack then I deserved."

"I imagine war changes a man." Olivia kept her voice soft and steady despite the temptation to scream. Of course he'd been with other women. Believing otherwise would be naïve. But having him tell her about it was far from easy. Sensing the importance of hearing him out however, the need he had for someone to hear his confession, she told him gently, "Your father clearly understood that, or he would have been more demanding."

"Life carried on around me. I put off the visit Papa requested. Instead, I enjoyed the company of friends and of a woman who later turned out to be married." He shook his head. "Selfish. Heartless. Unforgiveable."

"No."

"I was in bed with her when news of Papa's death arrived." He practically spat the words, his anger so palpable Olivia flinched.

She gasped, a reaction he seemed to take as proof that she'd changed her opinion about him. He scooted back as if preparing to rise and she scrambled forward, catching him around his waist and holding on with all her might. The pain he'd suffered, first in the war, then afterward as he'd attempted to deal with the mark it had left upon him and later when he'd become riddled with guilt, was more than she could bear.

It made her want to stay near him forever, to reassure him for the rest of his days that while he may have faltered, he wasn't a terrible person. If anything, he was the best man she knew. The remorse feeding upon his conscience proved it.

"It takes strength and courage to admit one's mistakes," she murmured while breathing him in. His heart thudded wildly in his chest, knocking against Olivia's cheek. "And it takes great resolve to change the course of one's life as you've clearly done."

He drew a tight breath, released it slowly. His fingers wove through her hair, loosening the tight chignon at the nape of her neck. "I'm sure I don't deserve you."

Instead of responding with words, Olivia rose onto her knees and pressed her mouth to his, pouring the love she harbored for him into one perfect caress. Only silence existed, accompanied by their unified heartbeats, until he emitted a throaty growl and hauled her against him, taking their kiss to a whole new level.

CHAPTER THIRTY-EIGHT

Grayson hugged Olivia close, savoring the honeyed flavor of cake and wine on her lips. There was an added depth of emotion to this embrace, a shared acceptance of heart and soul, a sense of unity and profound understanding born from the truth. By daring to show her his flaws, he'd gained a level of freedom he'd not known since childhood.

Beauty, personified by Olivia Poole, surrounded him and filled his senses. She made him want to give her the world, whisk her away from any hardship, rid her mind of all suffering, and bring her joy. No one was more deserving, no woman more humble or kind. Being allowed to hold her and kiss her, to soothe away any concerns she might have, was a gift not to be squandered.

So he drank from her lips, sought refuge in her

embrace, and welcomed the fervor with which she responded to his caress. He loved the way she arched against him, the slide of her fingers as she raked his hair, and the throaty purr of approval she gave him when he slid the hand at her waist even lower.

He drew her hips flush with his own, allowed her to feel the effect she was having on him, and just like that – between two heartbeats – everything changed. The kiss transformed with the scrape of her teeth teasing over his lips, her wanton sigh when he nipped at her ear, and her hands stealing under his jacket.

Grayson's stomach tightened. Her delicate touch – the innocent hesitance with which her fingers roamed over his back – was so bloody thrilling; it threatened to drive him wild. Hunger, basic and far more acute than ever before, stoked a fire so fierce he feared it would engulf them both.

"Olivia." Her name a half gasp, half prayer. He was older and ought to be wiser. He had to be the one who set the boundaries, the one who warned her where this would lead if she didn't show more restraint.

Instead of responding, she tugged at his shirt, and Grayson started falling into a state of complete surrender from which there could be no return.

No.

He shook his head, refusing to take advantage.

"Olivia." He spoke her name with force and curled his fingers around her arms. Reaching for the last vestiges of control, he pushed her back, panting for breath while he stared into her moonlit eyes.

"Yes," she whispered.

For a second he thought she was asking him what it might be he wished to say. But before he could find the right words, she repeated herself. "Yes."

He still wasn't sure what she meant, his mind too muddled to make sense of anything at the moment. Until she withdrew her hands from under his jacket and started undoing the fastenings at the front of her gown.

It was bloody hard keeping a cool head when he was kneeling before her, watching her strip. Concerned for her innocence, he knew he had to make certain she understood the ramifications of her actions. "If you undress... Olivia, I...please, just stop for a moment."

Her hands stilled and her gaze met his, so full of need it tested his every resolve. Still, he took deep breaths and fought to hold firm. "I need to know you've thought this through."

"Are you having second thoughts about me?" she asked, her voice low, hesitant.

He shook his head. "God, no. I want you with a desperation unlike any other I've ever known."

"Good." A sultry smile cast aside all hints of doubt from her expression. "I've made up my mind, Grayson. I want to share this experience with you."

"Bloody hell." It was all he could manage as she continued undoing her gown. Mouth dry, he watched the fabric part, the sleeves slip from her shoulders, and the gown pool low around her knees, leaving her in her chemise and front-tying stays.

Her fingers toyed with the laces and Grayson emitted a helpless groan in response to the sparks of sensation igniting his blood. "Would you like me to help?"

"If you'll allow me to remove your cravat."

Grayson's stomach tightened. His heart was no longer racing. It was flying so fast he could barely keep up. Unable to wait any longer, he reached for her, carefully tugging and pulling, undoing her stays while she went to work on the knot at his throat.

Her fingertips teased his skin as she unwound the long length of fabric, increasing the anticipation of what was to come. Never before had he wanted a woman so much. Never before had a joining been more important. Her pleasure was so damn vital to him, he began second guessing his prowess.

What if he hurt her? What if he lost control? What if he failed to last as long as required?

Heaven help him. Olivia was the only woman who'd ever been able to get to him in this way. She was under his skin, embedded in every corner of his mind, and dangerously close to owning his heart.

That heart gave a happy thump at that possibility. But when he tried to examine the sensation closer, Olivia pulled his cravat away, scattering all his thoughts as she leaned in to place a kiss on his throat.

It felt as though he'd been cast back into the eye of a storm as urgent desire took hold once more, spurred by the velvety softness of her lips sliding over his skin.

Yanking her stays away, he cast them aside before

shrugging out of his jacket. His waistcoat soon followed and then those eager hands of hers were tugging his shirt from his breeches, bunching the fabric and pulling it upward until she found her way underneath.

A hiss of air stole past his lips as her palms settled over his spine, infusing him with her warmth. Needing more, he gathered her in his arms and pressed his mouth to hers with hungry abandon while reveling in her response, in her throaty moan, the way she yielded beneath his touch.

His fingers twisted her chemise, sliding it upward, over her hips. She gasped when he scraped her skin with his nails, so he did it again while dragging the fabric higher. Leaning back, he caught her gaze, noted the neediness there – the fiery desperation matching his own. Without hesitation, he swept the chemise over her head and tossed it aside.

Trembling, he reached for her and allowed his hands to explore the perfection that was Olivia Poole.

"You are by far—" His voice cracked with emotion. Undone by the wonder he felt in response to the gift she offered so freely and overwhelmed by the hunger rising inside him, he crushed his mouth to hers and kissed her with all he was worth. She would be his tonight and by God, he could scarcely wait even though a small voice at the back of his head reminded him to take care.

He could not rush this. He must take his time. Even if it killed him.

So he did his best to ignore his rising discomfort,

394   SOPHIE BARNES

which worsened the moment her fingers dipped inside
his waistband.

"Christ, Olivia." He caught her wrists and pulled her
hands away, struggling to catch his breath. "Don't touch
me there, love."

"Forgive me." Her voice shook." I've no idea what I
was thinking. I—"

"Stop." He gritted his teeth and held himself utterly
still for a second while doing his best to regain control.
When the wave of arousal she'd stoked with her touch
diminished, he finally managed to say, "You have the
most potent effect on me. That's all. It's not that I do
not like your touch, but that I fear I shan't last if you
tease me so. Do you understand?"

The worry he'd seen in her eyes disappeared and she
nodded. "You have the same effect on me."

"I'm very pleased to hear it," he murmured. Catching
her around her waist he kissed her again while
lowering her body until her head rested on one of the
pillows. He knelt beside her, his gaze sweeping the
length of her shapely figure. His heart trembled.

Swallowing past a knot in his throat, he ran his
fingers over her skin, beginning the slow seduction
intended to make her insensible with desire. It was true
he'd been with dozens of women before, but this was
different. This time he cared. His heart was engaged,
and ensuring she had the best experience he could
deliver mattered far more than appeasing his own
desire.

And when they finally came together, it would not be the sort of rutting he'd always engaged in before – a distraction from the past and the means by which to satisfy his biological needs. No, he knew without doubt that with Olivia it would be so much more – a coming together of body and soul.

She gasped when his touch grew increasingly intimate and determined. He watched her face, savored the flush in her cheeks, the silent plea on her lips. His muscles flexed when she tilted her hips as if seeking more than what he presently offered.

"Please." She started writhing and Grayson pulled back, sweeping his shirt off while she sobbed in protest.

Shaking with restraint, he fumbled with his placket, undoing each button with clumsy movements he'd not experienced since his first time with a woman. Olivia stared at him, her eyes widening with apprehension when he pulled his breeches down over his hips.

"Don't worry," he assured her, his voice unusually raspy as he tossed the garment aside. He reached between her thighs once more and spoke to her gently. "You and I were made for each other. It may be a little unpleasant at first, but after that I'll make sure you love every second."

"Is that a promise?" Her breathy voice assured him she was responding to his touch and that she was coming closer to her crisis.

"Yes." Removing his hand, he positioned himself between her thighs and prayed he'd live up to his word.

Capturing her mouth in a heartfelt kiss meant both to distract and convey how he felt in this moment, he found his way home.

CHAPTER THIRTY-NINE

Clinging to Grayson with all her might, Olivia reveled in every sensation, including the brief pain he'd warned her about. The perfection of their merging was indescribable, the closeness she experienced with him as he explored uncharted parts of her body so utterly profound it brought tears to her eyes. With every movement, each touch and impassioned kiss, he bound her to him, heart and soul.

Whatever love she'd imagined she harbored for him before expanded until it consumed her. It filled her with equal amounts of yearning, comfort, and torment, for no matter how wondrous this moment might be, heartache was destined to follow.

Casting these thoughts aside, Olivia wound her legs around his thighs and gave herself up to the pleasure he offered. Her eyes met his and the dark desire she found there brought every pleasure he'd given her thus far into a dense conglomeration. She arched in response and tilted her hips, eagerly seeking that euphoric feeling he'd given her when they'd first kissed.

"Yes, Olivia." His voice was strained, the muscles in his back rippling beneath her fingers with each move he made. "Let yourself go."

He bowed his head and kissed her deeply while reaching between them. With the skill of a man who knew what she needed, he helped her toward the precipice, and pushed her right off the edge.

"Grayson!"

It was the only word she could manage. Stars exploded behind her eyes and sparks of dizzying light poured through her. She trembled and heard him groan her name while tensing above her, muscles straining.

A deep exhale followed as he collapsed onto his forearms, keeping his weight off her while panting lightly against her cheek.

"My God," he murmured, sounding as though he'd just run a race. "That was...extraordinary."

She trailed her fingers down his back and over his hip, loving the way he sighed when she flattened her palm against his firm buttock. "I know."

He rose up, braced himself above her again, and gazed at her in wonder. "Do you?"

A smile crept over her lips. "It was incredible."

"It's more than that. This...What we just shared..." He cleared his throat and shook his head as though unsure how to explain. But then his eyes cleared and he told her simply, "Imagine searching for paradise all your life and not only finding the door but being invited inside. I've never experienced anything like this before."

Awed by his confession and rather satisfied knowing she stood out among all the other lovers he'd had in the past, Olivia drew him down for a tender kiss and enfolded him in her arms. Lord, how she loved this man and oh, how she wished they could have the future she wanted. But at least they would have this – a moment in time no one would ever be able to take from them.

He rolled off her a little bit later, drew her against his side, and covered them both with a heavy wool blanket.

"I'm so glad you came to Sutton Hall," he whispered against the nape of her neck.

"Me too," Olivia murmured while bone deep languor pulled her into a light doze. She was vaguely aware of him speaking endearments as she drifted deeper, but failed to untangle the words as sleep claimed her.

Nothing could ruin Grayson's good mood the next day. Not even Nathan informing him that Miss Howell and her parents were back from Scotland and that they had come to call. Instead, he grinned, unable to stop the image invading his mind of Olivia waking him with sweet kisses at dawn, of how he'd encouraged her to straddle his hips and—

"What's happened?" Nathan asked.

Grayson blinked and focused his gaze on his brother. "Nothing."

Nathan frowned. He angled his head and then his eyes widened. "You finally did it."

"Did what?" Grayson attempted to brush him off with a nonchalant tone.

"You bedded Miss Poole." There was no escaping the accusation of that statement.

"I..." Grayson had meant to lie if for no other reason than to protect Olivia's honor, but what was the point? Nathan obviously saw straight through him. He sighed. "Yes."

Instead of pressing him further, Nathan merely offered a thoughtful nod before striding toward the door. "Come, brother. We've guests to attend to."

They entered the parlor moments later.

"Good afternoon," Grayson said, noting to his annoyance that Delilah was also present. "Please forgive my delay in joining you."

"It's quite all right," Lady Oldbridge said. Her features were tightly drawn with disapproval. "You're here now, prepared I hope to offer an explanation."

Grayson's insides tightened with alarm. He glanced at Nathan who looked as though he too had taken note of the strained atmosphere. Another look at Delilah and the wicked gleam in her eyes and the smirk she attempted to hide behind her teacup assured Grayson there would be trouble within the next second.

Bracing himself, he took the expected leap and asked, "Pertaining to?"

"The fact that you've a young widow residing beneath your roof when you are supposed to be courting Edwina." Lady Oldbridge narrowed her gaze. "Mrs. Newhurst claims to have come here with the understanding that she will soon become part of the Grier family."

Grayson clenched his jaw while grappling with the strategic move Delilah had chosen to make. He'd murder her for it later, when there were no witnesses present. For now, he had to come up with something – something that would dispel the idea of his marrying someone he loathed. If he went along with it, if he let the Oldbridges think he'd asked for Delilah's hand in marriage, then it would be real.

And yet, to call Delilah out, to show her as the liar she was, might prompt her to say something damning. If she revealed Nathan's secret, it would have far-reaching effects upon the entire family. Everyone bearing the Grier name would suffer. Matthew's political aspirations would be ruined, his children's prospects severely diminished. Mama's social status would crumble; she'd lose the donors her charities needed. Juliana's reputation, so firmly linked to his own, would collapse. Worst of all, Nathan could die.

Grasping for inspiration, some means by which to

avoid an intolerable outcome, he thought of coming up with an excuse to leave, buy himself some time to think.

Everyone stared at him, awaiting his response. He opened his mouth, prepared to say something yet still unsure what that something should be. "I—"

"She's absolutely correct," Nathan said, directing attention away from Grayson. "I've recently asked for Mrs. Newhurst's hand in marriage and she has accepted. The two of us are engaged to be married."

Grayson's jaw dropped. He turned to his brother but Nathan wasn't looking at him. He was smiling at Delilah with love in his eyes while she stared daggers at him in return.

"Did you not make that clear, my pet?" Nathan asked.

"I didn't believe it necessary," Delilah gritted.

Lady Oldbridge's expression softened a fraction. Relief filled her husband's face while Miss Howell herself sent Grayson a timid smile.

"I'm glad to have misunderstood the situation," said Lady Oldbridge. She raised her chin and gave Grayson a sharp look. "For a moment there I feared you might have broken the promise you made Edwina."

"I—"

"Instead, Lord Oldbridge and I shall look forward to another wedding announcement in the near future."

Holy hell.

Grayson fisted his hands and clenched his jaw while trying to think of some means by which to regain control of his life.

"A summer wedding would be ideal," Lady Oldbridge continued. "We'll host it at our home on Grosvenor Square so everyone who's in Town for the Season will have the chance to attend. There's plenty of space for a string quartet on the terrace and with the roses in bloom at that time of year it will make for such a romantic setting. As for the honeymoon—"

"My lady," Grayson said, his voice unavoidably harsh on account of the picture the viscountess painted. "I dare say your daughter and I will want a say in this matter."

"Oh, but of course." She stared at Grayson as though she'd forgotten who he might be for a second and then, without missing a beat, she turned to Nathan and Delilah. "Congratulations to you both. Engagements are such joyous occasions." Her husband and daughter seconded her remark while Grayson stood motionless in the middle of the room.

He couldn't quite grasp what had happened. A hasty decision on Nathan's part, to be sure, and a pickle Grayson would have to try and help him out of later. If doing so were even possible. Right. One problem at a time. He directed his attention toward Miss Howell. "Would you care to walk with me in the garden?"

CHAPTER FORTY

It had occurred to Grayson during Miss Howell's absence that his best course of action where she was concerned might be to appeal to her kindness.

Her face lit up in response to his question. "Indeed, I'd be happy to take a walk with you if Mama and Papa approve."

"Of course we approve," Lady Oldbridge exclaimed before her husband could get in a word. The poor man simply sighed and gave a weary nod.

Grayson pitied him. It couldn't be easy having a wife who was so domineering. At least Miss Howell didn't take after her mother. He held out his arm when she stood and together they quit the parlor. The rest of the party gradually followed.

"I've always considered you a lovely young woman," Grayson said, keeping his voice low as he and Miss Howell began their stroll along a path that would lead to the orchard. "You've a sweet disposition."

"Thank you, Mr. Grier."

Her tone was soft, her cheeks a deep shade of pink. Grayson recognized her as pretty, and yet her looks did not appeal to him. These days his preference lay toward black hair and more shapely curves.

Shoving that thought aside, he told Miss Howell, "I know your parents desire a match between us. Your mother has indicated to me that this is because of your own desire to wed me. Is that true?"

She glanced at him. A couple of finches darted past them, racing through the sky before coming to rest in a nearby tree. "Without question."

"May I ask what your motivation might be?"

Her eyes turned dreamy. "You're exceptionally good looking and charming."

It was as Grayson feared then. Hoping to dispel whatever romantic notions she might have crafted in her head, he said, "I'm four and twenty years older than you."

"I never consider the difference in age when I'm in your company."

"You've not spent a great deal of time in it," Grayson pointed out. "The truth is, I am a serious man, marked by war, death, and the duty that sits upon my shoulders. I have no interest in diversion. I fear you would be bored silly if you were to wed me. Hypothetically speaking," he hastened to add.

She sent him a wry smile. "If you imagine I'll need

entertainment or that I shall seek to host elaborate parties, then you are mistaken. My only interest is in you."

"I can't imagine why," he muttered.

"Isn't it obvious?" she asked. When he merely frowned she said, "I love you, Mr. Grier. I've done so since the very first moment I saw you."

"I beg your pardon?"

"I was twelve, I think, and you were riding past Oldbridge House just as I was returning from a walk with my governess. You looked like a prince, so handsome and dashing, with the afternoon sun glowing behind you. The smile you gave me while tipping your hat in my direction sent my heart flying, and that's when I knew. You, Mr. Grier, were the man I would grow up to marry, which is why I failed to make a success of my Seasons. Because there could be no one else. No other suitor lived up to your memory."

Strike that part about it being as he'd feared. This was worse. Much worse. The poor innocent girl had squandered her chance of marrying well because she'd held a false hope of becoming his wife. Good lord. "Do your parents know about this?"

"Of course." Something apologetic shone in her eyes. "I know Mama can be very insistent, but she's only trying to make me happy."

Grayson considered those words as the pair passed a flowerbed filled with hydrangeas not yet in bloom. He cleared his throat. "Has it not occurred to you that my interest might lie elsewhere?"

She gave him a smile, the disbelieving sort that suggested she thought he was jesting. "If it did, I'd imagine you would have acted upon it by now."

Her reasoning wasn't irrational. Still…

"Miss Howell. You have your entire life ahead of you yet. I would urge you, as a friend, not to waste your most precious years on a man who will only ever marry for love."

"But I do love you. I've said so just a few—"

"You mistake my meaning, Miss Howell. The thing of it is I would have to love you in return."

Her face fell. "Oh." She bit her lip, which had no effect upon him whatsoever. Not the way Olivia's doing so had. A frown followed before it suddenly cleared and her eyes brightened. "You could grow to love me. I'm certain of it if you'll simply give me the chance."

Grayson's heart ached for her. He knew what it meant to be young and deluded. Miss Howell didn't love him. How could she when she barely knew him?

Deciding to help her as best as he could, he said, "If you truly desire a love match, you'll want to take the following into consideration. It's important for you to be able to spend endless hours with your partner without ever tiring of their company. Your interests need not be the same, but you should be able to find joy in his while he should be equally able to find joy in yours. Compromise is imperative or one person is bound to feel like they're giving more than they are receiving."

She seemed to consider this for the next few paces

before eventually saying, "You've always struck me as sensible, dedicated, and kind. I'm sure I shan't regret marrying you for any reason. I'm also confident in my ability to be a wife you can be proud of."

He obviously wasn't getting through to her. Perhaps a firmer approach was required. "Miss Howell. The day will come when our difference in age will be hard to ignore. Imagine your life when you're five and forty and I am approaching my seventieth year. It's possible my health will be in decline while you remain strong and vibrant – eager to go out riding while I'll be unable. Have you considered what it will mean for you to have an ailing husband? I'll expect you to sit by my side and feed me broth. No visits with friends. No trips to Town for the Season. No stylish new gowns."

"We'd simply stay home and do nothing? But there is a chance you'll remain in good health well into your dotage," she said but her words were spoken with hesitance now, as though this had never occurred to her before.

"Are you acquainted with anyone over the age of seventy who doesn't struggle with their mobility, eyesight, hearing, or some other affliction?"

She bit her lip. "No."

"Were you and I to marry," Grayson pressed, "I fear you would sacrifice your happiness for mine, and that will not do. Instead, I recommend you set your sights on someone whose thoughts and passions align with your own.

"Let me ask you, for instance, to describe how I

made you feel when you took my arm and we started walking."

She gave her shoulder a slight shrug. "I'm not sure what you mean."

"Exactly." He forced himself to smile at her, to show her the same degree of kindness she'd offered him. "You deserve more than I shall ever be able to give you, Miss Howell. You deserve to want your husband with the same degree of hunger that he wants you. I mean, imagine climbing into bed with me."

"Mr. Grier." Miss Howell glanced around, a panicked look in her eyes. "How can you speak of such things?"

"I can assure you, if you truly desired to be my wife, you'd encourage me to say more on the matter, not less. But you're right, bringing it up was unforgivably inappropriate of me. I merely did it to prove a point."

"Which is?" she carefully asked.

"That you and I are ill–suited. You may think you love me, Miss Howell, but you don't."

"How can you say that when you are the only man I've ever considered taking to husband?"

The look in her eyes implored him to be direct. "Imagine if I were to die tomorrow."

She instantly paled. "Good grief, Mr. Grier. Are you unwell? Is there anything I should—"

"Calm yourself, Miss Howell. I'm perfectly well at the moment. I merely ask you to consider how you would receive the news of my sudden departure from this earth."

She slowed her pace. Heavy grooves creased her brow. And then she said. "I would be sad to hear it. And I would mourn you of course, for a respectable period."

"And that's how it should be. But if you truly loved me, you would be crushed, unable to carry on, wracked by sorrow and regret. Your life would never again be the same."

Concern strained her features. "I'm sorry, but I can't say I would experience what you describe. Oh, dear. How horrid of me to confess such a thing."

"Not at all. It simply proves that you are meant for someone else."

She blinked, too rapidly for Grayson's comfort. "But if I don't wed you, whom will I marry? I am twenty years of age, Mr. Grier, nearly on the shelf. To find the sort of match you speak of could take a long time and—"

"Allow me to help." What in the world was he doing? "How?"

Grayson cleared his throat and considered the lilacs growing nearby. "I'll, um...I'll host a ball."

Miss Howell's eyes lit up. "Truly?"

"Absolutely," Grayson said, warming to the idea. A ball could serve his own purpose too. "On the condition that you agree to dance with the gentlemen I introduce you to."

"Will they be handsome?"

It took a great deal of effort for him not to roll his eyes. He was tempted to tell her that looks weren't everything, that there were more important characteristics to consider. Instead he said, "Attraction is subjective. I cannot possibly know how you will find them, but I promise they'll all be suitable options for you to consider in marital terms."

She gave him a dubious look. "While that may be true, they won't be you."

Grayson considered his next words carefully. He had to convince her somehow. "Based on what you've said, regarding the first time you saw me, I suspect you've dreamt of a great romantic fairytale wedding for some time, Miss Howell. Is that correct?"

"It is," she admitted while blushing profusely and shying away from his gaze.

"Then you shall be disappointed if you and I marry, for that isn't something I can give you. But I can help you fulfill that dream with someone else."

"Do you truly think so?"

"I wouldn't suggest it otherwise."

Her lips twitched and she finally smiled. A nod followed. "Very well, Mr. Grier. I shall accept your assistance and...oh, what's that?"

Her question shook his mind free from the guest list he'd have to come up with. He dropped his gaze to the spot Miss Howell was pointing toward.

Hmm...

Lowering onto one knee, he reached beneath the hedge and retrieved a small wooden box. He frowned at the seesaw style lid a moment before peeking inside. The box was empty. "It looks like a mouse trap."

He returned the box to its spot and glanced up at Miss Howell.

"A trap intended to capture the creature alive?" Miss Howell smiled down at him. "How positively ingenious."

Grayson grinned at her. He managed to rise just as her parents reached them.

"Mama," Miss Howell said with excitement. "Mr. Grier will be hosting a ball. Isn't it marvelous?"

"An engagement ball, I trust?" Lady Oldbridge asked.

"Mama." Miss Howell glanced at Grayson before informing her parents. "I've had a change of heart. I'll not be marrying Mr. Grier after all. Indeed, I just refused his offer."

Shock descended on Grayson for the second time that day. First Nathan and now Miss Howell? It seemed surreal. One hour ago he'd been trapped by two women yet now he was totally free. He stared at Miss Howell, too afraid to utter one word. He'd known she was kind but this act of selflessness truly overwhelmed him considering he was the man she'd recently wished to marry.

"If this is because he desires the governess," Lady Oldbridge remarked as Nathan and Delilah drew nearer.

"Who desires the governess?" Delilah asked, revealing she was the only one who'd not been paying attention of late. Most likely because she'd been too caught up in her own scheming.

"Mr. Grier," Lady Oldbridge said as if this discussion were perfectly normal. And then, "I cannot believe you haven't noticed the way his attention wanders whenever Miss Poole is near."

Grayson groaned. Despite his oncoming headache he opened his mouth, prepared to deny the accusation.

Before he could utter one word however, Delilah said, "How positively scandalous."

"I heartily agree," Lady Oldbridge said. She raised her chin while giving Grayson a forceful look of disapproval.

At which point he squared his shoulders and told both women sternly, "I urge you to avoid any mention of this to anyone lest it lead to a negative impact upon yourselves. You want your daughter to make a fine match, Lady Oldbridge. A task I am prepared to help with though one I daresay shan't be successful if rumor has it I've taken advantage of one of my servants. And you, Delilah. Do you truly want your future brother–in–law to be a man of ill–repute? Just take a moment to consider how that will affect you."

"And if that's not enough to sway you, my dear," Nathan said, "you ought to know that we'll be reliant upon Grayson's generosity regarding our allowance."

Delilah clamped her mouth shut while giving Grayson the sort of obstinate look that finally hinted at why she'd sought to entice him into marriage. The woman was clearly desperate. He couldn't help but wonder why. But that didn't stop him from finding some satisfaction in having the tables turned.

Miss Howell took her mother's arm. "Mama, please don't press the issue."

"We've never actually seen him act inappropriately," Lord Oldbridge said, stepping into the conversation for the first time.

"I suppose not," Lady Oldbridge muttered after what seemed like a great deal of contemplation.

"And since I shan't be marrying him," Miss Howell added, "I'd really like for us to attend the ball he's agreed to host."

Lady Oldbridge met her daughter's gaze squarely. "As your mother, it is my duty to guide you and offer advice when needed. Which it clearly is now. Please, take a moment to reconsider Mr. Grier's offer, Edwina. It's what you've always wanted, what you've dreamed of, and what we have worked toward for so long."

"I know, Mama, but the thing of it is, I no longer wish to be his wife." When Lady Oldbridge stared at her daughter as though she'd gone mad, Miss Howell added, "Upon further reflection, I don't believe he'll make me happy."

"But—"

"Don't worry, Mama. I'll make a different match – perhaps even a better one now that I'm open to other options."

"Are you absolutely certain?" Lady Oldbridge asked her daughter while giving her a skeptical look.

"Perfectly so," Miss Howell declared.

Lord Oldbridge shook his head and muttered something about the confounding whims of women.

Grayson glanced toward the house. A footman wielding a basket of firewood leapt into motion and hurried toward the steps when Grayson's gaze found him. Dismissing him from his mind, Grayson began making mental notes regarding the ball he'd promised. Considering what Miss Howell had just done for him, he could not let her down.

CHAPTER FORTY-ONE

N umbed by what she'd just witnessed, Olivia
stepped back from the window and took a sharp
breath. There could be no disputing that Grayson had
made Miss Howell an offer outside in the garden. He'd
been down on bended knee, gazing up at her while she
smiled at him.

Olivia pressed her hand to her mouth and swallowed a sob. Her heart might as well have been ripped
from her breast. Not even a day had passed since she'd
given herself to him on the roof, and now this. Her eyes
stung at the memory of what he'd once said.

I hold you in the highest esteem.

How could he when he so easily bedded her one
moment only to ask another woman to be his wife in
the next? It went against everything she'd believed
him capable of, revealing him to be the sort of man
who took a woman's virtue without second thought

while whispering all manner of sweet things in her ear.

Never in her life had she felt so betrayed and yet…

What on earth had she been thinking? That Mr. Grier would remain unmarried forever – that this strange relationship of theirs would go on indefinitely? That giving herself to him would remove the threats he faced and convince him to wed her instead? That somehow she would miraculously be worthy of him in the eyes of society?

Of course not. To imagine as much would be ridiculous.

Truthfully, she had no reason to be upset, no right to feel as though she'd been denied the man she wanted when she'd always known he could never be hers.

Men like Mr. Grier were born to marry women like Miss Howell. It was expected and fitting.

"That doesn't mean I don't hate it," Olivia told the empty conservatory.

The very idea of watching him marry another woman would probably kill her.

Which gave her no choice but to go. Pack her bags and run, leave Sutton Hall behind for good and never think of Grayson again.

A pitiful laugh rose in her throat. How naïve of her to suppose such a thing might be possible when he'd marked a place deep inside her. There would be no forgetting him or Juliana, but hopefully, with time, she'd manage to move on. Just as she'd done after Agnes had died.

Grayson couldn't wait to find Olivia, but first, he needed to speak with Nathan.

"I've been thinking of how best to get you out of this mess," he said as soon as dinner was over and they were alone in the library. A cozy fire burned in the grate.

"And what mess would that be?" Nathan asked, a teasing twinkle in his bright eyes. Leaning back in his seat, he set his glass of brandy to his lips and drank while waiting for Grayson's response.

"Your engagement to Delilah," Grayson said. "What else?"

Nathan put his glass aside slowly. "What makes you think I want to get out of it?"

"Nathan, you can't be serious. I mean...don't you want to...that is to say..." Grayson scrubbed one hand over his face. The subject in question was deuced uncomfortable, but he was determined to address it regardless. Only to have his words fail him.

"It never truly occurred to me how difficult life must be for you, always worrying over those nearest and dearest," Nathan murmured. "Rest assured, brother, I've made my own bed and am more than ready to lie in it. You needn't trouble yourself where I'm concerned. Hell, I think you've got enough on your mind as it is."

"Telling me not to worry doesn't mean I won't," Grayson said. He drummed his fingers against his crystal tumbler. "Delilah is a scheming liar. You cannot honestly want her as your wife."

Nathan produced a dry chuckle. "It's not as though I'll want another woman in future, so it might as well be her given what both of us stand to gain if I wed her."

Understanding dawned. "She'll be forced into silence."

"Indeed."

Grayson hated the sacrifice Nathan was making. All because of Delilah's threats. He shook his head. "We could blackmail her in return."

"A fine suggestion if we had something equally damning on her."

"We could reveal her unfaithfulness to her husband."

Nathan gave Grayson the dubious look such a foolish suggestion warranted. "Nobody will care and Delilah knows this. With her husband dead and her indiscretions behind her, what does it matter?"

"I doubt if they're all behind her," Grayson muttered. "Knowing her, she probably left several lovers in London when she chose to come here."

A brief silence followed that comment before Nathan said, "You're not wrong."

"What?"

Nathan tilted his head. He took a deep breath as if trying to harness the strength required to speak before he revealed, "She's increasing."

Grayson stared at his brother, his mouth wide open in shock. "You have got to be joking."

"I found out while we were away in Taunton. That was her reason for trying to re–kindle things with you. We had a row, you see, and she let it slip."

"Nathan." Grayson blinked while he tried to come to terms with what he'd just learned. "You cannot mean to spend the rest of your days with her. You'll be miserable."

To Grayson's surprise, Nathan grinned with genuine humor. "On the contrary, dear brother, I daresay I shall be perfectly satisfied."

"How can you possibly say that when—"

"This is my chance to have a child, Grayson."

"Another man's child," Grayson reminded him. "And at what cost?"

Nathan stretched out his legs and crossed them at the ankles. "Stop fretting about me."

"That's easier said than done," Grayson muttered.

"It's not like I would ever be able to marry for love anyway." Nathan pointed this out with an annoying degree of practicality. "At least this way I'll have a son or daughter to dote on. In truth, I daresay we'll all be quite content."

Grayson held Nathan's gaze. "I wish with all my heart you could live the life of your choosing."

Nathan expelled a hard breath and relaxed against his seat. "By marrying Delilah I'll have the next best thing – the illusion of being like everyone else. Delilah and I have already discussed the matter. It actually helps that she knows the truth because it allows for a certain clarity I would have been denied otherwise."

"So what's the plan?" Grayson asked even though he knew he was probably overstepping in light of the subject at hand.

"Are you certain your delicate constitution can handle the truth?" Nathan took a slow sip of his brandy. When Grayson nodded he said, "I shall have my valet and she shall have whomever she chooses."

"Your valet?" Grayson choked, his face turning hot.

"Henry and I have been together for almost a year."

"Good God. You're practically..." Grayson waved his hand about in a helpless attempt at finding the words he required. Failing, he asked, "Why haven't you said anything?"

Nathan sent him a disbelieving look. "It's not exactly the sort of thing one bandies about. However, it does mean I'm able to sympathize with you. There's little worse than having to sneak about with the person one loves, of not being able to step out with them in public, but at least you've one advantage I'll never have. You shan't be sentenced to death if you're caught kissing Miss Poole."

Grayson slumped, nearly spilling his drink. "Nathan, I—"

"Stop it. Stop trying to fix everything all the time. You went to war, men died, a close friend of yours included. Nothing you do will ever bring him or Papa back. You can work yourself to death trying to make up for all the guilt you carry, and miss out on life in the process."

"I have a duty," Grayson said, annoyed by how blasé Nathan was being.

"Everyone does in some form or other, but there's also a truth that you've been ignoring."

"And what would that be?"

"That your tenants are happy. That Juliana's education is coming along splendidly. That Mama, Matthew, and I are all provided for thanks to your hard work and lucrative investments. You've already done what you set out to do. It's time for you to put yourself first."

"Not until Juliana has—"

"Now, Grayson. Before it's too late." When Grayson kept silent, Nathan added, "I suspect I know what you feel for Miss Poole, and if I'm correct, you'd be a fool to let problems that only exist in your own head interfere with this rare chance at a love match."

"You make it sound so simple."

"Good." Nathan's lips stretched into a wide grin. "Because the biggest obstacle in your path has always been yourself."

Nathan's words stuck with Grayson. He pondered them long after the two men parted ways. However difficult his decision, it was nothing compared with the hardship his brother went through every day. Lord help him, he couldn't imagine what it must be like, hiding his true self behind a façade, keeping his feelings for Henry a secret, living in fear of discovery.

By comparison, Grayson's concerns seemed laughable. Although to be fair, worrying over Juliana and how his actions would affect her held merit. But what if he was exaggerating the issue? Olivia was his servant, yes, but she was also a respectable woman – a vicar's daughter. And maybe with his mother's assistance...

Grayson held his breath as the very solution he

needed popped into his head. Why the hell hadn't he thought of this sooner?

Excited by the prospect of setting everything to rights and claiming the future he wanted, he spun on his heels and went in search of Nathan once more.

Finding him on the terrace with Delilah he told them both, "Pack your things. We're leaving for London tomorrow."

CHAPTER FORTY-TWO

O ne of Olivia's greatest regrets was the price Juliana would have to pay when she left. The girl didn't deserve having a new governess foisted upon her. Olivia had spent several hours considering this, wondering if perhaps there was some way for her to stay, to sacrifice her own happiness for the sake of the girl.

Eventually, she'd realized that doing so wouldn't be possible. Not when she knew her feelings could not be pushed aside or ignored. They would fill every aspect of her life for the foreseeable future, preventing her from being the governess Juliana deserved.

It was therefore with a heavy heart that she penned a letter to bid her farewell and wish her luck with the future. "Please believe me when I tell you that you are ready to take on the world," she assured her in the note. "I am so proud of what you've accomplished and of the woman I know you will become."

Her letter to Grayson was harder to write, but after five attempts, she managed to get it done. Swiping tears from her eyes, she folded it and placed it on top of the one for Juliana.

Determined to carry on, she got up. The tray she'd brought to her room sat on her bad, the meal on her plate almost untouched. She'd had no desire to socialize tonight, less so when she'd heard the other servants talking about the engagement.

So she'd claimed a headache and retreated, but that didn't mean she didn't have plans for the evening. With everything already packed and the letters ready to be delivered come morning, she quit her bedchamber and walked the short distance to Grayson's.

Reaching his door, she paused for a moment. Could she do this? Was it right? He'd made his choice and it wasn't her. Then again, she'd known it never could be. He would marry Miss Howell, share his life with her, but until he spoke his vows he remained a free man. And because Olivia desperately wanted a chance to say goodbye on her terms, to embrace the finality with all the love she harbored for him, she accepted this justification and let herself into his room.

The space lit up in response to the oil lamp she'd brought, revealing a solid four poster bed placed squarely in the center. A wide armchair stood near the fireplace, a blanket flung over one armrest. There was a round table next to it with an unlit oil lamp, a carafe, and a glass placed upon it. Velvet curtains, already closed, hung in thick folds to block out the world.

It was an orderly room devoid of clutter. Despite Grayson not having a valet for assistance, his clothes were not strewn about, his shaving utensils neatly placed on a shelf above his washstand.

Olivia soaked up every detail, mapping each corner while letting her fingertips memorize all the textures. Polished wood, smooth silk, and glazed porcelain were packed away in her mind for later, along with the plush comfort of the armchair and the slight itchiness of the wool blanket.

As soon as she was satisfied she would be able to visualize everything later upon demand, she undressed, climbed into Grayson's bed, and sought comfort in his scent, which lingered on the pillow. She'd no idea how long she waited before he arrived.

Half an hour? More? It didn't matter.

He froze as soon as he entered the room and quickly shut the door, his eyes widening with dismay when she rose up onto one arm, allowing the bed sheet to slip to her waist.

"Olivia." Desire roughened his voice. "I've been trying to find you."

She'd suspected he might so she'd made herself scarce, fearing she'd burst into tears if she saw him before she conquered her emotions. When they met, she wanted to be in control.

"Congratulations on the engagement." She was

grateful for the strength with which she delivered the words.

"You know?" He looked surprised but must have decided a servant had heard and passed on the information, for he immediately added, "Then you understand why I must go to London at once and inform my mother?"

He was already shucking his jacket. Olivia watched it fly across the room and land in a heap.

"Yes," she said, forcing her attention to his cravat as he untied this next. Anything to distract her from the loss infecting her veins.

The length of linen came away from his neck and flittered toward the floor. "When do you leave?" she asked.

"At dawn."

"I see." She'd thought to be on her way before he woke, but this was even better. By leaving later, she'd ensure he would not follow.

"Don't fret," he whispered, closing the distance to brush his fingers across her cheek. "When I return, you and I will discuss our future together. I promise."

A future in which Miss Howell became the mistress of Sutton Hall while Olivia lived as Grayson's mistress – a shameful secret for him to visit whenever his fancy struck.

No. Not in this lifetime.

Without offering him a response, Olivia rose onto her knees, bracing them slightly apart as she faced him.

His gaze darkened. "I'm impressed by how quickly you've mastered the art of seduction."

Burying her pain, Olivia forced a smile to her lips and reached for the buttons securing his waistcoat. Five minutes later, he tumbled onto the bed, rolling her over while kissing her with abandon.

Intent on making this memorable for him, of ensuring he'd never forget her, she maneuvered herself between his thighs and proceeded to taste every inch of his perfectly toned body. A kiss right over his heart for bearing her set–downs, one to his stomach for helping her with her list, another against his hip for sharing himself with her.

"Dear God," he moaned while clutching the sheets. "Olivia. You really don't have to…ah…bloody hell."

Oh, but she did, and the fact that he fisted his hands in her hair would suggest he didn't quite want her to stop. So she focused on branding him in this way – in a way she doubted the proper Miss Howell would ever do. Until he caught her under her arms and tumbled her sideways.

He landed upon her before she could register what had occurred, his mouth meeting hers as he suddenly claimed her. The hunger she'd stoked in him was evidenced in his tight movements, the rapid flexing of muscle, and harsh exhalations. This wasn't anything like the sweet seduction she'd known last night, but rather a primitive taking – precisely what Olivia needed in order to deal with the hurt.

It was depleting, both physically and emotionally,

and as soon as it was done, Grayson collapsed. He muttered something, words Olivia couldn't discern, and then his breathing eased as he drifted off to sleep.

Olivia took a moment to savor his warmth, to luxuriate in the intimacy of the moment. She took a deep breath and expelled it, then slipped from the bed and dressed, his gentle snoring accompanying her movements.

On her way to the door she paused to consider the long length of linen haphazardly lying on the floor – his cravat. Swallowing past a tight knot in her throat, she stooped to pick it up, then gave his sleeping form one final look before exiting the room.

Philip Dover stuck to a moderate pace while escorting Mary back to Sutton Hall. After seeing Mr. Grier, his brother, and Mrs. Newhurst off, they'd escaped to the woods for a brief reprieve. The morning air was fresh with the promise of afternoon warmth – perfect for picking mushrooms with a marvelous woman.

Chuffed, he tightened his hold on her arm, drawing her closer to his side. If only they could delay their return a while longer, pretend the future was still as bright as it had been before Roger burst into the kitchen yesterday afternoon to inform them that Mr. Grier had proposed to Miss Howell.

Later, Betsy had told them of Mr. Nathaniel's engagement to Mrs. Newhurst.

"I suppose we ought to prepare ourselves for the inevitable," Mary said, putting words to Philip's very own thoughts.

He sighed. "I know you hoped for a different outcome. I did too, but at least Miss Howell is pleasant. I'm sure she'll make a fine mistress."

"I suppose," Mary agreed, "but that doesn't mean she's right for Mr. Grier."

"No, but he's made his decision and we must respect that."

Neither said anything further as they arrived at the service entrance. Philip opened the door for Mary and followed her into the hallway. An earthy aroma of newly collected herbs wafted toward them, mingling with the scent of recently scrubbed floors.

After they delivered the basket of mushrooms they'd collected to Mrs. Bradley, Mary turned to him. "I don't suppose you might delay your duties another ten minutes for a quick cup of tea?"

"I'd be happy to." An extra ten minutes with Mary was much preferred to supervising the footmen polishing the windows.

He followed her to her sitting room and waited for her to open the door.

"Oh." Mary stopped in the doorway while Miss Poole, who'd apparently been waiting for her return, leapt to her feet.

"Forgive the intrusion," said Miss Poole. Her face was set in grave lines and the shadows beneath her eyes suggested she'd not slept well, if at all.

"There's nothing to forgive," Mary assured her as she entered the room.

"Perhaps I should come back later," Philip said. He took a step back, prepared to leave the women to their conversation though he regretted giving up those additional minutes he'd hoped to spend with Mary.

"Please stay," Miss Poole said. "You've both been so kind to me during my time here, it only seems fitting."

Philip hesitated briefly. There was something in Miss Poole's voice – a slight catch – that filled him with a sense of foreboding. Nevertheless, he shut the door, briefly noting the hinges needed oiling, and encouraged her to proceed.

"I've come to offer my resignation and to—" Miss Poole swallowed while fidgeting with her hands "— collect my outstanding pay. If possible."

"You wish to leave us?" Mary could not have sounded more surprised or more deflated.

"Yes."

"But…what of Miss Edwards?"

"She's more than prepared to make her entrance into Society." Miss Poole met their gazes unblinking, as though she'd put a mask in place and meant to keep it there. "As a lady who made her own debut a few years ago and Mr. Grier's future wife, Miss Howell, I'm sure, will not only sponsor Miss Edwards but will also offer any additional advice she may need."

"You're leaving because of her, aren't you?" Philip hadn't intended to speak the question out loud and yet, he had.

"My reason for leaving is of a personal nature. I will not say more on the matter, just that I must go and that I hope you will both respect this decision."

"Of course." Mary sent Philip a look that seemed to implore him to do something. But what could he do? If Mr. Grier was set on wedding Miss Howell, what did it matter if he and Mary believed he'd be better off with Miss Poole?

"We're sorry it's come to this," he said, hoping his words would offer some consolation.

"Thank you." Miss Poole managed a smile that didn't quite reach her eyes. "I appreciate your saying so more than words can express."

CHAPTER FORTY-THREE

"I can visit the *Mayfair Chronicle* to have our wedding announcement posted while you see the archbishop about the special license," Delilah told Nathan while the carriage tumbled along the country road.

Grayson bit back a curse and glanced at Henry, who sat beside Nathan across from Grayson and Delilah, just in time to catch him rolling his eyes. They were only one hour into their journey and already Delilah had spoken of plans to host an engagement party, select floral arrangements, as well as her idea to have several wedding gowns ordered since she would be hard pressed to pick only one design, and, of course, the food.

At least her latest comment addressed the decision she and Nathan had made to get married quickly for the sake of the baby.

However…

"We'll not be in London more than a day or two at most," Grayson said. "The sole purpose of this trip is to gain Mama's support. Once this has been done, the special licenses and wedding announcements may be seen to in short order before we return to Sutton Hall."

"But what about all the shopping I plan to do?" Delilah asked.

"We're not going to London to shop," Grayson informed her.

She huffed. "Why make me come then?"

"Because," Grayson said, "I would not dare leave you to your own devices. You'll remain under Nathan's, Henry's, or my supervision until you've spoken your vows."

"Well." She shifted in her seat. "Just so you know, I'm actually rather pleased with how everything has worked out."

"You are?" Grayson asked, surprised.

"Certainly. I mean, I wasn't trying to marry you because I loved you, Grayson."

"I am aware."

"Indeed, I wish I'd have thought to suggest a union with Nathan right from the start. In hindsight, it does make more sense, seeing as it serves everyone's purpose."

Nathan smiled at Delilah. "Quite right, my dear. I'm sure the three of us and whoever you choose to include at your leisure will be quite happy together."

It didn't escape Grayson's notice when Nathan

allowed his hand to brush Henry's or the fact that Henry blushed. Made slightly uneasy by it, Grayson gave his attention to the view. He'd no desire to ponder the intricacy of two men being lovers, but it did please him to know that they'd found a way to make their relationship work. If only behind closed doors.

Thankfully, Delilah soon fell asleep, allowing him to enjoy some proper conversation with Nathan and Henry. When Delilah awoke, Grayson took his nap, permitting him to reach London without having to pay her too much more attention.

They pulled up to his townhouse where they were greeted by Aldwin, his London butler. At ten o'clock in the evening it was too late to visit his mother. Instead, Grayson stopped by his club to find out if his friends, James and Colin, might be in Town. As it turned out, both had been spotted in recent days, so Grayson sent them a couple of missives in the morning before heading over to Grosvenor Square with Nathan.

"Mama," Grayson said when he entered the parlor and spotted her. She was holding a watering can and fussing about some potted plant on the window sill. He opened his mouth, prepared to launch into the explanation of why he was here, then recalled his previous visit and paused. Clearing his throat, he moved toward her and dropped a kiss on her cheek. "You look lovely this morning. That, um, color suits you extremely well."

"It's good to see you too, Grayson." She glanced past him and reached for Nathan's hand. "And you, Nathan, though I doubt you're here to marvel at my choice in clothes."

Grayson frowned while Nathan raised their mother's hand to his lips for a gallant show of affection. "Quite right. The fact is...Well, I suppose I should start with Miss Poole, or would it be best to begin with Miss Howell? Nathan, why don't you take the lead?"

Good God, it was hot in here. His cravat was uncomfortably tight all of a sudden. Needing to move, he paced the length of the room.

Mama sent Grayson a hesitant look then turned to Nathan. "I've never seen him so agitated before. What's happened?"

"You may want to sit, Mama." Nathan gestured toward the settee. "I'll ring for some tea."

The tea arrived soon enough along with a plate of lovely biscuits. Grayson walked to the fireplace while Mama filled three cups. He crossed his arms, uncrossed them again, and fiddled with a porcelain dog while trying to put his thoughts in order. He desperately needed Mama to agree with his plan and offer her help.

"I suppose I should start by mentioning Paris and—"

"No, no," Grayson said, turning sharply to face his brother. Both he and Mama froze, their teacups raised as though both had been about to take a sip. "There's no need to make this story longer than necessary, Nathan. Suffice it to say, he's to be married, Mama."

Mama's mouth fell open as she lost her grip on her teacup. The fine piece of porcelain fell to the floor, spilling its contents. Much to Grayson's surprise, it remained intact, cushioned by the plush silk carpet.

"You cannot be serious," Mama said, finding her tongue as Grayson and Nathan both leapt to clean up the mess. "To whom?"

"To Mrs. Newhurst," Nathan informed her while dabbing the carpet with his napkin.

"Mrs. Newhurst?" Mama's eyes widened. "Is she not a...um...former acquaintance of yours, Grayson? As I recall, you introduced her to me and your father once when we happened upon the two of you in the park."

"Yes. Well. That was a long time ago." Heat flooded Grayson's face while the old familiar guilt returned to gnaw at his conscience. "She is now Nathan's fiancée."

"But...does she know what marrying you will entail, Nathan?"

"Yes, Mama. She does." Nathan returned to his seat while Grayson set Mama's cup back on its saucer.

"And she is all right with having a husband who will not...I mean to say who cannot...I mean..." She waved one hand as though trying to put off a swarm of flies. "Oh, you know very well what I mean."

Nathan pressed his lips together as though attempting a serious mien, but his eyes danced with laughter. Suppressing a groan, Grayson removed himself to one of his mother's armchairs, an ornate piece upholstered in tasteful cream silk.

"I believe Mrs. Newhurst and I shall get along splendidly," Nathan informed Mama. "My intention is to secure a special license while in Town. It's important I make her my wife at the first opportunity, seeing as she is increasing."

"Good lord." Mama sank against the back of her chair. "Dare I even ask how that's possible?"

"The child isn't mine," Nathan explained while Grayson wished himself a thousand miles away. He was rather impressed by how calmly his brother was handling the subject, seeing as he himself felt as though he might need smelling salts soon. And then Nathan gave Mama a direct look and told her bluntly, "Mrs. Newhurst and I have made an arrangement."

Mama immediately straightened. "I see."

Grayson frowned. Did she really? He seriously doubted his mother could even begin to imagine the life Nathan planned to lead with Delilah as his wife.

"But enough about me," Nathan said, sending a jolt through Grayson. "I am not the only one with wedding vows on his mind."

It took a split second for that to sink in before Mama's gaze found Grayson. Joy filled her eyes in a way he'd not seen in years, not since before Papa died. "Is that true?"

"It is," Grayson told her. He sent Nathan a hesitant glance before giving Mama his full attention. "I've met someone – the most wonderful woman in all the world —and I...I love her, Mama. I love her desperately and want more than anything for her to be my wife."

Mama tilted her head and studied him with sharp-eyed precision. "And who, pray tell, is this marvelous creature who's managed to do the impossible?"

"She's, um," Grayson swallowed, took a deep breath, and forced himself to tell her, "Juliana's governess."

Mama blinked. For a second Grayson feared she might have a stroke. But then she asked, with the sort of drawn out exaggeration suggesting her patience was being severely tested, "Does she have a name, Grayson?"

"Oh. Yes. Miss Poole. Olivia Poole, that is." Nathan snorted as though he were choking on laughter. Grayson sent him a scathing look which didn't seem to help in the slightest. "She's a vicar's daughter, though her parents are both dead."

"Does she have connections?" Mama asked. A delicate frown had appeared on the bridge of her nose.

"No. She was forced into service as a means of survival but she is..." He tried to think of the right word to use and found himself struggling to do Olivia justice. Eventually he settled on, "Extraordinarily brilliant."

"She's fluent in French, German, and Latin," Nathan said. "In fact, I dare anyone to find a woman more educated than she in Society."

"Really?" Mama seemed to consider this piece of information with great interest.

"She's a survivor, Mama," Grayson added.

"But she's also a servant," Mama pointed out. "People will probably talk, if only to wonder how your romance came about. They may even think she took advantage of her position. After all, you would be providing substance to every upper-class lady's fear of her husband's being tempted by the governess."

"And that is without worrying how all of this will affect Juliana," Grayson murmured. He eyed his mother, noted the look of interest in her eyes, and dared to say, "I realize you have no wish to return to Sutton Hall and that you are also incredibly busy with all your charitable projects, but if you could—"

"Yes." Mama gave a firm nod. "I'll do it."

"But I've not even told you what 'it' is," Grayson said.

"Might I assume it involves bringing Juliana to London to live with me? Of putting some distance between the two of you for the foreseeable future?"

"She's remarkably clever, our mama," Nathan said, munching on a biscuit.

"Frighteningly so," Grayson agreed. He nodded. "Do you think it would work?"

"I do," Mama assured him. "Provided you sack Miss Poole before you ask for her hand in marriage."

"Sack her?" Although Grayson knew Olivia's position would change the moment she became his wife, he'd not envisioned dismissing her first.

"So she's no longer in your employ," Mama explained as though he were daft. "That is the main issue here, is it not? Wedding a servant would be improper, but wedding a vicar's respectable daughter, well, that's rather beatific really. Wouldn't you say?"

Grayson allowed a slow smile as happiness stole into his heart. "Yes. Yes I would."

CHAPTER FORTY-FOUR

Although the weather was in Olivia's favor when she left Sutton Hall, so much warmer and brighter than what it had been upon her arrival, a storm brewed in her breast. Clutching her bag as though it were a lifeline, she'd walked the tree–lined driveway toward the main road, unable to breathe past the massive knot in her throat.

Tears streamed down her cheeks when she stopped and turned for one final glimpse of the sprawling estate. When she'd first seen it, the building had been nothing more than an architectural splendor of carefully placed stone. Now it had been filled with happy experiences, wonderful memories, and love.

Love.

She'd nearly choked in response to that word and what it now meant. Once, not too long ago, her heart had been filled by Agnes. Now it contained Juliana, Nathaniel, and Grayson, as well as all of the Sutton Hall servants. In some ways, this love was worse for it was within her grasp and yet, she could not accept it, could not bear the suffering she would endure when she saw Grayson with Miss Howell and any children the pair might have.

The very idea had already crushed her heart.

So she'd turned away, forced one foot in front of the other until she'd arrived in Varney. And then she'd boarded the first coach out of town, finding some solace in knowing that even though she felt her life was over, she would move on. She had to, not just for Agnes this time but for herself.

Grayson was beyond thrilled by the time he returned to Sutton Hall. In the space of three days he'd gone to London, obtained his mother's cooperation, secured two special licenses – one for Nathan and one for himself – plus seen his friends. He grinned as he remembered James. It was remarkable how much their lives had changed since the last time they'd met. Despite James's adamant disapproval of Mrs. Lawson—which the divorced Mrs. Hewitt now called herself—the man had become as smitten with her as Grayson was with Olivia. All that remained was for Colin to meet his match.

"The ball you intend to host had better make up for

this trip," Delilah said as the carriage approached the Sutton Hall driveway. She shifted in her seat. "I've never heard of anyone leaving Town at the crack of dawn to travel for twelve hours straight without stopping for proper meals."

"Time was of the essence," Grayson informed her, excitement brimming inside him. He'd soon declare himself to Olivia. He'd whisk her away to some private corner, outside perhaps? And then he'd tell her his plan and how all would be well in the end and...

She would agree, would she not?

He shot a desperate look at Nathan who instantly straightened. "What?"

Grayson shook his head. He couldn't voice his concern with Delilah present, but the fact was he'd taken Olivia's innocence without properly discussing the implications with her. All he'd said was that she should consider them, but that had been before, when they'd both known he might not be able to wed her.

And later, after the fact, when he realized he loved her and would do what he could to secure her hand in marriage, he'd not really made himself clear. Because he'd not wanted to raise her hopes in case he failed.

"Grayson?" Nathan's voice prodded while Henry feigned deafness by turning to stare out the window.

"It just occurred to me," Grayson said. "I'm not sure Miss Poole knows how I feel."

A long moment of silence followed, interrupted only by the sound of the carriage tumbling along.

"Are you honestly telling me," Nathan slowly asked,

"that you've not told the woman you want to marry how much you love her?"

Delilah gasped.

Grayson shook his head. "There were you and Delilah, Lord and Lady Oldbridge, Miss Howell, my worry for Juliana and I...I think it may have slipped my mind."

Nathan's jaw dropped while Delilah snickered.

"Prepare to grovel," Nathan told him. "A lot."

Grayson stared at him but all he could think of was Olivia and how incredibly stupid he'd been not to share his thoughts and feelings with her. But he'd been distracted the last time he'd seen her and then he'd fallen asleep. When he'd woken she had been gone, back to her own bedchamber, and he'd set off without further ado.

Damn.

He leapt from the carriage as soon as it came to a halt and raced up the front steps, bursting into the foyer and nearly toppling Dover who'd come to open the door.

"Where is she?" Grayson asked, searching the foyer as though expecting to find her there. His gaze landed on the table and his heart immediately stuttered as dread crept into his bones. There were no flowers, not even a vase.

"Miss Edwards?" Dover asked. "She is in—"

"Miss Poole," Grayson blurted, turning to face the butler while hoping, praying, the void he felt was simply a trick of the mind – the product of his own fears.

"I cannot say," Dover told him, the hint of regret about his eyes like a spear to Grayson's heart.

He shook his head, vaguely aware of Nathan and Delilah entering the foyer. "Then we must ask Mrs. Hodgins."

"If I may speak out of turn, sir?" Dover's voice was annoyingly calm. It clashed with the turbulence whipping through him. Hands balled into fists, he gave a swift nod. "Miss Poole's decision to leave surprised us. I also believe it affected Miss Edwards greatly. Perhaps it would behoove you to meet with her first?"

"Right. Yes. Of course." He tried to breathe, to force some much-needed air into his lungs. "Fetch Mrs. Hodgins and meet me in the parlor."

Heart thumping, Grayson went to find Juliana. The girl was in her room, stretched out on her bed, staring up at the ceiling. She didn't so much as flinch when Grayson walked in.

"Juliana?"

"Yes?" She didn't glance at him.

"Are you all right?" He moved a bit closer.

"She didn't even say goodbye. All she left was a stupid note."

Grayson's breath caught. "A note?"

"I thought she was happy here but—" She suddenly sat and glared at him as though he were the vilest person she'd ever met. "I've turned this over a great deal, Grayson. You take off for London and then Miss Poole leaves? Without a word of explanation?"

"I…" He took a step back, startled by the anger snapping in her eyes.

"What did you do?"

"I can explain." He glanced around, desperately seeking something. "The note she left you. Where is it?"

"Why?"

"Because I'm looking for clues as to where she might be." When Juliana merely narrowed her gaze, Grayson explained, "I need to find her, Juliana. So I can ask her to be my wife although that will mean—"

The air was knocked from his chest by Juliana, who'd launched herself into his arms. And then she hit him. "You beast. Why didn't you say something sooner?"

"That is indeed an excellent question." One he would no doubt ponder for years to come.

Juliana rolled her eyes and collected a folded piece of paper. "Here. There's not much to go on."

Grayson accepted the note and scanned it on his way out the door.

Dear Juliana,

It pains me to tell you I must leave, but as you well know, a governess's position is fleeting. Please believe me when I tell you that you are ready to take on the world. I am so proud of what you've accomplished and of the woman I know you will become. And since I detest the permanence of goodbyes, I prefer to say, au revoir.

With fondness,
Olivia.

Juliana followed Grayson and together they went to meet Dover, Mrs. Hodgins, Nathan, and Delilah in the parlor.

Dover handed Grayson another piece of folded paper upon his arrival. "She left this for you in your study, sir."

Grayson took it and read the few lines.

My Dearest Grayson,

Meeting you changed my life. The months I've spent with you here at Sutton Hall have been a most wonderful gift. Thank you for the friendship you offered, for the understanding you've shown Miss Edwards, and most of all, for helping me keep the promise I made my sister.

You are the best man I've ever known and I shall miss you greatly.

Affectionately yours,
Olivia.

Grayson stared at the words until they blurred. It felt like someone was gripping his throat. And then, to his absolute horror, something wet slid over his cheek. Good God. Was he actually weeping?

Dipping his head, he closed his eyes and fought for control. He needed to think, to figure out what to do, not fall apart. A handkerchief materialized before him and he snatched it, gave his face a good dab, and tested his throat with a cough.

When he looked up, he saw that all eyes were

trained anywhere but on him. Enough of this. He needed to act. "Mrs. Hodgins. Did Miss Poole meet with you before leaving?"

"She did. I paid her what she was owed and wrote a letter of character for her."

"And during this conversation," Grayson pressed, "did she at any point mention where she might be planning to go?"

"No, sir. I did ask, but she wasn't very forthcoming. In fact, the only thing Mr. Dover and I were able to discern was her reason for seeking employment elsewhere."

"She was unhappy," Grayson muttered. And he was to blame.

"I fear it's worse than that," Mrs. Hodgins told him. She sent Mr. Dover a hasty glance.

Grayson shifted his gaze to the butler just in time to catch the quick shake of his head. He stood. "What is it, Dover?"

"Nothing, sir."

"I dare say I'll be the judge of that," Grayson informed him. "Out with it."

Dover stiffened in response to the obvious reprimand but kept his chin up. "Begging your pardon, sir, but we were all surprised to learn of your marital plans."

"I dare say Miss Poole took it harder than anyone else," Mrs. Hodgins piped in.

Grayson froze. "Marital plans?"

"You did propose to Miss Howell, did you not?" asked Mrs. Hodgins, concern now tingeing her voice.

"Miss Howell?" Grayson croaked as the incident in the garden rushed to the front of his mind. He'd been down on bended knee. One of the footmen had seen him, but he'd pushed the incident from his mind, and now everyone believed he intended to marry *her*. Christ have mercy, it was what Olivia thought.

"You've got it all wrong," Nathan said, coming to Grayson's rescue since he couldn't find the right words at the moment. He felt like howling, but it was as though his tongue was made of lead and his mouth had been filled with sand.

"Grayson wants to marry Miss Poole," Juliana said.

"Oh!" Mrs. Hodgins clapped her hands together. "But that's marvelous news."

"It would be if I knew where to find her," Grayson managed.

No one seemed to have anything to add to that statement, so Grayson gave his attention back to the note Olivia left him and read it again. He stared at the last part.

Thank you for the friendship you offered, for the understanding you've shown Miss Edwards, and most of all, for helping me keep the promise I made my sister.

The promise I made my sister.

Grayson's heart gave a hard thump. Was this not her ultimate goal? To complete the list she'd made with Agnes. It was what brought her to Sutton Hall in the first place.

"Visit another country."

"What's that?" Delilah asked.

Grayson ignored her and tried to think back.

A memory stirred. The list had been Agnes's idea, but some of the things on it had also been Olivia's dreams. What was it she'd said when they'd been on the beach?

I'm fluent in French and German, yet I've never left England.

The longing in her voice had been palpable. And Bristol wasn't far. In fact, it was much too close for Grayson's liking – so close she might be well on her way to France or Germany by now.

He considered this as a possible option. It made sense. If Olivia's heart was broken and she was trying to run from him, from the memories they had made here together and from her belief he would marry Miss Howell, she'd want to put as much distance between them as possible.

And if that were indeed the case? Hell, he'd scour the world until he found her.

He looked at Nathan. "I need you to go to Treadmire in case she may have returned there. In the meantime, I shall travel to Bristol and inquire if anyone's seen her."

"Bristol?" Delilah asked. "Would London not be a more logical destination for a young woman attempting to find a new position as governess? It's where most of the people looking to hire will be right now, what with the Season underway and all that."

"Which is why I shall head there myself if I find no

trace of her in Bristol." He turned to Juliana. "I promised Miss Howell a ball and I'll not let her down. If you could please send out invitations during my absence? Invite everyone, especially the bachelors."

Juliana's eyes widened. "The bachelors?"

"Not for you," Grayson quickly informed her in cased she'd misunderstood his intention, something that seemed to be happening quite a lot these days. "They're for Miss Howell. Oh, and the date, Juliana. You may set it for…one month from today."

"Yes. Of course." Juliana straightened her back and smiled. "I'd be honored."

"And if I'm not back by then I'll trust you to plan the event. Mrs. Hodgins and Dover will help you of course." The two servants voiced their agreement while Juliana positively glowed in response to the faith he was showing in her. He turned to Nathan. "Can I count on you and Delilah to host the ball in case I'm not back in time?"

Nathan didn't hesitate. "Of course."

"Good. Thank you. Once I return, we'll see to getting Juliana to London."

"I'm going to London?" Juliana asked with wide-eyed dismay.

"Nathan will explain the plan," Grayson said, not wanting to waist one more second. He turned to his butler. "And Dover?"

"Yes, sir?"

"Have someone fetch the vicar the day after tomorrow. Nathan should be back from Treadmire by then and will surely want to use his special license."

Satisfied he'd addressed the most pressing matters, Grayson left the room and went to prepare himself for his journey, ever conscious of the fact that he faced an almost impossible challenge.

CHAPTER FORTY-FIVE

I t took longer than Olivia expected to reach Bristol. She had to change mail coaches three times before she arrived in the noisy town where street vendors shouted to make themselves heard and throngs of people shoved their way past each other without apology.

Her confidence wavered when she stepped down from the coach with her bag, not knowing which direction to go.

Someone bumped her shoulder, jostling her so she nearly slipped off the pavement and into the street where horses were ready to trample careless pedestrians. She steadied her stance, tightened her hold on her bag, and approached a plump, middle-aged woman who swept the front steps of a nearby shop.

"Excuse me," Olivia said, drawing the woman's

attention. "Can you point me toward the harbor please?"

The woman gestured toward Olivia's right. "It's that way, luv. About a mile I should think."

Olivia thanked her and headed off. She kept her pace brisk, her resolve firm, even though she was sure the walk was at least twice as long as she'd been told.

When she finally spotted a mast peeking out from behind a low rooftop, she smiled and hurried forward. The afternoon light was beginning to fade. Soon, evening would set in. She quickened her step and was panting for breath by the time she entered the ticket office. Her feet ached, but at least she'd arrived before the place closed for the day. She'd purchase her ticket and head to France where she would start over, make a new life for herself and, most important of all, avoid having to hear about Grayson.

"Is there a decent inn nearby?" she asked the clerk as soon as she'd paid for and received her ticket. Hungry and exhausted, she looked forward to a hot meal and a decent night's rest.

"The Howling Rooster's not far. Just head right to Brick Street and take the second left after that. You can't miss it."

Olivia thanked him and left. But as she turned onto Brick Street, footsteps clicked against the pavement behind her. She glanced over her shoulder. Two men, their heads bent low beneath caps, shoulders hunched and hands in their pockets, kept pace with her strides.

Discomforted by their presence and by the fact that

the rest of the street was empty, Olivia increased her speed. She didn't like being alone with two men. She needed to locate the Howling Rooster and the safety she hoped to find in a larger crowd.

She glanced back again. The men were closer. Her heart kicked into a mad gallop as genuine fear pricked at her skin. Despite the evening chill, heat burned the nape of her neck, sending flashes of unease down her spine.

Breaking into a near run, Olivia started to cross the street, only to be yanked back, her body jolting as it connected with brick. Pain shot through her head and shoulder. She opened her mouth and started to scream.

A smelly hand covered her mouth while another grabbed hold of her arm. "I'll take that bag."

The voice, low and threatening, caused the air around her to tremble. A menacing chuckle followed and then a large hand settled over her waist.

Stale breath fell heavily on her cheek as the other man spoke. "Ye're a pretty little thing, ain't ye."

Olivia jerked her face away from him while fighting a sudden wave of nausea. Pressing herself into the wall, she tightened her hold on her bag and kicked the nearest man in the shin.

Neither man budged.

Instead, the grip on her arm tightened. "Let go of the bag and we'll not harm ye."

Olivia didn't believe him, yet what could she do? She, alone against two men? The odds weren't great but to give up her bag wouldn't do.

Tears welled in her eyes even as she stubbornly tightened her jaw. The bag contained her diary and the list she'd made with Agnes. She could not lose either item. Never mind the money intended to help her survive until she found a way to earn more.

Desperate, she kicked at the men again and twisted against their hold.

"Oi! What's happening there?" someone called.

Olivia nearly sagged with relief. She would be rescued from these villains and—

A howl of pain shot past her lips as the man who'd been holding her wrist snapped it backward with sudden force. Stars danced behind her eyes and Olivia's legs gave out. She fell, aware of only one thing: the bag containing all that was left of her sister was no longer with her.

Grayson headed straight to the docks upon his arrival in Bristol.

"Are you in charge?" he asked a clerk at the second ticket office he entered.

"For the next five hours I am," the clerk replied. He was a skinny lad who looked to be in his late twenties, with thin blonde hair, and spectacles perched on the bridge of a pointy nose.

"Perhaps you can help me then. I need to know if a Miss Olivia Poole recently purchased passage."

The clerk raised his chin and pushed his spectacles,

which had slid forward, back into position. "I'm afraid I can't disclose such information unless you're with the law."

"Understood." Grayson placed a couple of pounds on the counter. "Perhaps this will persuade you?"

The clerk eyed the blunt with enough interest to encourage Grayson. He added another pound and the clerk's eyes widened. "You said the magistrate sent you?"

Grayson nodded. Whatever pretense the clerk required in order to give Grayson the information he needed was fine by him. He blew out a breath when the man took the money and started searching his ledger.

"Olivia Poole, you said?" The clerk shook his head. "There's no one here by that name."

"She's in her mid–thirties, petite with raven black hair and dressed for mourning. Perhaps she used a pseudonym." Grayson tried to think and suddenly blinked. "What about Agnes Poole. Is that name there?"

"Hmm…that name does ring a bell. And a woman exactly as you described did purchase a ticket the other day." His finger slid down the list of outbound passengers. "Ah yes, here we are. Agnes Poole."

Grayson's pulse leapt with excitement. He'd found her. He was certain of it. "Where is she bound?"

"It says Le Havre but…" The clerk frowned.

"What?" Grayson leaned forward, attempting to see what was written.

"The ship departed yesterday but Miss Poole wasn't on it. Look for yourself." The clerk pointed to a notation made to the right. "Her ticket, marked as number seventeen, was never collected."

Whatever brief joy Grayson experienced in response to knowing Olivia must still be in England, that he wouldn't have to chase her to France, was swiftly replaced by dread. Because if she hadn't used the ticket she'd purchased, then where was she, and what had altered her plans?

Increasingly worried, Grayson straightened himself and thanked the clerk for his help.

"I'd recommend looking for her at the Howling Rooster," the clerk told Grayson. "I suggested the place when she asked if I knew of an inn."

"Thank you." Grayson handed the clerk an extra pound, made a note of the directions, and took his leave. Olivia had set off alone, without a companion. Good lord, any number of awful things could have happened to her, all of them his fault because he hadn't been clear.

He'd *thought* he had been, but considering she'd believed he was to marry Miss Howell, then his suggestion that they discuss their future when he returned from London could only mean one thing. That he meant for Olivia to be his mistress.

Furious with himself and terrified on her behalf, Grayson got back on his horse and made his way to the Howling Rooster.

"I'm looking for a woman," Grayson informed the innkeeper once he found him.

The man, an older pudgy fellow with a missing

front tooth and slicked back grey hair, chortled. "Ain't we all?"

"No, I...I need to find a particular woman. Her name is Olivia Poole. She's roughly this height, five and thirty years of age with raven hair and dark eyes. She would have been wearing black or grey and probably carrying a bag. It's my belief she recently spent the night here."

The innkeeper frowned, which gave Grayson hope. At least the man appeared to be searching his brain.

Grayson held his breath until the innkeeper shook his head. "Can't say I've seen 'er."

"You're sure?"

The innkeeper scratched his ear. "We've 'ad a family of four, two university lads, a solicitor, and three sisters with their maid during the past few days. None of the females looked like the woman ye've just described and none were alone as ye say she was."

"Then I...I don't know where to look." He'd counted on this place to give him a lead but the trail had already gone cold and now. He shook his head. There had to be other options – something he wasn't considering.

"I 'ate to suggest this," the innkeeper said, a grim expression on his face, "but one of the regulars came across a muggin' three nights ago, just one street over. Said a young woman was left in a bad way."

Grayson's stomach plummeted. Olivia had left the ticket office intent on coming here, spending the night, and leaving for France in the morning. Instead, she'd gone missing. Was it possible for her to be the woman the innkeeper now referred to?

He hoped not, but it was the only possible trail at the moment, so he had to ask, "Do you have any idea where she might have gone?

"St. Bridget's would be my bet." The innkeeper glanced toward the taproom and nodded at one of the servers. "I'll just be a moment."

"Saint Bridget's?" Grayson pressed, directing the innkeeper's attention back to him.

"It's a charitable 'ospital servin' the poor," the innkeeper said. "Seems like the right place for someone who's lost all their blunt to get treated."

Gut twisting, Grayson thanked the innkeeper and set off again.

By the time he climbed the front steps of St. Bridget's, he almost hoped all of this was a ploy intended to keep him off Olivia's trail. That she'd suspected he'd hunt her down no matter what and had made a ruse to keep him chasing until she'd managed to get away safely.

Until he mentioned her name to a nurse and described her appearance.

The small nod of confirmation that followed was like a lance to his chest. His ears clogged up and his vision grew hazy. It was as if the world was spinning too fast and he was in danger of losing his balance.

"Sir?"

"Yes," he gasped, attempting to come to terms with the fact that the love of his life had ended up here. Hurt and alone.

"She was pretty bad off when she was brought in, but our bone–setter did his best to make sure she'll retain the use of her arm."

Grayson felt the blood drain from his face. He feared he might be sick. "Bone–setter?"

"Miss Poole was attacked and—"

"I need to see her." He glanced around wondering which direction to head in. "Where is she?"

"Perhaps if you'd tell me who you are and how you're related to her?"

Grayson drew himself up and glared at the nurse. His whole body was shaking and he was doing his best to keep his voice level and to convey a calm he did not feel. "I'm Grayson Grier, master of Sutton Hall, and Miss Poole's fiancé."

A gentle, barely there touch, drifted across Olivia's cheek. Floating somewhere between sleep and wakeful-ness she sighed, enjoying the warmth that surrounded her, unwilling to face the pain that awaited when she became fully conscious.

Another caress, so brief it scarcely registered, then nothing at all.

She moved, instinctively seeking the tenderness

someone had shown her, so achingly familiar and yet, how could that possibly be?

"Forgive me." Warm breath tickled her ear, pulling her out of her slumber. The voice...oh, that wonderful voice, so rich and velvety smooth.

Impossible.

Disillusioned, she dove back under, swimming beneath the surface before plunging deeper, seeking that soothing place where the world disappeared and dreams began.

When she finally opened her eyes, she realized two things. One, the room was dark, and two, it was a different room than the one she'd fallen asleep in. That room contained nine other beds while this held only hers.

She moved to sit and immediately wished she hadn't as sharp pain lanced through her skull, shoulder, and arm at exactly the same time. A scraping sound alerted her to another presence, and then she saw him, a large dark figure rising toward her from one corner.

Olivia's heart jolted and then she screamed, begging for someone to help her as she began scrambling out of the bed. Whoever had stolen her bag must have come back to finish her off. Wasn't that what those sorts of men did?

"Shhh... Olivia. It's just–"

She slipped in her hurry to get out the door but rather than land on the floor, her fall was broken by two strong arms. Warmth and security kept her safe and she finally registered whose voice she'd heard.

"Grayson?"

"Yes, my love." He swept her into a careful embrace, making sure he didn't touch her bad arm. "I'm here. I've got you."

"Is everything all right?" someone asked from behind her.

Olivia pulled away from Grayson and turned to the night guard who stood in the doorway. She gave him a nod. "Yes. Sorry. It was just a nightmare."

The man held up his lantern and swept the warm light across the room. His gaze landed on Grayson before returning it to Olivia. "Don't hesitate to call if you need anything."

"A flint would be helpful, if you have one on you."

He stepped farther into the room and set his lantern on the table where her oil lamp stood. "You can keep mine and I'll take yours."

Olivia thanked him and then he was gone. She sagged against her bed and Grayson's hands were immediately there to offer support.

"Easy does it," he murmured, slipping an arm around her.

"They took my diary and the list," she cried, emotion flooding her on account of his presence. "I've lost them, Grayson. My dearest possessions."

"I'm terribly sorry." His voice was raspy, filled with regret as he hugged her to him. He lifted her as though she were made of glass, and settled her on the mattress. Her blanket was gently tucked around her. A large hand brushed over her hair. "All of this is my fault."

"You're not to blame for what those men did." She wouldn't allow him to wallow in guilt for this too.

"Perhaps not directly but—"

"No, Grayson. It wasn't your fault."

A kiss was placed on top of her head and when he spoke next, his voice shook. "I'm so glad I found you."

"I...I don't know how you managed." But she was glad too, although... She grasped his hand and gave it a squeeze. "I'm not coming back to Sutton Hall with you."

"Olivia, I—"

"No." The word was awkwardly loud in the otherwise quiet room, but it was important she stay firm, that she prevent him from using her weakened state against her as he could so easily do. "I won't be your mistress."

"Olivia you—"

"Do you not understand, Grayson? I love you. I love you with all my heart, more than I've ever loved anyone else in my life, and I'll not be able to bear it. I'll not be able to stand seeing you with Miss Howell, watching you raise your perfect children together."

"I love you too."

"Oh, God." Her heart broke all over again. Fresh tears slid down her cheeks and every breath she took clawed at her throat. "Please don't say that. Walking away was hard enough before. Please, if that is how you truly feel, let me go."

"I'm afraid I can't do that." He perched himself on the edge of the bed and swiped her tears from her cheeks with his thumb. "Olivia, there's been a terrible misunderstanding. I dare say I'll never forgive myself for it, considering what it has led to. But the truth is I'm not engaged to Miss Howell. I never was and I never will be."

Olivia stared at him through bleary eyes. "I don't understand. I saw you propose. As did Roger."

"No." A mixture of painful regret and yearning creased the corners of his eyes. "What the two of you saw was me crouching to look at a box beneath one of the hedges."

"Juliana's mousetrap." She tried to recall exactly what she'd witnessed given this new information, but there was still no denying the fact that it had looked as though he'd been proposing. "You weren't crouching, Grayson. You were down on bended knee while speaking to Miss Howell."

"I was only telling her what I'd discovered." His gaze intensified as he raised Olivia's hand to his lips for a gentle kiss. "Olivia, I swear to you, my heart will never belong to anyone else but you. Marry me and I vow to spend the rest of my life making up for this blunder. Because the truth is, the only woman I want to marry is you, my love. If you will have me."

Elation swept through her. "Of course I'll have you, but what about—"

The kiss he gave her was slow and tender, filled with love and hope for the future.

"Nathan will marry Delilah," he told her, answering her unspoken question. "They've made an arrangement which should work well for them both."

"Are you certain?" Olivia found his position hard to believe. "Your brother is such a wonderful man. It's a pity if he's denied the chance to marry for love."

Grayson sighed, the sort of sigh that suggested a heavy weight rested upon his chest. He held her hand loosely and brushed her knuckles with his thumb. "There's something I ought to tell you. Something you need to know so you can help keep him safe."

"I don't understand." He wasn't making any sense. "Safe from what?"

"Your father was a vicar and you have led a sheltered life, so what I'm about to tell you will most likely shock you. There's also a good chance it will change your opinion of Nathan for the worse, but if you are to be my wife, I want no secrets between us. Just promise me you will never share what I am about to tell you with anyone else."

"I promise." Sensing his distress, she turned her hand over and laced her fingers with his.

He hesitated briefly, alerting her to the difficulty of the subject at hand. And then his gaze latched onto hers. "Nathan has no interest in women."

Olivia frowned. "What does that mean?"

"It means," Grayson spoke, his voice measured, "that women do not appeal to him."

It took her a moment to comprehend what he was implying. Her lips parted. "But...but that's—"

"A mortal sin, punishable by death."

"Oh, Grayson." She scarcely knew what to say. The burden he carried was so much greater than what she'd believed. But to say she was sorry felt wrong, like a confirmation that Nathan was somehow defective, when nothing could be further from the truth. He was simply...different. "No harm shall come to him if I can help it."

He expelled a deep breath. "Thank you."

A sweet kiss followed before Olivia dared to ask about Miss Howell.

"She freed me from all obligations when I made her realize what she feels for me has never been more than infatuation. I've promised to host a ball to help her make a more suitable match. Juliana is in charge of the preparations."

"How good of you, Grayson." Honestly, she didn't think she could love him more than she already did and then he went and surprised her. "I'm sure she appreciates your trusting her with such a big responsibility."

"I must confess I'm eager to see if she can pull it off."

"How can you possibly doubt her?" Olivia smiled at him before adding, "You know as well as I that she's had a marvelous teacher."

He grinned, then kissed her again, promising her without words that all would be well and that the happily ever after she'd not dared dream of would soon be hers.

CHAPTER FORTY-SIX

S tanding at the periphery of the ballroom with a
glass of champagne in his hand, Grayson had to
admit Juliana had done an incredible job. She'd had
help of course. Not only from Delilah and Mrs.
Hodgins, but from his mother too.

Much to Grayson's surprise, Mama had been at
Sutton Hall when he and Olivia returned from Bristol
one week later.

"It isn't easy," she'd told him when he'd inquired
about her decision to come, "but it's time. Your father
and I shared such wonderful moments here. A pity if
one painful memory should overshadow all that.
Besides, I made a promise to you regarding Juliana.
When Nathan wrote that you'd gone off in search of
Olivia, I thought it best to come here at once."

"I'm glad," he'd told her.

"Me too. Olivia is a delight, Grayson. I'm so incredibly happy for you."

Pleased to know he had his mother's approval and the love of the best woman he'd ever known, Grayson sipped his champagne and glanced at the dance floor where Nathan was leading Delilah in a quadrille. Their wedding had been hastier than his and Olivia's, who'd had to wait for their return to Sutton Hall to use the special license issued for use in Varney parish. The piece of paper had practically burned a hole in Grayson's pocket by the time they stood before the vicar.

Miss Howell, he noted with some satisfaction, was dancing her second set with Mr. Price, a charming young man and an excellent candidate for a potential suitor.

"It's almost time for our set," a soft voice said as the music started to fade.

Grayson smiled at Olivia, catching the twinkle in her green eyes. His breath caught with the pleasure of knowing she was his. Dressed in a lilac silk gown, her hair held in place by the comb he'd made and with the diamonds he'd gifted her sparkling against her skin, she looked exquisite despite the splint she still wore – like a dessert he'd like to take his time savoring.

Her lips curved with knowing interest. "Later, Grayson. When we're alone."

"Is that a promise?" he murmured, loving the flush that crept into her cheeks.

"Of course."

He dipped his head, not caring if anyone saw him being affectionate with his wife or what they might think, and placed an open mouthed kiss against the side of her neck.

"Wicked man," she chided, her blush deepening.

"Just a reminder," he told her as he began leading her onto the dance floor.

"Of what?"

He spun her into position and sent her a roguish grin. "Of everything to come."

The music started and Grayson swept Olivia into the dance and toward their awaiting future.

Standing in her sitting room later that night, Mary wound her arms around Philip and accepted his kiss. Filled with love and hope, it offered her endless amounts of comfort.

"I am so blessed," she whispered against his lips before hugging him close.

His low chuckle vibrated through her. "Me too."

"And to think everything turned out as we prayed it would." She leaned back so she could meet his gaze. The glimmer she found there made her smile. "It's rather marvelous, wouldn't you say?"

"Without a doubt."

"Mr. Grier has married a wonderful woman."

"I'm hoping he won't be the only one to do so," Philip murmured. When Mary tilted her head in question he reached up to cup her cheek. "Marry me, Mary. Be my wife and let me love you for the rest of my days."

A fountain of joy erupted inside her, filling her veins until she was certain she must be sparkling. "Nothing would please me more than to have you for my husband."

Dipping his head, he brushed her lips with his in a tender caress that warmed her from the top of her head all the way to the tips of her toes. To think such happiness should be hers at her age.

Well, it was just as splendid as the man who presently kissed her as though he were a fairytale prince who'd just won his princess.

EPILOGUE

O livia clasped her husband's hand as they strolled through the churchyard. The childish laughter behind them brought a smile to her lips. She met Grayson's gaze, warmth filling her breast in response to the answering love in his eyes. Gone were the rigid lines that had dominated his expression when they'd first met, replaced by heartfelt contentment.

They walked to the gravestone where she'd once stood alone in the cold March rain before setting off for Sutton Hall. So much had happened since then and she wanted to share it with Agnes

As expected, her throat closed the moment she saw her sister's name, etched in the granite and partially covered by some sort of vine. Grayson made quick work of the plant, pulling it away so Agnes's name could be properly seen. He stepped back and took Olivia's hand once more – gave it a little squeeze as he so often did when he knew she needed reminding that he was there with her, ready to give her strength and support.

She took a shaky breath, then reached out to trail her gloved fingers across the cool granite. "I've done it, dearest. I've completed the list we created together, but not without help from a wonderful man." She sniffed and accepted the handkerchief Grayson offered. "We found each other, thanks to you, and I learned how to live by taking your dreams and making them mine. Sweet Agnes, the gift you've given me cannot be put into words. It has given me love, a husband whom I adore beyond measure and children…"

"A son who will soon turn five," Grayson said, helping Olivia when her voice cracked. "We named him Francis after my father."

"Our daughter, your niece, carries your name," Olivia whispered and shifted her gaze to the three-year-old girl who was trying to hide behind the statue of an angel, unaware of the fact that her bottom stuck out. It wouldn't take long for Francis to find her.

Returning her attention to the gravestone, Olivia let go of Grayson's hand and sank into a crouch. She'd considered bringing a pretty bouquet to brighten the gravesite, but hated the idea of wilted flowers eventually marring the ground.

Instead, she reached inside the basket she'd brought and retrieved a trowel and some bulbs. Come spring, a lovely display of yellow would brighten the spot when the daffodils bloomed.

Once they'd been planted, she brushed off her hands and collected the basket.

"Ready?" Grayson asked after a moment of silence.

Olivia turned to him with a smile. "Yes."

He took the basket from her hand and swept an arm around her shoulders, then called for the children to join them. Holding Olivia close to his side as if sensing she needed the added affection, they started back toward their awaiting carriage.

"I love you," he whispered close to her ear. "More and more with each passing day."

"As I love you," she told him fondly while Agnes skipped past. Francis jogged after his sister. Olivia shared a look with Grayson and she grinned, happy knowing that while they had both suffered loss, they'd been lucky to find each other. The wealth they'd built out of love could not be measured. And it would keep growing as long as they were together.

∼

Thank you so much for taking the time to read *Mr. Grier and The Governess*, the second book in my **Brazen Beauties** series. If you enjoyed this story, you'll also enjoy **The Crawfords** in which three independent minded women, shunned by Society, find love and happiness. The first book in this series, *No Ordinary Duke*, is FREE if you sign up for my newsletter! Head on over to www.sophiebarnes.com and get your complimentary copy today.

Or, if you haven't read my **Diamonds In The Rough** series, you might consider *A Most Unlikely Duke* where bare-knuckle boxer, Raphe Matthews, unexpectedly inherits a duke's title. Figuring out how to navigate Society won't be easy, but receiving advice from the lady next door may just be worth it.

You can find out more about my new releases, backlist deals and giveaways by signing up for my newsletter here: www.sophiebarnes.com

Follow me on Facebook for even more updates and join Sophie Barnes' Historical Romance Group for fun book related posts, games, discussions, and giveaways.

Once again, I thank you for your interest in my books. Please take a moment to leave a review since this can help other readers discover stories they'll love. And please continue reading for an excerpt from *Mr. West and The Widow.*

Get a sneak peek of the sequel!

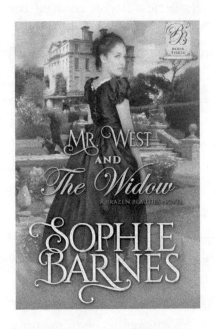

CHAPTER ONE

Colin West finished the tangy tomato and mutton stew he'd been served and downed the last of his Bass, the left side of his face deliberately turned away from the rest of the Screaming Rooster's guests. The roadside tavern was fuller now than when he'd arrived, the tables near him occupied not just by men, but by women and children too.

Inhaling deeply he glanced through the beveled glass window beside him and studied the sky. Additional clouds had gathered since his arrival, their murkiness heralding rain. Wildflowers dotting the bar ditch with shades of blue, yellow, and red, swayed from side to side. A gust of wind caught hold of a tree and ruffled its leaves.

Setting his jaw, Colin retrieved the payment he owed from his pocket and dropped the coins next to his bowl. Time to go if he was to get home before the storm hit. Woodstone Park wasn't far now – a two hour ride at most. He grabbed his hat from the chair beside him and set it upon his head, pulled his greatcoat collar as high as he could, and stood, hoping to make his escape without any fuss.

Head bowed and with his chin tucked to his chest, he moved toward the door. The smell of melting lard, roast meat, and charcoal swirled in the air around him. One of the servers called out an order. The well-worn floorboards creaked beneath his boots. Laughter erupted from the table to his right. A young boy, no more than eight years of age, rocked back in his chair and blocked Colin's path.

Damn.

"Excuse me," Colin said, his voice gruff.

The boy twisted in his seat, his gaze directed at Colin's waist.

"Steven," a large bearded man, most likely the boy's father spoke, "get out of the way."

Steven shifted as though prepared to do as he'd been told but lost his balance in the next instant. His eyes widened in panic, his small hands frantically trying to grab the edge of the table only to have it slide from under his fingers. With a yelp, he fell while the bearded man scrambled to grab him.

Colin swooped forward into a crouch, catching the boy before he hit the ground.

Steven stared up at him and gasped, eyes wide as he pushed away from Colin as though he'd come face to face with a monster.

"What's the matter with you?" the bearded man asked.

"Nothing," Steven stammered while scuttling away from where Colin knelt.

"Forgive me," he muttered, his chest tight. "I only wanted to help."

"And we thank you for it," a woman said from somewhere nearby, her voice pleasant but firm.

Colin closed his eyes briefly, expelled a deep breath and rose, acutely aware of the silence – the fact that all eyes were on him. Straightening, he raised his chin, directed his gaze at the man he presumed to be Steven's father, and allowed him to see what had frightened the boy.

Alarm pulled at the man's features. His hand settled firmly upon Steven's shoulder as he drew him closer, away from Colin. He gave a stiff nod – a show of appreciation that also told Colin to leave.

Colin held the man's gaze for an extra beat, hands fisted at his sides, before swinging away and heading toward the door. Cutlery clattered behind him and sighs of relief escorted him out. He pushed through the heavy oak door, straight into a gust of wind that nearly knocked his hat off his head. He pressed it back into place and strode to the stables where he collected his horse, Midnight. Dipping one hand inside his great coat pocket, he selected a penny and tossed it to the groom. Unlike the travelers inside the tavern, this young lad did not retreat from his presence – something which lifted his spirits immensely.

"If you ever need another position," Colin told him as he swung up into his saddle, the leather squeaking beneath his weight, "come to Woodstone Park."

"Thank ye," said the groom and offered a toothy grin.

Colin snatched the reins, tightened his grip and kicked Midnight into motion. The beast reared its head with a snort, stepping sideways in agitation until Colin turned him about so they faced the right direction. Then, loosening his hold to give Midnight power, he urged him into a gallop.

The country road stretched for miles, twisting and turning through endless fields. Chased by the worsening weather, Colin whipped the reins and pressed Midnight to run faster. Rain was already falling, splashing into his eyes so he struggled to see. Thunder cracked from above and rumbled around him. A flash of light lit up the darkening sky. The rain fell harder, like water poured from a bucket, drenching Colin and turning the tightly packed dirt road to mud. The wind whipped across his head, taking his hat with it much like a naughty child bent on mischief.

Colin muttered a curse and gritted his teeth. Another flash of lightning revealed a massive collection of branches and leaves in his path, and Midnight was barreling straight toward it.

"Halt!" Colin pulled on the reins and leaned back with all of his might. Midnight skidded, his hindquarters dipping as he responded to Colin's command. An unhappy whinny followed before Midnight straightened, rearing up onto his long hind legs while tossing his head with displeasure. His front legs landed with a hard thud, sending a jolt up Colin's spine.

"Easy does it," he murmured, leaning forward to stroke Midnight's neck. "The bridge is blocked. We'll have to go around."

Pulling Midnight sideways, Colin steered the horse to the right, across a waterlogged meadow, away from the road. They'd have to follow the river until they reached the crossing at Pinehill, which would add at least ten more miles to the journey.

Damn.

Slowed by mud, Midnight plodded forward at a steady gait. Colin squeezed the reins, his body tense in a hopeless effort to ward off the chill in his bones. Midnight snorted, fogging the air, and Colin wiped his brow in a futile attempt to get the water out of his eyes.

A heavy sigh pushed its way out of his chest. He glanced around and then he saw it, a glow immediately to his right, slightly obscured by a cluster of trees.

"Come on." Although he knew he'd likely be turned away at the door, Colin directed Midnight toward the house in the distance. Drenched to the bone, he'd happily risk being spurned for even the slightest chance of getting warm.

Ordinarily, he favored the autumn, winter, and spring – the cooler climate these seasons allowed for. With summer came heat and the flood of memories taking him back to Aboukir – to the desert sand beneath his boots, agonized screams of men getting slaughtered, and the cloying stench of death so thick it still made him wretch.

He shuddered and buried the thought by focusing

all his senses on Midnight's solid stride, the smell of wet dirt and the stubborn splash of rain.

The house in the distance grew larger, stretching and transforming as he made his approach, until it loomed before him – a large square block with a pitched roof and a single light burning behind a downstairs window.

He swung from his saddle and landed upon the ground with a thud. After giving Midnight a well-deserved pat, he grabbed his saddle bag and walked to the heavy front door. The partially washed away gravel beneath his boots shifted and crunched with each step he took.

Fisting his hand, he positioned himself with his left side turned away from whoever might answer his call, and knocked. Water fell from the roof in cascades, splashing onto his legs before turning into rivers that ran down the front steps.

He knocked again. Thunder cracked and lightning flashed. Midnight shifted and shook his head with a whinny.

"Stay," Colin commanded.

He prepared to knock once more when the door eased open just enough to reveal an older woman with narrowed eyes, thin lips pressed into a firm line, and creases etched upon her brow by age. Her white cap and black serviceable dress suggested she was a maid.

"Yes?" she asked while staring at Colin with pale demanding eyes.

"I'm sorry to bother you on a night like this, but

the bridge back yonder is blocked by a tree, preventing me from reaching home anytime soon. With the weather being what it is, I'm hoping you might be willing to give me shelter for the night, even if it's in the stables."

The maid stared him up and down, then glanced past his shoulder at Midnight. "Name?"

"Colin West of Woodstone Park." He reached inside his greatcoat and retrieved a calling card, embarrassed to note that the corner was bent. He handed it over nonetheless.

"One moment," she said upon taking the card. The door closed with a thunk.

Colin cupped his hands and breathed warm air onto his palms. It didn't do much. He'd need a good hour in front of a fire before he expelled the damp chill coursing through his veins.

The door swung open once more and the maid moved aside. "In you come."

"What about my horse?"

"It will be taken to the stables."

Colin thanked her and crossed the threshold, taking care to keep the left side of his face averted. The door closed and the maid dropped her gaze to the large puddle forming around his feet.

"Sorry about the mess."

"I wager you'll want to get out of those clothes so you can get warm," she said, looking back up. "A hot bath will help."

"I don't want to burden you." It hadn't escaped

Colin's notice that there was no butler or even a footman in sight. "A fire will serve just fine."

"I have my orders," she said. "A bath will be prepared soon enough. This way, Mr. West."

Colin followed the maid through a sparsely furnished hallway toward the stairs. The carpet runner was old, filled with patches where tufts had been worn away to reveal the backing. Not a single piece of artwork adorned the walls though discolored marks showed where several pieces had once hung.

The steps creaked and moaned as they climbed to the first floor landing where a hallway extended in both directions with six doors leading off it. Windows at each end provided natural light, though this was greatly dimmed now due to the weather.

"You'll be staying here," said the maid once they reached the door furthest to the right. She opened it to reveal a sizable space containing a double bed, a dresser, an armchair, and a table upon which an oil lamp sat alongside a flint box. A brass tub stood to one side, waiting to be filled.

"It's perfect," Colin assured her despite the thick smell of mildew harassing his nose. He moved so she only saw his good side, and set his satchel on the floor.

"If you're able to build your own fire, I'll see to heating some water and having a meal prepared."

"Thank you but–"

"Like I said, I've got my orders."

She was gone before Colin could argue.

He stared at the door, then swept his palm across his

face and raked his fingers through his sodden hair. Moving swiftly, he shrugged out of his greatcoat and hung it on a wall hook, then crouched before the fireplace and selected a log from a discolored iron rack. After getting the fire going, he warmed his palms for a moment, then grabbed the white linen towel that hung by the washstand. He rubbed it over his head with rough movements to dry off some of the water.

A knock sounded and Colin deliberately turned so his left side faced the wall. "Come in."

A man with thick white hair and bushy brows entered, a steaming pail in each hand. He had to be well past sixty. "Water for your bath, sir."

Colin stepped forward at an angle. "Allow me to help."

The man hesitated. "Doesn't seem quite right seeing as you're the guest and all."

"That may be, but I'm not the sort to take advantage. Please. It would make me feel better."

"Well in that case…" The man set the pails down and rotated his shoulders. "As regrettable as it is, I'm not as young as I once was. But the exercise does me good. Name's Reynolds. Mark Reynolds."

"I'm Colin West."

"Aye. So I've heard." Mark watched while Colin grabbed both pails and emptied them into the tub. "Thought you might like to know that your horse is safely secured in the stables. Gave him some fresh hay myself."

"Thank you."

"Think nothing if it." Mark reached for the empty buckets. "I'll fetch some more water."

"I'll assist you."

Mark looked as though he'd like to accept but felt like he ought to protest. "Pouring the water's one thing. Having you fetch it is quite another. Not really the done thing, if you know what I mean."

"I really must insist," Colin said. No way in hell would he let the old man trudge up and down stairs, carrying water, while Colin lounged on his arse.

Mark hesitated briefly, then shrugged one shoulder. "We'd best get on with it then if you mean to take a hot bath."

Ten minutes later, after two additional trips, Colin peeled his wet clothes from his body and sank into heavenly warmth with a sigh.

He hadn't met other servants while helping Mark with his errand. Not in the stairwell or in the kitchen. When he'd commented on it Mark had replied, "We've got what we need."

Which got Colin wondering about his host.

What sort of man ran a house this size with a skeleton staff?

A frugal one.

Or one with financial troubles, considering the threadbare linen he'd found on his bed and the otherwise lack of wealth on display.

He climbed from the bath and went to dry off in front of the fire. Warmed by the dry heat from the flames and the humid steam rising from the water, Colin retrieved a clean set of clothes from his satchel and dressed. He paused briefly before the oval mirror that hung on the wall and stared at his face – one side perfect, the other side ruined forever by meaningless war.

Except it was more than his face that had been destroyed on that fateful day in the desert heat. Lives, not only of the wounded soldiers, but of their families waiting back home, had been forever changed. And then there were those who hadn't made it.

His good friend Richard Hughes had been at his side. They'd been heading up the beach together with James Dale and Grayson Grier in pursuit. Until a quick shot to the head from a sniper had struck Richard down. Colin had barely registered his demise before a cannon blast sent him flying.

Closing his eyes he blocked out his tarnished reflection and took a calm breath. It was, he'd learned, the quickest way to ward off the anger that twisted inside him whenever he let his mind linger upon that long ago day.

Best he get out of the room too and away from the mirror. The meal the maid had promised would offer a welcome distraction as well, so he made his way downstairs and went in search of the dining room.

The first door he opened led to a parlor, the next to an unfurnished space where faded curtains and an equally faded carpet seemed to serve as a reminder of better days. He shut the door and continued his progress through the hallway. His hand reached out toward another door handle.

Someone cleared their throat and Colin froze.

"That room is off limits, Mr. West."

He turned his right side toward the maid, who'd approached with a near silent tread. "I was attempting to find the dining room."

"Last door on your right," she said. "If you make yourself comfortable I'll fetch your meal."

"Thank you...Miss."

"Mrs. Reynolds," she corrected.

"Mark's wife?"

She folded her hands and raised her chin. "He's never been one for formalities, but you'll not have my given name, Mr. West."

"I wouldn't expect to." He withdrew his hand from the door handle he'd been about to use and walked to the door at the end of the hallway.

The solitary place setting Colin found suggested he would be dining alone. Did that mean the master was presently absent or that he deliberately chose not to join his uninvited guest? He decided it must be the latter once his meal arrived – a savory dish consisting of roast lamb, buttery potatoes and steamed vegetables. It seemed unlikely servants would offer up such fine food unless they'd been ready to serve their employer.

"May I ask who the owner of this estate is?" Colin inquired when Mark came to clear his plate. "I should like to know to whom I'm indebted and offer my thanks."

"Leighton, is the name," Mrs. Reynolds said before her husband had a chance to reply. She'd brought a trifle, served in a chipped glass bowl, which she set on the table in front of Colin. "We'll be sure to pass along your appreciation."

"Thank you Mrs. Reynolds but I–"

"When you're done eating you may take a drink in the library. It's just across the hall from here. You cannot miss it." She gave him a pointed stare. "I would ask that you not wander about the rest of the house. This is after all a private residence, not an inn. Several rooms are off limits. Is that understood?"

"Absolutely. It was not my intention to overstep in any way. As I explained before, I was merely trying to find the dining room."

"Good. I shall leave you to enjoy the rest of your supper then. Please ring the bell when you're finished." Moving briskly, her posture stiff, Mrs. Reynolds turned and quit the room.

"Don't mind her," said Mark. He set Colin's used plate and cutlery on a tray. "She's very protective of our employer and unaccustomed to having guests."

"Her loyalty is commendable. I take no issue with it."

Mark smiled, added a nod and took his leave, allowing Colin to savor his trifle. The berries, sherry soaked sponge cake, and custard, delighted his taste buds.

Once done, he pushed back his chair and stood. Following Mrs. Reynolds' request, he rang the bell pull, then went in search of the drink she'd offered.

Contrary to the rest of the house, the library turned out to be a wondrous work of art, lined with bays of shelving. Portraits of philosophers and poets bordered the ceiling cornice. An ornate marble fireplace and large bay windows interrupted the shelving and offered comfortable reading corners.

At the center of the room stood a wide oak table with a globe set upon it and books stacked to one side. The silver tray beside them contained two crystal decanters. Colin selected one, removed the stopper, and sniffed the contents. Brandy.

Satisfied with his choice, he poured a good measure into a glass and took a large sip, his senses jumping to life in response to the spicy flavor. This brandy had more of a bite than what he was used to, burning all the way down his throat and heating his chest.

He took another sip and picked the top book from the pile on the table. Books could tell all sorts of stories. Maybe this would give him a better idea of who his host was.

After flipping it open he leafed through the pages. It detailed farming and agricultural practices with a green ribbon marking a spot pertaining to water supply for crops. He gave a soft grunt. Apparently they shared an interest.

Setting the book aside, he reached for the next one.

Roman aqueducts and Archimedes' system of raising water along with instructions on how to dig wells.

Colin's curiosity grew, especially when he glimpsed the title of the third book.

Sense and Sensibility.

An odd choice for a farmer. Perhaps it belonged to his wife?

Mystified by the strange assortment of books, the lack of servants, and low maintenance in the rest of the house, Colin could only conclude that his host was in financial straits, possibly even infirm, and that he loved books. It showed in the library which, although of modest size, appeared to be exceedingly well kept.

Having returned *Sense and Sensibility* to the table, he arranged the books so they were exactly as he'd found them. A log snapped in the fireplace and he crossed to one of the armchairs standing by the bay window. Heavy curtains crafted from sage green jacquard were pulled shut. The only reminder a storm raged outdoors was the drumming of rain against the glass.

Glad to be warm, dry, and well fed, he sat and dropped his gaze to the low table beside him. A chess set filled most of the space with a game already well underway. He studied the pieces. White was clearly the stronger player and would likely win unless black moved his bishop, setting up a three step opportunity to take White's queen.

Unable to resist, he picked up the piece and made the move.

Thunder boomed in the distance. The clock on the mantelpiece chimed the hour. Something behind him creaked and a flash of awareness stole over his shoulders.

Whipping around, he glanced at the doorway, certain he'd catch someone watching.

But there was no one.

The doorway remained empty.

Order your copy today!

AUTHOR'S NOTE

Dear Reader,

This book did not come together as easily as I'd expected. Although the plot and characters were clearly outlined in my head, putting Olivia's story to paper in a manner I found satisfactory, was far from straight forward. Her tale is one of self-discovery and growth. Telling it over the course of a regular length book became a challenge because I didn't want the romance between her and Grayson to feel rushed. I wanted their relationship to develop organically and also for Olivia's bucket list to be completed in a believable way without it becoming repetitive or boring. As such, this book for which I re-wrote the beginning and the ending while re-arranging the middle, is my longest to date.

All I can say is that I hope it hasn't felt that way for you while reading, but rather that you will agree the added length was necessary in showing the change

Olivia, Grayson, and Juliana underwent because of their interaction with each other.

I hope that you have enjoyed their story and look forward to sharing more adventures with you in the future.

SOPHIE

xoxo

ACKNOWLEDGMENTS

I would like to thank the Killion Group for their incredible help with the editing and cover design for this book.

And to my friends and family, thank you for your constant support and for believing in me. I would be lost without you!

ABOUT THE AUTHOR

USA TODAY bestselling author, Sophie Barnes, has spent her youth traveling with her parents to wonderful places around the world. She's lived in five different countries, on three different continents, has studied design in Paris and New York, and speaks Danish, English, French, Spanish, and Romanian with varying degrees of fluency. But most impressive of all – she's been married to the same man three times, in three different countries and in three different dresses.

While living in Africa, Sophie turned to her lifelong passion – writing.

When she's not busy dreaming up her next romance novel, Sophie enjoys spending time with her family, swimming, cooking, gardening, watching romantic comedies and, of course, reading. She currently lives on the East Coast.

You can contact her through her website at www.sophiebarnes.com

And please consider leaving a review for this book.

Every review is greatly appreciated!

CPSIA information can be obtained
at www.ICGtesting.com
Printed in the USA
LVHW112202080822
725485LV00022B/139

9 798201 927554